From Cath Christmas 2024

Summer Wars & Winter Schooners

Book I: *Summer Wars & Winter Schooners*

Book II: *Schooners Are Black & U-boats Are Grey*

Book III: *The Final Acts of Fogo's War*

By

Patric Ryan

"...The sands were the same. The horizon was the same. The North Sea was the same. They couldn't change the North Sea..."

The Fogo's War Trilogy

Copyright © 1990 by Patric Ryan

Copyright © Sarawak Studios & M.L. Ryan Publishing 1993

First printing 1994

Second printing and revised edition 2014
Released in separate volumes.

Book One: *Summer Wars & Winter Schooners*

Book Two: *Schooners Are Black & Submarines are Grey*

Book Three: *The Final Acts of Fogo's War*

All rights reserved by the publishers including the right of reproduction in whole or in part in any form including electronic, mechanical or storage in a retrieval system.

The Fogo's War Trilogy is a work of fiction. The names, characters, places and incidents portrayed in this piece are fictional or are used fictitiously. Any resemblance to actual events or locales or persons living or dead, is purely coincidental.

Sarawak Studios Press & M.L. Ryan Publishing
Illustrations by Patric Ryan
Cover design by Sophie Ryan

Canadian Cataloguing in Publication Data

Ryan, Patric D.M.

The *Fogo's War Trilogy*

ISBN 0-9698003-0-4

ISBN 978 09698003 0 9

1. Ryan, Patric D.M., 2. Germany & Newfoundland: 1913-1945. 3. Germany & Newfoundland at war. Drama. WWI, The Great Depression, WWII. Fiction.

Acknowledgements

To the girls in my life: Dorie, who shared the Newfoundland adventure and worked on the many facets of the Fogo's War stories; reading, proofing and listening, always supporting and encouraging. To my daughters, Sophie and Sarina, who have been very patient with Dad during the long process. The process includes the girls growing up and becoming editors and designers for Dad's books. To their Oma for her support and help. And most of all to the enduring memory of Mom who has been coach, cheerleader and benefactor in so many ways over so many projects.

To the memory of my dad, who loved his country and his granddaughters. Their Poppy was proud of his time in the Canadian Air Force during the Second World War.

To Dorie's dad, who was in the German Luftwaffe and a prisoner of war during the Second World War.

To our many friends in Newfoundland who showed Dorie and I such kindness, and taught us more than just the ways of the sea and that incredible Island apart. To Naaman J Humby, his wife Doris, and son Harvey. To Jimmie Mitchell and his family. The Trokes: Andrew, Jack and Florence, and the memory of their son Gary. George Collins. Harry Pardy and his family. Martin Legge and Annie. The Rogers, and many others who shared their stories. And finally to Hank and Thelma who are remembered in our memoir about Newfoundland, *Closing the Newfoundland Circles*.

Dorie and I experienced Newfoundland at a special time, the end of an era, just before the fish disappeared from the grounds. A time when our friends still told stories of sailing down to Labrador on the big schooners, a time of fierce independents, but in the shadow of the passing of the old ways.

Preface

The *Fogo's War Trilogy* is a story of love, war and tragedy, inner battles and personal survival. There is much humour, just as in real life. As in real love. The wars are within and between the characters and not great battles on foreign oceans and distant battle fields.

In August and September of 1914 Northern Europe went to war; a common occurrence over the centuries in an unstable Europe, but the scope of the conflict would cause the survivors and historians to call it *The Great War*. It was a local event in the present definition of global conflict but it was vast enough and disastrous enough to touch or destroy the lives of millions on both sides. As with most wars, WWI ended with a treaty but the Treaty of Versailles isolated Germany and her allies, and punished her for losing the war, guaranteeing that the German states could not recover socially, economically or emotionally. The consequences of a flawed treaty and France's harsh conditions and not the least, the isolationist policies of the United States, would eventually drag the world into another war. In between wars, the Great Depression, which began almost immediately for Germany after the First War, succeeded in crippling the world financially. The unsatisfactory end of the First World War and the malaise of the world Depression made the Second World War inevitable. The *Fogo's War Trilogy* is about my people caught up in the events from 1913-1945 that shape our world in the New Millennia but *Fogo's War* is not a war story. The novel is about Kurt Schulte and Pius Humby, their families, and the supporting cast members, caught up in the whirlwind of events, blown about like spume off wind-mad waves.

Although the *Fogo's War Trilogy* is fiction on a large stage, the story originated in 1986 with a modest idea; a premise for a short story. What *if* two young Canadian soldiers from the prairies were stationed as observers in a remote outport on the northeast coast of Newfoundland during the Second World War? The premise was attractive because in 1981 my wife and I spent many months in an outport on South Twillingate Island, rebuilding an old fishing schooner. The little village was no longer remote but to us it was a New World, peopled with a cast of characters at once delightful and puzzling. We came to love their old world ways and simple values. In 1981 the outports of Newfoundland were still fishing communities and we learned the hard lessons of life lived on the margins. When the fish declined the fishermen endured, and found ways to make a life on the water pay. The big runs of fish are gone but as long as there is a living to be made by the sea, the fishermen will go out in boats.

So, what happened to the original short story? It grew and grew. The premise wasn't large enough to contain the characters I created. The Germans entered the piece in the original screenplay because my Newfoundlanders needed an enemy, besides the sea. I introduced a submarine commander who was supposed to be a villain. Organically he grew and grew also until Kurt von Schulte emerged as a very interesting and sympathetic misfit; a tragic figure, flawed and vulnerable, plagued by human failings and fears. Once created he had to be redeemed.

The Newfoundland outporters are decent, direct and generous people and Pius John Humby emerged as a composite sketch of my ideal fishing schooner captain. He lived and suffered, struggled and sometimes lost. Then he met a man who should have been his enemy but whose life and troubles were almost exactly parallel. How could they be enemies? It's possible that decent human beings cannot remain antagonists when they face each other with jeopardy in common. Then how can wars happen?

Fogo's War doesn't try to answer the question or establish a moral high ground. The characters offer their opinions and act in accordance with their life lessons; and the answers to the question and resolutions of their conflicts can be found for every character.

The World Wars and the Great Depression have been documented many times. I make no attempt to retell the story of those terrible events other than as they relate to my people and only as a backdrop to their personal wars. At one level it's the story of two men who meet under odd circumstances in two wars and the Great Depression. On the surface Pius and Kurt could not be further apart philosophically, socially, emotionally or morally. There is no reason for these two men to become friends. On other levels the members of the supporting cast, like the enigmatic Anna, the wonderful Lady Bright Tifton, the pompous Captain Wilkinson, the Urchin Pimp of Hamburg, the tragic Rosie and the unfortunate Jimmy, grumpy Uncle Saul and the irrepressible Eric, and not the least, the arch Nazi, Karl Kessel, come and go and swirl about the main plot line like dancers at a wedding feast. Always in motion, adding and taking away, but so necessary to the piece that without one of them the piece would be diminished.

The *Fogo's War Trilogy* evolved from the short stories and screenplays. Like all good things, it had a life of its own and once the idea was set in motion the story took over. The spirits of Pius and Kurt told me about their lives and I offer their story as I interpreted their logs and journals.

BOOK ONE

Summer Wars & Winter Schooners

If I had known then what I was to learn about Fogo Island, and other islands, would I have begun the voyage? The journey into the past and other lives?...

FOGO HARBOUR

September 20, 1981: The day of the Iron Cross. Fogo Harbour, Newfoundland seemed a peaceful enough place that day. Boys in oversized rubber boots were fishing for Tommy cod from the town wharf. A rare, sun-warmed breeze wandered across the island from the southwest, pushing at a string of dories moored off the skidway; their battered, paint-neglected hulls fretting at the end of slime-grown tethers like forgotten puppies at market. Sun-dappled hulls of white speed boats danced on the clear water. Spindly stages of spruce poles, holding up red fishing stores, lined the waterfront and close by brightly coloured frame houses, perched on bare rock, stood out against the ochre-tinged hills. Work-a-day laundry in a back yard waved at laundry in a neighbours' back yard. Fogo looked like every other Outport I had visited that week, with one exception; the funeral of the German, Kurt von Schulte.

The cemetery of the Catholic church held a gathering of villagers, perspiring in their Sunday clothes, standing shoulder to shoulder around the open grave. The Stuckless grocery store was closed for the burial service. Beyond the store and the shambling picket fences staggering up the rocky slope, odd patches of emerald grass gave the village a civilized look.

I had been detailed by my Dublin publisher to get a sense of why so many Irish emigrants chose to settle the remote islands in the Western Atlantic so I was dutifully touring the coastal villages of the main Island, once a part of the European continent, even more remote and difficult than the Aran Isles, themselves cut adrift from the ancient coasts of Ireland. I was also instructed to sound out the expats about the Irish Question and their IRA affiliations. I thought it odd and foolish to interview Irish descendants who had left their homeland hundreds of years before the Troubles began. My knowledge of Newfoundland was peripheral and circumstantial; the Rock was famous for fog, poverty, seals and salt cod, known to the locals as *fish*. I was told by locals in Twillingate that many Irish families settled barren Fogo Island; just visible from Long Point Light, beyond Bacalhao Island, about as far east as one can get in North America.

In the early years, when the fishing fleets arrived from Europe in the spring, young men often jumped ship to escape indentured status, scratching out harsh lives in isolated settlements called Outports, eventually populating every cove and rock that could support a tilt and fishing stage. Fogo Harbour is the largest village on Fogo Island and all I knew about the history was that it had something to do with the Portuguese White Fleet and fires.

Since most of the villagers were collected in one place I walked up the hill toward the white church. The service was special to one old man who leaned in close to say goodbye to a friend or relative. A frail but handsome woman held his arm as he placed an Iron Cross on the casket. The legendary black cross with the silver border gave the plain wood a finished look, and I remember thinking it was too fine a day to be dead, but more, I was curious about the German Iron Cross.

Pius and Mary Humby made the slow journey up the hill to their white house with blue trim...*the blue between a Mediterranean sky and the elusive turquoise of a glacial lake; the result of mixing blues and greens arbitrarily*...the colour spoke of a stubborn independence in its creator. When I asked Pius Humby about the Iron Cross he said simply that it was time for tea so I followed at their slow pace.

Pius Humby's stride and rolling gate said he had been a leader, someone to be trusted in a tight spot. Strong in his seafaring days, now shrunken with age, narrow shoulders thrust forward from long hours on deck, leaning into the wind looking for landfalls. The deeply-lined face veined by wind and sun. His gnarled hands disfigured by hard work. A fisherman? An easy guess in the outports. Mary held Pius' hand to guide him through the gate and reminded him gently that the gate needed mending. *"See to it first thing,"* he said. She reminded him every time because it was something he could look forward to doing.

Mary Humby was a quiet woman, with an easy grace born of knowing she was beside her man, in her own house, mistress next to God. In appearance Mary was everywoman, sparse of frame, like Pius, with plain features that didn't give away her age. Her quiet strength the glue that holds the outports together. She hovered near Pius while tending to her kitchen work, only a heartbeat away from his side.

Pius sat me near the window with a view of the Harbour. Mary put the kettle on and spread a lunch of fresh baked crusty bread, margarine, bake apple jam, cold sliced herring, a can of milk for the tea and a sugary cake from the mainland. It was a wonderful, cozy feeling to be wrapped in the warmth of the Humby's home but I wasn't getting near the Irish Question. The Humby clan are English through and through.

"...My name's Pius. Pius John Humby, if that's any consequence? Mother called me Pius, with some hope. John was my father. I'm ninety-three years old, and aside from the time away fishing or in the Navy, I've lived in Fogo. A good enough place, as the outports go. There's been a lot of changes since I was a lad. Most of the Humbys're gone now. Aside of young Thomas, my brother's lad, up in Toronto, who we raised like a son. I guess I'm about the last of the Humby men on Fogo Island. There's Humby's over to Bonavista, but they're another bunch. A good crowd just the same. Boat builders, understand, and good ones. There's Jimmy, my sister's boy, he's a White. Still, he's got the blood. We lost a good number in the wars, and more drowned at sea during the peace. Had my own schooners then. Never lost a one sunk or wrecked. The ones I lost otherwise? That's a story. By'n'by we'll get to the stories. Mary's got tea on...Wouldn't I love to see one of my old schooners at the new wharf? 'T'would be fine to walk a deck once more before I go over to join the Commander...'"

A tea bag waited in each cup for the kettle to boil on the ornate, nickel-bound stove, recently converted to oil. Pius said the food tasted like it was cooked in the engine room of his schooner. He preferred wood fires but it was too hard to keep a supply since the neighbours had given up their old cook stoves and no longer got together to cut and stack wood, as they did in the old days.

"...I can see good enough in one eye. See the new wharf? That crowd up in Ottawa built that last election. Won't do 'em no good though. The old wharf was good enough; the one we built in...what year was that Mary? Before the war...doesn't matter. We built it ourselves and it was bigger. Take a schooner either side. Or a submarine. We always looked *after our own selves. Didn't need to ask nobody for a thing, sir. Then Joey got us hooked up with that crowd in Canada. You don't want to hear about that sure..."*

Pius rummaged in a drawer for a tattered scribbler filled with almost illegible handwriting, a salt-stained log book from the schooner days. I drank my tea, acid-strong, while leafing through the yellowed pages, deciphering the words slowly, much like learning to understand the outport dialect. And I missed the reference to the submarine.

"...You'd be some interested in the Commander's books. Can you read German? Neither can we b'ye, so I never knew what's in'em, except that Kurt, that's the Commander, told me most of the stories, I suppose. We had many years to share out the stories. At least the Commander always had a one to tell..."

Pius watched the harbour and a motorboat doing tight circles at high speed; some older boys blowing off steam after the quiet of the funeral. I watched his face, waiting for him to go on, torn between deciphering his handwriting and curiosity about the Commander. What stories? Where were the Commander's journals? Pius' scribbler was only a sketch. A catalogue of events.

"...The Commander's books? Where're them books to, Mary? My son, he was one for writing. Did it all his time see, when we weren't talking the ear off one another, or out for a walk. Course, the Commander spent a lot of time with Jimmy White at first. The lad couldn't do for himself see, not after the accident. It weren't an accident, really. More like it was bound to happen. Jimmy was in a bad way for some years but by'n'by he got better. The Commander had looked after him, so when the Commander got on, like, Jimmy turned about and looked after him. It was,

at first, like the Commander was the father and Jimmy just a child. Don't know what Jim's going to do now. You can go up around for a visit if you've a mind. I'm no good for it. My legs see. Too many years keeping the deck. The legs just give out. You go on up. Might cheer Jimmy up some. He's got himself a tilt up in the hills. Wanted to get as far away as he could from the ocean, see. He never could bide the water, after that time..."

That time? Pius showed me pictures of his schooners and talked about the sea. As much as I liked hearing about the boats I was dangling over a cliff of curiosity about the Commander. Pius left me hanging there while we talked about the weather and the decline of the Grand Banks fishery. But eventually the stories had to come out. He began with a brief reference to Kurt's story as a young man in the East Frisian Islands, off the northern coast of Germany.

NORDERNEY ISLAND

August 21, 1913: (Translated by Jimmy White from Kurt von Schulte's journals): '...*Today I walked the north side of the island. The wind was*

strong. I wanted to walk into the water but the wind kept pushing me back. Back and back into my childhood until I was looking at my father's red face. I felt naked. Cold. His rough hands were cold. Mother put the blanket over me. Father pulled the blanket off. He inspected me again. The old Jewish maid said that I would catch pneumonia. Father ordered her to let me lay in front of the open window for an hour each day after my bath. Toughening, he said. He laughed and his big moustache jumped around. He looked like a clown with a boozy nose, but he wasn't funny. He smelled like a horse. He smelled like brandy. The monster crowded my dreams. I was a great disappointment. He had another son...My brother Willie.'

Kurt scratched out the last line and dropped the pen. Ink flecked the page. Then he picked up the pen again and wrote: '*...dropping the knife across the plate can say many things. The maid whispers to the cook. If they are Jewish and care about their jobs they will try to appease. Swallow bile. Appease the one who pays for you...*'

Kurt poured a large brandy and drank it without bothering to swirl and savour the essence. He knew how it would taste. He put on his coat to go down to the beach.

He walked the tide line, soaking the bottoms of his careless white pants, wondering why he could never stand up to life. The sand felt good but the water was cold and frothy. Bubbles came out of the sand as the waves pushed higher and ran back. Life was returning with the tide. Life went on. Why was he always pushing the wrong way? he wondered. Looking into the misty nothingness of the North Sea was easy, the reason he feared leaving Norderney for Berlin. In exile there are no apologies and he preferred the clean difference between the sand and the moving sea to a boulevard of lights and noise. Middle ground came with the retreating tide. The time when the sand flats are neither land nor sea and each step could be a surprise.

The tide turned and Kurt followed, unaware of time, as if the moon was pulling him away from the land. He walked and walked and tried to ignore the feeling, the thing he feared, swelling into his head like angry wasps. The tide retreated until the North Sea was a constant roar in the distance. The sea birds, self absorbed and busy on the flats, knew what they had to do...content to play their part, as unconcerned as he was unaware. Kurt followed the tide and tried to imagine what it would be like when the tide came back. The small ripples would rush at his toes, chasing the sandpipers back to the island. The ripples would become cold waves leaping at his legs, climbing higher until he was fighting to keep his balance against the surge of the big waves. He was looking up, watching the breakers foam overhead, surrounded by the silver fish that flashed as they turned to avoid him, holding his breath. He wasn't a fish...Kurt turned his back on the sea, retreating toward the beach, stopping to inspect the dead-white carcass of a rotting eel, shivering under the gaze of his father; crying for Mother to come and cover his white, cold, nakedness.

One day he would follow the tide all the way out and when it turned he would not present his back but continue at a processional pace, and meet his sea mistress, consummate the unholy alliance, mingling his useless body fluids with the cold sea. Why couldn't he do it today?

His feet were numb by the time he reached the beach and turned west, against the occasional sun. The weather hadn't been good. Norderney was nearly deserted by the end of July leaving only a few bathers to spoil his view. Some days the sun broke through in late afternoon, too late to be of any use to the stubborn visitors from the mainland who sat through mist and rain waiting for summer. It was time to go to the cafe for a cognac and a small dinner, if he felt like it, then he would see the doctor. The timing was precise.

Kurt walked slowly back to Norderney town. The sand was cold but his feet were colder because he refused to put on his shoes. The pain crept up his legs until his knees ached. He would tell the doctor the pain caused him to crawl the last mile to the café. The doctor would shrug and tell him to wear boots. He wasn't a foolish child. No, he wasn't a child, he was twenty-six, but refused to become a man to spite his father. It became a habit; then a way of life.

Norderney had two cafés. One served the fishermen, the traders and the crews of the galliots; the sturdy ketch-rigged freighters that carried everything from mail to apples among the Frisian Islands and into the Baltic. The other café served the wealthy visitors who came on the ferry for an experience. During the winter the fishermen had their choice of cafés but left behind their smells and stains. The visitors absorbed the smells and stains without the bother of socializing with the uncouth fishermen.

Kurt preferred the fisherman and their plodding talk of fish and the sea, their endless games of checkers and their rude philosophies. He tried to imagine his father sitting in a cloud of coarse tobacco smoke, drinking dark beer or a scalding brand of cognac. No, it wouldn't happen. Fantasies played out in Kurt's mind until reality and fantasy lost their boundaries and in his confusion he sought the sea. The difference was absolute…The young waiter approached his table.

"Good evening, Herr Schulte. The usual poison?"

"If you guarantee it."

"Herr Schulte makes a joke. That's good."

"I have a doctor, thank you."

The young waiter cleared the table, handling the dirty glasses with unveiled distaste. The previous owners of the grease-smeared glasses had been eating smoked eels. "Would Herr Schulte like a smoked eel? They're very fresh."

"Are they dead?"

"I guarantee it!"

"Just sausage. I saw enough dead eels on the beach."

"Herr Schulte's been walking today?"

"And yesterday. And the day before. What else is there to do on Norderney?"

"In your state of mind? Really, Herr Schulte..."

"You'd make a wonderful maître d'hôtel in Berlin," he said, emphasizing the French version for the waiters' benefit.

"Ah, Berlin! Herr Schulte's so lucky."

"Drop the Herr Schulte. Kurt's good enough."

"I'm sorry."

"You should work down the street."

"They're just fat pigs," said the waiter, appraising Kurt's long, trim body under the careless white uniform.

"Rich fat pigs," answered Kurt, uncomfortably aware of the waiter's intimate look and his own disastrous propensity for slumming.

"Not all, like yourself."

"Cognac," Kurt said abruptly, then added almost gently, apologetically; "...and a double bock, please." The waiter smiled knowingly, Kurt was in a hurry to get drunk, and left, hip swinging between the tables. Kurt noticed but didn't care. He had come to Norderney on orders to cure himself. The waiter's problem didn't interest him. He watched the fishermen and the sailors whose lined faces were wind burned and opened with coarse laughter. Smoke rose up in clouds; a fog that softened their rough lines. Why were they always so damned happy? Damn them! The waiter returned with two glasses; one cognac, the other dark beer, and a plate of sausage and another plate of sauerkraut and bread. Kurt drank off the cognac and placed the glass back on the tray. The beer he set in front of him and looked into the dark liquid. The waiter arranged the plates of sausage and sauerkraut on the small table.

"Am I expecting company?"

"The sauerkraut helps you sleep."

"Nonsense!"

"All right, don't eat it."

"I never sleep."

"See?"

"You're in the wrong business. My doctor won't touch my balls."

The waiter giggled. "Did you hear, Kurt?" he whispered. "A tragedy today…" Four galliot hands at the next table leaned close to hear. The waiter leaned away to share his news. "…An old man, a mainlander, shot himself, in the testicles. On the beach, at sunrise."

"Is there something significant about the sunrise?"

"I don't know!"

"Then why tell me the time, if it's not significant?"

"It was significant to his testicles."

"Obviously."

The waiter giggled behind his hand. The four galliot hands laughed and raised their glasses to the poor man who'd shot off his own balls. Kurt stood up holding his beer and a thick garlic sausage above his head. "A toast to the old bugger's balls! May they rest in peace, where ever they are! Fortunately my friend here was able to save his dick!"

Kurt bit the sausage, the juice running down his chin. The waiter danced around the table, grabbing at the sausage. The sailors roared. Kurt drank beer with them and forgot his appointment with the doctor.

August 22, 1913: Kurt opened his eyes in total darkness that stunk worse than usual after drunk sickness, and the bed whirled but also tilted. A new sensation. The sound was different too. Things creaked and groaned with the motion. Kurt felt for his eyelids and recoiled when his finger touched a bare eyeball; he was blind. Kurt screamed in panic. A door opened and a stabbing shaft of light made him recoil again. If he wasn't blind, then he must be dead. The stinking doctor with garlic breath probed for life with a candle in a lantern. Kurt passed out again, slipping deeper into the nightmare.

'...*Once, when I had a fever, Father held a candle close to my face to see if I was dead. The hot wax dripped on my eye. I screamed of course. Mother and the old Jewish maid entered by different doors. Father was at least apologetic...*'

"Herr Schulte? You awake?" breathed a voice heavy with tobacco and garlic.

Kurt was looking at a dark beard with bad teeth under a seaman's cap. The light behind the man was square, like a window. Odd, it didn't look like a window and the sun swung slowly back and forth. Which dream was he in?

"You have it bad," said the black beard.

"Worse than bad. I'm still alive."

"A nightmare?"

"No dream ever smelled this awful."

"You jumped into the harbour. The tide was out. You would have drowned in the mud."

"This is better!?"

"We didn't know what else to do. Your death would have caused the harbour master great problems."

"Perish the thought!"

"He's a friend of ours."

"Do I know you?"

The sailor laughed. A wave of bad breath washed over Kurt. The motion of the galliot and the natural stench of the black fo'c'sle made his stomach turn.

"We are sworn brothers, you and I," declared the sailor.

"It could be worse."

"Yes?"

"You might have pushed me."

"Not without first taking your money."

"Practical." Kurt looked beyond the sailor to the gangway and the swinging sun. "We're not in the basin."

"Going to Wilhelmshaven. Three days, we'll be back to Norderney."

"What time are cocktails?"

"I'll bring coffee."

The sailor patted Kurt's arm, chuckled and climbed the ladder to the deck. Kurt watched the sun swing back and forth until his eyes hurt, happy not to be blind. The strong coffee gave him the will to reach the fore deck.

A child can watch the waves and listen to the sea for hours. The sea speaks a language a child can understand. Kurt sat on the greasy wire windings of the windlass listening to the sea curling away from the bow. A Morse code of splashings, without the boredom of rhythm. Repetitive but each different. Some insistent. Others suggestive, urging the ship to complete the passage. Offering peace in a safe harbour if only the laws are obeyed. The ship, enchanted, plows ahead; a hopeful suitor to the enchantress. Sometimes fatal but ever optimistic, only fatalistic if the journey ends badly. No sooner home than another journey begins and the lovers resume their game.

To starboard, beyond the Frisian Islands, the low mainland shore, an unending line of marshes and sand dunes, broken only by narrow creeks and tidal harbours, was an uninteresting grey smudge on the horizon. To port Kurt watched other galliots and steamships and the blue North Sea. He imagined its depth, not in real volume but in abstract space. He imagined diving into the cold water, the astringent North Sea washing the bad taste from his mouth and the depression from his spirit. Only the sea could be penetrated in so many ways. He had tried to dive into sand. Floating on grass was inconclusive and swimming on air was impossible. He was closer to the fish than to the birds.

Sometimes, when bedridden with one of his frequent childhood illnesses, he turned the house upside down and walked on the ceiling. The piano didn't fall if he was careful to keep it in place. He was forever forgetting and something would fall. The chandelier was a crystal Christmas tree with the candles upside down. The wax dripped on his bare feet and sealed the ribbons on their presents. The gift from his father was a dead pigeon. The one he and Willie had stoned to death when they acted out a Passion Play. They were thrashed by their father. Willie had thrown the stone that killed the bird but neither would say. Willie gave Kurt his favourite glass ball as a reward for his silence. Kurt wished Willie could walk on the ceiling and step over the door lintels and pretend they were stowaways on the Imperial Fleet battleship, heroes who saved Germany when the crew had been killed. They steered the huge ship into the Queen of England's battleship. Kurt thought it amusing that England had a Queen. Willie thought it made them soft and Willie didn't like ships. Willie liked horses and would join their father's horse guard when he turned sixteen. Sixteen was years away then, although Kurt noticed how round and soft the young Jewish maid's breasts were. He pretended to be asleep so he could put his head between them and let his hand rest on her warm thighs. It wasn't as interesting as walking on the ceiling but he liked the feeling, and it happened more often. Mother seldom held him. She only touched him when he had a fever. He tried to fake fevers but only managed headaches.

"It clears the head! This air, huh, Schulte?" said the black bearded sailor who was one of the drinkers in the fishermen's café from the night of the sausage. Kurt grunted, annoyed by the change of plans. He had been plotting how he would get his hand under the Jewish maid's skirt without Mother finding out. The Jewish maid wouldn't object. He understood only instinctively the politics of pleasure then. The plotting was a recent development.

'...*The young Jewish maid* was *let go when Father caught her with her hand under my blanket. She only wanted to sooth me. Father wanted me to freeze to death...*'

"Yes, it clears the head. When I recover I could steer, or climb the mast," said Kurt, sarcastically. "Work my passage."

"You don't have to work your passage. You're my guest."

"I was Shanghaied!"

"Ungrateful bilge rodent! I should throw you to the fish. That would wake you up."

Kurt laughed. The sea was working its magic and he felt hungry. "When do the prisoners eat?"

The sailor dredged a hard biscuit from the pocket of his canvas coat. Kurt squinted at the square cake the size of the man's hand and shook his head. The sailor shrugged and bit off a corner, working the chunk around in his mouth. It was necessary to let it soak until it softened. The sailor repositioned the chunk.

"Cookie has a fish soup on. The best!" He dipped the biscuit into air and carried imaginary pieces of fish to his mouth. Imaginary drops of broth ran down his thick beard and splattered his canvas coat. Imaginary sea creatures were nourished in the tangle of hairs. Hideous heads poked out, mouths open for the next torrent. Kurt was afraid the creatures would eat his host if Cookie didn't make enough.

"You are lucky bastards, you know that," said Kurt.

"Yes, we know."

"Know what? I didn't say why."

"You think this is for fun!" said the sailor, grinning. "You love the water, Schulte, I can tell. It's freedom for someone from the land. You think we're free to come and go!" The biscuit chunk went down with a dry gulp. The sailor took a filthy looking green-bottle flask from another pocket, pulled the cork with his teeth and held it out to Kurt. He was a good drinker but the body was too abused. The sailor pressed the bottle into Kurt's chest.

"Go on! You need it."

Kurt swallowed sea air. It was pure and clean. The bottle was passing through his rib cage. It may be necessary to drink the liquor or die of internal bleeding.

"Are you saying you're not free?" Kurt asked, with an effort.

"*Phuff!* The weather. Tides, dishonest agents, impatient customers. Always the boat needs work."

"Why do you do it?"

"In this bottle is my freedom. But out here, on the sea, on the deck of my boat, I'm in love. Are you free if you marry a woman?... no! You say, *I give up my freedom for this and that, and I'll do for you this and that*. And she has babies and you do this and that, for them. Why?"

"Because you have to?"

"No! Idiot! Because you love the woman!"

"Oh," said Kurt. The pain in his chest subsided. The sailor held up the bottle. It became a jewel. A chalice. The sea sung the Angelus.

"See this bottle! It's not how it looks. The best French cognac. Old. Rare. You are skeptical, my fish food. A story then...Once, in the old days, there was a consignment of cognac from a corrupt French official to an equally corrupt German official. They butter each other's bread, huh? And demand more taxes from us, their plentiful peasants. It wasn't a coincidence that the cargo travelled by canal to the Dutch lowlands and was shipped by galliot to Hamburg. Well, almost to Hamburg. The galliot in question laid over in Norderney to wait out a gale but had an *unfortunate* stranding on Neuwerk Sands the very next day." A long, experienced pull on the bottle lowered the water line by a quarter. The aroma was not of the rough peasant brandy Kurt drank and he began to have doubts. The sailor deliberately replaced the cork and slipped the bottle back into his pocket, noting that Kurt's eyes followed. Lingered. He had him! "Stranding on the sands is dangerous," the sailor continued. "With a falling tide and another gale on the horizon, it was lucky some galliots *happened* to be close by."

"Happened?"

"My dear, Schulte! You don't imagine collusion among honest seafarers? Hard done by we might be and the Good Lord knows we're at the mercy of agents who rob us at every turn."

"Then the galliot in question was fortunate to lay over in Norderney," said Kurt sarcastically.

"Many were held up. It happens. We all left on the next tide. We were overdue in the estuaries, as you can imagine. The impatient customers? The captain of the galliot imprudently attempted to cross the Neuwerk Sands. We tried to warn him off but to no avail."

The bottle reappeared. Kurt flinched. The sailor was a master of suspense. The ritual of the drink was artistic and prolonged.

"The *rescue*?" urged Kurt.

"Of course! We're brothers."

"Of course."

"His was a deeper draft galliot, you understand. We nosed in, at great peril to ourselves, until we were alongside. The sea was very rough. Any moment we could have been smashed to pieces."

"So, you saved the crew."

"*Phuff*, no need! These galliots are built to take the ground. We simply lightened his load. When the tide returned he floated free. The light keeper on Neuwerk Island swore to the facts of the *accident*. Unfortunately, many of the rescuers were scattered to safe harbours by the coming gale so not all the cargo could be accounted for. The insurance company settled for a percentage. Everybody was happy."

"Not to mention safe," said Kurt sarcastically.

"Of course. Safe! It's the unwritten rule of the sea!" He offered the bottle again.

Kurt accepted and an experimental taste proved the sailor's tale.

WILHELMSHAVEN

The weakening sun went down over the North Sea in a smothering haze and the air was hushed as if waiting for another gale. That evening the galliot hung at anchor on the outgoing tide in Jade Bay near the approaches to Wilhelmshaven. Kurt sat on the main hatch with the crew as Cookie's fish soup digested. Coarse bread and strong wine circulated. Smoke hung over the deck and the talk was easy. Good times, bad storms, shore women and sea men. Their children. They bragged about their children even if they were bad.

Kurt felt good. He felt so good he didn't want to spoil the evening by remembering that he had worked and schemed to be bad. It was his way of punishing his tormentor. He felt better than he had ever remembered as a child, or adult for all the privileges of family. Meals taken with High Command officers and important politicians at his father's table had failed to nourish him. But fish soup and local wine? He might have been a different person. He might have been one of them, a simple fisherman.

"So, Schulte, we've been friends all this time but we still know nothing about you," said the skipper. The other sailors waited for new entertainment. The cook appraised Kurt as if he were a side of pork curing in a smoke house.

"Yes, a long time. Since you Shanghaied me."

"Saved your miserable carcass from the harbour mud! Never forget. We always come to the rescue of those in distress."

"Oh, yes! If the unfortunate one has a load of booze aboard."

The sailors laughed. This Schulte was worthy of rescue. At the café in Norderney he bought the double bocks and provided uproariously funny sketches with garlic sausages.

"You'd be a good sailor, Herr Schulte."

"Then I'd be good at something wouldn't I?"

"I'll show you how to tie a knot a woman could never get out of," offered another.

"He means marriage. Pay no attention."

"Idiot!" commented another.

"What were you doing in Norderney? You're not like the rest," said the skipper.

"Taking the cure."

"Have some of France's best," he laughed, holding out the green bottle. "It'll cure whatever ails you."

"Do I drink it or pour it on?"

"Depends who you want to pour it on."

The talk got rough. Kurt gave as good as he got and his troubles swam away. These sailors from the Baltic seemed to have no problems to hoist up the mast, keeping them instead in the bilge with the rats.

August 25, 1913: Kurt's room at the inn. Doctor Gluck motioned for

Kurt to undress. Kurt pulled off his pants and sat on the dresser so the doctor would not have to manipulate his balls. The examination was a ritual but the doctor was more terse than usual. He was from Berlin and Norderney was to be a vacation, of sorts, with his family in tow. Treating Kurt was a favour to his father and the doctor was impatient to return to the city. The summer had been a disaster. His family left on the ferry vowing to holiday in Spain if Germany persisted in being damp at the wrong time. Then there were the rumblings of war with France and England. The doctor held a commission in the German Imperial Army and, to be in line for promotion, it was necessary to be on the ground. "There's nothing more I can do. You're cured."

"I'm not ready to go home."

"You're wasting your father's money here."

"He has enough."

"You're healthy, considering your unhealthy habits."

"Am I really cured?"

"I'm not a psychologist, Kurt."

"Have a cognac with me?"

"Thank you, no."

"Doctor..."

"I must return to Berlin, soon. You can do as you like. Good day."

Kurt didn't bother to dress. He poured a large cognac and stood at the window watching the persistent rain. A wet cat passing under the street lamp wore a halo of mist and the puddles on the cobbles made an odd checkerboard pattern. Otherwise, Norderney town was black and silver and lifeless. The cognac failed to bring warmth but Kurt wouldn't dress. He showed the town his genitals. Cured, the doctor said. The disease was defeated but the patient was dissolving from cancer of the spirit. He picked up the brass sextant, celestial navigation his latest hobby, and pointed it at the harbour. The sea-distance between

Norderney Harbour and Norddeich on the mainland was a gulf he couldn't yet cross. The rain continued and Kurt drank to compensate, waiting for the red and green running lights of the ferry to approach the wharf at high tide. It would be easy enough to walk to the pier and board the Norddeich night boat. He would stay on the open deck in the rain and wind. One hour of exposure, tasting, savouring the salt spray, avoiding the other passengers. Punish his body with the elements. He poured another large cognac instead.

That night Kurt wrote: '...*Father prescribed toughening for the weakling child. Five minutes in an icy bath followed by an hour of naked exposure in front of the open window. He and Mother battled constantly over the issue, as I lay freezing to death. Mother never picked me up. The old Jewish maid left the house in disgust; replaced by another Jewish maid who was warm and pretty. She held me close when Father and Mother left me to die. She opened her blouse and pressed me against her warm breasts. I drowned in her bosomy warmth. I longed for the icy bath if only to be brought back from the brink of death by her body...*'

August *26*, 1913: Kurt slept late and was awakened by sunlight streaming into his room. He dressed and had a small breakfast of coffee and rolls at the café, sitting at a table on sidewalk in the rare sun. Visitors from the mainland drifted off to the beaches or sat on benches and talked about the weather, or idled about the market in a daze. Kurt watched the locals go about their business, writing in his journal while waiting for the fishermen who would come to the café when their work day was done.

A week-old Berlin newspaper on the next table showed bold headlines about naval buildups in Britain and France, without mentioning Germany's rush to build capital ships; hulking steel gun platforms of the new Kriegsmarine designed only to instill fear and hurl death at the enemy. The aging generals of the High Command still clung to the old ideas of warfare, thought Kurt. Men like his father longed to get into battle to test their manhood. Dashing young heroes in gold-splashed uniforms astride rearing war horses. War, according to his father, was as much show as strategy, not sweating young bodies in the bowels of ships, passing coal or explosive shells and muslin bags of cordite. Kurt decided to go to war to relieve the boredom but horses repelled him. He would join the Imperial Navy to spite his father, but not on one of the capital ships. Something small that dashed about having an adventure. That decided, he threw the paper on the ground. "Reading about war is depressing when it's not happening," he said to no one. Kurt finished his coffee, took his sextant in its black case and walked to the harbour.

The familiar smells of wet-mud and rotting fish drifted over the harbour with the sea breeze. Stout masts of the fishing fleet in the basin sprouted drunkenly this way and that like a flailed forest, their hulls laying on the thick mud where they were dropped by the tide. Visitors avoided the harbour at low tide but Kurt was drawn by the atmosphere of the working quay where men went about their routine without the need to analyze everything to prove they were alive. He dangled his legs over the edge of the pier and let the rough planks dig into his flesh. It was pleasant to feel the sun-warmed sharp edges. To run his fingers over the weathered grain. Few trees grew on the islands so, like Kurt and the tourists, the planks were foreigners also. They may have come from one of the countries who traded with Germany in peacetime and become enemies in war. It was a good system, he decided. It perpetuated commerce. Build it. Blow it up. Rebuild it. He wouldn't think about the war.

Boot prints traced the routes between fishing smacks resting on their bilges in the black ooze. Fishermen crawled about the slanting decks doing the endless jobs required by working boats. Nets needed mending. Running gear had to be repaired. The pace was unhurried, purposeful. Further out in the offing a few deep draft galliots waited for the tide, the crews stretched out in the sunshine stitching sails. Kurt framed the scene and imagined a palette of greys and ultra marine for the old timbers and shadows of the piers. The hulls in black with yellow trim. Umber and ochre for the mud. Blue-grey for the sky and pools of water. A splash of red for a shirt or a flag, like the Flemish painters do. How would he paint sunshine? Painting was another of his failures. Life was so complicated he thought and looked through the sextant for the simplicity of endless crenellations on the horizon.

A blank sheet of paper gazed back at Kurt. A stack of paper waited at the side of the writing desk. Kurt stared at the cracked plaster walls of his room, at the dirt filling in the cracks, not disguised by the white wash, left behind by indifferent scrubbings. If the wind blew a seed into the crack a wildflower might grow. Then the crack would be interesting. Kurt wrote a few lines about wildflowers; a topic about which he knew nothing, then tore the sheet in half. He stared at the crack where his imaginary seed languished. Angrily he swept the stack of paper off the desk. It took a few moments for the sheets to settle, arranging themselves like a spent wave on a beach, while his anger rose to a panting plateau. He reached for the bottle of rough cognac and knew how the night would end.

August 27, 1913: Dawn in Norderney Harbour. Kurt arrived in the dark and waited at the pier for the fishermen. He felt lousy from the drinking but wouldn't let his body recover; a form of penance that seldom freed him from the guilt. Fishermen can drink themselves to sleep and make the first tide, always moving within the laws of the physical universe. It is simple because tides are predictable and cycles reassuring. Decisions depend only on variables such as wind and weather. Storms are confronted or avoided. They fuck their wives and have the children to prove it. And the risks are acceptable.

An old fisherman named Glimpf, bent with age and arthritis, approached the wharf at his steady, determined pace. Kurt had spent an evening in the café with the old man and his crew. The old skipper nodded a greeting. Talk, like coins, was calculated and spent reluctantly outside the café.

"Good morning, Herr Glimpf," said Kurt. The old man stopped. "The other night? You said to come aboard...fishing."

The old man remembered. "Ah, just so."

Herr Glimpf continued along the pier to his smack, its deck now level with the pier. Kurt followed since the invitation hadn't been revoked.

The two young deck hands, Manfred and Axel, had come down earlier to draw the smack up to the pier for their skipper. Kurt was tempted to help the old man over the rail but decided against it. The taciturn Manfred and Axel had drunk with Kurt and made an uproar at the inn but hardly said a word to him as he stepped aboard and retreated to the stern. Perhaps in his usual drunken condition he had offended them.

The galley stove under the fore deck was already burning and water boiled for coffee. Foul weather gear was laid out. Herr Glimpf inspected the beam trawl net hanging from the mast, his fingers racing over the heavy black cord, feeling as much as seeing. Even a small hole meant lost fish. Lost money. Pennies added up when the work was hard and life lived on the margins.

Kurt watched the old man and his boys methodically going about their routine. Their hands were calloused and tough. His own hands were soft. He felt out of place but he longed to glide out of the harbour under the patched sails of the smack. Needed to be born along by the tide, rocked gently by the swell, blown clean by the cool wind, always with the tang edge of brine. You only had to lick your lips to garnish life's experience. He wanted to experience what these men took for granted every day. He still believed in the freedom of the sea and felt cheated that he was born to privilege with its strictures and obligations, politics and facades. The aristocracy fed upon itself, bred within tight ranks and fostered idiots. It also fostered the idle sons of the rich who played at life and wasted their talents pursuing visions. His mood collapsed in self recrimination. Kurt stood up suddenly and stepped across to the pier as the lines were thrown clear.

"I'm sorry, Herr Glimpf. I can't go with you today. Something I have to do."

The old man shrugged. It was of no consequence. Manfred and Axel hauled up the sails and coiled down their lines as though Kurt never existed. It was another day of work. The smack dropped down the harbour with the tide until the wind filled in around the town and puffed at the sails. In the offing, small whitecaps raced along with the morning breeze. It would have been a sparkling sailing day. Kurt, pouting, still punishing himself, tucked the sextant case under his arm and walked back to the town.

'*...Father took me to a Jewish merchant who sold fireworks. I was afraid of things that made noise and he treated me like a gun-shy hunting dog. Father, in uniform, strode ahead in his imperious manner while I ran at his heals as he marched to the merchant's store. Something about the occasion of buying bombs for his son to blow up baby birds required full military honours. It was a wonder his Horse Guards weren't lined up abreast as we entered the merchant's shop. Inside was an armory of Burmese crackers, flares, rockets and Chinese fireworks in chains. Father ordered a box of miniature Burmese bombs. He said his friends complained that their children kept them broke buying bombs for blowing up rabbit holes and pigeon nests. I couldn't understand blowing up pigeons when he had thrashed Willie and me for stoning a pigeon. What was the difference? Were bombs more manly? Did children learn to be good soldiers by attacking baby birds? I don't know. When I asked for sparklers Father refused, at first. Sparklers were for girls. I cried. He bought me the sparklers but the triumph wasn't enough. When we left the store I let the bag slip and some of the sparklers clat-*

tered to the floor. Father didn't notice that I was pouting, punishing myself in an attempt to be bad. The merchant noticed. We exchanged knowing glances. He didn't attempt to replace the sparklers. I thought it was because he was my confederate. I realized much later that he saw a chance to increase his profit by selling them twice. Lessons come hard when pain is self inflicted…'

Late evening: Kurt was on his hands and knees among the scattered sheets of paper on the floor. He wrote a few lines then rocked back on his haunches. He crumpled the page and sat with his back against the cracked plaster wall. He was damp with sweat. Was it just fear? Can't let the fear in, he thought, reaching for the bottle. He drank and unfolded the crumpled sheet.

'…There is a void where my life should be. If I step into the void I know there is nothing beyond. Yet, if it's where my life is…I must go there…'

It took a moment before I realized Pius was talking to me, explaining the story I was already lost in.

"…That was before he met the woman. Anna he called her. My son, the Commander was tormented something awful by that one. And it didn't stop there. He believed her spirit was so mean it followed him here, years later, see. A fine man like the Commander didn't deserve to be tormented so. Mind, he was young then. A young man troubled by life. He told me how he was tormented by his father too. Terrible cruel that man. An officer of some kind, the Commander said. Had a bunch of men all his own. Horses and such. It's all there in them books I suppose. You get Jimmy to read the books and you'll get the whole story. I only know what the Commander told me…"

Pius wanted to rest for an hour. He showed me the path that lead up to Jimmy's house and told me to come by later. I started up the hill, turning and twisting between the rocks. The harbour spread out below like a diorama in a museum. The dories and motorboats were models on a glittering lake of plastic. I tried to imagine Pius' big Grand Banks schooner at the wharf and the spindly spruce drying flakes covering every available space between the houses. All gone. I climbed again, wondering what Jimmy would be like. Pius had given me glimpses of his story, although Jimmy's was much later. And the Commander's books. Pius seemed reluctant to ferret them out. Perhaps they didn't exist. Pius said that Newfoundlanders stockpile things, like old log books, fishing gear and the endless pieces of marine engines. It was a result of being thrifty by nature. Then there would come a day when, on a whim, a fisherman would clear out his store and carry the lot to the end of the stage and send it along with the tide; the daily flush.

There was another presence in the hills and I wasn't ready for Jimmy White. Too much lay between. The woman, Anna, once insinuated into the story, wanted to make her story known. Pius seemed reluctant to talk about her but I decided to pursue that direction. I waited an hour in the lee of a rock just taking in the view of sparse hills and sparkling ocean that some would call a wasteland, until the sun dropped too low for warmth. I retraced my steps, deep in thought, shivering from a sudden chill wind.

"...Well sir, I don't know. 'Tis not a good thing to talk about another man's private affairs, 'specially those to do with a woman. I never liked to when I was young, and I don't say I understand all of what the Commander was getting at, see. It so pained the man to speak of her..."

Mary was laying out the evening tea, moving about her domain with that quiet assurance, tolerating the male presence as Pius' reward for a life of toil. Pius agreed to tell me some of the story; but only by way of understanding the Commander. He had great respect for the German and I sensed a kinship. He mentioned the strikingly similar losses in their personal lives. The Commander's bravery. Humanity. I deciphered unspoken dignity. He wanted me to understand that the German was a good man, also the enemy, with human flaws.

"...It was the woman, see. Kurt was a young man when he met up with her, twenty-six, thereabouts. And at just the worst possible time. My son, don't it heap upon us when we can do nothing at all for ourselves but slide along, like falling off the backside of a Jesus big sea. There's nothing at all in the world to stop that now. She picks you up when you're not watching your stern, and first you're looking down the hill, then under she goes. Well my son, you can throw the wheel this way and that all you want but she's stalled see, and nothing for her to bite into. By'n'by that big sea runs under your keel and you're looking up to Heaven with nothing but a Jesus big hole under your counter to fall into. And just when you needs a bit o'wind she fails you too. That's what the Commander was up against. My son, that man had a time!..."

August 28, 1913: Mornings tormented Kurt the most. A body too often punished by brandy and self doubt cringes at the dawn. The ruthless light stabs at swollen eyes and probes the vulnerable places, making demands on the will. Kurt forced himself off his sweat-soaked bed and dressed in stages, each step calculated to achieve pulling one pant leg on, then the other, then pulling all together and securing buttons with trembling fingers. The belt. *Never mind the belt!* The belt seemed important. It was on the floor but he tried to avoid the scattered pages, fearing what they said. The truth was unavoidable. He found the cognac bottle under the chair. A drink remained but he avoided that also.

The old street sweeper and his dog occupied the town. Kurt envied their self-purpose but wanted to lecture them about satisfaction. *Be content that you are content.* The dog investigated smells at the fish store and at the bakery and the cheese shop. The street sweeper stopped to relight his pipe, leaned on his broom and watched Kurt out of sight as he turned the corner for the North Beach.

Kurt began running at the edge of town. He ran to the end of the cart road then along the trail to the grass covered dunes. He ran hard, harder than he ever ran playing games at school. '*...I disliked hurting myself for goals with the headmaster yelling at me, with expectations, like father. Disappointed when I failed. At dinner Father would grunt when I answered questions about the football game. Willie excelled of course but little Kurt participated at half speed, taking short runs at life, reducing my own disappointment. I hated kicking the ball. Most of all I disliked being kicked by other boys because I wanted to retaliate. But retaliation meant hurting. I could see no point to hurting someone for the sake of a game. Father grunted. The grunt said many things. Later Willie would tease me. Willie could run like the wind and manoeuvre the ball. When he made a goal Father praised him. I was told to be more* *like Willie. Still, I loved Willie and I was happy for him...'* He was running beyond feeling the pain in his lungs. The soft sand of the dunes made his legs hurt but he ran through that pain and ignored the salt rivers streaming into his eyes. Soon he would be in the North Sea, plunging into the cold depths, eyes stinging from the salt and the cold water. He would force his eyes open. The water at high tide was clear and blue, but he fell at the top of the dune and rolled to the bottom, forcing himself to get up before the burning in his lungs stopped and he felt good again, too good to go on. It had happened before. Laying on the sand in the sun looking up at the tumbling clouds and wheeling sea birds. It was too easy to give in when the pain went away. But it was only an illusion. One pain substituted for another. Physical pain would go away if one simply stopped causing it. The other had to be exorcised. The early morning sun was not warm so the sand was cold and the message on the paper too clear. He stopped only long enough to catch a breath, to ease the ache in his side, but the other aches remained.

Kurt ran again on the hard flat sand at the edge of the sea, running beyond the pain. Legs working hard. No longer his legs. Ahead was a fog bank moving over the sea to the sand. Into the fog he ran, his feet no longer touching down. There was no sensation of contact. The hammering blows to the back of his head ceased. He floated in the fog. Peaceful fog, gliding over the sand; no sound. He stopped breathing and spread his arms.

Kurt sat on the wet sand facing the oncoming waves. The sea would return as it always did to claim the flats. Today it was only Kurt in the way; a small thing for the sea to deal with. There had been others. Desperate characters who fooled themselves. The sea was not the solution. True, it could dissolve anything, given time, but only in transition. Out there in the fog the North Sea crept closer. Every wave pushed further along and he could hear the pipers' excited chirping as they scurried ahead of the onslaught. Out of the blowing mist the birds came. The advance guard detoured around Kurt without a pause in their work. Kurt became impatient. *Go out to meet her.* He could not. It had been a victory just to establish his ground. He was dug in. If his nerve failed he couldn't survive another defeat.

'...I heard Father tell my mother, as they watched the Jewish maid tuck me in, that I lacked survival instincts, which is why I was sick so much of the time. Mother said, nonsense, but Father wasn't listening as usual. He asked the maid if I'd had my cold bath that day. The maid lied. Yes, she said. And did I get my hour by the open window? Yes, she said, but it was only a half lie. She had wrapped me in her shawl. Father forbid blankets in the nursery from 0600 to 1930 hours. That's how he spoke of time. As if Willie and me were little soldiers in training. Willie thrived and our sister was spared by gender. Father left her to her fates, meaning Mother. Mother did her best but it didn't prevent Dear Sister from growing up to be a calculating social climber. I will say that she was pretty, well mannered...when it mattered...and cultured. Everything calculated to survive well. She succeeded. She treated me well though, and for that I thank her. In one small corner of her socially corrupted psyche she had compassion for my problems. The motherly instinct. When she became a mother herself she could not be faulted for the way she handled her large, savage, beautiful brood. Indulged and spoiled but they were loving, delightfully rambunctious children. It all proves nothing. What do I remember most about my own childhood? I remember cold water and our Jewish maid's warm, soft breasts...'

The North Sea crept closer, the large swells tripping on the sands and crashing down, shaking the earth. Kurt imagined a monster coming toward him out of the mist. Soon the water monster would rear up and fall upon him and it would be over. He looked hard into the mist and a cold wetness flowed around his bare feet. He recoiled instinctively. The next wave surpassed the first and soaked his behind. He shivered. Where was the sun? A pale orb barely penetrating the mist but luminescence could be colder than darkness. In darkness there are no expectations of warmth. It was all relative. On a cold day the sea feels warm. The sea changes very little so it must be perception that changes. Kurt began to have doubts. Had his perception of his wasted life been correct? Or was he just caught in a down draft? Was this premature? *Losing your nerve, Kurt?* he asked himself. Then he said it out loud: "Losing your nerve, Kurt?"

A plover stopped following a receding wave. The plover didn't have the answer. Birds seldom suffer self doubt or kill themselves because they cannot write. They could die of loneliness from the loss of a mate perhaps, but they are too busy securing their own survival to dwell on it. The plover hurried on.

One wave followed another and soon Kurt had trouble sitting. The waves pushed at him, pushy little waves, impatient waves, with a destination on the beach, resenting this pointless interruption. *It's stupid to humanize the elements.* Nature is spared because Nature is perfect in its indifference to human existence. Patience or impatience were not a part of the infinite universe. But Kurt was human and he resented being pushed about by the waves and crawled forward to meet the sea on it's own terms.

A big swell survived the sands to break over Kurt. He tumbled backward, rolled under and was pounded against the sand. Fighting the instinct to save himself he let the next wave drive him down again. He opened his eyes for a last look at his beloved water mistress but the sea pulled back and Kurt was left rolling in the foam, racked by a coughing fit. The next wave pushed him higher on the sand. He didn't struggle nor would the receding water pull him back. Stalemate. Another defeat. He had used up his manhood and nothing was left in reserve, an empty shell cast up on the sand by an indifferent ocean. *Again, the attempt to inflict human values on nature,* he wanted to shout. The ocean was neither caring nor indifferent and he wanted to scream at its, what? There's nothing to shout at that listens. Only conceit could allow him to think he had some communion with the other world. Kurt stood up, angry at himself. Angry with the sea. The gods. The fog. The ineffectual waves. His father.

"Where are you!?" he shouted at the fog. A flock of ghost-white gulls wheeled out of the mist, chastised him, and disappeared. He cursed them.

The screaming gulls hurled back the epithet and the waves mocked his impotence. Kurt waded into deeper water until the coldness lapped at his crotch. He raised his fist. "Damn you!" In answer a wave broke, knocking him down, and Kurt's resolve collapsed. "Isn't there anything I can do…?"

The clouds drew away like a scrim cloth on Act One. Kurt sat waist deep in foam, bathed in sunlight, with a prickly feeling on his back; where the tingles go when a ghost is disturbed.

A woman in billows of white silk hovered in the mist, and her hair, framed by the sun, like a flaming henna halo streaming out as battle pennants. His heart stopped. Or was he already dead? Another wave rolled him over. He tried not to take his eyes off the vision that smiled down at him like the Blessed Virgin appearing to a child. An appearance of the Virgin had been accepted by the Church in France. The little girl, Bernadette of Lourdes, recently honoured by Rome. Adoration was next. Veneration would follow, then she would be declared Blessed and Bernadette's canonization assured by miracle cures. Springs of holy water. He didn't believe the miracles of course. What should he believe? What do you say to the Virgin Mary?

"Where have you come from?..." he heard himself ask. "Does it amuse you to watch a man drown?" She held out her hand in that peculiar way. *Was she just pointing the way?* "Are you pointing the way? I know the way."

She moved up the beach toward the dunes, fading into the low morning sun. The mist curled around her feet and she floated above the sand. Kurt was transfixed. The story had said, *'...the children were transfixed by the apparition...'*

'...I was hiding in Mother's armoire, in the act of stealing one of her silk undergarments as a bribe to the maid. Father and Mother were having one of their arguments about Little Kurt. Mother was defending my lack of enthusiasm for all things military, which wasn't exactly true. I had a fascination for sailing ships and sea battles, which of course grated on Father. We were Prussian, gentry with traditions to uphold and the sea was abhorrent to Father. He had connections at High Command and could have placed me on a capital ship but saw no advantage in having a son disappear into the bowels of a floating fortress. He insisted I join the family Horse Guards. I could be resplendent in gold braid before my eighteenth birthday. Leadership qualities? None. Social advantages? A good marriage with connections of course. Political advantage? Considerable.

Father was losing the battle for my soul. Little Kurt wasn't going to be a cavalry officer, but a good soldier knows when to cut and run. So, when Mother offered the compromise of Kurt entering the priesthood Father was merely silent, weighing the options. I was left in the darkness, inches from discovery, while Father decided my future. It would have been an enormous joke to pop out and surprise them, take the whipping and retire to my bed to savour my wounds. At my young age I had a well developed sense of freedom; and the loss of it. The priest-

hood!? I imagined breathing clouds of incense during endless Holy Days while the priests made mystical signs, chanting Latin and swinging the gold censer. My job was to carry the incense boat, at a distance, because the smoke made me gag. My school chums and I guessed that the skinny priests who looked like bats hung from their feet in tiny dark cells. What did they feed them? We never saw one eat so we speculated they drank blood to wash down the thin dry wafers of the Eucharist. The bishops were very fat because they ate little children...Mother broke the silence. Kurt might become a bishop, she said. I imagined my Father's face lighting up. His moustache twitching with anticipation. Yes, he said, a bishop in the family wouldn't hurt...'

After the bishop decision, Catholic doctrine was drummed into Kurt, but the more his mother pushed the more dissolute he became. At fourteen he was admitted to the seminary in their St. Hedwig Parish, centre of the powerful Berlin Archdiocese which, like the state, had been formed in conflict and politics, as was much of Germany. St. Hedwig's was a bastion of wealthy Prussian military families, perfect for his father's intentions. Kurt rebelled, failed miserably and at age sixteen was rejected by the seminary as unfit for service, to everyone's relief. He, in turn, rejected the Church and its mysticism. So Kurt was not convinced the vision in the dunes was the Virgin Mary of his youth. Something else was stirring in his body. *"Don't go!!"*

The fog bank rolled in thick and black, further dimming the weak sun. Kurt, abandoned by the light, forgot dignity and crawled into the dunes, climbing, falling, climbing, in desperation like an animal; all instinct, sinews and muscle, the prey in hand. He would drive it to ground. Not the way the cat crawls; slowly, deliberately, calculating the moment. Kurt scrambled, escaping as much as pursuing, over the top of the dune and down the other side to land in a heap at her feet. He stood up, teetering like primitive man experimenting with his back bone, and was staring, mouth agape, like the village idiot of Norderney.

Pius brought us back to the present. *"...I'm not saying she was real, sir. The Commander said maybe the woman was a dream, like. Fantasy, he called her. I'm only telling you what he told me so's you'll understand how things stood for Kurt. He was in a bad way, and according to anything I know when a man's driven too far, well sometimes he sees things, visions. Happened to Jimmy after his bad time. Now, the next part, well...I can't bring myself to tell you half what the Commander told me, and he said he left out a lot in respect for my religion. But it's in them books, see. So if you want to know the private stuff you've got to go to the books. I'm not a moral Holy Joe, it's just that, I couldn't tell it the way the Commander did..."*

Mary sat on the day bed knitting. A neighbours' girl was due and every child born in Fogo started out life wearing Mary's knitted booties with leather soles cut from the soft tongues of old work boots. It was seal skins in the old days. She said that now most of the women bought mainland clothes for their babies. Pius made a sign and presently Mary gathered up her knitting and went to visit Aunt Sally who was ninety-six and feeling poorly. Pius poured us another cup of tea, dashed in a generous dollop of rum from a bottle on a high shelf in the pantry and settled himself in his chair with a view to his harbour, and the past.

"...The Commander was just twenty-six. Same age as me, see. A grown man but still a child. That's how he told it, and the woman was younger. But he said she was older in her ways. Did I tell you her name?...Anna? Pretty name just the same. From one of those northern countries, so she claimed. I thought they was all fair in those countries, but Kurt said she had hair as red as a sunrise. He used to laugh about

the old saying, red sun in the morning, sailor take warning..."

Kurt died the death he had longed for. His soul fled. His heart ceased pumping but the blood coursed through his body. Her face was pale and smooth as sculpted marble and he could feel her power, irresistible, dominant.

"You're her!...my sea mistress." The woman laughed, a teasing laugh, like warm chimes. "You mock me." Anna put her hands on Kurt's shoulders, kissed him and forced him gently to the ground. She cradled him in her arms, The Madonna and Son, taken down from the cross. Head rolled back, unconscious in surrender. The picture was incomplete. Roman soldiers and weeping peasants, cowering disciples and lightning would not have been surprising. Then she lay Kurt on the sand and kissed him as if her breath could bring him back to life. Waves of silk smothered him. She worked him over like a technician, then mounted him like a Persian horseman, pounding Kurt's shell into the sand.

The spent body of a man was stretched out on the bed, moon-shot, dead fish white and motionless. Breathing in short, cautious breaths as though unwilling to be discovered. A creaking sound from the halfway startled him. The door opened slowly and Anna flowed into the room, moonlight tracing her flawless body as if the nightgown was a transparent vapour. The vapour slipped silently to the floor in a pool of quicksilver. She gazed through Kurt, the tigress sure of her power, gold-flecked eyes showering sparks over the room and Kurt's eyes darted about looking for a place to hide. Her breathing was slow and deliberate, like a trained assassin, a sleeping victim wouldn't feel the slightest discomfort. Kurt's breathing became erratic. In his imagination he ran, fleeing across the grasslands, bounding through the moonlight until his heart burst with fear and flight. Diving into the crystal river in panic. Then Anna was upon him, pealing away the layers of doubt and self pity. The lioness killed well and true, discarding the body to find its own salvation. Kurt drowned in her flesh as he had longed to drown in the sea. Drifting, turning, down to the mysterious, destructive depths to dissolve in sweet release.

August 29, 1913: Kurt's room faced east. The promising morning sun, pouring through the filmy curtains, followed the path of the moon. But the morning light was more honest. The room was a shambles as if Kurt had been savaged by an expert and the victor had withdrawn from the field leaving the survivor naked at his desk writing down the details of his death. Purplish welts crisscrossed his back but he felt nothing of the physical pain.

The pen worked its way over the page in an unrecognizable scrawl, the word *void* repeated over and over. He got slowly to his feet and poured water from the big jug, watching it swirl around the wash basin. A small cockroach trapped in the basin was caught in the maelstrom, legs flailing. The swirling subsided enough for the cockroach to get a foothold and the small creature tried to pull itself clear. *Water is like glue,* Kurt thought. But when the roach was close to freedom Kurt put his finger into the water and stirred the surface into another whirlpool. The insect spun round and round, helpless, and Kurt watched in fascination. Kurt stirred again and the cockroach flailed faster. Was it panic? Survival instinct? Or was the thing simply tired of going around in circles? Kurt wanted to help the creature but hesitated, inflicting his will on a lesser being. The whirlpool slowed and it found a crack, a tiny toe-hold and pulled itself clear, painfully, exhausted.

"I know how you feel and there's not a damned thing you can do about it!"

The bug gained the fluted edge of the bowl, tottered, then fell to the dresser with a wet *tick* and scuttled away to a dark place. Kurt looked at himself in the mirror, turning his head slowly. The grey-blue eyes were too far back in the sockets. He was the prize fighter after a beating, disfigured even in victory. Kurt hadn't won. He had the familiar empty feeling; hollow, tired. Knowing it was an uneven contest and losing was part of the game. He also knew it wasn't the end of the game. He washed his face and splashed at the fouled water.

Kurt put on a clean white shirt because he couldn't find the one he had been wearing. He couldn't remember if he had lost it in the water or in the dunes. It didn't matter. He sat on the bed to put on shoes, fingering the covers, testing the texture of the heavy linen. Her musk still clung to the room. It was like no other. Certainly not like the girls in Berlin.

Kurt finished dressing and went down to the café to drink a coffee. The rich smells of bread and sausage and frying fish from the shops couldn't penetrate the presence of Anna and the coffee had no taste. Only Anna. Then she was there, across the street. Kurt put down his cup. What should he do? He felt foolish. She was baiting him. *How could she!?* He waited for a gesture, some sign that the person who spent the night devouring him at least recognized him in the morning. She was occupied by a window display of fashion. Kurt was confused, then angry. Then Anna looked back. Was it the gesture he had expected or a challenge? Kurt seethed with impotence. *Damn the woman!* Anna moved on, slowly, deliberately. Every motion tore into Kurt like claws.

Kurt wasn't certain she had gone to the beach until he saw the footprints. His heart pounded like an engine out of control, every step was a further descent into oblivion.

"Madness! Go back..." he might have said aloud. The end would be the same as the day before but he tried to shut out reason. If it had been a game between equal antagonists, and the excitement of the chase a reward, it might have made sense. But with Anna it was an execution and the beautiful assassin tricked her victims into running themselves into the ground, weakened like the gored bull that continues to charge the lance. And like the dumb bull, Kurt hurried to his fate. He didn't believe in fate. It was his choice. So many times his nerves had failed and he could not turn back.

The footsteps suddenly veered into the water. He scanned the sea to the horizon.

"Anna!"

The gulls screamed back as Kurt waded into the water. "Anna!!"

A large sea broke and rolled up the beach, erasing all the footsteps. "Don't leave!" A bigger sea reared up. Kurt retreated up the beach before it crashed down. *"Anna..."* he whispered like a man giving up.

Warm laughter drifted over the wind from the dunes, a gentle summons and he followed like a man sleepwalking to his execution.

Behind the barrier of the dunes the change was abrupt. The wind was silenced, the sun was hot and the sand burned his bare feet. The other change was the sound of the sea. The roar of the North Sea faded to a dull, prolonged booming. It takes the senses time to adjust to the comfortable warmth of the sand and sun, recognizing the other elements as accessories to pleasure. But if the body is racked by doubts and fears and already given up for dead? Oblivion.

A wary circle of seagulls watched as a land crab approached the body lying face down, arms flung out where it had fallen. The crab scuttled over Kurt's back investigating possibilities. A seagull advanced obliquely and took an exploratory tug on a finger. Kurt woke, recoiled, and the crab tumbled to the sand, spiny legs flailing the air. He cursed the crab and pitched the creature at the seagulls. In a chaos of wings the gulls lifted into the air, wheeling, accusing.

Kurt sat up and looked around the silent dunes expecting to see Anna stage managing his further humiliation. His disappointment was a mystery. He should have been relieved that there were no spectators for the final act of the Passion Play. Instead he felt abandoned, at the bottom of the spiral, his only relief a spiritual numbness, another set back. The mist was behind his eyes this time but he forced himself erect and began the slow trek to Norderney to await the adjudicator's critique.

September 3, 1913: The day was grey with a cold drizzle from the Nor'east. Kurt walked down to the harbour with doctor Gluck who was mercifully silent, like the visitors waiting for the ferry, subdued by the heavy atmosphere. Kurt had no strength to make the doctor's departure less awkward and there were no lectures. The doctor knew Kurt's habits but he had done his best, the disease had been arrested and physically Kurt was cured but the woman, real or not, was the curse of Kurt's heritage. The doctor understood that every woman Kurt introduced to the family had been scrutinized by his father as if she were a prospective brood mare. Women lacking the necessary pedigrees were driven from the field. Kurt had few options in life, so, even the acceptable young women looked elsewhere. What mattered to the practical young ladies of German society was the long run. Expectations were high. Germany was a power in Europe and Kurt offered social stability only as long as he remained under the family roof. He looked further afield but seldom brought the women home. He did bring home the disease. The doctor didn't mention it. He was silently concerned about Kurt's mental state. There was nothing behind those vacant eyes but loneliness. Kurt would have said *void*, but Kurt didn't mention it either.

The interminably foul weather and crossing conditions were discussed with vague references to families and getting together for a drink. Kurt wanted to apologize for...what? The doctor's misspent summer? He was well paid. The doctor's family rebellion? That was nothing to do with Kurt. He couldn't apologize for the weather, so they shook hands, relieved when the ferry's shrill warning sounded. The tide was turning and the captain of the Norddeich boat was impatient to be going. The doctor stepped aboard and Kurt was left to deal with his spiritual disease.

Anna appeared on the upper deck wrapped in a somber cape, the hood quenching the flames of her hair. She looked ordinary, huddling under the overhang of the bridge to escape the drizzle. She didn't wave, offering no smile or alluring look. She was just Anna; beautiful, pale, vulnerable...human. The expression was sad. Regret at leaving? Perhaps Anna wasn't the real tormentor. In his fragile mind she had offered him life, he believed. In his confused state he could not fathom the offering. Had he created Anna in order to kill his own spirit, to give him an excuse for failure? Anna's eyes were not searching the quay for anyone. There was a man beside her who looked like a banker. Kurt thought she was crying, or were the tears just raindrops misplaced? The boat's leaving whistle jarred the harbour and wet lines snaked aboard. Kurt slumped against a lamp post and watched until Anna faded into the drizzle and the brown turbulence of the outer channel quickly closed over the ferry's wake. He had finally reached a lower plateau of desolation but was still spiraling down. He sought solace in the only space he knew; the verge between sea and sand. He walked in a trance to the far end of the island, following the tide along a sand spit until there was nothing left but the sea. Water and sand.

And the void. Black storm clouds drove in from the west and crashed down, buffeting his emaciated spirit until he crumpled under the onslaught, crawling after the retreating tide, defeated again. Even the sea had deserted him.

"...A man can't get much lower than that, sir, and still be alive. You'd have cried sitting there, just where the Commander was sitting when he told me that. My son..."

Pius watched darkening Fogo Harbour in silence as if offering Kurt Schulte a moment of peace in a tortured existence.

"...And that was the one he called Anna. She jumps into the story now and then but she never was that real again, if you takes my meaning. No? Do you believe in spirits? Ghosts and such like? I won't say I do, then I won't say I don't. I've seen too many times when there was no other way to explain a thing. As to Kurt? He's suffered cruel, and the worst of it was he did it to himself. He tried to explain, but I've no capacity for understanding what happens in a man's mind when he's tormented nearly to death. We watched our Jim go through that, sir. She was the same thing I suppose. Doctors study up on the thing but 'tis not for a simple man to try to get handy to it. What about Kurt? Mary's coming up the road there, see? We'll have a bite to eat now. Didn't realize the time had got on so... "

The time had but I wasn't aware. I was still on Norderney, in a driving rain storm coming off the North Sea, with a man lying at my feet. Lights came on around the harbour and the ocean changed from blue to grey. Big clouds walked toward the Island from seaward. The wind changed too. It would be colder and probably rain, Pius had said. The brilliant September day slipped away while I was captive on an island no more than a big sand bar, three thousand miles away. And what of the rest of the story? It continued but frequently Pius would stop and gaze out the window to the cemetery where the fresh mound of brown dirt was visible through a gap in the crumbling fence, as if he was waiting for help from the Commander. Mary began serving out our evening tea. After the meal we talked about schooners, fishing and ice hockey.

"... *You don't mind if I take a pipe? I should've give it up by now, if I was going to. Don't suppose it'll hurt me now. Nothing the Commander and me liked better than to have a pipe and a drop o' rum. He smoked cigarettes most often. Had this gold case. Pretty thing, from his brother. We liked our smoke, and talk. Mary'll tell you. We spent a good many hours sitting here, sir. We watched Fogo change. The young ones couldn't leave fast enough when they seen the television. It's fine in its place I suppose. I never was against progress. We enjoyed watching the hockey best. The Commander always pulled for the Montrealers. Me, with so many of us gone up to Toronto, I had to pull for the Maple Leafs. Some fun we had brother. Yes sir, but the Commander always had the best of it with his Canadians...*"

I found it very difficult to make the mental leap from Kurt von Schulte, cringing on a sand spit on Norderney Island, on the brink of self destruction and Commander Kurt Schulte cheering for Guy Lafleur and Larry Robinson on ice in the Montreal Forum. I was anxious for Kurt and Pius must have sensed my impatience. He settled himself in his rocking chair by the stove, lit his pipe and picked up the tale. It was now dark. Lights on the wharf bounced on the restless black water, rain rivulets ran slowly down the windows and soon we were back in Germany.

September, 1913: Kurt awoke on his side, knees drawn up under starched white sheets. His first awareness was the smell of his childhood. He watched the cook and the maids prepare meals. It wasn't the smell of food that came to him but of the caustics they used to clean the kitchen.

'*...I remembered the disinfectants because the young Jewish maid smelled like that if she'd been working late after a weekend of guests who made a mess of everything. Her hands would be rough from scrubbing but she'd rub nice smelling cream on before she put her hands under my covers. I could still smell the disinfectant though. It wasn't a bad smell and it had better memories than how my mother smelled when she used the expensive perfumes Father ordered from France. He said there wasn't anything worth smelling in Germany except gun powder. He was wrong. I liked the garlic sausage smell when the servants ate their meals in the kitchen. We weren't allowed to eat garlic sausage because Father said it would make us smell like peasants. The cook would give me a piece of sausage and some parsley herb to chew. Sometimes the cook saved me the ends of the sausage and let them get dry and hard by the fire. I put them in my pocket and went for long walks in the woods with our pointers. I'd feed some of the hard sausage to the dogs but they wouldn't chew the parsley so Father would smell their breath when they jumped up on him. He'd be furious with the servants. The servants accepted the harsh words and the threats and never told on me. I liked the smells of the peasants and I love garlic sausage still, but I remember the disinfectant, creamy smell of the Jewish maid best of all...*'

Everything around his bed was clean and bright. Kurt wondered if he was in a mist with sun shining just above, the way it did on days when the fog was close to the sand. There were voices, muffled and far away. He reasoned he couldn't be on the sand because the scraping hollow sounds were footsteps that echoed off the walls. He had an impression of high ceilings. He was not on Norderney either and that's all he cared to know. For the rest of the day he stared at the clean white sheets and tried not to think. *Do not think about Anna.* He didn't have to think about her. Anna was a feeling and the feeling was of great loss.

BERLIN

March-May, 1914: Kurt languished within the walls of the Institute for Mental Aberrations for several months in a state of induced indifference. The hospital was small and efficient. Somnolent male patients wandered the halls and gardens. None of the two dozen people he saw daily appeared to have injuries or disabilities. He wondered why they were there. *They must be loonies.* Kurt knew *he* wasn't crazy. He had been through a difficult emotional episode but, other than exhibiting a certain lassitude and indifference to his surroundings and fellow inmates, there was nothing wrong with Kurt Schulte. He didn't remember Norderney or Anna specifically but floated in a state of euphoria with only hints of depression. A nurse would give him pills and the depression went away so situation was not unpleasant.

Kurt had a private room with fresh linens and flowers daily. The hallway outside his room was bright even on cloudy days. There was a bench with leather pads and a long skylight whose axis was north and south. And even on the days it rained Kurt liked to sit for hours watching the rivulets trace patterns from one leaded pane to another. It was a never ending fascination to try to guess which way the next rivulet would run. He must have spent the winter in the Institute because some days the skylight was a familiar luminescent glow, although Kurt couldn't remember why. There was a common room with heavy tables and good chairs where he and the others took meals or sat evenings watching the shades of light change from day to night. In the spring the weather was warm and if he wanted the sun he could go through the common room, out the heavy glass doors that opened on a courtyard gardens and set beside a reflecting pool. The older inmates tended the gardens. There was a lot of discussion about roses. Kurt had never been interested in things that had to be cultivated. Benches were arranged in the centre of the courtyard near the pool and some along a high stone wall. The cut stone was covered with ivy vines. When the ivy leaved out in May the stones almost disappeared. Kurt liked to sit on the west side in the morning and the east side in the evening to keep the sun on his face. It reminded him of something. He was very particular about directions. He asked for a compass and his sextant but the orderly just laughed and said Kurt didn't need a compass to find his way around the garden. Kurt gave it up because he didn't know himself why the compass seemed important.

In May and June Kurt had daily sessions with a doctor who knew a great deal about his medical history. The doctor said that Kurt would be allowed to remember if he promised to work on a problem. He was gradually brought up to his time on Norderney but the process stopped short of a full disclosure of his hallucinations. He accepted the doctor's prognosis that his problem had been induced and that there never was a real Anna, but for a complete recovery it would be necessary to stop denying that the mythical Anna existed and give her a theoretical life purely for the therapeutic value of exorcising her once and for all. Kurt agreed to try. He had nothing to lose if the demon never existed in the first place. After a session he would station himself on a bench in the courtyard working up fantastic female demons in robes with henna hair like snakes. The doctor said it was great progress. Kurt, however, was losing Anna twice.

After a wet, cold spring in Northern Europe, the temperature rose like the political climate. On June 28 the Austrian Archduke Ferdinand was assassinated on a street in Sarajevo. June melted into July. The weather turned hot and Berliners sweated while they read the news about the assassination in Serbia and the inevitable ultimatums. Kurt worked hard everyday at writing. He filled books and improved so quickly the doctor said he could be going home before Christmas. Kurt wasn't sure he liked the idea. Home meant bitter memories, although he never hinted to the doctors that home was anything but the well ordered domain of one of Germany's most respected military minds and his analyst didn't mention that he consulted with the good Doctor Gluck. His days were spent in blissful ignorance while his mother worried about social standing. Kurt's condition had been kept a family secret. Friends were told that Kurt was convalescing in a sanitarium in the south of France, for a spot of tuberculosis. They wouldn't doubt the possibility of a sanitarium but they didn't for a moment believe the official version. Kurt simply vanished. July continued hot. Kurt wrote and improved.

As summer progressed rumours of imminent war gripped Germany. Diplomatic missions flew about Europe with accusations and ultimatums. Inside the walls the inmates tended their gardens and fed the pigeons. Newspapers were allowed, though few of the patients were lucid enough to read, content to whisper the rumours. Kurt read the papers on good days. He worried about Willie. Would Willie be at the front with his regiment? In daylight Kurt saw brightly dressed Horse Guards, banners flying, drummers and buglers sounding charges and alarms. He visualized the battles as scenes from an opera with staged pageantry, the singing and the chicken blood. And when the war was over the characters would get up, take their bows and the audience, satiated with bloody culture, would applaud. It was nonsense, Kurt decided, but the coming war troubled him. At night, in his dark dreams, he saw grey masses of men cowering in the mud as heavy artillery pounded them into a bloody pulp until neither side was recognizable. A new kind of machine driven warfare, the newspapers had warned. During these dreams Kurt sought the safety of the cold depths of the ocean in a steel machine that floated in a protective void. He would awaken shivering, cold, and depressed. The war was coming after him. General Freidrich von Schulte rode a black horse with fire in its eyes, at the head of a van whose sole purpose was to find Kurt's hiding place and strip his clothes away so he could freeze to death in a ditch. The walls weren't high enough. He pestered the orderlies with questions. He planned ways to barricade his room. Fear of his father caused him to slip back to the simple division of sand and water, to drink with the fishermen or go to sea. To distance himself from the land where his father stalked his dreams. Then one day he was standing knee deep in the reflecting pool. Faces came toward him out of the mist. A red headed nurse was calling to him. Her hair ignited. The flames shot out. General Schulte and a host of flaming riders closed in for the kill...

"Herr Schulte, you must come out. It is forbidden to be in the pool."

Kurt wanted to run but there was no way out. Orderlies gently pulled Kurt from the pool, babbling about water and war, but after a day of sedated rest he resumed his writing. A few days later, recovered sufficiently, he received a visitor.

July 25, 1914: The heat of the city was subsiding. Late summer and fall predictions promised to be golden but it would be wet, soaking the fields of France and Belgium where the armies would dig in.

A young army officer was shown into the courtyard. The nurse pointed out Kurt sitting on a bench beside the reflecting pool, concentrating on his writing. The officer nodded and strode at a smart pace to Kurt's side as if by walking quickly past the other inmates he could avoid catching diseases of the mind. Kurt continued writing, unaware. Willie, awkward and uncomfortable out of his element, watched him for a few moments. He hadn't expected to see Kurt dressed in street clothes, looking older but normal, totally absorbed in work. Willie hesitated to disturb his brother and looked around the courtyard at the old men shuffling about aimlessly in gowns and slippers. Kurt didn't belong in this place.

"Kurt?"

Kurt almost jumped with surprise, "Willie!" he shouted, dropping the notebook. "It's so good to see you!"

Willie sat beside him and took his hand in a prolonged handshake that said much to Kurt. It was Willie's apology.

"How are you feeling today?" asked Willie, cautiously. He was still suspicious about Kurt's condition. Afraid it was one of Kurt's play acting phases.

"Wonderful! Really. Look!...I've been writing."

Kurt held the notebook out for Willie's inspection. The smile on Willie's face faded as he scanned the pages filled with one word, *Anna*. Willie handed the book back, searching for words of his own.

"Kurt, it's...only a name."

"But don't you see? I'm writing again." Kurt beamed like a child excited about a new discovery. He studied Willie's face for a hint of approval. Willie watched a pigeon land near an inmate for a handout. The old man on the bench tossed a small stone on the ground. Then another, and another, grinning maliciously. The pigeon tried each one without catching on that it was a rude trick. Kurt sensed Willie's disappointment and tried to explain.

"The Doctor said, if I could confront my demons and name my fear, even if it never existed, it would go away...she would."

"God knows I don't like the idea of you being in here! Father thinks you're playing games. Are you Kurt? Is this just to punish us?"

"Did he send you to ask me that?"

"No! I'm sorry for not coming sooner. I couldn't get away." Then Willie blurted out the news. "There's going to be a war! You know the Austrian Archduke's been assassinated." It was his turn to be excited.

Kurt understood without question. The Schulte's have always thrived on war. It was in their blood, their heritage and birthright. It made them wealthy and kept them in demand. Kurt was the only barren twig on the illustrious family tree.

"Yes, I know. I have the papers. That should make Father happy." He looked at Willie and smiled, happy for his older brother, the soldier. "You're going of course."

"Of course! It's my patriotic duty."

"Your idea of good sport, you mean."

"Won't you join us, Kurt? Father would be so pleased."

"Would he?"

"You know he would."

"I'm a prisoner here."

"Don't be foolish! You can leave any time you like. Look, say you'll join up. Father just has to say the word. Kurt?..." *In the dark ocean depths his sea mistress waited. It was silent and peaceful. Silver and gold protector fish swam around, ever vigilant...* "Kurt?"

"Oh, I was thinking about something else. What did you say?"

"Father can get you out of here and into our unit."

"No."

"You wouldn't have to fight. A posting in Berlin. Father's Aide-de-Camp."

"I'm not afraid, Willie! Do you think I'm a coward!?"

"I didn't mean that!"

"Poor little Kurt. I'm not afraid to die, Willie!"

"You won't die!"

"I might."

Willie opened a gold case and offered Kurt a cigarette. They were French and well made of the harsh sweet Turkish tobacco. Kurt took the cigarette. Willie struck a match but Kurt shook his head. He ran his finger along the smooth cylinder, looking at it end on, holding it level then tilting it toward the reflecting pool, gliding it to the surface. They watched the cigarette drift away and break up.

"Submarines," Kurt breathed, almost reverently.

"You're not serious!?"

"Will we fight the English?"

"Yes, if they object to annexing Belgium."

"We'll need submarines. I've been reading about them."

"I don't know much about the new service but Father won't hear of it. He has a dim view of the Kriegsmarine as it is, but submarines!?"

"Surely you won't deny me the choice of my own destruction?"

"Must you go on about it?"

"You go on about it. Endlessly! You eat and drink war, you and Father."

"It's not the same thing."

"Isn't it?"

"You're so clever. Try being sensible as well. Stop play acting and being the martyr. Come home and make peace, for all our sakes. It's not pleasant being around him when he's constantly making remarks about your unsavory life style, and this...place!"

"He sent me here!"

"No, it was Mother. You know what Father's solution would be."

"Yes, of course," said Kurt, laughing, mimicking his Father. "Get a horse. Cure anything, and if the venture fails you can always eat it."

Willie laughed. "I have to go. My regiment's mobilizing outside Berlin. They leave for the frontier tonight but I'll join them in a few days. You can join up and go with me."

"It's already been decided then...the war, I mean."

"Yes. It was decided a long time ago. We're just waiting for Austria to move on Serbia."

Kurt sat in the garden for awhile after Willie left. The sun went below the stone wall but Kurt didn't move to the east side of the courtyard. He thought about submarines. It would be dark in a submarine and he had to get used to going without sunshine. He faked his medications, slept during the day and wrote at night. In the deep ocean he could be close to his sea mistress. The reflecting pool was too shallow. Kurt needed depth to be safe. Emerald, blue-black depths, where nothing could reach him.

Day by day the war clouds gathered and the horses thundered closer. The walls were breached in screaming nightmares until Kurt had to run because he was too lucid once free of the narcotic drugs. He slipped out one night and made for the sea by train. It was surprisingly easy. Why had no one thought of escaping?

August 2, 1914: Germany declared war on Russia the day before Kurt walked away from his prison, took a tram to the Friedrichstrasse station and boarded the local train for Norddeich at nine o'clock that evening. The central station was busy and the train heading west for Bremen was crowded with military personnel. He found a compartment with two sailors going as far as Emden and had to step over their sprawled legs to take his seat by the window. One sailor, a young man with an innocent face and a patchy blonde beard, studied him with red-shot eyes. The other, a dark-bearded, tough looking boy of eighteen or twenty, just stared, dumb-drunk, a bottle of wine cradled between them. They had spent the day drinking their way through the brothels before shifting for their base. Kurt thought they were too slovenly dressed for German sailors until he noticed the insignia of the submarine service and the battered forage caps tucked in their belts. Only boys and already hardened veterans of the crumbling peace.

Kurt, still in civilian clothes, had been stared at as he walked to the station. He felt naked again. All the eyes accused him, a fit young man not in uniform, and he was glad to shut himself up in the stifling train, a narrow tube of steel, like a submarine. He felt enclosed by the solid structure and the heat. He pulled the heat around himself and longed for the oblivion of sleep, knowing that the dreams would soon wake him, sweating, screaming, or so he imagined. It didn't matter. He was free and on his way to Norderney and would see only cold, clear water.

The air was golden when the train pulled out angling into the dusty sunset. To the west armies were poised to hurl themselves at the enemy; Germany was invading tiny Luxembourg as the train cleared the ornate station, but Berlin was somnolent in the dying summer heat. Kurt was surprised that the city looked normal, the way it had always appeared from their carriage windows. Was he dreaming about the war? Street vendors with carts went about their business in slow motion. Old women and young girls in big feathered hats walked in the Tiergarten like strutting birds. The old men occupied their benches and talked. The few young men to be seen, clerks from the war office, were in uniform. Confident. Self possessed...*they could afford to be at ease. They weren't going to the Belgium frontier*...walking smartly to attract the young ladies but not too fast to out distance them. The air stood still and heavy with portent, Kurt imagined. After all, Willie had said the war was poised to begin, looming on the horizon like an advancing thunder head. Kurt thought of the days on Norderney, waiting for the big grey clouds to rush in from the North Sea.

The blonde sailor with the innocent face pulled the cork with his teeth and offered the bottle to Kurt. The other sailor continued to stare. Kurt tasted wine for the first time in a year. It was a good, heavy-bodied red from Spain, the Castilla region. He could taste the warm yellow and blue south. It had been a long time since that boozy summer with his dissolute friends; anarchists, artists and writers, searching for the spirit of Saavedra. They were twenty and life was a promise they could put off. They did Spain, then the South of France and Italy *for experience*, they said. *One has to experience life to create it.* They set off with high hopes and their parent's money to pursue culture in its lair. In reality they spent their time chasing down the best local wines and the worst local girls. Their money flew away and they crawled home in disarray before much damage was done. Culture was unharmed as well, although art was mauled severely late at night in bars in Barcelona and Madrid and small harbour towns.

"...Thank you. It's good," said Kurt, reluctantly handing over the bottle.

"You look like you need a drink."

"You're very generous to share, with a stranger."

"We've drunk so much today, you do me a favour."

"Still, I thank you."

The blonde sailor waved him off. The tough sailor stared. Kurt was becoming uncomfortable and he couldn't get away from them.

"Why is your friend staring at me?"

"Who? Him?...not staring...dead," the blonde sailor said, grinning like an idiot. "Dead drunk. If he moves he'll probably puke all over you. Be happy he's just staring."

"All right, I'm happy."

The tough looking sailor blinked, then shut his eyes and slumped against his mate. Kurt was alert in case the boy pitched forward to be sick. But he didn't wake again until they changed trains for the local line at Bremen. The blonde sailor didn't seem to mind.

"Are you going to Emden?" asked the sailor.

"No, Norddeich," answered Kurt hesitantly, not wishing to explain.

"What's in Norddeich? Your home?"

"The boat to Norderney."

"Ahh, then Norderney's your home?"

"No," said Kurt. "I'm just going to Norderney."

"Shit! What for!?...nothing there! This albatross and I went there on leave once. Somebody said a lot of birds went there on holidays, and I don't mean the kind with feathers. Nothing but sand and wind. Awful!"

"Precisely."

"You like that shit!?"

"Yes, something in here does, although I don't know why," Kurt lied. He wished he could have another drink of the good Spanish wine. He did know why he had to go to Norderney; the feeling named Anna had been there but it couldn't be explained, except the sand and water. "Norderney's all right, if you want to be quiet."

"You're too young to be quiet," said the sailor. "You can be quiet when you're dead. The war's on you know! That's why we're going back. Cut our stinking leave short. Had another two weeks, then we get told to hump it back. Say, you're not a spy are you?"

"Are you doing something secret?"

"Shit! Top secret. We go out in our goddamned stinking little U-boat and float around like a whale on his back with his dick out of water. Some fun, I'll say."

Maybe it was fun, thought Kurt. The blonde sailor laughed, held out the bottle of wine for Kurt, then snatched it back. "Hey, how is it you're not in the goddamned Kriegsmarine!?...or something?"

"Well, tell you the truth, I just got out of a mental hospital. I escaped, actually. Haven't had time to join up."

"Shit! If you're hungry to join up you must be crazy!"

Kurt eyed the wine bottle lying in the sailor's arms like a nursing baby. The sailor handed the bottle to Kurt and waited for the explanation. Kurt took a good long pull in case it didn't come back. The sailor motioned he should drink more. Kurt tried and topped up too fast and red wine ran down his chin and soiled his only good shirt.

"Out of practice," Kurt explained, laughing. "It's been a long time, since I've had the pleasure of good wine. Of anything come to think of it. A year I think. They must have kept me pretty well knocked out at the Institute."

"No wine?! No women!? Shit! How did you stand it!?"

"I don't remember. Never thought about it much," he lied again. Anna was never far away. The feeling of Anna, rather.

"You poor bastard! I know a crazy man from our town. He gets it all the time. He has a reputation...know what I mean? Dick like a horse!"

"I had a problem, but it's gone...I guess," he lied a third lime. Kurt wanted to change the subject. "Do you like the submarines?"

"Shit! I don't know. Joined up when I was sixteen. It was that or reform school. Lots of trouble. I beat up an old man for a lousy bottle of schnapps. The old bastard nearly died. It was service or reform school. What a choice! One's as bad as the other, we live like moles with webbed feet and never see the sun. And stink? Shit! You wouldn't believe the stink. It's worse after leave when the boys are still drunk. Then it gets very bad. Sick again...sea sick."

"But you stayed, so you must like it."

"Maybe. I don't know." The sailor took a reflective drink. "Say, why don't you join up!? The boat needs a clever boy like you. Our navigator keeps getting lost. We have to stop ships to ask them where we are." The sailor laughed and passed the bottle.

"That would be funny," said Kurt, taking another drink. "Stop a

British battleship to ask directions home before you put a torpedo in her guts!"

The young, innocent face, that had beat an old man nearly to death, laughed and poked his mate in the ribs. The tough looking sailor slept on. Kurt and the blond sailor drank and laughed for a few minutes but Kurt feared the next, obvious question. He wondered how he would answer. He felt the wine working and couldn't think straight.

"So, a good looking crazy man in Berlin. Truth? I think you must've had lots of women."

"Yes, hundreds. The doctor prescribed one a day for my cure."

The blonde sailor thought it was very funny. He laughed, encouraging Kurt to drink up. The crisis passed. They settled in to finish the bottle, talking nonsense.

The night train to Emden was late. A troop train from Prussia crossing to the Belgian frontier had priority. They changed trains and waited at Bremen for the crossing train. The tough sailor slept on. The passengers, mostly soldiers and sailors, stretched their legs and speculated that the tracks had been blown up by British saboteurs working for the Belgians. Or Belgian saboteurs working for the Dutch. They also stared at Kurt and whispered.

"Come on, before they turn you over to the police," said the sailor. "I'm starving. We'll have to liberate some captive bread." Kurt and the blonde sailor left the train.

There were no shops open so the blonde sailor forced his way into a bakery. Kurt watched through the window. The fire boy was asleep beside his oven. The sailor, silent as a ghost, took two loaves; a long, heavy rye that the peasant farmers eat and a pumpernickel, like a brick, with big moist grains you could chew for a long time after eating the bread. Kurt held the liberated loaves while the blonde sailor liberated some sausage from the butcher's and two bottles of wine from the wine merchant. Kurt was getting nervous.

"Cheese?"

"No! We'll end up in prison for sure."

"Shit! There's a war. We're in training; survival training. You, a suspicious looking civilian, they might shoot on sight though, in which case I'll carry the wine."

Kurt liked the blonde sailor. *Good German youth,* he thought. Resourceful, sense of humour. He decided to leave the train at Emden, short of Norddeich. He'd been thinking about submarines. It was an opportunity to see the beast close aboard. He discounted fate putting him in the compartment with the submarine kids. *Still, he wondered...*

"Look out!" whispered his companion hoarsely.

"What!?" Kurt was jolted out of a reverie that was about to take him down some dark, mentally useless road to a predictably erroneous conclusion.

"Shit! Military police. Run for it!"

They ran into the darkness. Kurt expected a bullet in the back so he ran low, juggling the bread and sausage, stuffing dangling sausage links into his pockets as they stumbled blindly down a lane beside the tracks. The lane was a light mud with dark puddles defining the holes to avoid. The sailor leaped into a ditch beside the tracks. Kurt tumbled in beside him, laughing.

"Good going, mate! A few nights in a decent whorehouse and you'll be back in shape."

"*Phew!* Now what? No train. No luggage."

"I saved the wine. Got the bread?" Kurt nodded. "Huh? Good!"

"Good!? We could be shot and left in a ditch like rabid dogs."

"I resent being called a dog." The sailor broke the neck off a bottle with a sharp blow of his knife and offered Kurt the first drink.

Kurt shook his head. "You pinched it. You deserve the first drink."

"I never drink first. In case of glass."

"Thank you very much."

They stifled laughs and shared the wine. It was a cheap white wine with no character, except for the taste of the acid. They agreed it was no time to be particular but the sausage was local and good. The rye bread was stale but edible. They spent an agreeable hour making small talk, enjoying the protection of the dark ditch, listening to the rhythmic panting of the steam engine idling beside the station. Dim figures moved about the platform. There was no sign of the train moving soon. Or of the military police.

"Shit! Typical German thinking," said the sailor. "The Frontier train has priority. We could've been half way to Emden by now!" He took a long pull of the wine in compensation. "Look, when that train starts moving you watch me. It's still going slow here. But be careful, a slip, under you go. Hard to catch a train with no feet."

"You've done this before?"

"It gets boring on the night train. No women travel these days. The train always stops at Bremen. We're always hungry."

"Was there really a military policeman back there?"

The blonde sailor laughed.

August 3, 1914: Germany declared war on France. The train was five hours late arriving at Emden. A mechanical problem had stopped them again between Leer and Emden. The blonde sailor wanted to walk but the tough looking sailor wouldn't wake up. It was too bright to sleep so Kurt and the sailor had breakfast of sausage, the rest of the wine and the heavy pumpernickel. The foul taste of cheap wine and cigarettes and garlic sausage clung to Kurt's mouth like alum. He felt used up and longed for a bath and good bed. Or the North Sea. The dark sailor, who woke up grumpy, taking only a cigarette, resumed staring at Kurt.

Emden was as busy as Berlin was subdued. Carts and lorry traffic moved in and out of the harbour at a measured pace but there was the electricity of war preparations in the air. Kurt wondered if the scene was the same in other German harbours on the North Sea and the Baltic; Wilhelmshaven, Hamburg, Cuxhaven and Kiel. And was it the same in France and Britain? He wondered about Russia, their unpredictable back yard neighbour, the unfathomable behemoth, the Great Russian Bear of legend, that all Germans feared. Germans, like the French, could never hope to succeed in Europe without dealing with the Bear because Russia had an almost inexhaustible supply of cannon fodder to make up for their leaders' lack of finesse. Czar Nicholas was faltering, the anarchists threatening to topple the autocrats and his father had chauvinistically dismissed Russia because Germany was fixated on the Belgian coast. Britain would have to be engaged to take and hold them unless the British could be finessed. Doubtful, the newspapers had said as soon as Germany engaged the French. Long and bitter relations existed among Europe's restless nations and war was necessary to settle accounts. Kurt felt no ill will toward the French. He drank their wine and loved their women. In temperament he was more French than German, but he *was* German so he would find the office of the submarine commander before he changed his mind.

"Not so fast my friend," said the blonde sailor. "We've got four hours before we have to report and there's a good whorehouse in Emden. You can't just throw yourself at the Navy and say, here I am, a virgin!"

"I'm not a virgin!"

"A year without pussy? Same thing."

"I'll see your commander, then I'm going on to Norderney. The war can wait."

"Have it your way, mate."

His new friends lurched off in the direction of Emden's brothel. They both died in the first month of the war when their U-boat was run down by a trawler. However, the whores of Germany, and the world, would be busy. There are priorities even in war and some personal pursuits are more important than being at the front on time.

Kurt followed the supply carts down to the harbour and as he rounded the corner of a warehouse he checked his steps at the sight of so many grey killing machines gathered in one place; tug boats, gunboats, frigates, a pair of new destroyers, and submarines, an untidy, unGerman-like assembly of tiny ships scattered about the basin, tied to every possible floating object, and attended to by an army of protective ants. The submarine flotilla's headquarters were in a red brick office building attached to a big warehouse, recently occupied by the British Atlantic Shipping Line. No one had bothered to pull down the sign. There was no guard at the door so Kurt entered the reception area; sealing his fate, if he believed in fate.

Petty officers carrying papers and dossiers, went in and out of small cramped offices, *just like a submarine would be,* Kurt thought. A tall, thin korvettenkapitän entered behind Kurt and gave him a thorough looking over as he passed. The korvettenkapitän entered a door at the end of the hall.

Pictures of German submarines and smiling crews covered the walls of the reception area. They seemed a slovenly lot compared to the spit and polish of the German Army. There was a cutaway model of a submarine in a glass case. Kurt wondered where forty crewmen would stand up or lay down in the cluttered space. The magazine pictures Kurt had poured over while in the Institute didn't do the clutter of machinery justice. The slender tube seemed to be all pipes and gauges and engines. In another glass case was a model of a British freighter, with gleaming white superstructure, red bottom and yellow Sampson posts and derricks; the flagship of the British shipping line. Some humourist had painted a bull's-eye amidships below the bridge, and written, *Up yours Cousin George* across the grey hull. To Kurt it seemed a sacrilege. Worse would be done to the real ships and real men. If he had doubts he could still walk away and take the train to Norddeich.

Kurt's perversity to reason and danger prevailed. He wandered down the hall looking in open doors. Clerks looked up, some even said hello or smiled, then went back to their work. Everyone was busy but the pace was relaxed. If they were preparing for war there was no great hurry. Kurt began to relax. This was different than the rigid atmosphere of the august chambers of the German Imperial Army in Berlin where stiff old officers, dripping with braid and medals, posed in groups planning a war. His father had exposed Kurt to the great men in hopes that the grandeur would rub off. Instead Kurt was repelled by the decorative excess and the pomposity of old men playing at war. The Spartan offices of the former British Atlantic Line were more to his liking. He reached the end of the hall and the door to the Commander's office. The upper panel was pebbled glass and inside forms of men wavered as if they were under water. *Appropriate,* thought Kurt. A title and name, Kapitän zur See, Ernst Müller, was roughly stenciled above the title of Commander Submarines. Kurt knocked. A tenor voice bellowed at the door.

"Christ! If you have time to knock it can't be important! Go away!"

Kurt knocked again.

"Damnit man!...if you insist, come in!"

Kurt opened the door feeling immediately at ease. Only a man with a sense of humour could respond like that in a German uniform. Three young men stared back at him. The commander, Ernst Müller, not much older than Kurt, sat with his feet up on the big desk of the shipping company manager. Another man, Walther Schwieger, a hard nosed veteran of submarines wearing his officer's cap pushed well back on his small head, occupied an overstuffed easy chair, one leg thrown over the arm. The korvettenkapitän was standing to one side reading a document on a clipboard. He was about the same age as the commander but looked older because he sported a full blonde beard. He had piercing-blue, no nonsense eyes, but laugh wrinkles around the eyes gave him away. The uniforms were, to say the least, casual. Battle jackets open to shirts without ties, leather boots, rumpled, comfortable fatigue pants with large pockets. They were the young Turks of the fledgling submarine service. Outlaws of the German military.

"A civilian for God's sake! Grab him!" said the veteran. The other two just grinned as if civilians were only for entertainment.

Kurt studied each face separately and liked what he saw. These men would be at home in the fisherman's bar on Norderney.

"Yes? Well, what do you want?" demanded Commander Müller.

"I would like to buy you a drink, at my café on Norderney," Kurt answered spontaneously. The commander was puzzled. The korvettenkapitän laughed. The lines were there for a good reason.

"Business must be very bad at your café," said Schwieger. He was joking but Kurt detected a hardness in the man. He would soon have a chance to put his hardness to the test. Kapitänleutnant Walther Schwieger was the submarine commander whose *U-20* would torpedo and sink the *Lusitania* a few months later. But at the moment the submarine service was a long way from glory.

"Oh, it's not my café. The fishermen go there to play cards."

"Fishermen!? What are we waiting for!?" said the korvettenkapitän. "We could Shanghai a few to fill out our rosters." The korvettenkapitän waved his document. "I'd give two petty officers, plus my cook, for a damned navigator who could find his way from the nearest pub to the boat without falling in the gutter."

"What are you complaining about, Schrader? You've got the best coxswain in the fleet," said Schwieger. "I'd trade all my petty officers for a good coxswain. Indispensable!"

"Yes. Damned right!" responded Schrader. "A good coxswain can get you off the mud when your idiot navigator runs you aground. But I'd rather not be aground!"

"Now Alfred, we have no sympathy," said the commander. "He put you on the beach not a hundred meters from the best whorehouse on the coast. And on a falling tide. What did you do for twelve hours?"

"And why didn't you radio for help sooner?" needled Schwieger.

"My radio operator was knocked out of commission, in his own bunk, during the grounding."

They had a good laugh. The kind of laugh men can have when they trust each other. Kurt laughed too. He longed to be in the society of men who could laugh while getting ready for war. If war was inevitable why not enjoy it?

"Are you from Norderney?" asked Müller. "You don't look like a fisherman."

"No, sir. I met a couple sailors from one of your boats on the train."

"I suppose they told you all our secrets. Well, we have very little to hide. We're desperately under crewed..."

"Under screwed you mean!" said Korvettenkapitän Schrader.

"Under supplied," continued Müller. "Our boats are falling apart. The war is about to begin and the High Command ignores us."

"In other words, situation normal," said Schwieger and Schrader in unison.

"One of your sailors only mentioned that his boat needed a navigator."

"Are you a navigator?" asked Korvettenkapitän Schrader.

"Navigation's a hobby."

"A hobby!? This's a goddamned navy, not a social club!"

"Have you done much sailing?" asked Müller, ignoring the jibes.

"Some. Yachts...galliots."

"Yachts and bloody galliots!?" repeated the commander, in mock disgust.

"A goddamned yachter playboy!" laughed Schwieger.

"Can you work a sextant plot?"

"I perfected my sextant work on Norderney."

The commander stifled a laugh. "Is the island still where it's supposed to be?"

"Ah, yes! Every time."

"Good enough! I'll take him," said Schrader.

"Hold on!" said Commander Müller. "Shouldn't we ask the gentleman his name before you throw him into your boat?" He looked at Kurt, trying to be serious. "We need to know your next of kin so we can send them your personal effects."

"Formalities," said Schwieger, leaving the room. "We'll fight the war with paper work. I have some of my own. They want me to shift to Wilhelmshaven in the morning. Join us tonight for my farewell party and see how foolish submariners can be when they're drunk."

"Thank you. But I have other plans..."

"You don't have plans in submarines," said Schwieger. "Only reactions...And consequences. Goodbye then. Good luck!"

Schwieger closed the door. Kurt wondered if Schwieger was being prophetic or just somber for his benefit. Kurt would remember Schwieger's parting comment about reactions and consequences in other circumstances. At the moment he was amused by the offhand comments and casual attitude of the submarine men into whose midst he had been thrown. He still wouldn't admit to the possibility of fate. He could have stayed on the train and gone on to Norddeich.

"Well?" inquired the commander. "What *is* your name?"

"Kurt...Kurt Schulte, sir." Kurt looked at the two officers. "To be accurate, I'm afraid there's a *von* in there."

"Von Schulte? Hmmm...Prussian." Kurt nodded as if ashamed to admit to his heritage. "*The* von Schultes?" asked Müller.

"Yes. My father...the General," Kurt admitted reluctantly.

"Schrader, what would General Freidrich von Schulte's son be doing in the mud of Emden trying to join the submarines?"

"Good question," answered Schrader. "His only prospect's misery, or at best a quick drowning. No glory."

"I can't ride a horse," offered Kurt.

The commander and the korvettenkapitän laughed. Schrader sat down on the leather couch and motioned for Kurt to take the chair vacated by Schwieger. The conversation was absurd for the military, even for the submarine corps, but whatever the future held he wasn't apprehensive about the company.

He may be entering a war with an untried and dangerous force but he felt further from danger or death than he could remember, having born the burden of his mortality too long to have confidence in his own survival. To compensate he had once chosen self-destruction. Now, the war and Emden could be his undoing or his salvation. Life was becoming simple, at last. *Follow orders and be able to locate a position on a chart by knowing the day of the year, the time and your position in respect to a heavenly body.* Kurt sunk into the stuffed chair, melted into the heavy brocaded fabric and felt his body dissolve. The comforting mists from his commander's cigarette enfolded him and said, *I will protect you, Kurt.*

"You're in luck, Schulte," said Müller. "The only horses you'll find in our little boats, besides the engines, are in the sausages. And they can be hard enough to keep under control."

"Do you allow garlic sausages, the stink and all?"

"Stink? Perfume of the god's compared to the rest," answered Müller, still trying to be serious.

"A few days at sea and you'll put garlic sausage up your nose for relief," teased Schrader.

"You'll sleep with it and think it's the pure smell of a virgin, but no funny business. Talk. Only talk," said Müller.

"Tell lies about your exploits with the women. It's every man's duty to keep the spirits up. It helps to get through tight spots, such as when the boat's diving and she won't pull out and the only thing between you and the bottom of the ocean is a kilometer of cold, black water, and you know the pressure hull will collapse at two hundred meters," said the korvettenkapitän gravely.

"Do you like sunshine and fresh air?" asked Müller quickly.

"Yes, but..."

"Forget it!" said Müller. "Think like a troll. Sun is the enemy. Darkness is your friend."

"Of course," offered the korvettenkapitän, "as navigator you must go on the bridge to get sights and when you come below the others will ask you to describe the waves."

"I don't understand. Describe waves?"

"Most patrols that's all there is to see," the korvettenkapitän assured Kurt.

"Hot meals on time?" asked Müller.

"Forget it!" answered the korvettenkapitän.

"Toilet facilities when the bladder is ready to explode?" asked Müller.

"Forget it! Piss in a boot. Your own!" said the korvettenkapitän, seriously.

"A hot bath or even enough putrid water to wash your face?"

"Forget it!"

"Clean linens?"

"Forget it."

"Except for the first day out."

"And hope your bunk mate doesn't have crabs."

"Letters from home?"

"Forget it!"

"Do you have a woman? A wife? A mistress?"

"No, and...yes," stammered Kurt.

"No and yes!?" echoed the korvettenkapitän.

"Tell lies about what you do with your mistress but we don't talk about wives. Too dangerous. Your mistress might be someone's wife. And don't show pictures to make the others jealous."

"It's better to just tell lies about whores. Less chance of insulting somebody's wife."

"Chance of promotion?"

"Impossible!"

"When the Kapitän dies, everybody dies."

"If the Kapitän lives he won't let go of good men."

"Chance of survival?"

"Slim," answered Schrader.

"Chance of being decorated by the Kaiser?"

"Also slim. The Kaiser doesn't know he has submarines."

"And the High Command, although they are forced to admit we exist, refuse to understand what we do."

"Why do you want to be in submarines, Schulte?" asked the korvettenkapitän abruptly.

Until that moment Kurt thought he knew why; to be near his sea mistress, but confronted with the comforting reality of men in a real war, the possibility of a mythical lover blew away like ground fog in the morning sun. He wasn't discouraged by the litany of horrors recited half in jest. He wasn't afraid of dying nor did he have aspirations for promotion, and personal discomfort was a way of life for a part time ascetic. He would have to tell the truth: "I'm afraid...I can't give you a good reason."

"You're not running away from anything are you, Schulte?" asked the korvettenkapitän. Kurt shook his head.

"Good!" said Müller. "Then there's no baggage to drag along? No brooding over grievances or broken promises?"

"No. I was just going to Norderney."

"Excellent! If only it were always that simple to put yourself in harm's way. A clear conscience. An open mind. No fanatical dedication to a cause. Believe me, Schulte, in the submarines you won't need causes. Your own survival is all you'll ever need to make you want to fight," said Commander Müller.

"It's not even necessary to know why we're fighting. The old bastard of a Kaiser might be wrong but we are Germans and we fight for Germany. Period!" asserted Schrader.

"Schulte, meet your Commanding Officer. Korvettenkapitän zur See, Alfred Schrader."

"Welcome aboard, Schulte." Korvettenkapitän Schrader offered a soft, almost delicate looking hand but the grip was strong and sure. Kurt felt a certain power in the tall, slender man he had liked immediately. Schrader would not have been out of place behind a violin. He had intelligent eyes and the strength he felt was in the eyes, a man to be trusted and followed to the end. Kurt would never forget the moment. He didn't exactly go soft and mushy in the man's presence but he would have been happy to have a father like Schrader.

"Thank you, sir. I hope I'm some use."

"You'd better be," said Schrader, winking at Müller. "We can't afford to haul around frivolous cargo. I'll give you a chance to prove yourself. You're duties at first will be strictly navigation. You must learn the details of your incarceration on the job and take your turn with the others. Is that clear?"

"Yes, of course..."

"Good! You have five days. I suggest you go home and tidy up business. Your family will want to know what it is you've gotten yourself into. My regards to your father, the General; he won't remember me."

"Sign this paper, Schulte." The commander turned a document toward Kurt. "Then swear to do your duty."

Kurt, in a daze, signed the document that had something to do with offering his body up to the Imperial German Navy without question, duties, consequences for failure, internment, court's marshal. He was under a spell and the enchantment was too pleasant to spoil by asking mundane questions about legalities. "I swear."

"You are a German sailor now. If you fail to come back in five days the military police can track you down and shoot you for desertion," said Müller, teasing again.

Kurt laughed. He had already been in the sights of the military police, or so he believed, and lived to volunteer his immortal soul to the Fatherland.

"That might complicate things," said Schrader, with a mischievous grin.

"It wouldn't look good on your record," said Commander Müller.

They all had a good laugh. Kurt's spirits soared to heights he had never imagined. He followed Korvettenkapitän Schrader out of the room. Schrader put his arm around Kurt and they continued laughing as they went down the hall, getting astonished looks from the clerks as each office doorway flipped by like framed portraits of young men.

"You have time for a drink before the Norddeich train. If I had less work to do I'd join you on your little excursion to Norderney. I'd like to meet your fishermen."

"I'd be delighted to have you're company, sir."

"No need to call me sir, yet. You're educated, Schulte. If you have the spirit you have a future with the navy, despite what we said back there. Hard work and good humour; most of all good humour. It sometimes succeeds where too much discipline fails."

They passed out of the office building to the busy harbour. Coal smoke from trains and derricks and ships hung over the docks like a pall. Kurt stopped to watch the harbour scene from a new perspective; a sworn member of the U-boat service. A half dozen slim, dangerous looking, grey U-boats lining the nearest floats of the basin, appeared to be ready for sea, their crews lined up on the after deck at ease waiting for the order to cast off. Workers still poured over them, supplies disappeared into them, and everywhere there was activity, like an ant hill girding for a long winter. Ships of all sizes moved up and down the misty River Ems. Beyond was the frontier and Holland and beyond Holland, the Channel and the North Sea, the moat guarding England, that must be fought over and controlled to hold Belgium. It was all wrapped in smoke and mist and speculation. Kurt's future was somewhere out there and the vehicle to take him into that uncertain future was somewhere in the oil and soot-grimed harbour.

"Come on! Stop staring at them," said Schrader. "They aren't very pretty anyway. Plenty of time to see your boat when you get back. You'll be so sick of seeing her you'll get to shore and never look back. That's her over there in the dry dock."

Schrader's submarine looked naked and vulnerable on the blocks.

"I've read everything I could find about submarines," said Kurt, as Korvettenkapitän Schrader steered him toward the officer's club across the road. They dodged a wagon load of gleaming torpedoes. The slender cylinders reminded Kurt of cigarettes in Willie's gold case. What would Willie think? He couldn't wait to tell him. Submarines!

"Submarines are the new science of warfare," said Schrader, as they took chairs at a small table in the officer's club. "Pure physics applied to the transportation of men and torpedoes for the express purpose of killing the enemy. What will you drink, Schulte?...Rudolf! We have only a short time to get this man drunk before he changes his mind!"

"Cognac," said Kurt.

"Excellent! I'd be disappointed if you'd started with beer. Besides I'm buying. Always take advantage and never give an inch but be generous to your friends in all things, except women; and be compassionate to your enemy only when he can no longer hurt you."

"Sums it up pretty well," said Kurt. "Can I quote you?"

"Why? Are you a writer or something?"

"Yes, I'd like to think so."

"Rudolf!! Quick! It's a real emergency. Just bring the bottle. We have to get Schulte drunk before he starts writing. Or thinking!"

Submarine officers at other tables laughed at Schrader's joke. They sensed a raw recruit already in Schrader's good books. Kurt didn't mind. He felt a part of their society. Rudolf arrived with a bottle and Schrader poured destructive amounts of strong French cognac.

Schrader held up his glass in salute. "Dive! Dive! That's an order from your Commanding Officer!"

Kurt was determined to get the cargo down the hatch in one offering. Before the measure had stopped sloshing about in his empty stomach his head was beginning to reel from the brandy and the fatigue that follows excitement. It's a common problem. You can go on nerves just so long, but when it's all right to relax the body collapses at the first opportunity. Kurt didn't just relax, he crashed. Not immediately. He had the experience to stay with it for a few glasses but it was a losing battle. In the end he had the distinction of being carried to the train by Korvettenkapitän Alfred Schrader and a pair of ranking officers who would be dead within a month. Schrader was the only decorated commander to turn down a promotion to stay with his boat and crew, only to be lost near the end of the war in a freak accident. He would be decorated many times over for his exploits. But the war had to be started and fought and all the players located properly on stage, waiting for the directors and stage managers to give the signals. "Long live Imperial Germany!" shouted someone. *Vive la guerre!* Kurt said to himself.

Kurt had only a vague recollection of the train ride to Norddeich, wearing an assortment of service dress donated by various officers at the club, complete with a battered officer's hat. A note pinned to the coat instructed the trainmen to take good care of him because Schulte was a famous Konteradmiral on his way to Norderney to defend Germany against an invasion force from England. Kurt was dumped on the platform of Norddeich station with his valise and turned over to the night crew of the Norderney ferry.

Kurt arrived on Norderney relatively unscathed, with the euphoria of recent events competing in his brain with the mundane immediacy of a monumental headache. He found his way to the café; was greeted with cheers and handshakes, the delinquent returned, and settled in with his fishermen to get really drunk.

August 4, 1914: Germany declared war on Belgium for refusing to let her armies march on France. Kurt woke in his old room at the inn. He recognized the cracked plaster as familiar things came into focus. The writing desk; scene of struggles and defeats, started up the memories before he was ready to deal with Anna. The dresser where his sextant case had resided, also where he sat for the doctor's inspection of his diseased parts. The heavy planked floor where he sat among the papers trying to write or make sense of the encounters on the beach. He smoothed the covers on the bed where another battle had been fought. He tried to visualize the unequal skirmish in the moonlight but the image was indistinct. It could have been a picture painted by someone else; seen but only vaguely remembered as though it hadn't left an impression. He was surprised by the lack of spiritual pain as indifferent memories of Anna drifted through the room. He pulled himself to his feet, waiting through the stabbing pain and pounding blood, and began the awkward ritual of dressing in unfamiliar military clothes; even the shirt and pants. He didn't remember how he got them off. He had a vague recollection of the young waiter from the café. A moment of panic swept over him until he remembered the coarse hands of his fishermen who had dragged him across the street to the inn. He was convinced by the disarray of the serendipitous uniform...the queer would have folded the clothes neatly and tucked him in, among other things. *Never drink yourself into oblivion, again,* he vowed. He wondered which submariners in the officer's club had contributed, a mannequin puzzle assembled by drunkards.

Adjusting the battered officer's cap to the back of his head, as Walther Schwieger did, so as not to look too serious in the role, he went about the business he had come to Norderney to finish. The first encounter with the morning-after had been encouraging. It was easier than he imagined. The year of diffused shadows and destructive therapy hadn't dulled his senses. He felt alive. More alive than he had dreamed possible during the cold months when his mind had been numbed and his body isolated in a cold womb for its own protection. He accepted the condition because he was too weakened to protest. The dreams had finally forced him to run and a real war was his escape from the nightmare, and the woman. War was his therapy. Or so he thought in August of 1914. First he would write it all down, just in case he died, or survived to tell the tale. He took the black, leather-bound journal out of his valise and sat down at the desk. He put down the words honestly...nothing dangerous at first.

Later Kurt walked the surf line on the north beach. The sun was different from the year before. It shone clear and bright and optimistic. Proof that nature was not in concert with the human combatants. As Kurt scanned the sharp horizon German troops were crossing the Belgium Frontier and people were already dying on the ground. Britain was mobilizing in response, the gauntlet had been dropped, or thrown down in anger at Germany's deliberate provocation. As the tide slid higher up the sand, Britain's North Sea squadrons were preparing to sail for Scapa Flow to blockade the Baltic. The larger blockade of the North Sea region was beginning and U-boats were getting under way from German harbours to harass the British fleet. Kurt saw only sea birds and whitecaps on the blue sea. Big white clouds with grey centers owned the sky. The sand was clean and no one had died of the war in his ocean. His sea mistress was still a virgin. He chuckled at that thought.

Kurt relaxed, more sure of his place in the scheme of things. No ghosts came at him out of the distant mists. No self doubts clawed at his insides. Anna remained an enigma but in the background and he had taken a step into his future, free from the stifling demands of the family. He wondered if it wasn't to spite the family.

Kurt began running along the beach, skipping over the foaming waves, shouting with relief. He was happy to be going to war; the happiest man alive. He ran faster, kicked off his shoes and sprinted on the hard sand until his borrowed officer's cap flew off. He unbuttoned the jacket and flung it up the beach. He ran as if he were leaving Kurt Schulte behind. If he ran fast enough the wind would tear away his features and he wouldn't be Kurt Schulte at all. He could be anybody he wanted to be. He could be Maupassant, Renoir, Dante, Munch, Monet. Conrad! Kurt stopped running and bent forward, hands on his knees, until he could breath again, laughing and gasping with the happiness and the effort.

"Conrad!" he shouted, laughing at the silliness. "You understand my ocean! You could have explained her to me. No, I have to make a fool of myself, in front of a flock of seagulls, who'd tell anybody. No shame those birds of yours. I can be like you. Damn right! What are you, Joe!? Just a Russian sailor who writes! What are you, Claude? Just an old French fart who slaps colours around on a canvas. And if you weren't so old you'd have to fight this goddamned war too and maybe we'd have to kill each other! Wouldn't prove anything would it? But, since you don't have to fight you can go on being great, while I, Kurt Schulte, bad writer and worse painter, get experience so I can be great too...while you get fatter! And probably greater. I'll never catch up. But I don't care!"

Kurt laughed until his side ached. He felt good. It felt very good to hurt for art but the running made him light headed. It was cleaner than the wine and didn't have an after taste. Art must be pursued. He chased art and ran hard again until he collapsed under the weight of culture and didn't see the men from the Institute approaching...

That night in his room at the inn, when he had recovered from the beating, Kurt wrote in his journal: '*...Art is a gigantic cunt you keep sticking enormously creative dicks into until something gets created.*

Some art is a real bastard though. Nobody wants to admit to it. No, look at us! We pushed things around until this bastard, creative war gets started and nobody wants to take the blame for its creation. We're little blobs of colour being pushed around on a big canvas. I don't know what the goddamned picture's going to look like...'

And at the same time he wrote: *'...One day I was painting in the garden all alone. I remember it well...I was twelve, an awkward age for an awkward child. Mother always scolded me if I got paint on my clothes. My sister teased me. She was better at it, but she was older and should have been more charitable. My brother Willie, the critic, threw mud and grass on my paintings. Father was usually disgusted when he caught me painting. But this day I had set up under an apple tree; there were blossoms, and I had the hedge between me and the terrace. Father liked to sit on the terrace in the evening outside the conservatory, to smoke before the guests arrived. We always had guests arriving. I was set up to get the light on the pond, with the ducks in reflection and in silhouette. I'd seen a painting by an old French master, not very interesting, but the light in his painting was good because it had a sparkle on the water that made me squint. I couldn't understand how a painting could make you squint if it wasn't real light, only paint. I wanted to try. I worked hard for a long time but it wasn't right. The more I tried the more wrong it became. I was cursing out loud. Father came up behind, quietly, and watched me daubing away, too angry to notice him. I was ready to chuck the whole mess in the pond when Father startled me. He said I wouldn't make much of a painter until I could paint as well as I could swear. He said I could swear better than some of his officers. I wondered if it was a compliment. Then he said if I insisted on daubing I must learn to paint well, so as not to disgrace his name. When I asked him if he would let me go to an art school in France he grunted and walked away. I never found out what it meant. The grunt...'*

His own name, shouted from somewhere down the beach, startled Kurt. In seconds he relived Norderney in the way he was trying to forget. Months of therapy sessions were undone in a single shout. He wanted to escape into the sea but ran for the protection of the sand dunes.

"Kurt Schulte!!"

A group of men were hurrying along the beach; two of the men were policemen. The robberies at Bremen station? His submarine career was in ruins. Where else could he run? Two of the men were dressed in white. He recognized the orderlies from the Institute. How could they have tracked him down so soon? He thought about his nighttime flight from Berlin. A blind bloodhound with defective olfactory glands could have followed the scent trail. The fifth man was the young waiter from the fishermen's café.

"Herr Schulte! Take it easy," soothed the bigger of the two orderlies. He was the mean one. He's the one they would send after a fugitive. The orderly was like a caged animal at the Institute because there was a rule about beating the wealthy inmates. Out here they could drag him behind a sand dune and beat him senseless and only the sea birds would know. Surely the police would protect him. Wasn't he a valuable member of a German submarine crew about to enter the war? What did a few sausages matter in a time of national crisis?

The queer! What if he lied to them because Kurt wouldn't play his dirty little games? They came closer, a knot of men looking ridiculous in their uniforms. And his own uniform? The queer was holding Schrader's cap, the officer's coat and Kurt's shoes. Surely the uniform would protect him. But how would he explain the odd sizes? They would say he stole everything. Kurt longed for the protection of the deep water. The old feeling of irrational fear crept over him. "Take it easy, Herr Schulte. Don't run again. We only want to take you back so you can rest," soothed the big orderly.

He scrambled to the top of a dune. "You can't! I belong to the Imperial German Navy! That is my uniform!"

They looked at the uniform pieces held by the waiter and they looked at Kurt in his wine-stained officer's shirt and trousers and bare feel. They looked at each other.

"So, Herr Schulte's play acting again?" asked the big orderly.

"I'm sorry, Kurt," said the young waiter. "I told them, because I was afraid you'd hurt yourself."

Maybe he was wrong about the waiter too. The boy was reaching out to him in a very human way, for whatever reason. Kurt was momentarily strengthened by the addition of an ally, but the doctor had mentioned paranoia. He hated being stripped bare by the doctor...not just naked...worse than naked. Vulnerable. Standing in a circle of light, surrounded by people in the shadows. He couldn't see their faces. Each accused him in turn. He was dissected piece by piece until only his soul was left standing in a refuse heap that used to be his body. Then the doctor would tell Kurt to put himself back together, piece by piece, like little toy blocks. Kurt believed the doctor and tried. Then he felt silly, mentally reassembling his pieces as if he were a child with his tiny building blocks that kept slipping through his fingers. At night he would take himself apart and put himself back together. In the morning he would wake up to discover that the pieces were all wrong. The doctor said it was great progress.

"Leave me alone! I don't need you now!" he yelled down at the men.

The beating in the dunes was stopped by the police only at the waiter's insistence. The police took charge of Kurt and checked with Commander Müller in Emden to confirm that Kurt really did belong to the Imperial German Navy. The orderlies left empty handed and

Kurt was allowed to leave Norderney for Berlin.

August 7, 1914: Kurt sat alone in the back seat of the family touring car, legs stretched out, smoking, enjoying the freedom of leaving the city, looking out at the rolling farmland as the Mercedes accelerated quietly along the narrow country road southeast of Berlin. They had been delayed several times by convoys, but once the fields opened up slowdowns occurred only when a farm cart straddled the road or cattle ambled across, attended by an old man or a young girl. *Life is a series of patterns,* thought Kurt. *Everything is arranged and ordered, except my own life.*

He relaxed in the familiar comfort of the big car. The back of the chauffeur's head was also familiar and comforting. The chauffeur never spoke to Kurt, showing disapproval on principle, but Kurt was happy to be quiet, to stare at the back of the chauffeur's head or out the windows at the patterns of fields and fences. He knew the names and the histories of each estate. He ticked off the moral degenerates, the hypocrites, the morons and the frauds. He knew them all and despised their self-satisfied pretentiousness. Then he realized he was being unfair. *Who was he to call anybody a degenerate?* Some of the best minds and hearts of the German nobility lived in the big manor houses. Without the aristocracy holding the country together, the peasants would be adrift in chaos like the poor buggers in Russia. *How could two countries be so different?* he wondered. How could two countries want to go to war in this excellent countryside during this glorious summer? What would it be like by autumn? He imagined the forests aflame, not with colour, but with gunfire and smoke and blood.

The battle had been joined but it was to be a short, decisive war, many predicted, with Germany victorious. Kurt had two days to be at home with his family before they all separated for their respective positions in the drama; Kurt to his submarine, Father back to his office at High Command in Berlin and Willie to his regiment poised on the frontier waiting for its turn to smash into Belgium. The Schultes could move about at will...Kurt touched the plush velvet of the cushions, the nicely worn leather under him and the smooth hand-crafted wood of the door frames. There were advantages to wealth. How easy it would be to slip into the habit of being rich and powerful...The war was progressing as planned. Father summoned Willie; the dispatch saying that he was needed in Berlin to consult with the High Command, because he was a Schulte. Kurt had no power or rank, just a piece of paper saying he was in the navy, and given a trial as navigator on a questionable adventure. But bottom of the barrel or not he had to break the news to the family.

The black Mercedes turned onto a long, winding drive bordered by manicured lawns with correct trees; like the lawns of every other manor between the Schulte estate and Berlin. Maybe there was a law in Germany that prescribed how the facades should look. There were strict rules about how the inhabitants should be seen to conduct affairs. Kurt broke the rules and paid the price. A social outcast among the families who ruled the invisible kingdom. Even the chauffeur refused to acknowledge Kurt, beyond his duty. And for appearance's sake the family would receive Kurt cordially, so long as he obeyed the rules and played the family game.

Kurt had wired his parents from Norddeich so they were expecting him and plans for his home-coming were developed quickly in response. No one outside the family would visit the Schulte manor for the next two days. Kurt was in isolation, a social quarantine. He didn't care. He hadn't seen his parents for a year and a half even though his father's office in the War Ministry was only six blocks west of the Institute. Father wrote Kurt off, made no apologies and Mother remained in the sanctuary of the country home, although in other years she could find dozens of excuses to be in Berlin. Operas, benefits, weddings or shopping. There was going to be a war and preparations demanded her attention on the home front organizing sheet tearing sessions with the ladies of the district. Bandages became crucial months in advance of hostilities. Father had suggested the timing of the opening of hostilities; it was top secret information, but everyone knew. Bandages were the clue. Preparing bandages was akin to publishing the war in the social gazette. Only Willie had found time to visit him with the news so Kurt thrived on benign neglect and the family fortune substituted for parental love. *Don't be bitter, Kurt,* he said to his reflection in the window.

The Schulte mansion, a study in tasteless excess, opened out of the trees looking like a large, pink concrete box with wedding cake decorations stuck on. Architectural history could be studied by walking around the edifice. The Greeks and Romans were represented with strong columns, patios and urns. It could have stopped there with some success but the graceful vertical lines of the Doric columns were spoiled by pastries that gave the whole an uncomfortable feeling of impermanence. The carnival could strike its tents and steal away in the night leaving behind a cellar of memories. The stucco façade was borrowed from the Italians. General Schulte had been in Italy for a small war. When he returned the traditional German red brick was plastered over. Painting it was his mother's idea. It was her way of punishing her husband for having affairs with Italian whores; while she entertained the young officers of the General's Home Guards. *It worked,* Kurt thought. It was embarrassingly pink.

'...Father and Mother discussed the stucco colour in private, which means they fought. It was my sixteenth birthday. I had just escaped another form of imprisonment in the seminary and Willie and I drank a bottle of French champagne in the cellar and got silly drunk so we missed the actual battle. Sister said it was a dreadful row, with missiles as well as words thrown about. Mother won of course and Father never mentioned it again...the pink stucco...'

A fine drizzle of welcomed rain made the pink manor stand out against the hedgerow green and harvest brown of the fields. It might have been attractive, in Lombardy. Willie, who was waiting under the French portico in full dress uniform, looked splendid. The Baroness posed in the open doorway, hand on the ornate handle as if ready to flee, but it was a greeting of sorts. She could withdraw if Kurt did anything rude. *He had to stop seeing everything in a paranoiac haze,* he told himself, as he stepped from the car under the umbrella held by the manservant who avoided looking directly at Kurt. Again the paranoia! Of course the manservant looked away. He wasn't supposed to judge, or speak unless spoken to, and Mother was in the doorway because it was raining. She was afraid of pneumonia and could contract it at convenient times.

Willie was smiling and Mother seemed happy to see him. Where was Father? Kurt looked up at the study window. Father was looking down on him. *The old bugger did it on purpose! Never give an inch. Who had said that? His new Kapitän, Schrader.* Kurt the profligate, the dissolute, diseased, mental degenerate, had come home to beg forgiveness. They were duty bound to receive him for appearances. *Oh, for God's sake, Kurt! Get a hold of yourself. Look, Willie's smiling. He's coming forward with his hand outstretched.*

"Hello, Kurt!" said Willie cheerfully. "Welcome home. You look splendid in a dinner jacket."

Yes, I do, Kurt said to himself. *Wait till you see my new uniform,* he almost said. He had stopped at their tailor in Berlin for the suit and a uniform. For a premium the tailor worked day and night to finish it. Some major's glittering uniform had to wait. *My Father is General Schulte!...* "Hello, Willie!" Kurt replied. "It's good to be home. Hello, Mother! Go in before you catch your death. Where's Father? Oh, there he is! Hello, Father!!" Kurt shouted and waved knowing it would annoy the old bugger. It was indecorous to shout and wave from the portico where statesmen entered for important meetings and booze ups. The Kaiser himself had almost visited but an urgent state crisis forestalled the event. Kurt gave his father a twisted smile in self defense and put his arm around Willie to go in. Mother accepted a light kiss on both cheeks. She still wouldn't hold him. Didn't know how; from lack of practice. Funny how she could hold diplomats, strangers and cavalry officers tight enough to extract whatever it was she needed. *Stop it Kurt. You're home. Mother's here. Cast no stones. Keep your paranoia under control.* He decided he liked the term...*Paranoia*. It was new. It summed up everything nicely and put it in a box labeled: *Kurt's current problems.* He put the lid down.

'...*The rest of the family arrived later. Our sister, her husband and the children and Willie's wife and children. The meeting with Father went rather well I thought. We were polite. He must have put his feelings in a box of his* own. *The children were a pleasant distraction. Willie has three under twelve. Sister has three over twelve and two under twelve and all delightfully over indulged. Well balanced bunch, we Schultes. They, the children, made a great commotion so that talk was almost impossible. A great relief. It saved me from having to pretend to be interested in Sister's husband's ridiculous views on the war and Willie's wife's hysteria about the deprivations of war. Would chocolates be in short supply? What if they rationed sugar? She knows I hate chocolates. The box opened a crack but when no one was looking I sat on it and shot the bolt...*'

Dinner was another matter. By Schulte tradition formal family dinners were subdued affairs. The General presided from the head of the table and conversation was confined to the logistics of eating or restraining the children. However, if important guests were present they were allowed to talk, laugh, spill drinks and molest maids as much as necessary to keep up morale. Kurt gave up trying to start up small talk. It was impossible to change a lifetime of cynicism growing up under the dual system of values. So, when he realized the family took turns staring at him, as if he were about to spontaneously combust, he protested. "For God's sake! Will you all stop looking at me like I was the constipated Kaiser himself. I'm fine. It's not contagious."

"That will do!" said the General sharply. "We do not speak about the Kaiser in jest!"

"Please, Kurt!" Mother said quickly, sensing a disaster. The warning flags were up and the first salvo fired.

"I feel like I'm the prime exhibit in a freak show."

"Kurt, not at this time," Willie began.

"I'm cured! I'm rehabilitated!" said Kurt.

"You haven't changed!" responded the General. "A tour at the front might cure you. Out there real men have no time for frivolous games of the mind!"

"Father, may I speak?" Willie tried again. "Kurt's not interested in..."

"Don't take his side, Wilhelm!"

"I'm not taking sides, Father. I merely offer a compromise."

"Diplomacy doesn't become you."

"If Kurt were to enter a non-combat service."

"He'll join the Horse Guards!"

"I abhor bloody horses!" said Kurt too loudly.

His reentry into the fray caught the General off guard. There was a shocked silence around the table as eyes darted about searching for a diversion or escape from the inevitable. The children waited expectantly for the best entertainment of the summer. The General regrouped for a counter attack but Kurt kept the advantage. "I can't stand the stink of them. And besides, I don't have the facility you have for staying on the bloody beasts!"

The General changed colour from his neck to his forehead. "Your grandfather created the Horse Guards! The horses are specially bred in Ireland."

"Yes," he replied. "Breeding horses, like whores." Heads snapped to Kurt. "I'm surprised Schultes have time for children."

The Baroness tried to mediate. "Kurt! That's unfair. Apologize!"

"Yes, Kurt, do apologize," pleaded Willie. "That was uncalled for."

Kurt scanned their faces. Father was deepening in colour, his moustache shifting from side to side. Mother's lips trembled slightly and moisture was building up in the corners of her eyes. Willie looked disappointed but Sister glared at him while her husband sat back and wiped his lips with a napkin to cover a smirk. He loved to watch the Schultes savage each other. Willie's wife watched carefully, committing every detail to memory. This was going to be a good story to tell and retell over coffee and cake. The children of course were enjoying every moment. The homecoming was about to become a wonderful disaster.

"Apologize? What have I done!?"

The General chewed his words carefully. "You, young man, have made it your life's work to embarrass this family. We've tolerated your indifference and indulged your whims, in the hopes that some day you'd grow up. At every turn you've thwarted our attempts to include you in family affairs. You'd rather throw away your future, and our reputation, with debauchery at levels I wouldn't want to know about…and find an excuse for your laziness in drunken excesses. That is as polite as I can be." The General sat back, satisfied.

Kurt was tempted to catalogue some of his parent's public and private excesses but it would have accomplished nothing in the context. "I'm sorry if I have displeased you," said Kurt, in mock humility.

Only the children missed the subtlety, then, perhaps not. Kurt was being bad. He wished he wasn't but it was too late. The box was about to spring open as Kurt lost the will to keep it closed. The years of bitter defeats at the hands of his father swept through him like a cold wind. He was feeling cruel at a time when he should be calming the waters, explaining step by step his recovery and how he arrived at the decision to join the submarine service, asking for understanding and the family's blessing, instead he baited the General who was at a tactical disadvantage. The General committed the unforgivable, for a military planner, and let his emotions determine his time and method of counter attack, drawn into the field with all his colours showing.

"Displeased me!!?" shouted the General. "You have never done anything but displease me! You fought against my every effort to make a man out of you. Your sister would make a better soldier!!"

"Had you paid more attention to our Dear Sister and left me alone with my books you might have been rewarded with a more normal daughter and a less degenerate son!!?"

Kurt's sister flashed daggers at him. Her husband was unable to mask his delight realizing the situation was rapidly descending to the level of a pit bear fight. Kurt sensed he was gaining the advantage, tempted to go for the kill but lacked the instincts to inflict that much pain; deserved or not. After all, his sister had often taken Kurt's side. She had helped him wage the war of the blankets on the battlefield of the nursery. He regretted having drawn her into the arena.

"Dear Sister, it's unfair of me to suggest that you're anything but normal. You did your best to save me from physical destruction when I was helpless in a house of torment. What do I mean by that? I mean, Father, your attempts to make me a man, as you call it, would be considered abusive in a court of law."

"Now you're accusing me of being a bad father!? You ingrate! Look around you! Do you have any idea what it means to have a heritage like the Schulte name? I gave that to you freely. All I asked in return was a small commitment to maintain the Schulte name in honour and dignity, as all your ancestors, myself and your brother Wilhelm have done. Was that too much to ask? Yes, apparently! Now it seems you have some further apologies to make and you'd better start with your mother!"

The tide of battle swung quickly. Kurt was off balanced by the counter attack that touched a nerve. He knew his father was right. Conscience had always been a problem for Kurt and to be truly bad he had to overcome the urge to be good. Being good would have meant giving in. His stubborn nature prevented him from giving in. Now he was torn again by all the conflicts he had known since he was a child. To be a good German he should respect and obey his parents and the Kaiser. Those were rules of the game. He also wanted to love his parents because they were his parents. Nothing to do with the rules. He stood on the brink of a conscious understanding that the obligation to be at least a reasonable son meant he should put an end to the mental anguish of being the profligate in order to punish his tormentor. It would be easy. If he threw himself at the feet of his father, asking forgiveness, the crisis would pass. They would drink to Kurt's moral homecoming and he could announce that he was joining them in Germany's time of need, to fight alongside the family ghosts, to die in honour by war and spiritually live happily ever after in the bosom of the family. They might even hang his portrait in the Grand Hall alongside the stern faced ancestors who chastised him from birth with their silent, accusing eyes. *Kurt, seize the moment.*

"Of course, Mother. I'm sorry..." he said, hesitating, hanging out the apology like a flag. It was the colour of the flag that mattered now. It was all there for the asking; the forgiveness, the clutching, tearful embraces as the family gathered around to welcome Kurt into their midst with vows to forget the past and start anew. Onward for Germany! Father and sons astride magnificent chargers, helmets agleam, banners flying, spirits soaring like the Black Eagle of German heraldry! But he hesitated, and in that second the decision was taken away from his rational consciousness. Suddenly there was Anna standing above him on the dunes of Norderney laughing at his weakness. Weakness instilled in him by the relentless attempts to make him a man. He had always tried to hate his father. He plunged on: "...I'm sorry you didn't have a horse instead of a bastard son. I don't belong to this family!! That should be obvious!"

Kurt hurled the challenge at his father. The General rose to the occasion as Kurt knew he would.

"Enough!! Leave this table until you are cured in the manners too!!"

Kurt threw down his napkin. The family froze with anticipation. A Rembrandt painting would have conveyed the opposite picture because Kurt picked up his wine glass and held it aloft in a salute. An angelic smile set off his slightly puffy lips, a reminder of the recent beating, as he addressed each face deliberately. Kurt was struck by the notion that, had it not been for the hurtful statement, the picture could have been exactly what it implied. He smiled but inside the anguish of the approaching finalé was acute. Pride was as difficult a taskmaster as revenge and hate.

Kurt watched the scene from a distance as if he had died and stepped out of his body. It was his way of not accepting responsibility for the pain he was about to inflict on himself and his family, but at the last moment he stepped back in. Whatever his regret he would live with it. And, so, the toast, and the announcement.

"To my Schulte family heritage, in all our tradition-bound splendor! May there always be a war to bring us together." Kurt took a sip of wine too grandly, but it was difficult to maintain the pretense. Control was slipping away under the glare of his father's rage. "And I have an announcement. With Willie's blessing, at least, I hope...I have enlisted in the Submarine Service. I leave immediately to join my boat at Emden to sally forth, as the bloody British say, for God, the Kaiser, and glory. Or given my history, ignominy. But, not before I have toured the brothels of Berlin and disgraced myself to the best of my ability, for God and country! Then I can do my duty as a properly debauched submariner. Perhaps I shall avoid ignominy and die a horrible but heroic death and you can hang my portrait in honour." Kurt saluted the stern portraits of Schulte military men and drank off the bitter wine, poised to throw. The silence was oppressive. He felt completely foolish flinging the glass into the fireplace, the crystal chimes still resonating as he turned his back to stride out of the room, and probably out of the family for good.

Kurt's lasting image of the family during the coming war was the look of disappointment on Willie's face. That was his real regret. Willie was the one person he could love. The imagined loss of Anna and the rejection of Willie would haunt him for the next four years. Kurt went to war in pain and no terror in battle could cause him more.

"...And that's how the Commander got into it, see? No way for a man to go to war, running away from himself as he explained it, but himself was always there, see? A man who doesn't care if he lives or dies can be a

terrible enemy. *And that's just the way the Commander felt, my son. He didn't have a blessed thing to live for so you can't scare him into getting out of your way. That's how we come to meet. In the war...*"

I didn't understand exactly what Pius was getting at. He had made a reference to the Commander being an enemy in two wars and now the question of their relationship demanded an answer. Pius looked tired out but when I asked if he wanted me to go he said no. He got up stiffly and led the way to the door and out to the porch, the *bridge* as he called it. He said we just needed some fresh air.

The village and the harbour were well picked out with lamp light and I wondered how the village had looked before electricity came to Fogo. The lights on the government wharf reflected off the black water. The wind had died and the rain had stopped. Even the restless ocean held back. Only an occasional smooth swell spilled onto the pebble beach, sounding like a sigh. Was the tide coming or going? I'd lost track of time but I and the atmosphere waited, breathless, for Pius to continue his story.

"*...That's the year I was gone first mate with Skipper George Small out of Seldom Harbour. The year the war started. The Great War. I was lead hand onto the* Sarah B, *our own schooner, see, but Naam White, that was my sister's man, he was mate alongside of Father on the* Sarah *when I was ready to go first. Well, sir, you don't put family out of a berth so I went along with Skipper George on the* Clara Ridgeway. *She was down from Boston and named for the builder's daughter. Skipper George never wanted to change the name. T'was bad luck, see. I never thought it was bad luck if you gave a boat a new name what meant something. Give her a spirit she can hold onto, see. It's not like starting a voyage on a Friday. Not the same thing t'all. Or wearing blue mittens. Then you're just asking for trouble. Don't mean it'll happen but you'd* *best keep a sharp eye because if it's going to happen that's a good time. I know of plenty boats tempted fate like that and some of the b'yes had the Devil's own time to get out of a scrape. Some didn't. I'd been with Skipper George that season, see. We'd gone for seals in March month. Then we had a load o' dry fish for the Portogeese. Some trip that was! My son! A hurricane chased us all over the Jasus ocean. Then we had no wind left to bring us back. The ocean can torment you sometimes with contrariness. Well, by'n'by we get home and lay into St. John's to get our salt and gear for the Labrador. There was a lot of talk on Water St. about the Germans and the French getting a war up. The big worry was that England might be getting into it too and some said the Germans was too strong for the whole bunch and they'd get at England after they cleaned up the French. They wanted the Empire, see. They was right put out that England had all that coastline and all the colonies to boot. We was making a good run of it down to Labrador in August month when I made up my mind to go. Lets see, I was twenty-six, or thereabouts, and had a wife, Mary, and one son born and lost, another son, Harry, and a daughter, Jeannie, born. I didn't have to go. If you fished you was supposed to lay by. The b'yes got to eat, war or no war. If everybody joined up to fight then the war'd be over soon as the b'yes got too hungry to fight. But I had to go. Something about them Germans pushing everybody around. I don't like that, sir. Not a bit. The Commander was one of them, sure. But I didn't know him then. Later I lost a brother killed by a submarine..."*

August 23, 1914: The Grand Banks schooner *Clara Ridgeway* thrashed to windward in boisterous seas, trailing chevrons of jumping foam. The big schooner's bow bit into the waves and threw green water aside; the wind flung it back over the decks as sparkling crystals. The rough fishing life had its own rewards and a true sailor could enjoy the power of his ship competing freely with the elements.

Young Pius Humby held the weather rail and faced the wind. The chaos of spray and foam, straining canvas and creaking spars can be a tonic to a sailor. A well found schooner in the prime of life is a symphony of sound as long as the rules are obeyed. An equal contest between man and sea but beating down to Labrador isn't for timid souls. Pius was raised on the decks of fishing boats; could handle the wheel by age six and set a topsail before his thirteenth birthday and was no more superstitious than any of his mates. He loved the ships and the sea more than anything in life aside from his family. He was a good man on deck or in the fo'c'sle and expected to sail until they put him ashore as an old man. The only cloud over his life was the death of his oldest son, Roy, age seven, on his first trip to the ice. Pius blamed himself for letting the lad go, but he was six himself on his first trip to the shore seals. They had lost Roy before Pius turned twenty-five. Then the First War happened and changed his life, the way it changed the lives of so many.

Pius said a brief prayer for Roy and took the spray full on his face as if testing his spirit. The ship was headed for Labrador but his thoughts were far to the east and the battle for Europe.

Later that evening, after their meal and the watch changed, the wind backed to the southwest and the schooner ghosted along with a light breeze on her quarter. Pius and the skipper were alone on the aft deck and Pius told Skipper George Small that he intended to join the war.

"You don't have to go," said the Skipper.

Pius stared across the ocean to the war he only imagined. Newspaper accounts of the bloody battles in Belgium filtered slowly through the island. They spoke of hordes of grey-clad Germans pouring over the harvest hills of Western Europe, sweeping Belgian and French troops ahead of them. But that was the early stages, before the rains came and the war became a stalemate and the troops mired in the muddy trenches. The most distressing news was of German battleships and submarines in the North Sea blasting helpless merchant ships. The talk in St. John's had been inflammatory speculation, but unfortunately prescient.

"It's only some foolishness," continued the Skipper. "A skirmish! Be over before you get there."

"Buddy says the Germans'll do for England, if they get the chance."

"Aye, son, suppose they would. Been waitin' this long while"

"The Kaiser has a wonderful big army. Navy too!"

"The Kaiser wouldn't take on the whole bunch of us, sure? Be daft to try it!"

"Newfoundlanders'd give he a run for 'is money."

Skipper George put the helm up a few spokes to correct the course. Pius continued to stare across the sleepy waves. The Skipper put his knee against the wheel while he relit his pipe. The smoke trailed forward to join the wisps rising from pipes of the men sitting on the hatches enjoying the fine fall evening. The schooners weren't all hard work.

"You're determined to go then?" asked the Skipper. Pius nodded. "We'll miss you, son. You're the best mate I ever sailed with, and I've seen a few."

Pius was embarrassed by the compliment. The Skipper repeated the ritual of the pipe and Pius knew the signal. Advice was given in carefully measured amounts but they were lectures just the same.

"The navy's a hard enough go," Skipper George began. "The British Navy's stood the test of hard times. They take the measure of them selves before ever they face the enemy, see. England's always stood alone, in the end. She's depended on the navy for three hundred years, and more. This muck up with the Germans is only another fight she's got to get through, and the ships be iron now to match the b'yes on deck. What I means to say, lad, the navy's the thing!"

"Aye, could be no worse than running around in the mud carrying a Jasus big rifle," Pius concluded, "likes a sealer in slobby ice."

The pipe was out again. The Skipper struck a match. The wind had slacked off so that the match hardly needed cupping in his big raw hands. The schooner, with everything set, was idling along under barely ruffled canvas, resting before the next howling gale. The sun was sliding behind the dark mass of the Labrador coast to port and the moon coming up in the east was full and bright.

The ocean was calm that night but it was the last season a seaman could relax on deck. Sailors of every nation would learn to fear the full moon and feel vulnerable at a time when a sailor's soul should rejoice to be alive. Instead he would pray for black nights with running seas and reduced visibility so that the enemy in dark submarines, slipping under the surface, could not blow their ship out of the water without a warning. Neither the Skipper nor Pius thought about their own familiar coast becoming a battle ground where fishermen could perish in a violent explosion. It was a foreign notion. Innocence was dying by degrees.

"Stick to what you knows best," the Skipper said. "You tell them fellas you wants to join the King's Navy. Newfoundlanders weren't bred to die in the mud. 'Sides, according to anything I know, if this conflagration they're getting up is anything like that skirmish with the Boers, a soldier's lot's to wait around like a bitch seal just asking to get shot. No sir, you get yourself on a good ship. The Skipper paused a moment to puff up his pipe. "...I'll put you off to the first boat that's headed for St. John's," then added, "I wish I was going with you, son."

"...The Skipper was as good as his word. We spoke the Bessie and Grace *out of Greenspond, she was Billy Windsor's boat then...just off Battle Harbour, the Labrador, coming up with her fish for St. John's. Billy and the* Bessie and Grace *drove ashore down in the Caribe with a cargo during the war. Every soul was lost aboard of her. Not just the Germans killed us, sir. Funny ain't it? That we should lay off Battle Harbour to put me over to the* Bessie an' Grace *'cause I wanted to go to that blessed war? If I'd changed my mind then, or the* Bessie and Grace *had been someplace else then I'd have been someplace else besides where I was two years later when the Commander and me first met up. But that's the way of it, sir. Coincidences, like. Never a breath you take what doesn't have some effect on the way of things. Some smart fella on the television said that one little thing out of place can change the whole universe. I don't know about that now. I'm not clever about things I ain't never seen. But Billy Windsor came along and I went aboard and he carried me up to St. John's where I soon got a smart steamer to England with a load o'fish. Dried cod that is. They're what keeps this old island going. They say that's coming to an end too. I don't understand it. Do you? How in God's name could them fish just suddenly up and disappear when they'd been on this coast for hundreds of years? Terrible year for fish. Some of the lads is ready to give it up. But I suppose they'll try again next season. I'd like to see another season, and the fish come back. My son, she's a hard go sometimes. But that's all up with me. No good for it, see. They say our folks was fishing this coast a long time before she got discovered by that skipper...Cabot. They got a statue of him down to Bonavista. We steer on his light trips up to St. John's. Easy to see how he found his way in, when the fog's not hung around the Head, see. How in all that's holy could he claim to discover us when we wasn't lost!? You tell me, son. Did you know we used to call ourselves Vinelanders? The Norse, see. The Vikings* was here long before Cabot came

over. But they didn't stick it long enough to leave their mark I suppose, but still, they should get the credit. Anyway, Skipper Billy put me off in St. John's and I got a ship for England. I told you that, didn't I? I can't recall the name of that steamer. She was a smart new iron ship, a beauty, and fast. I heard she got sunk on her next trip over. Submarine caught her by herself off the Irish Coast. A God forsaken place if ever there was one. The Irish Sea that is. No place to run, see, if you can't get clear of her. Terrible storms in there in the fall of the year. She was coming in to Liverpool as I understand, but she wasn't the only one to be sunk by the Germans. Wasn't the Commander though. He was mostly in the Channel, where we met up, and he said he never liked to sink a merchant ship...he gave the Navy what for just the same. He hated to do it though. He loved the ships, see. Said it was a shame to sink them but it was his job. And it was our job to sink him...Terrible what we do sometimes...Makes you wonder how God puts up with us..."

Pius was tired now. It was the sound of his voice, slowing down. I asked if he was cold. The light breeze off the ocean had an edge of fall and a touch of mist. The cool ocean air easily penetrated my impractical summer clothing. Newfoundland weather is changeable in the extreme and it only depends on the direction of the wind. The cold Labrador Current churns by just offshore and a wind from that direction could be cold and damp at any time of the year. Pius didn't seem to notice, having lived with it for ninety-three years. I said perhaps I should go. He seemed willing to continue the story but I felt guilty. I misjudged an old man's resilience. Then there were the books and the journals.

"...Them books? Up at the Commander's house I suppose. Tom's old house. Rose lived there, after Tom was killed. Before the Commander came. She's another story b'ye. Poor young thing. Rose never liked us well enough to learn to stick it. The measure b'ye..."

Pius wanted to explain about taking the measure. It was important to him, I suspect, because he saw so many young people giving up on Newfoundland without a fight and leaving for the mainland and the promise of a better life in the cities. More stay away than return although they know there is more to life than a paycheck when your heart is on the Home Island. But there are realities. Dignity dies when there are no prospects for the future. My Newfoundland is a dream of days gone by; an old colony where hard work and self-sufficiency ruled with a heavy hand and dignity and self-worth was something accomplished by having done it the hard way. The boats are gone. The fish are gone, and consequently the jobs. The children of the old schooner men couldn't survive on their parent's memories no matter how much the good old days are dredged up by romantics and dreamers. Pius had given me hints of these feelings. He nodded and said it was, "...about handy to it..."

"...You come around another day, and if I'm still alive we'll see if we can scare out them books of the Commander's..."

We said good night after Pius saw me to the road and held the broken gate, saying that it would want a bolt soon. I looked back once and Pius raised his arm but he seemed to have diminished in shadow. I was afraid he'd vanish and leave the story in limbo. The scribbler had only suggested an intriguing series of events, beginning with Pius' trip to England and the war years. It was merely a sketch, a seaman's log book but the events fired my imagination. I had left the scribbler on the table hoping to return and pick up the narrative. Newfoundlanders expect you to come around when it suits you. *You're as welcome as if you'd never come.*

I walked down to Mrs. Penny's Bed and Breakfast with the tantalizing story teasing my brain. I looked up to the hills above Pius' house where a light in a window revealed the location of Jimmy White's cabin. Jimmy would be in his sixties. Pius mentioned that he had suffered a terrible debilitating illness. Would he be able to fill in the details if Pius?...I wouldn't think about it.

A dog barked from the darkness between two frame houses recently clad with aluminum; except for their distinctive low-roofed shape they could have been bungalows in Oshawa, Ontario. The silver-blue glow from the windows spilled out on the street, the occupants watching televisions and not interested in a stranger walking by on the new blacktop auto road where horses used to pull loads of firewood up from the *bully boats*. David Letterman, moronic commercials and all. I couldn't imagine what people on remote Fogo Island could possibly see in the glitter culture of New York or California. Pius might be settling down to watch a fantasy commercial full of intense young people having fun, a red sports car screaming around corners at illegal speeds. He seldom slept, he said, preferring to cat nap and keep an eye on the world. It's all right for mainland dreamers to imagine long-dead Grand Banks schooners tied to rotting wharfs. The new wharf, with its garish mercury lights, was provided by the Department of Fisheries and Oceans; probably designed by a college graduate from Alberta, doodling in the safety of civil servant haven, who went home at four o'clock and didn't worry about vanishing cod fish and German submarines.

Mrs. Penny, a big woman in her forties, let me in the front door. I apologized for being late but she said it was all right. Baseball season was grinding to a conclusion and the Toronto Blue Jays were being mauled by the Detroit Tigers. My team, those Tigers, having grown up forty-five miles from Detroit and an American by default. Newfoundland came close to being an American state in 1949, by choice.

Despite the cultural gulf between South Western Ontario, where I grew up, and Newfoundland I could pretend I was fifteen again and sit down with Mrs. Penny to watch my Tigers trounce the mythical Blue Jays and dream of owning the red corvette being assembled a few miles away in the Motor City. I was tired but Mrs. Penny wanted to talk. She offered to make tea. I declined. She followed me to the foot of the stairs.

"If there's anything you needs, my dear? We don't get many visitors this time of the year. Mostly in July month, you know? Folks from away come mostly in summer. The weather's better then. Did you have a nice day?"

"Yes," I said innocently.

"That's good, my dear. Did you go around by the church? They say she's the oldest church on the Island, aside of the Portuguese church in St. John's. The sailors built it, the one in St. John's, the Portuguese, like? Some kind of a shrine. They used to fish around here some while back I suppose. Had a crowd of 'em in the harbour once, when I was a girl. Big white boat it was too, but all running with rust and scuzzy like? Some kind of sailboat, I suppose. The boys were some fun though. They never spoke no English 't'all, the most of 'em. They came in one day 'cause their boat got handy to iceberg. They was here some little while. You look around the harbour you might see some dark eyes, if you know what I mean?"

"Yes. That's life, I guess..."

"Yes, my dear man! Some fun it was too. And some commotion a few months after that boat left. There was some explaining to do when a couple young girls got in the family way and their men away fishing. It was some wonderful how them Portuguese boys got around. We don't talk about it though. Right touchy subject it is. I won't say you'd get a straight answer if you was to ask. What did you find to do then?"

"I walked around the harbour and took some pictures. I, ah, met an old skipper, Captain Humby. He told me some interesting stories..."

"Old Pius! My son, that man can tell some stories! And tall ones at that. Did he tell you about the old German we buried today? My dear, them two was the biggest pair of leg pullers you ever seen. Queer pair they was. And Jimmy White!? My son, he'd scare ten years growth off you if you met he on a dark night. Sits up there and watches us he does. Only comes down at night, 'cept for the Mummer's times. Then he gets a dress on and covers his face with a veil like. Every one's scared to death he's going to come to their door. The children are right frightened. If you ask me, that one should be sent to St. John's and kept in one of them homes. He'll die by'n'by and save us the trouble I suppose. I hope Old Pius didn't waste your day with the nonsense. Well, good night. You just call if you needs anything. My sister's at the game. Said she'd wave."

Mrs. Penny turned up the volume; a commercial, full of noise and healthy young people in an upscale bar, swam around the house and bounced off the walls. I felt light headed and sick in the pit of my stomach, but not from the frantic music. So Pius' story might be just the elaborate concoction of an old man whose failing memory is padded-out with fantasy. A big lie. I finally dragged myself up the stairs and fell on the bed. Intuition told me there was too much to Pius' story to be a fabrication. Besides, I had seen them burying the German.

I came *to* with a deep feeling of depression, in a cold sweat from the effects of a bad dream. I had been running in the hills above Fogo, stumbling in the darkness on unfamiliar trails, tripping over the long dress I was wearing, my vision impaired by a lacy veil cut from an old curtain. It smelled of dust and moth balls. So did the dress. At first I was running to get away from the smell, then there was a shadow. It didn't come for me but skulked from rock to rock, sure footed, nimble, and knew every hiding place. I tripped over scrub trees. Finally, I fell off a cliff on the other side of the hill into the *back harbour*, as Pius described the back door to the main harbour. I think I was screaming when I woke up.

Mrs. Penny was knocking on my door. It was difficult to get up with a weight on my chest that took an enormous effort to move.

"You all right, my dear?" she asked through the closed door.

"Yes, I think so. Bad dream."

"I come to see if you wanted something to eat. You missed breakfast but I can put you up an instant coffee an' some little cakes I got from mainland."

"Just a cup of coffee, please."

"Oh, and, I thought you'd like to know? There was trouble up to the Humby's this morning. They took old Pius away in ambulance. Aunt Sally thinks it was a stroke. Might have been…he drank, see."

I didn't see; nor did I wait for coffee. I sensed old Pius was getting a bum rap and doubted the odd drop of rum he used in his tea had anything to do with anything other than a good excuse to talk. I left Mrs. Penny in my wake still offering the breakfast that goes with the bed.

Mary met me at the gate. "Come in, come in…You heard the news? I have something for you." I followed her into the kitchen which was diminished by the absence of the skipper by the stove. "Pius said you were to have these and you're to look for an old iron box up to Tom's house."

Mary put the scribbler and a key in my hand and sat down again with her knitting.

"It was the last thing he said before he went down, my dear. He felt poorly at breakfast. Wouldn't touch his porridge. Then he just went down. He looked so pitiful there on the floor, t'would make you cry to see it. It's the one thing Pius feared, getting old and being a burden."

"Where will they take him?"

"Ambulance went on the ferry. They'd go on to Gander, or maybe to St. John's. They couldn't say. Depends on his condition, see."

"Would you like to go? I could drive you."

"No, my dear. Pius wouldn't want me to make the trip. He'd love to see you of course, even in his suffering. Always likes a visit. I'll wait for him to come home."

"What happened?"

"They thought it was a stroke...maybe was his heart found."

"I hope it wasn't my fault," I said, thinking of the long conversation the night before.

"No, my dear, he knew something was coming, see. He stayed with it as long as he could, so's you'd know."

"Why would he tell me...a complete stranger?"

"Pius has a way of knowing about people. He must have known you'd be interested and maybe do something he and the Commander always talked about."

"If I can. What did they want?"

"Someone to write it down. The Commander, he used to do it but something happened, oh, a long time back. And he was never able to get on with it...other than to talk about it with Pius."

"I'll try," I said, not realizing what lay ahead.

"I think the spirit just went out of him when the Commander died. They was as close as that, see. I won't say they never argued. Both stubborn as the day is long. Would astonish you to know how those two shared their lives...being bitter enemies so long. But it's their story. Anyway, go up to Tom's house. There's the key. Never used to lock the old house but times have changed since the Commander come to bide with us after his stroke, when was that?...a dozen years ago I suppose, spring of the big herring run and then the squid come in so thick that summer, but it never stopped him talking, the stroke I mean. My what a dear man. So polite. So good to the children. He taught them as long as he could get to the school. There's many of them gone off this island to the universities and such, would never have got nowhere without he helped them. And never took a penny for it. Not one. Said it was for his keep. The way his own boys did for us during the war. But that's all in the books sure. I'm not as good remembering. You go along now and God bless you."

The Commander's house, Tom's house, was a typical Newfoundland outport home, except for the new taller roof and dormer, a mainland touch, but on a smaller scale, as though there were no plans for a large family. It was weather-beaten from the harsh climate but the cod oil and salt-soaked spruce had stood up well. It had once been painted a courageous colour scheme of reddish pink clapboards, green-blue trim...that must have come out of the same can as Pius' house trim...and red-ochre skirting boards that looked like a high tide line. The shed was a promising salmon pink with brown trim. The whole works peeling, showing more wood than paint but there was some mercy in that. Most, except for Tom's home, were topped by a shallow pitched roof, but nestled in the village of similar imaginative paint jobs it looked quite natural.

I felt strange unlocking the door, entering another man's life but I was there to find evidence of the past. The stories. Pius, the Commander and the whole gang of characters had to be verified.

The bright kitchen was neat and clean, as though the Commander had gone on vacation. I opened closets and drawers quietly, afraid to waken the inhabitants, and felt a little prickle on the back of my neck every time I reached for a handle. I don't know what I expected to find. The Commander? Tom? The new name, Rose? Anna? Walther Schwieger, the killer of the *Lusitania*? The enigmatic Jimmy White? I felt ridiculous. There was an old fisherman's coat, a hat and boots in a closet and a well worn peak cap on a peg behind the kitchen door. Two walking sticks, one broken, leaned against the wall. The usual homey sayings in chintz frames hung on the wall over the simple green painted pine table. Lace curtains graced the kitchen windows. A faded plastic rose perpetually bloomed in a cracked sugar bowel on the window that faced the harbour. A stub of a pencil had rolled into the crack between the window sash and sill. Perhaps it was put there purposely to stop the window from rattling on stormy nights while someone rocked in the big chair beside the stove, reading by lamplight, the oil lamp perched precariously on the edge of the warming shelf. Ashes still lay in the bottom of the fire box. A few sticks of well dried spruce waited in the wood box behind the big, life giving stove, the first thing you'd notice entering any outport home, in the old days.

The low-ceilinged, open-beam kitchen was bright and shiny, like the interior of a working ship. There were no light bulbs or electrical fixtures in the Commander's house. There wasn't much evidence of the clutter of modern living. Nor was there an iron box. It meant prying deeper into the interior and, although it was a small house, it was as daunting as a medieval castle with legends and secret passages.

The miniature parlour with its dark antique furniture gave up no secrets. I would have to climb the stairs and search the bedrooms but when I put my foot on the first step I felt the familiar prickles. Foolishness? My overtaxed imagination was having a wonderful time. An incident a few days earlier, while exploring a small peninsula on the Big Island, made me cautious. It was a typical settlement; rugged rock peninsula thrusting bravely into Bonavista Bay with Indian Arm to the south, the ocean rolling in on jagged rocks. A cluster of abandoned houses huddled forlornly on a grassy hill. One of the abandoned buildings, left open to the winds, was furnished as if the inhabitants might come back. Pictures of the family hung uneasily on the walls, their eyes following me from room to room. I passed the stairway twice before deciding to investigate the upper bedrooms where people store their private lives: births, deaths, wedding nights, pain, joy, sorrow or long nights of waiting while the wind howls off the ocean. It was probably just a freak of the wind blowing in broken windows, but when I put my foot on the first step all the doors in the upper hallway slammed shut. I don't believe in ghosts but I don't take chances with spirits.

However, if the iron box was in the Commander's house it would be in one of the upper rooms. The stairs creaked ominously.

I had a choice of three rooms and chose the right hand door; imagining people screaming in my head, shouting numbers, and entered a room with a ceiling so low I hunched down, feeling foolish but not alone. There was a bed, made up with a quilt that would bring a high price in the city, a small chair, a chamber pot under the bed and an empty closet. I shut the door quietly, returned to the hallway and opened door number two.

A steamer trunk huddled below a small window which looked out on the hills. The lace curtains were dusty and delicate but there was a piece cut out of one curtain, about the size of a man's head. I thought of Jimmy White. It might have been his room. There was nothing else in the room but the trunk; not an iron box.

The trunk contained women's dresses; colourful, like the outport houses, in a gaudy way, old but well made, wouldn't look out of place in a stage musical. Probably costumes for the Mummer's days, I surmised. Mrs. Penny had mentioned that Jimmy White dressed up in women's clothing. That would have to do for an explanation, but it didn't explain where the dresses came from originally. I lifted them out of the trunk carefully so as not to upset the spirits, and there, on the bottom, was a small sampler photo album. I put the arm load of dresses on the corner of the trunk to lift out the album. The dresses cascaded to the floor like flowing water and made a colourful puddle on the linoleum. Sorry, whoever?

The album crackled when I opened the thick cover. The first pages were portraits of a young man and woman facing each other. Wedding day pictures taken many years ago, but holding up well. The man had strong features, not handsome, but large jawed and broad-nosed, like a bull dog. The eyes narrow and dark. Mean, I thought. The woman was pretty enough but had sad eyes. The next page was a group picture taken out of doors and the urban background was not Newfoundland. The man and woman had aged. They were surrounded by children and the man was wearing a uniform. A sailor or a lawman perhaps? The next page had a picture of another young woman. Very pretty. Short curly hair. Would be wavy if it were long. I guessed red. I don't know why, the face just seemed to go with red hair. Age, about twenty, but possibly younger. I flipped back to the family picture. Out of a litter of seven children there was the face on a little girl, about nine or ten. The hair was long and hung in ringlets, wavy if brushed out. The face of the young woman was hauntingly beautiful. The eyes were probably green. I looked at the pile of dresses on the floor. Yes, they belonged to the face with the red hair, the innocent green eyes and the sparkle of a spirit that had expectations. *Rose*. Pius had mentioned a Rose, another character in the piece, but where did she fit? Rose seemed out of context in a Newfoundland outport. Pius had said: *"...Rose never liked us well enough to learn to stick it..."* I could imagine there were other reasons why she didn't fit; she was from away or had some connection with the Commander, Jimmy White or Tom, Pius' younger brother, the one who died in the Second War. I was in Tom's house, but it was also the Commander's house, after Tom died. And also Jimmy's house before he moved to the hills. I flipped the page. The last photograph was of Rose dressed in a fancy gown, not much older, but the eyes had changed. The sparkle was gone; small worry lines had appeared and a hint of desperation replaced the innocence. It was a publicity photo; the kind every hopeful entertainer has made up with their last dollars to spread around to talent agencies. Rose was a stage performer, probably a singer judging by the gaudy dresses. The old dresses, left behind, became costumes for the Mummer's Days. An interesting sidetrack, but I didn't need distractions, I was looking for the Commander's journals. I lifted the publicity picture out of the corner mounts but there was only the name of a Toronto photographer, an address and the date, November 28, 1939. I returned Rose and her career to the trunk.

Although I had put Rose back in her trunk she wouldn't get out of my mind. There was a story; expectations, desperation. Her mother had sad eyes on her wedding day, perhaps foreseeing the future; seven children and a sailor, and one of her beautiful children also had expectations of life.

Room number three. Opening the door I wasn't surprised to see the small iron box bound with iron straps, waiting beside the bed, below the window that looked out over the harbour. The Commander's room. The iron box had an engraved plate riveted to the top, the brass recently polished. The eagle and swastika were etched in black above Gothic lettering, and a serial number. I guessed that it was the document box from the submarine and expected to find holes in the bottom so that it would fill with water and sink quickly, taking information about the submarine, logs, orders and code books to the bottom in the event of imminent capture. I lifted the heavy lid carefully but it swung away and slammed against the wall leaving a gouge in the wainscoting. The house shook. I apologized to the spirits. I was about to enter into Kurt Schulte's personal life.

On top of the contents was a chart, folded flat and badly worn on the edges. It was a British Admiralty chart from the 1930's, with German words and symbols stamped along the bottom. There were many notations in pencil, in a strong German hand. Most of the notations, symbols and numbers were clustered around the Strait of Belle Isle, the adjoining Coast of Labrador and the waters between the Strait and Fogo Island. The rest of the chart was worn and dirty from handling and stained with salt water and dark brown rings. I conjured up a vision of sea water pouring down the hatch of a pitching U-boat and the navigator and the skipper hunched over the chart sipping tepid coffee while they plotted the destruction of an enemy convoy.

The trail to the story was hot now and I dove deeper into the treasure chest. More charts, rolled up and difficult to handle, but evidently detailed charts of harbours, most with French names. One showed the approaches to the fjord leading into the harbour of Bergen, Norway. Others were mid-ocean charts with depths and bottom symbols and a grid with letters labeling each rectangle. I surmised that they were for locating a point on an otherwise featureless expanse of ocean. One grid rectangle was marked with an 'X' and the name of a ship; the *Aegean Trader*, Liverpool. Latitude and longitude coordinates, 28° 22" W & 52° 17" N. The date, August 23, 1944, 2015 hrs., and the tonnage, 12,000 GRT. There was also a scrawled notation, *Keine Schwimmer*. I could understand that much German. *No survivors*. It marked the death of a ship and its crew; not just a mid-ocean sighting. The convoy had gone on its way leaving the victims to the mercy of the sea. Suddenly the story of the Commander took on a deadlier meaning. It was the Second World War and the Battle of the Atlantic when people died violently and Commander Kurt von Schulte was the enemy.

There were more charts of the coast of Europe; the waters of the Northern countries. Another was a detailed chart of Bergen Harbour, Norway and a notation. There was a North Sea chart with a crude, childish cartoon of Adolf Hitler astride a torpedo about to be swallowed up in a dark patch between ample female thighs. A bored seaman's fantasy? The Commander? Another North Sea chart caught my attention. The Frisian coasts of Holland and Germany were strewn with a bewildering system of channels and mud flats between islands. The island of Norderney was circled. There was a short notation and latitude and longitude calculations at what appeared to be the northern side of the island. There was an 'X' close by and another short notation. The only word I understood was *Anna*.

Here was something at least, the name of the girl Pius mentioned in one of the Commander's stories, but no journals; only an old, moth eaten blue seaman's sweater folded on the bottom of the box. I picked up the unexpectedly heavy sweater. There was a package wrapped in the ancient wool. I fumbled in haste to unwrap the brown paper tied with thick twine. The Commander's diary I hoped. The twine was too tough to break and my impatience made the task twice as difficult. When I finally slipped the coarse paper off the book I was staring at a mint edition, hardbound copy of a novel, dust jacket and all. The title, *Der Republik Des Teufel*, the author was Kurt von Schulte. I turned the book over and there was a picture of an aristocratically handsome young man in his mid thirties. It was a good photograph but the picture couldn't hide the pain and loneliness behind the eyes. I had a fair idea why. If Pius' tale of Kurt von Schulte's ordeal on Norderney were true, the eyes were telling some of the story. I opened the cover to the frontispiece. There was an autograph, but it wasn't Kurt's. It seemed to be a dedication from another person, Frank Heppelmann. A new name. Another sidetrack. I would have to get used to those. The publisher was a Berlin house, Deutsch Redefreiheit Verlagsgesellschaft, and the year, nineteen thirty-four. When I opened the book the bindings crackled as if it had never been breached. I was holding a rare gem for a book collector but I wasn't interested in collector's items. There were no journals. No cryptic messages. Pius said the Commander spent all his time writing. So, where were the results?

I rewrapped the book and set it aside, dumped the sweater and charts back into the box, closed the lid carefully and began a more thorough search; despite the spirits. I opened the closet and was rewarded with a German officer's uniform. A pair of mouldy sea boots sagged against the door and fell out at my feet, dark and rodent-like, about to attack. The uniform was thread-bare and the brass buttons and submarine insignia were tarnished, as was the campaign medal, dated 1914-1918. Beside the medal were two tiny holes and a dark cross shape on the faded material, probably left by the Iron Cross I saw Pius place on the casket. On a hook at the back of the closet was a leather belt and holster. I recognized the type from watching old war movies. The holster was empty. Another puzzle. Where was the Luger? The leather was splotched with green mould but the owner's initials were still visible; F.V.S. Freidrich von Schulte? Kurt's father? As Pius explained it, Kurt was the least likely inheritor of the father's gun, but the gun was not present and accounted for, and where was the officer's hat? Why didn't they bury the Commander in his uniform? I closed the closet on more questions than answers.

There was nothing else in the room to ransack so I clutched the Commander's book, retracing my steps through the other rooms, finding what I expected to find...nothing. I sat down in the rocking chair by the cold stove in the kitchen feeling frustrated and lonely. Why lonely? I was surrounded by spirits. I rocked for inspiration. Should I start tearing up floor boards?

Rocking, watching the harbour and sifting through my mental storehouse of confusing information, added little. Something sinister had happened in the village during the war. The Commander had cared for Jimmy after an *accident*. Pius had amended the statement to mean something more than an accident. Inevitable? Premeditated? Attempted murder? There is a big difference. Jimmy looked after the Commander in turn when he got old. Jimmy had therefore lived in the house before he built his retreat in the hills. There was Rose. I couldn't dismiss Rose but Jimmy was the key now. Pius had suggested I go *up around* and visit his nephew.

Summer Wars & Winter Schooners

On my second attempt to visit Jimmy White I had more reasons to be apprehensive. It wasn't just the unnerving feeling of spirits in the air and behind the rocks, Jimmy White was an image drawn out in my mind's eye after Mrs. Penny had intimated he was crazy, dressed in women's clothing and frightened the children.

Jimmy White's rough shack had one window and a door, but it was strongly built by hands that obviously knew the ways of wood. Built to withstand the extreme winds of hurricanes and winter gales. I shuddered to think what it would be like to ride out a full Atlantic gale on the exposed cliff above the harbour. Sanctuary, was all I could call the place. There were no approaches other than the steep, torturous route around the jagged rocks. There were no trees, only scrub spruce, stunted and twisted by the constant winds. They offered nothing in the way of shelter or firewood. I caught my breath at the top of the path near the shack, wondering how Jimmy White survived in such a place. I was summoning the nerve to knock when he opened the door. My mental image hadn't prepared me for the sight.

Jimmy's twisted face was frozen in a grimace of perpetual terror. The white hair, more a fringe, was coarse and spiky. He twitched as if unable to control his limbs but when I was able to focus on his eyes they looked completely normal. He motioned me into the shack with a jerk of the grizzled head and I accepted the invitation with some misgivings.

The interior of the shack was simple and well organized; the compact home of a careful man. Jimmy indicated a chair beside the window that would have had a grand view of the harbour and the ocean to the Northwest but there was a piece of oiled canvas tacked over the window with only an inch or so at the top to let in some light. He saw me trying to peer over the cloth for the view. "I don't like to see the ocean, sir."

Jimmy made tea from water already boiling on the small wood stove called a Shipmate. Made in Lunenburg, Nova Scotia, the embossed letters said. He put out a loaf of bread and tiny pot of jam, everything seemed to fit a small lifestyle, and poured the tea. We sat looking at each other silent, while Jimmy twitched sporadically, but the longer we sat quietly the less he twitched. Many minutes passed with not a word. I started to introduce myself. He nodded: "I knows who you are, sir."

"You do!?"

"Yes. Uncle Pius told me."

"But...how?..."

"I heard you talking."

"Then you must have been with Pius...when he, went down."

"Yes, my dear, man."

Boo Radley. I couldn't help thinking about the recluse in the classic story *To Kill a Mockingbird*. Harper Lee's enigmatic character was only a shadow and imagination is far scarier than a cardboard monster.

"Then you know why I'm here?"

"Yes, I knows."

"And about the Commander's books?"

"Of course."

Jimmy White was remarkably fit, for a wizened ogre. When his body wasn't twitching it was easy to imagine him as a young athlete. He was also a puzzle. Jimmy had a refined way of speaking, slipping in and out of accents from Newfoundland English to cultured English to German and back to a Newfoundland dialect that seemed out of the Middle Ages.

"You lived with the Commander."

"Twenty-four years we did. 'Til the stroke and I couldn't look after him no more. The people were afraid of me, see. The Commander went to live with Uncle Pius and Aunt Mary. I went down at night though. We continued to read and write."

"To read and write?"

"The books. I'd read them to the Commander after Uncle Pius and Aunt Mary went to bed. He'd make corrections and I'd write them down. Uncle Pius didn't know about the reading. It was our secret."

Where were the journals? I wondered.

"The Commander taught me to read and write German. It was how he helped me back, from away…in my mind, so to speak."

"The accident?" I asked, prodding to assemble the pieces of information.

"A part of the story, sure. 'Tis all in the books, my dear man. The Commander was going to write a real book, but he never did, only kept adding stories to the *journals*, as he called them."

"Ah, did he make the stories up?"

"I know that some of the ones he wrote, after I come back, were real because they were about us. He might've made up some others."

"When did you, come back, as you mentioned?"

"December, 1953. We were listening to the radio, at Uncle Pius and Aunt Mary's. It was Christmas, a choir singing. Then, like a miracle, I was back in the cabin of the *Liza and Mary,* on our way to St. John's, but it was nine years later. I didn't remember much about those nine years. Do you have any idea what that's like?"

I had no idea. Jimmy nodded as if he had read my mind. I was a little spooked to say the least. "Do you remember the accident?"

"The Commander and Uncle Pius told me most everything, I suppose," Jimmy continued. "They both knew parts of the story and what one didn't know the other did, see. But sometimes when one of them forgot or was a bit hazy I'd be able to tell them what happened, though

I couldn't tell you how. And I couldn't remember things after I'd told them, like."

"Is this all written down, the stories I mean?"

"Yes, every word."

"Did you know that the Commander had written a book that was published in Germany?"

"No, sir, I was not aware."

I handed Jimmy the brown paper package. He unwrapped it slowly, almost fearful of discovering the contents. He looked at the front cover and then at the picture on the back cover. "Is that the Commander?" I asked.

"Why, yes, that's the Commander. He were just a young man then."

"But he never mentioned this book?"

"He never mentioned a book to us, sir."

"I found it in the iron box, in a bedroom of...your house."

"Yes, 't'would be the place. We never looked in his box, sir."

"I'm sorry, I was told..."

"That's all right. Uncle Pius wanted you to find it."

"Why is it the Commander didn't want Pius to know you were learning German?"

"Uncle Pius hates the Germans, see."

"But, the Commander, Kurt von Schulte, was a German. Wasn't he?" Maybe I had missed something along the way, just firing along on assumptions. Jimmy read my thoughts again.

"No mistake, sir. The Commander was a German through and through. I don't know how to explain it but Uncle Pius and the Commander loved each other like brothers, but they was still the enemy, first and last. It was a kind of long truce neither of them wanted to break. Then the Commander died the other day and I thinks Pius has gone off to do the same."

"Of course, you'd know what happened this morning."

"He was adrift, Pius was. Knew he was having a spell and he wanted me to make sure you got the journals."

Finally. "That's wonderful!" I said, trying to contain my excitement. "I'd like to get started." It was a great relief to achieve my goal so easily. "I'll take them with me."

"No, sir. You can't take them away."

"But...ah, I thought...?"

"Mind's not right. I forget easy. Every time I get too close to the ocean I'd forget, see? The books help me remember."

Jimmy began to twitch. I changed the subject with the intention of solving the problem of possession later.

"Can you tell me something about the Commander's book?"

"Come back in three days," he said, and closed his eyes.

I was shown to the door and reluctantly started down the hill, somewhat deflated, with the option of waiting out the three days or leaving Fogo Island and giving up the whole affair. It was becoming increasingly complicated and the legitimacy of the Commander's stories were in question and I only had Jimmy to sort out the truth from the fiction. But I had handled Pius' scribbler, which I had left on the table of Kurt's house. I was anxious to retrieve at least that document and the charts.

I expected to find that an agent of a dark power had slipped into the Commander's house, while I was distracted on Jimmy White's hill, and made off with the scribbler and the charts. But the scribbler was on the kitchen table, although not on the table as I remembered leaving it. In the bedroom the charts were tumbled into the iron box as I had left them. I selected the charts I wanted and left the room, closing the door gently, as I had done previously to the doors of the other two rooms, which were now *open.* Something was missing from room number one. The quilt was not on the bed. I hadn't touched the bed. It never dawned on me that the journals could have been stuffed in a mattress. But the quilt was definitely gone. I closed the door and approached room number two. Nothing appeared to be amiss. I opened the trunk. The dresses were folded neatly. I *hadn't* folded them, am incapable of folding clothing that neatly. I dug down to the bottom of the chest. The photo album was gone also.

Mrs. Penny was a study in restrained curiosity when I announced that I would be staying another few days, at least. She was thoughtful and quiet, weighing the news. While she was musing I tried to explain that I needed more time to take pictures and get to know Fogo and I would gladly pay extra to take meals with the family. I couldn't abide another day of greasy fried chicken and French fries from the new outlet across the road from the new finance and loan office. Mrs. Penny looked troubled. Perhaps she would tell me to go back to the mainland and stop nosing into the business of the outport.

"My dear man, you're welcome to stay but you'll have to shift for yourself. We're gone away this week next. Every year we takes a spell over to Gambo to visit my husband's crowd, see. He's not from Fogo. My husband come over to look after the fish plant 'bout ten years ago. He's a Gambo Penny. There's Penny people all up and down the coast. Some gets together in Gambo for a reunion, like. Know how to cook yourself a meal, my dear?"

"Yes, I can get by."

"I'm sorry to put you out, like, but if you've a mind the house is yours. And since you've got to shift for yourself you pay only half, and if any others come along you charge them the same, unless you got to cook for them, you know? Then you charge them regular, aside what it costs for the food. Just tell Reg at the store...you know the one I mean over by the church...put it on my bill. Just lay the money in the box. Oh, and the cat will want a bite now and then. And wouldn't hurt to look at the plants once or twice. It'll save Vera coming in. I hope you aren't put out of your way?"

"Ah, no, not at all. I don't mind," I said, flustered and amazed by the trust the woman put in a stranger.

"Good, then, we'll be off in the morning first thing. I'll leave your breakfast in the oven, dear."

I wasn't put out by the arrangement. I could spend my *waiting time* without having to answer questions or risk having my already shaky confidence in the story, shaken further. However, Mrs. Penny's parting comment was a warning: "Stay clear of the queer place up in the hills. Jimmy White's to be avoided like the plague." I assured her I would take utmost care of myself, her house, her guests, her cat and her plants.

I spent the three days pouring over Pius' scribbler and puzzling over the missing quilt and photo album. I took pictures. I walked in the lower hills, and photographed the colourful boats and stages in the back harbour where the wind was more subdued, avoiding Jimmy's hill as instructed, by Jimmy. I sat on the fish plant wharf when the sun shone and watched the children fishing for Tommy cod after school. The children complained that there weren't many Tommy cod that season. Seems the string was running out on them as well. The village was quiet with the fish plant closed down. Families were leaving in cars packed for long distance travel and I doubted they were all going on vacation. Joey Smallwood's wish was being fulfilled; the fishermen were coming ashore and burning their boats but there was nothing ashore for them to do either. From my perspective on the wharf and in the hills I was seeing a way of life coming to an end. I thought of Pius and the schooners, imagining the glory days of sail and wind-toughened fishermen. At night I concentrated on Pius' scribbler and tried to fill in the blanks until it was time to pay my respects to Mary Humby and get the news.

Mary sat me down at the kitchen table spread with the usual comestibles; hot tea and fresh bread. The hospital had called, she said quietly. Pius was transferred to St. John's over night in serious condition but now stable and resting comfortably. There was some paralysis and it had been a near thing with his heart all the way to the hospital in Gander. Mary wondered if it had been the right thing to do. Perhaps they should have let him go in peace instead of being wired up and rushed here and there by strangers. I didn't say anything. I genuinely hoped he recovered, if he could still enjoy life, and if not, slip away on them to his rest.

Pius and I had been talking about old schooners and the mainlanders who come to Newfoundland looking for the old derelicts. I mentioned a few old schooners I knew about that found their way to Ontario and drove their owners crazy keeping them afloat. Pius smiled and nodded. He understood the fascination but he was more realistic. A fishing schooner, he said: "*...is built to do a job of work and she's given just so long to do it, and when the time comes she's no good for it, you puts her ashore, strip away what you can use and let the old hulk go peacefully to her rest on the beach. It's where the damned things try to get on you all their life...*" He said it with an affectionate chuckle, so the meaning was clear. It was the inevitability of life he hoped would suit him in the end. We were welcome to strip away from him what we could use and let him go. Not leave him adrift in a billow of cold, clinical whiteness, because it still leaves a man alone on the beach and a woman alone in her kitchen.

We tried to get away from the subject of Pius's passing. Mary was strong and didn't dramatize the personal pain, she just got on with the business of living. Then Mary mentioned the quilt and the photo album. She went to the parlour and returned with the folded quilt.

"Yes, I was at the Commander's place to find you but you'd been and gone. Can I ask a favour? Rose had this quilt that her mother made, it was somewhat special to the child, and some pictures of her family. I wondered, if it wouldn't be too much trouble to carry them back to Toronto and find a relative. Jimmy didn't want them."

And there was Rose again. I agreed to try. Apparently, Rose, and her history, were going to insert themselves into my story, and where would that road lead? Mary and I exchanged small talk about the weather and remedies for ailments and illnesses. It kept us closer to home. The only reference she made to the stories was something about how they used hot poultices in the old days to draw infections. She made a specific reference to Jimmy White and said a German custom of using garlic and mustard poultices had saved his life after the *accident*. She didn't elaborate. I didn't pursue the lead. It was obvious she didn't want to venture into memories while Pius was still in the present. Nor did I mention my dilemma about the journals and Jimmy's refusal to let them go.

It was time to make the pilgrimage to Jimmy's shrine but I felt like a dandelion seedling looking for a place to take root, blown constantly around by the wind, full of promise but at the mercy of the forces. I promised to return for the quilt and the photo album before I left for the mainland. There was a chance Mary would want to talk about Rose and it might be helpful, but I was sure I was only on the track of a war story and two unlikely companions who had fought on opposite sides.

Jimmy was waiting for me at the top of the path. He cast a long, defiant gaze out over the ocean, facing the enemy, his personal demon. I waited, watching with him. Was he testing my patience? (In all the thought I gave to Jimmy in succeeding years I could never fathom what was going on in Jimmy's mind, even after I learned the details). Finally Jimmy turned and walked toward the shack.

The cabin was almost as before; the kettle steaming on the tiny stove and a Spartan lunch spread on the table by the window, but now the canvas was pulled aside to let in the light. Kurt's book was lying open beside Jimmy's porcelain mug.

We sat at the small table and shared fresh bread while waiting for the tea to brew. There was something touching about the simple ritual of adding a handful of tea leaves to the brown tea pot from a tall brass canister; a four inch diameter brass shell casing. Jimmy said it was from the submarine. *The* submarine?

While waiting for Jimmy to go on, my eyes wondered into the gloom of the small shack. The sleeping area was only a narrow cot; a day bed. There was one blanket, no pillow and no clothing to be seen and there was no closet. What about cold weather? As my mind raced around these small puzzles and my eyes adjusted to the gloom, I spotted the iron box; a foot locker to Jimmy's cot. It appeared to be the same box I had rummaged through in Kurt's room but there was something about the way it sat at the end of the cot that spoke of permanence.

"Yes, they're in the box," Jimmy said, noticing my gaze.

"Good. That's good," I said, relieved.

I fidgeted in my turn. I looked out the window at the spectacular view of the Atlantic, imagining what the icebergs would look like, forming a phrase for the story...*I longed to be on the coast in the spring when the icebergs move down from Greenland with the Labrador Current, crashing through the pack ice, crushing anything in their way*...Jimmy poured out the tea and we ate in silence. I watched his face, accustomed now to the disturbing visage, encouraged by the sharp, intelligent eyes that seemed to smile at my uncontrolled curiosity. He wasn't toying with me, it wasn't a game for Jimmy. He had come back from something horrendous and lived in his own peculiar rhythm, on a hill, looking over the only world that mattered.

"I have read the Commander's book this last while, sir."

"Oh? What did you think of it?"

"There was a lot I didn't understand."

"I see. But, is it about Kurt? The Commander?..."

"No, b'ye. Not about he, about people in Germany though. I never heard the most of the names, except for Mr. Hitler. The rest was nothing to me."

"It's fiction then?" I asked, disappointed.

"I suppose that's what the Commander called it. A story, like."

"What was the story about?"

"The Jewish people, b'ye. Least that's what I could get out of it. Terrible time they had. Nobody wanted them, see?"

"Persecuted?"

"Yes, that's it! They was persecuted terrible, but worst of all in Germany. The one family, the woman's, had been well off but the Germans didn't like them. Made life hard and worried them until they nearly gave up. But they had friends, see, and when they was down they climbed out of it and was sailing free again until Mr. Hitler and his crowd got a hold of the country and that poor family was knocked down until they was no more. They was drove out, I suppose."

"After nineteen thirty-three?"

"I believe it was about right. I was only a lad, but I remember hearing something about it then, you know? Fellas come over on the boats for fish, like. They said it was hard times in those countries. Guess it was. We got a war out of it didn't we?"

"Yes, we certainly did."

"You weren't in that war?" asked Jimmy.

"No, I was born during the war."

"You don't remember anything about that war, sir?"

"I remember my father coming home. My uncles."

"Terrible thing, war," he said, with pathetic sadness.

"Yes," I agreed, but from a different perspective.

"We had our own war, right here in Fogo b'ye. I believe that's the story you wants."

So, it was beginning and Jimmy seemed ready to talk. He looked out over the ocean as if watching his war on a big movie screen. I wanted to see what he could see and I wanted someone to explain the war. I grew up in the aftermath of the Second War, playing war games with war surplus gear smuggled home by fathers and uncles. We had nine men in the service between my parents. They all came home. The real war hadn't bloodied us, not the way some families suffered, although there were wonderful stories, some hilarious, and I would hang on the periphery as they told their wonderful tales over beer and cigarettes. Their war seemed like a grand adventure.

"How old were you during the war?" I asked.

"I was twenty-five when I went away, in my mind, like."

It struck me then what the war had meant to Jimmy White. It took away a lifetime and left him with only a life. No family, except for the Commander, who cared for him, and Pius and Mary. No wife. No babies. No future, other than to skulk around at night, learning German from a man who might have killed him in other circumstances.

"Do you mind if I make notes?"

"Notes, sir?"

"So I can remember what we talk about, for the story I think I have to write."

"The Commander used to say that if you didn't live it you shouldn't write about it."

"If I don't write it who will?"

"That's so, b'ye. I couldn't do it."

"Let's say that I'm going to write it for Pius and Kurt."

"I guess that would be all right."

Jimmy seemed satisfied but whatever I took away from the Island was going to be laboriously gained and my interpreter had at least been on the ground for some of the action.

"Did Kurt's published book mention the First World War?"

"Some. Mostly it was after the Great War, and them poor Jewish people. The Second World War hadn't started yet but I think he was predicting it. The war…"

"What does the title mean?"

"Mean? *Der Republik Des Teufels?* The Devil's Republic. I think it means it was the Devil running the country, like."

"An apt title I'd say, considering what happened in Germany."

"My son! The Devil's work for sure. The Commander said so himself. He had no love for that fellow, Mr. Hitler."

"Did he write about his submarine service during the First World War?"

"No, sir, never mentioned a thing 'bout submarines."

I was afraid I'd hit the first stone wall. The doubts surfaced, like a whale too long under water.

"But don't you worry, sir. The Commander wrote it all down, see."

The doubts sounded again. Jimmy got up to open the iron box. His box had padlocks and the key materialized from somewhere overhead. In a village where traditionally nothing was locked it seemed odd for Jimmy to lock the box, but it was Jimmy's life and, fiction or not, it was all he had.

Jimmy set a stack of journals on the table. Large books with leather covers, like old fashioned ledgers, corners broken and torn and the leather scuffed and stained. Important looking documents with a history of their own that had that musty stench of age and time spent in damp places but they were Jimmy's icons and he their caretaker. Jimmy cleared a space and took the top book off the pile. It was maroon leather and his fingers lingered as though he was reluctant to expose Kurt's history. "This be the last book, sir. The end of Kurt's story." The next book was green; it went on top of the maroon book, the next blue and the last black.

Jimmy pulled the black book toward him and opened the cover. The first page was written in black ink with a straight pen that skipped and made little splatter marks. Jimmy turned the pages slowly, as if savouring the written word, breathing in life. In the margins were illustrations, the loose sketches Impressionistic in style.

"Pius told you the most of this part, sure. Some things to do with his family and a woman named Anna. I never understood what happened unless the Commander explained it, see. About his family and the woman. Pius told you some of that as well. This part here's what he wrote down about he and Pius in the First War."

I opened my own note book.

THE ENGLISH CHANNEL

May 31, 1916: The choppy, chatter noise of approaching propellers cut through the thin metal skin of *Unterseeboot-42* like ragged sheers. Commander Kurt von Schulte, sweating, concentrating, pivoted the search periscope. The crew, faces red in the glow of the control room battle light, watched impassively. He had to decide the course of their lives and whether they had a future or became blasted bags of skin; remembered only by loved ones, their brave submariners who had left Emden a week before to run the British blockade of the North Sea. Their orders were to demoralize the British Navy. Kapitänleutnant Kurt von Schulte had taken his submarine to the doorstep of Portsmouth Harbour to attack a destroyer in the Solent off the Isle of Wight and they were paying the price for the daring raid.

Three fast British destroyers pursued them relentlessly like angry wasps and the running battle lasted for twelve hours. It was now 0415. The crew had been at action stations for almost twenty-two hours as the battle was waged above and below the surface, until Kapitänleutnant Schulte had been forced into shallow water near Etretat. Claude Monet might be watching from the cliffs, Kurt chuckled. The crew looked at each other wondering what could possibly be funny about their impending destruction.

Kurt was thinking about the over-rich scenes of the colour drenched coast interpreted by the French and Flemish painters, while Kurt himself was far removed from beauty and decadence. He envied Monet, not because the Frenchman could paint better, but because Monet was good enough to paint badly if he chose and get away with it. He almost never did, paint badly, that is. Kurt always wanted to paint well but seldom succeeded. Perhaps he should paint something truly his own, like the view of the darkened sea through his periscope and the shadows of the destroyers dashing about, hunting him down like hounds on the scent, their signal lamps flashing, searchlights sweeping the black water like intelligent lighthouses. He would certainly paint the flares arcing across the night sky to burst in glory, showering the sea with sparkling petals from exploding flowers. Art of the moment. The artist painting his own death by violence…

Kurt von Schulte found his true vocation with the fledgling German submarine service. On his return to Emden after the disastrous family gathering, Kurt had gone to sea with Korvettenkapitän Alfred Schrader as probationary navigation officer and supernumerary. From their base at Emden they ventured out to harass the British Grand Fleet. The opening months of the war were heady and chaotic. Schrader rose quickly in the ranks, taking Kurt with him. Kurt's own promotions from probationary navigation officer to Oberleutnant zur See to Korvettenkapitän zur See followed in rapid succession. The war was deadly for both sides as the rules were thrown out, the deadly submarines operated further from their bases and the British developed depth charges and became proficient at sinking them. Kurt was given his own submarine and made Kapitänleutnant zur See in December, 1915.

At first his crew were suspicious of his rapid rise in the ranks. Kurt himself suspected the family name had something to do with it *...General Schulte reasoned that his son would not disgrace him by groveling in the bowels of a stinking submarine as a faceless sailor. His son would be an officer...*Kurt accepted the promotions and discovered he was good at commanding a killing machine. He enjoyed it, never hesitating to place his ship in harm's way and take the consequences. He vowed not to show fear during attacks, but instead thought of Anna and Norderney in defiance of the enemy, wearing Anna as his armour.

Kurt celebrated Christmas in the North Sea sitting on the chart table of his U-boat while depth charges rained down around them. Five months later Kurt was running out of manoeuvres and ideas in the Channel. It would be first light soon and they would lose the protection of the darkness. Escape on the surface was out of the question unless he could outsmart the enemy destroyers, beat them at their own game, and the old style submarines were not meant to travel fast or far submerged.

Kurt, at his battle position in the conning tower, turned the periscope slowly, stopping to focus, marking the ships he could see. He made three stops. One destroyer was going away, withdrawing from the battle. Two, he identified as Beagle Class coal burning, fast destroyers, remained in the hunt.

The destroyers, HMS *Savage,* Lieutenant Freddie Holmes in command, and HMS *Scourge,* Lieutenant Lord Howard Hedley, drove down on Kurt's estimated position, sure of a kill between them. Lord Hedley and Freddie Holmes were best friends, team mates on the Royal Navy football team. Lord Hedley, with Freddie's help, was keen to dispatch this German submarine quickly and punish the Huns for killing so many good men when HMS *Renegade* suddenly blew up as she cleared the Portsmouth fairway buoy. It had been a daring attack by an invisible German U-boat in the narrow corridor of the swept channel. In the Navy's front yard! There must be retribution before the ships could head back to Portsmouth.

On the bridge of *Scourge* Lieutenant Hedley replayed a match his team had recently lost to the upstart Marines by the narrowest of margins. He couldn't help chastising himself for missing a close in kick at a crucial point in the game. He had been playing well but let his concentration waver because of a minor detail that his Number One had brought to his attention before the game. Leading Seaman Pius Humby had requested a transfer to officer's training school. Hedley knew Humby was officer material but he was also an excellent quartermaster, a helmsman who could handle his ship with a rare finesse that made Hedley look very good on manoeuvres. Looking good is important to naval careers. Hedley himself was ready to move up and wasn't going to risk letting Humby get away. Now he was thinking about the match as he watched *Savage* astern, about to cross the track of his own *Scourge,* as planned.

Hedley swung his gaze away from *Savage*. He knew Freddie Holmes would turn his ship to port. He always cut behind Hedley to take a drop pass, then had the option to give and go. The manoeuvre usually caught the opposition off balance and Hedley would be credited with pretty goal. They were ready to make another run at the submarine to force it aground, on the mud, on a falling tide, a sitting duck for target practice. It was no way to fight a war but Hedley needed results.

"Mr. Humby, five degrees, starboard, if you please."

"Aye, five degrees starboard, sir," repeated Pius.

"Lookouts! Keep an eye on *Savage!*" Hedley said to the men scanning the four quadrants with night glasses. He turned to his first officer. "Freddie might pinch in a little closer this time around and try to pop a shell down his hatch."

"Good for him, sir," said the first officer.

"Well, Number One, we've got the bugger this time!"

"Right, sir. He's running out of water."

"I hope he'll bloody well run out before we do. I don't like this close in work. Too many chances to take out her bottom."

"The chart doesn't show wrecks in this area. We can follow him right up on the beach, sir."

"I trust not up on the beach, Number One, but there'll be a wreck to chart before dawn if we can force *him* up. Steady there, Mr. Humby, you've got the track now."

"Last run gave him something to think about," continued the first officer.

"Too bad we can't dump a calling card on the blighter, but it wouldn't look good to blow our own stern off. I don't trust these new depth bombs."

"It would be bloody funny though…sir, popping the Hun a bun, right out of the oven, as it were."

"Right. If it didn't happened to us," said Hedley without taking his eyes away from the binoculars. "There's his periscope!"

The telltale phosphorescence streaked the surface against the dark line of the French coast.

"Signals!"

"Aye, sir!" replied the almost invisible boy, already sending Holmes' number.

"Make to *Savage*. Target bearing green, zero-three-three. Follow me in."

"Aye, sir, green, zero-three-three."

"What if the German turns out this time?" asked the number one.

"Freddie's behind us to cut him off. He has to turn in, unless he's a fool. Then we've got him! Helm! Steer one-two-five, and lead him. Correct one degree to port at intervals of ten seconds!"

"Aye, sir. One-two-five. One degree port, at ten seconds," repeated Pius Humby.

Pius watched the compass card move as he turned the wheel. The lubber line at the top of the compass ring was the bow of the ship. He had to bring that line to the compass course of one-two-five degrees, then adjust the course to lead the submarine as it ran for its life along the coast of France. The periscope dipped out of sight. The deadly game continued.

"Guns!?"

A voice came out of the tube almost immediately.

"Aye! Guns here!"

"Guns, I want a single shot, dead ahead. Range, six hundred yards and closing at speed. Fire when ready."

Moments later the four inch gun turret erupted in smoke and flame and thunder. Hedley watched for the expected splash of the shell. Two seconds, three seconds: the sea rose up in a pale blue fountain, looking

Fogo's War Trilogy

clean against the dark background of the coast. The shell hit the water less than a hundred yards ahead of the submarine's calculated position.

"Close enough!" said the lieutenant. And to the voice tube: "Good shot. Guns!"

"A lucky one might do for him, sir," offered Number One.

"No wild shots. That was just to coax the German to see things our way. And we don't want to run him down, do we? Helm! Make your starboard turn in five seconds, Mr. Humby! Bring her around well outside Freddie's turn."

Pius counted then spun the wheel to starboard. The destroyer leaned away from the turn as the narrow hull dug into the water at twenty-five knots. *Savage,* following close astern, but angling to port, was pinching in to the submarine's course. Kapitänleutnant Kurt Schulte's harassed *U-42* was forced to bear off again toward the coast and shoaling water, or turn to fight.

In the control room of *U-42* Kurt Schulte and the navigation officer leaned over the chart assessing their options. They were limited. The hydrophone operator, spinning his directional wheel, was trying desperately to determine the bearings of the two destroyers manoeuvring ships-in-line and bow on to mask the second hull. It was difficult to guess their next move. The exact effect Hedley hoped to achieve. It wasn't in the Navy's books of manoeuvres but Hedley gambled that initiative was the path to advancement, if it succeeded. If it failed and a ship was lost, so was his future in the Navy. Most lieutenants went by the book. In the modern era of the British Navy, failure by the book was not punished as severely, if at all. The ambitious Hedley also believed that caution seldom won battles. His view was shared by the First Sea Lord, Winston Churchill, in the tradition of Lord Nelson, but their powers of self determination were vastly different. Three captains; one German and two British, threw their training, their crews and their ships, and most of all their instincts, into the battle and prayed luck was on their side. But Hedley could not second guess the enemy, only hope he was conventional.

Kurt climbed back to the conning tower to bring the periscope to bear again. There was no hope of shaking the destroyers this time. The crew prayed for the most basic of reasons. Survival. In the red light of the control room, sweat stood out on their young bearded faces like blood. Fatigue lines looked theatrical. They were characters in a play about the *Inferno*, caught in the lights, frozen for the moment, waiting for the protagonists and antagonists to make the next move. The script was being written as the play unfolded and the finalé was always a surprise to the supporting players. Kurt waited for Hedley to commit himself.

"They're just playing with us, Chief," Kurt said, speaking to the top of his pudgy, pink-faced chief engineer's head only inches below him. Eric Heidle's eyes never left the Papenberg tube or his hand the valve that controlled their depth and buoyancy. "They intend to drive us into the mud, Eric."

"The bloody British swine!" said Eric, with theatrical disgust. "They know we need some sleep."

"Ah, yes, Eric. I'd forgotten sleep."

Eric had been at his station directing the dive and trim operators for all of twenty-two tense hours. His youth conquered his bulk and he never wavered. Kurt looked down at the navigation officer who seemed about to collapse over his chart but was in fact picking out small numbers.

"He can't ram us in this close, unless he's very angry. He'll turn to starboard. Where's the bottom, Nav?"

"Only eight meters under the keel and shelving, sir," said the navigation officer, without looking up from his beloved chart. "Five hundred meters off the first bar."

Hedley had committed HMS *Scourge*. He was purposely too close to *U-42* and now turning away, taking his four inch gun out of play, but *Savage*, trailing, would be in position for a shot. Kurt made his decision. Time to act. He swiveled the periscope and locked on his target.

"That one's now predictable also," said Kurt, pulling his eyes away from the silhouette of the vulnerable destroyer, ignoring the one that had been bearing down on him. "He'll come in on us then continue turning to port." Kurt slammed the adjustor handles. "We'll attack." He turned to his helmsman in the conning tower, "Hard to port. Ninety." Then he addressed the coxswain and Eric waiting for orders at the ladder below him, "Torpedoes and deck gun. Run us up on the surface, Chief."

The red, theatrical faces in the control room seemed relieved. Kurt had just pronounced their probable end in a storm of smoke and gun fire, but it was action, snarling back at the dogs hounding them. The Chief gave the orders to adjust the hydroplanes. "Two degrees up, fore and aft," the Chief said quietly. There was no need to shout orders in the cramped confines of the control room or the conning tower. If the crew feared their future they didn't show it. Kurt watched Eric and his crew at work. He loved every one of his scruffy gang of seasoned submariners who never complained more than any seaman complains.

"What's the tide, Nav?"

"Falling. Two hours to low," answered the navigation officer, over the sound of compressed air squeaking into the ballast tanks and the gunners assembling at the conning tower ladder, ready to pour out on deck for their last go at the hated British.

"Currents?" asked Kurt, as if requesting a time check. He watched the depth gauge climb toward their destiny. He rejected destiny and knew he wasn't dying that day.

"Southwest by west, on this tide. Two to three knots. Two with no wind."

"Prepare torpedo tubes one to four, Number One."

"One to four, aye, Kapitän."

"On the surface," said the Chief.

"Right then! Let's go," said Kurt as if addressing his own football team.

Kapitänleutnant Kurt von Schulte, failed intellectual, dissipated young aristocrat and bane of his father, with the master sight under his arm, led the charge up the conning tower ladder.

The two destroyers were a third of the way through their sweeping turns. The *Scourge* had gone first and took the long way around her right turn while *Savage,* turning left, made a tighter circle. *Savage* would arrive at the junction point first, and lead the next run in. Freddie Holmes would then turn to starboard and Hedley to port completing the figure of eight. They had worked out the manoeuvre over pints of bitters in the officer's club. They reasoned that if it worked on the football field it could work on the ocean against any ship, surface or unter zee, as they joked. It set them apart from the other lieutenants in their flotilla at Portsmouth. The Brass didn't care for stunting, unless, in retrospect, it worked.

The destroyers were committed to their circles when the U-boat foamed to the surface as Hedley expected; the German was forced to show himself if he was going to make a run for it along the coast, or go aground, but his prey was facing the wrong direction. Lord Hedley could taste victory before the German showed himself and his course and speed prevented the German from getting off a good shot at his own ship. What he hadn't considered was an enemy who appreciated oddities. The bow of the sub, instead of angling off to the north and west, was pointing at the apex of the turn Freddie's destroyer would make and Freddie's stern was presented perfectly to the sub's deck gun. It was a narrow target in the half light of the predawn but a steady target for a good gun crew.

Young, courageous, impetuous, Lord Howard Hedley, watching from the starboard wing of his own bridge, realized his error instantly. Through his binoculars he could see the picture unfolding. The sub had surfaced in perfect position for a leading torpedo run and the gun crew were rapidly preparing for a stern shot at the *Savage*. His body went numb. Cold perspiration bathed his face and trickled down his sides. Colder realization that his friends life and his own future hung in the balance.

The submarine was a very small object on a dark expanse of sea with a coastline in the background to eliminate a silhouette. Freddie Holmes and his lookouts didn't see the submarine surface. Hedley's bold plan prescribed that they commit a cardinal sin of seamanship in warfare, they exposed the weakest chink in their armour.

"He's surfaced, sir!" said Hedley's number one.

Hedley could see too well. "Yes, Damnit! He's going for Freddie's stern!" breathed Hedley.

"Why doesn't *Savage* get off a bloody shot!?"

"Hard-a-starboard! Flank speed!"

Pius Humby spun the wheel the rest of the way to the stops. Number One rang the telegraph, a quick double ring for flank speed. The answering ring was almost immediate and alarming, as if the chief engineer deep in his control room sensed the emergency. The ship shuddered and heeled further to port and the circumference of the circle collapsed inward with Lord Hedley's plans.

"Guns!!" Hedley screamed into the speaking tube.

"Aye! Guns!"

"Rapid fire!! Target dead ahead, five hundred yards and closing! Fire! Fire! Got that!!?"

"Aye, sir! Five hundred. Firing now!"

"Signals!! Make to *Savage*…'*Torpedoes. Port side. Break off!*'"

The click and flash of the signal lamp was an impotent response to the flash of the deadly little deck gun pointed at your friend's ship. Click…Click…Click. The first shot from the submarine fell short of *Savage's* vulnerable stern. The column of water that rose up was no longer night-time-blue but dawn-grey tipped by first-sun orange. Worse still, the lookouts on Freddie Holmes' ship would be facing the new sun so the submarine remained hidden by the very thing that should reveal its ugly presence. Hedley watched as the gun crew of the sub slammed in another shell. The burst of smoke and fire sent the shell on its way. Hedley prayed for a hit on the tiller flat that would at least stop the dictated circle of death.

Pius Humby adjusted the wheel back to port, purposely over steering to correct the ship's momentum to starboard. The moment *Scourge's* bow came to bear on the submarine the forward gun roared out an answer to Hedley's dilemma. The submarine's next shell exploded on the after funnel of *Savage*. Dark pieces of funnel and mast and rigging and what looked like a man, rose into the air and fell back into the water, and left behind in the confused wake. Smoke obscured the stern.

The signal lamp clicked on, too fast. Signals repeated the message without the proper interval. *Scourge* fired her second salvo. A geyser of water was on line but short of the submarine's conning tower. Another salvo erupted from *Scourge's* guns as soon as the gun layer adjusted the range. Hedley swung the binoculars from the submarine to *Savage*. He had the morbid sensation of watching a tennis match.

Freddie, saw his friend's destroyer turn sharply but his young signalman did not understand the hurried signal from Hedley's bridge. Freddie clung to the plan. The battle was joined and he was carrying out the manoeuvre he and his trusted friend had worked out in a cozy, leather-rich officers pub, safely away from battles and worries. They were going to make a big splash in the Navy. Freddie Holmes was not from an aristocratic family. His parents were labourers and Freddie was riding to glory on Lord Hedley's coat tails. He would follow Hedley blindly, faithfully, to oblivion if necessary.

Kapitänleutnant Kurt Schulte, having fixed the master sight for aiming torpedoes looked up to find the situation altered. The first destroyer, well away on a starboard turn and almost obscured by its own funnel smoke against the dark horizon clouds to the south, suddenly changed direction but his target destroyer, the doomed HMS *Savage*, already trailing smoke from the destroyed funnel, was closer, sweeping in a graceful curve to port into the light morning sea breeze. The bow wave and stern tumble almost blending in the first light of dawn. Kurt set the master sight, calculated distance and speed and deflection. He coldly determined the spot the destroyer and the torpedoes should meet.

"Come right, five degrees," said Kurt calmly to the helmsman in the conning tower just below his feet. "Spread pattern, one to four. Open bow caps!" The orders were quickly relayed by the first officer to a man below the control room hatch. The orders were repeated along the line and the answers came back as expected.

"Bow caps open. Torpedoes one to four, ready, Kapitän."

"Fire torpedoes one to four," Kurt said with no more emotion than ordering four double bocks for his fishermen in the café.

The order was relayed to the torpedo room. Levers were pushed in delayed sequence followed by a hiss of compressed air for each torpedo launched and the bow rose in response to the lost weight. In the control room the Chief ordered sea water pumped into the forward trim tanks to compensate. The men and their machinery worked smoothly. Voice commands in even, practiced tones carried the messages. In a matter of coldly calculated seconds some of the enemy in their war machine would die horrible deaths and the reasons they were killed no longer mattered.

The four torpedoes sped away trailing happy bubbles from their propellers. It would take less than eighty seconds to run to their appointed rendezvous; not a long time to alter the future. Kurt was watching the effects of the deck gun's second shot on the funnel of the *Savage* when the first salvo from the *Scourge* rocked his own ship. Spray from the port side geyser drifted over the bridge. Kurt didn't acknowledge the shot close aboard, intent on watching his own gun crew fire and reload, noting the interval with satisfaction. Gunnery practice had paid off with efficiency of motion; a well oiled crew, as they might say in navy parlance, on both sides. Smoke. Thunder. Water. Kurt's first officer pointed to the *Scourge,* bow on, bearing down on them.

"Ship! Port beam!!"

The deck gun erupted again. Kurt let his binoculars drop. He stared at *Savage* whose port side was coming into plain view. Thunder. More shells from *Scourge*. Water. More shells into the stern and then the quarter of *Savage*. Smoke. Pieces of ship and men arched into sky and fell into the sea. Geysers rose up around the submarine. Thunder. The first officer felt the wind from a shell that overshot the bridge. Water. Kurt didn't feel it...*He wasn't there. He was on Norderney Island sitting in the foam of a retreating wave looking up at the beautiful woman in the mist...*

"Kapitän!! The Britisher will run us down!"

"Undoubtedly," replied Kurt, uninterested.

The deck gun was losing the range. Kurt looked at his watch. The second hand swept on. Still thirty seconds to run. Thunder. Time was compressed. Water. Time stood still. Smoke. "Guns, aim for the other destroyer's bridge!"

"We should dive!"

"No! There's no water," Kurt heard himself say. Kurt yelled down the hatch, "Come to port, eighty degrees!! Full ahead, both!"

"Madness!!" yelled the first officer.

"We can't outrun a destroyer," Kurt said, as if analyzing a boxing match, "So, we present our smallest target and attack! Guns!! Aim for the bridge! For the bridge!!"

On the open bridge of HMS *Scourge* Lieutenant Hedley knew it was too late for his friend. "Why doesn't he bear off? Turn away, Freddie, damn you!"

The time for distraction or salvation was beyond the control of the antagonists. Freddie Holmes continued the prescribed port turn as he watched his friend's destroyer bearing down on the submarine, suddenly realizing the game was up. His own ship was taking shell's aft but he was waiting for damage reports or a clear signal from *Scourge* before initiating evasive action. The Second Officer in the enclosed bridge below him reported the helm unresponsive. Time for action was passed. For Lord Hedley there was only time for retribution. "Humby, steer for the bastard's conning tower!!"

Pius didn't need to be told. He was using the fore jack on his bow as a sighting wire, the racing destroyer's sharp stem aiming for Kurt Schulte, the obvious target. The first shell from the submarine was high. The gun layer miscalculated the closing speed of both vessels. Pius saw the flash and knew the Germans were shooting at him. He wasn't afraid to die. He held the wheel with a death grip and willed the bow of the destroyer to carve into the bloody German commanding the submarine.

The next shell from the German exploded at the base of the fore deck turret. Orange flames and black smoke leapt out and blew back. The gun crew were reloading when the German's shell tore into them. A young seaman from Devon was holding the British shell. Someone set the emergency klaxon going. The strident *gronking* only added to the din of sirens and fire parties rushing about. The officers on the open bridge fell back from the intense heat. Smoke from the burning turret poured into the open doors of the bridge. Pius, shielded by the metal and glass of his enclosed steering station, hung on, eyes burning, choking, but no longer able to see his target. Lieutenant Hedley stumbled to the port bridge wing. "Hold your course, Humby!" he shouted into the speaking tube.

When the smoke cleared, the destroyer and the U-boat were still on a collision course. A German shell penetrated the wardroom below the bridge. Pius could feel the deck lift and then the wheel went slack. The lines to the steering motors in the stern had been severed. The signalman slumped beside his shattered signal lamp, still holding the useless flipper. Their well ordered world was turning into chaos as Pius fought his way to the starboard door, intending to reach the manoeuvring wheel on the monkey island above the bridge. As he climbed to the open bridge wing he had a view over their own burning foredeck to a bizarre sight. Their sister destroyer, *Savage,* rose slowly, almost majestically, on a column of water then settled back into her element and continued on, but mortally wounded, to find the beach below Etretat. Lieutenant Hedley turned away from the awful, career ending spectacle. He saw Pius staring, transfixed by the catastrophe.

"Mr. Humby!! Get back to your station!!"

Pius tried to shout over the noise of the klaxon. He motioned that the wheel was out of commission and pointed up. Hedley nodded. It was the last command Hedley gave; not a command really, an acquiescence. Another shell exploded. Lord Hedley, his Number One and the lookouts vanished with the port bridge wing. Pius was blown backward and fell against the outboard side of the starboard bridge wing. The next shell penetrated the armour plating in the centre of the wheelhouse and exploded behind the useless helm, killing the second lieutenant, the midshipman and a messenger. Smoke. Thunder. Fire. Then silence.

Pius sat with his back against the bridge awning, too stunned to move, staring in disbelief at the carnage and smoking ruins around him. *Was he the only one left alive?* Blood ran down the door frame and across the deck planks. Sticky bits of flesh clung to unusual places. The stench was acrid and sweet. Pius touched a crushed head and was sick to his stomach. He couldn't tell if he was hurt. He didn't feel anything beyond the nausea. The brain centre of the ship was dead but the engines still raced ahead, out of touch and out of control. He knew he should move. Bullets from the U-boat's machine gun tore jagged holes in the canvas, clattered and ricocheted around his world. *Useless,* he thought. They were already dead. Pius pulled himself up to the rail to see who was trying to kill him?

Kurt was also entranced, watching *Savage* rise and settle, then continue on thinking that German torpedoes had to be improved if the Kaiser was to prevail over British steel. Steam from a ruptured boiler swirled above the sea. Thick black smoke hung over the scene as if trying to hide the disgusting sight from the eyes of a God who must be dismayed by the stupid things His little people do in His name. The battered hull would survive to find the beach before it settled on the bottom with superstructure, masts and funnels showing above the surface at high tide. The ship would be salvaged to finish the war but Freddie Holms was dead. The flotilla flag on the signal yard waved at Kurt out of the smoke before *Savage* crossed behind the on coming *Scourge*.

Kurt felt the thud of bullets ripping along the wooden gratings of the foredeck. Someone on the destroyer was firing a machine gun at him. Bullets clattered around the conning tower. Pieces of metal flew in all directions. A machine gun close to Kurt answered. A body slumped over the railing. His first officer was sitting at his feet hugging the pedestal of the master sight, humming a marching tune and tapping the pedestal in time with his wedding ring. Blood trickled down from under his cap. Kurt looked around for the cause of his officer's injury only to see the bow of the destroyer towering above them and the gun crew scrambling away to save themselves. "Afraid to face your death, Heinrich?"

"I'm not afraid," answered the first officer. "I just don't want to see it."

"We must face our death like good Germans!"

The glancing blow caught the U-boat's hull just aft of the starboard torpedo tubes, collapsing the outer casing as the submarine was muscled aside, grinding along the flanks of the destroyer.

The destroyer was still racing ahead. The dead midshipman draped over the bridge telegraph. In the engine room the telegraph indicator rested on *Finished with Engines*. The chief engineer knew he should obey the signal but knew also the telegraph order was impossible. He sent a runner to find out what was going on topside. The runner never returned. The Chief was still waiting for an answer when he was thrown over the catwalk railing into the maze of steel and iron below. He died in a tangle of machinery; devoured by the long, gleaming piston rods of the powerful steam engine he loved and cared for like a doting mother. The wisp of steam blowing over his mangled body and the hot oil anointing his forehead could neither bring back life nor guarantee anything in another world.

Kurt wasn't braced for the collision either and was thrown forward against the bulwarks of the tiny bridge but the force of the blow was cushioned by the body of a dead sailor. He looked up at the grey, salt-streaked wall of iron sliding by. The faces of astonished or angry British seamen looked down at him but with guns silenced. At close quarters neither side felt like shooting. Then he noticed Pius Humby on the bridge wing. He shrugged, smiled and waved a salute to the enemy.

Pius looked back at his burning wheelhouse, remembering something Lieutenant Hedley had once said about never cursing the enemy. "I can curse you, you heathen bastard!!" Pius shouted down at the smiling German. "I can curse you a thousand times!!"

And Kurt's reply was simply: *"Lebewhol! Auf wiedersehen!"*

The battered destroyer limped toward the coast of France like a wounded whale, trailing smoke and bad wishes astern. Kurt watched until it also ran aground on a falling tide. Why didn't they back away?...*the Norddeich ferry backed away from the dock at Norderney on a cloud-heavy day when the mist couldn't decide whether it would fall as rain or drift into one's face and run down like tears. Was Anna sad to be leaving? Or was Anna sad because Kurt didn't understand...*The second officer and the coxswain were beside him waiting for orders. The dead and wounded had been cleared away. The U-boat was stopped while damage control repaired hull leaks.

"The Britishers are vulnerable, Kapitän," said the second officer.

"Yes, vulnerable, and helpless," Kurt said, staring at the *Scourge's* exposed stern. HMS *Savage*, further down the coast and obviously on the bottom, was an easy kill with the deck gun even in *U-42's* battered condition. The British would be occupied caring for their survivors. The *Scourge* was a sitting duck for a stern torpedo shot but the destroyer fought well and Kurt no longer had an interest in sinking ships...(The *Scourge* was also salvaged by British tugs and towed back to Portsmouth within a week. There was an inquiry. Pius testified to the events as he remembered them. Lieutenants Hedley and Holmes were commended posthumously for their actions against the unidentified German submarine. The log books were sealed. The matter was filed and forgotten in Admiralty archives).

On that May killing day in 1916 Pius Humby held what was left of the shattered bridge as his ship ran herself aground in impotent fury on the same mud bank the young Lieutenants had planned as the final resting place of the German U-boat. There was confusion about who was in active command. The chief engineer was the ranking officer but he deferred to Quartermaster and Leading Seaman Humby as the designated Deck Officer, in control of a stranded, demoralized British warship. Pius was in shock and only years of experience allowed him to organize the clean up and prepare to transfer what was left of the compliment of ninety-six sailors to the French beach. He didn't realize how beautiful the coast was or how many painters tried to dab its shifting colours on canvas and how many would succeed and how many fail. He had failed to run down the German and it would cause him much sole searching in the years to come.

Kurt had more immediate problems.

"What's our situation, Franz?" Kurt quizzed the second officer, who, on the death of the first officer while humming marching tunes, was promoted to Number One.

"Not good I'm afraid," answered Franz gravely.

"I surmised that. Can we keep her afloat?"

"Barely. Eric's been hurt. It's bad," reported the new Number One. "The main pumps are down and Eric's Number Two doesn't have the brains to blow his nose. The other boys just follow orders."

"Thank you," said Kurt, noting that Franz was taking his promotion seriously. "Send up the written report."

Kurt cast another long gaze at the smoking destroyer and the beautiful but hostile coastline, looking splendid in the sunrise. He was in enemy waters with a damaged submarine that could no longer dive to escape. A daylight voyage from Etretat through the Strait of Dover to Ostende or Zeebrugge was out of the question.

Although he was concerned about his chief engineer, Kurt had no desire to go back into the bowels of his dead ship just yet. He waited for the damage reports on the bridge, organizing priorities in his fatigued brain. He weighed the possibilities and gave the order to head out to sea, southwest then south past Le Havre. They would attempt a landing at one of the Normandy beaches under the cover of darkness. The topside crew assembled the dead on the after deck to commit the bodies of their crewmen to God and the ravenous ocean. Kurt rejected the notion of ravenous. It was just an ocean. He was idling in his mind, waiting for the burial detail to finish laying out the four bodies in their canvas enclosures. One sailor had fallen overboard during the battle and lay on the bottom nearby, but he would be remembered with his mates in the form of personal effects, a photograph of a sweetheart and letters from home.

The brief ceremony finished, Kurt climbed wearily down the ladder. He had been on the bridge for a long time. *Long enough,* he thought, *to damage or sink three destroyers, and kill hundreds of British sailors. In the process he sacrificed five of his own men. That's a long important voyage.* He was tired but there were too many details before he could sleep. The control room looked strange in normal light. He spoke to the recording midshipman on his way to the engine room.

"Make a note...*Action broken off at 0438. One enemy destroyer damaged by torpedo and aground. Visual. One probable sunk in the approaches to Portsmouth Harbour. One damaged by gunfire and collision and aground near beach below Etretat. My crew performed all duties. The enemy was valiant under fire. Proceeding south to beach the boat due to pressure hull damage. Taking water. Not possible to make base at Ostende or Zeebrugge*...You fill in the rest. Names, times, tonnage and casualties. Bring it to me when you're finished."

"Kapitän...?" spoke up the navigation officer as Kurt ducked through the pressure bulkhead. The navigation officer followed him to the Petty Officer's mess.

"Yes? What is it, Nav?"

"Kapitän, I want to say...you were magnificent."

Kurt opened the water tight door to the engine room. "Find me a sand bank on the Normandy coast. A nice flat one so we can walk ashore in the dark!"

"Yes, sir! Sir!! You *were* magnificent!"

The machinery noise of the big diesels in their small engine room was always a shock but on this occasion Kurt was thankful for the noise. He almost told the navigation officer they were all goddamned well lucky to be alive and it was no thanks to their *magnificent* Kapitän who was suicidal enough to risk everything on a surface attack and then black out with a memory-dream in the middle of the attack. He stepped over the high sill and ducked into the engine room.

The air was thick with diesel smell and blue with diesel fumes. *Would they ever find a way to vent engine rooms so the poor slobs could breath without choking down each breath?* What possessed sane men to fight in these conditions? Still, they had heard reports about the appalling conditions of the trench war in France and Belgium. Compared to sleeping in two feet of cold muddy water, with rats crawling over the dead and the living while waiting for the next shell to fall, submarines were a luxury cruise. He didn't mention the worsening odds. But the men knew. There were no secrets in the navy.

The Chief Engineer's feet were sticking out from behind the port engine and his pink, fat body propped against some pipes. He insisted they leave him to die happily beside his iron children. The medical officer was stitching a deep gash on the side of his head. Eric's eyes were closed and his teeth clenched tightly with the pain. It had been a hard day for chief engineers on both sides.

"How are you, Eric?"

Eric looked as if he had been kicked by a demented gang of toughs in jack boots. There was no place in an engine room to fall without hitting some projection or solid piece of machinery. Falling down meant injury. Eric's was serious. Kurt looked for the point of impact to avoid looking at Eric's blood-streaked face. *He had too much colour to be dead,* Kurt thought. Kurt hated the sight of blood and declined to look when the M.O. offered to show him the severity of the wound.

"You look. I'll take your word for it."

"He'll live if he gets through the first day," said the young M.O.

"The first day!?" retorted Kurt. "He has to be all right now...Eric!"

"I'm sorry, Kapitän, he's not fit for duty."

"Eric!!...It's Kurt!"

Eric opened one blood-caked eye and looked around his engine room. The eye came to rest on Kurt's face. He tried on a small grin which hurt. The grin and the wince of pain looked about the same. The M.O. began packing up his kit.

"I'm sorry, Kurt...I fell. Stupid, huh?"

"The M.O. thinks you're going to die on me."

"Hand me a spanner and I'll beat the bugger!" said Eric, trying to laugh.

Eric's laugh made the pain worse. His head felt like a thumping diesel piston. He coughed and spit into his hand. There were flecks of blood. He felt around his bandaged ribs. He could feel the sharp ends of bones. He coughed again and moaned.

"Take it easy, Eric," said Kurt, holding Eric's hand.

"I'm okay. Help me up."

"The M.O. says not to move."

"Piss on the M.O.! Whose body is it anyway!?"

"Right now it belongs to the German Navy and I'm in charge of it."

"Good. You can be in charge of the pain too."

Kurt was encouraged by Eric's intact sense of humour. "We need the main pumps."

"I suppose we're sinking?" said Eric in mock disgust.

"We will be if you can't get the damned water out faster than its coming in."

"Don't lecture me on hydraulics! I don't tell you how to steer."

"Maybe if you had we wouldn't be sinking."

"That's right! Screw up, then turn the mess over to the engineers..."

Eric coughed again and held his broken ribs. Kurt looked at the M.O. who was waiting by the door. Eric tried to open his left eye. It was puffed closed and caked with dry blood. Kurt took out a hanky and spit on it. The medical officer shook his head and left. He disliked patching up fools and war heroes. They were one in the same in his books.

"Can you tell the black gang how to fix the pump?"

"I don't know what's wrong with it."

"It won't work," goaded Kurt.

"You should be a bloody engineer!"

"Thank God I'm not, but you are and you're all I've got."

"All right. Get me over to the control panel. I'll check the systems first. Might be just a fuse, or a line break."

Kurt motioned for the two engine room artificers.

"I was so comfortable, just dying peacefully. But it's not time to go yet, is it?"

"No. I'm afraid not, old dog. There's no glory in sinking because one's head has a little hole in it."

Eric smiled weakly as the two ERAs helped him to his feet. He had learned his lesson about laughing. He vowed to avoid all jokes, even his own. There was nothing very funny either about a sinking submarine and a cold ocean.

Eric would do all that was possible. *It's too damned bad,* Kurt thought, *that really good men like Eric should have to die in wars created by fools. Only stupid bastards like himself should go to war; then it wouldn't matter. If he were the Kaiser he'd make a decree that only psychopaths and syphilitics could be in the war. The country would benefit. The war could be fought by specialists and the population strengthened by getting rid of the dregs. A perfect system. A master race would emerge by thinning the herd, cutting out the weaklings. The cream rising to the top...*Kurt was drifting off...The hypnotic thumping and clacking of Eric's babies were taking him into another world.

"Kapitän!"

Kurt was jerked back to reality. Something urgent was demanding that his tired brain function at peak efficiency. "What a joke!" Kurt said out loud to the engines. "Why is it that the body's expected to function at its best when it's at its worst?" He hadn't hit bottom yet so there was no excuse.

"Kapitän!!"

The new first officer was shouting over the racket of the engines. *The young man was eager and efficient and would probably make a good commander, if he survived, but why did he have to be so healthy about it?* wondered Kurt. *He never seemed to be tired.* Kurt felt used up. The Navy wasn't finished with his personal equipment yet so he pulled the elements together and pretended to be at least the efficient kapitän.

"Yes! What is it, Franz?"

"Enemy ship sighted, sir! Hull down to the northwest. Masts and funnels. Might be a British destroyer out of Portsmouth."

"Thank you! I want best speed! Maintain southwest by south!..."

Franz bolted away before Kurt could finish. Franz was a realist. He was now the Number One. The next step was command of his own submarine. *Too eager,* Kurt thought. *Acts as if the stinking war was created just for him. Well, why not? Germany needs all the eager young men it has to fill the gaps left by the dead, the dying, the almost living and the ones who wish they were someplace else.* Kurt had no wish to be relieved. When he was someplace else he wished to be right where he was. Franz was not going to get his job no matter how much Kurt messed up. *Degenerate or not, I'm the goddamned Kapitän! Thanks to Papa.* "Franz!!"

Franz jerked himself back inside the engine room like a puppy on a leash.

"Sir!?"

"Take down everything on deck, except the gun and the compass."

"Sir?"

"Cut everything down. Masts! Jacks! Railings! Lights! Throw a tarpaulin over the gun. And get some paint and splash it around. We have to change our profile. The French call it camouflage. A beautiful word, huh?"

"Sir?" questioned Franz again.

"Camouflage!...French. Never mind. Splash the paint around. The tarpaulin too. If the Chief can't get the main pumps working we'll have to dump all the ballast. We'll look like a pregnant airship. My apologies to Herr Zeppelin."

"Herr Zeppelin?"

"Ferdinand von Zeppelin! Invented the airship! A friend of Father's!" Kurt said with a straight face. "Prince of a guy! A Count actually!" Kurt couldn't resist. "Make something of himself if he could ever get his feet on the ground!" Kurt grinned at the first officer.

Franz stared blankly. Kurt burst out laughing. The ERA'S looked at each other wondering what could be so hilarious. Kurt was light-headed, giddy and beyond tired. Should sleep. Sleep before he did something completely foolish. Kurt groped his way to the door. He stopped at the sill and looked back. He burst out laughing again and howled until the tears rolled down his cheeks. The ERA's decided they had better laugh along with their Kapitän. Eric bent over the control panel in agony trying not to laugh. He understood. Then Kurt remembered that he wanted best speed.

"Give me speed, Chiefie! Put your boot up her drawers! If she can't take it we'll drive her to the bottom of the goddamned English Channel!"

Kurt disappeared into the galley, headed for the control room. A confused Franz, afraid he'd been promoted first officer to a madman, followed on his heels. The incredulous ERA's looked at Eric as if he was the repository of all wisdom to do with officers who might be cracking up from the strain. They would like to have kept laughing just for the exercise but Eric was about to pass out.

"You heard the Kapitän!!..." Eric shouted. The first artificer leapt for the throttles. "Half speed! Check the hull and the frames on the starboard side, from the torpedo flat to the control room. If she takes that we'll try three quarters. You, check the junction box for the port pump!"

The artificer bumped the throttle on the port engine, then the starboard engine and listened. He made adjustments until the two huge Korting diesels were in sync, not exactly purring; more like a massed drum corps pounding everything they had as hard as they could and doing it in perfect time. Talk was difficult at half speed. At full speed the engineers seldom had to worry about nuisance visitor from officers idling about, wasting precious time; while endlessly polishing brass in blissful solitude. No deck officer since the beginning of engine-driven sea travel has been able to understand engineers. Satisfied that all the moving parts of their roaring engines were sluiced with oil and happy, the artificers headed forward to sound the hull of their damaged submarine, much like a doctor doing a physical examination from inside the chest cavity. Eric was left to enjoy the sensation of his noisy engines. The incredible din soothed away the pain or perhaps it just deadened the nerves.

Kurt quickly read the midshipman's detailed notes, signed the rough form and climbed the ladders to the bridge. It was a triumph of mind over body to drag himself over the combing of the conning tower hatch. He wondered how Eric managed to get in and out of a submarine. He'd be the last man out in an emergency otherwise one false move and the fat chief engineer would be like a stopper in a bottle…Kurt began to chuckle again at the vision of Eric huffing and puffing as the crew tugged at his ears and nose trying to pull him free and Eric swelling up more and more with the effort and the only thing that would save him would be the years of grease accumulated in his pores…Then he accomplished the bridge ladder.

The sharp May air immediately cleared his brain of humour and fantasy. The wind and spray hit him full in the face as soon as he put his head above the combing of the bridge deck where the crew were busy demolishing their own boat and he was looking through a picket of legs at the racing ocean. The bridge shield was gone as were the railings and masts. The crew obviously enjoyed the activity of destroying something even if it was their own ship. He thought the coxswain was a bit too aggressive flinging the brass steering wheel over the side. It arced over the waves and disappeared with a silent splash. A seagull made an exploratory swoop in case it was edible. Kurt wanted the wheel as a souvenir; a relic of past glories for his old age. It was a bit premature, considering their delicate condition...*The wheel would have made a nice addition to a sailing yacht. Maybe he would buy a galliot and go cruising around the North Sea and the Baltic hauling apples...*

Kurt sat down on the cold deck gratings with his arms around the compass pedestal because the sighting compass was the only object left standing.

The wreckers finished disassembling the bridge and the painters were making a game of splashing the paint around. *Well, let them have their fun.* Kurt envied them. It would have been wonderful to splatter paint. Dark blue and grey and white. A dash of yellow. *Easy with the red there!* The ship was in danger of looking more like a spring garden gone wild than a hunter-killer submarine. What would a Frenchman say if they slipped into Le Havre and pleaded for sanctuary for his gang of lunatics escaped from an asylum for mentally deranged Impressionists? Red iron oxide dripped down the sides of the conning tower like blood. Kurt had read all the great naval battles. Stately ships of the line flying clouds of canvas, banners and heroics. Drummers and cannon fire. Two lines of ships standing in to battle at close quarters. *Fire when you see the whites of their eyes!* said the Swedish King and others in the bloody history of war, Kurt remembered from school days. In naval warfare it was an honour to be close enough to yell at the man you were about to blast out of creation. Blood ran out of the scuppers and turned the sea red, the books said. One of his heroes was the little British tactician, Horatio Nelson. *The bloody British! Why is it they always do things so well?* The French could be forgiven because they, like the Italians and the Spanish, had an endearing quality; they stumbled their way from crisis to crisis with style and colour. Their countries shared a warm sea and their colours were warm and clear. Their painters wallowed in Mediterranean yellows and oranges and burning blues and soft greens. The English were cold and calculating and precise and too much like the Germans, and therefore dangerous. And easier to hate, Kurt added. Kurt had a theory that Germany functioned on two levels. One level was their skill at organizing and building; the other level was their consuming envy of any country that also excelled at organizing and building. It was a burden Germany carried around like a cross…

"Kapitän!?"

Kurt's head jerked off the pedestal. Franz was looking at him from the safety of the hatch combing.

"Kapitän Schulte? Are you all right, sir?"

"My neck hurts. My head aches."

"Oh, that's good…I mean, I thought you'd been, injured, sir."

"Are you tired, Franz?"

"No! sir…Yes, sir, I'm afraid I am."

"Don't be afraid of being tired, Number One. It means you're normal. Machines don't have the luxury to just get tired. They must bang along until something breaks."

"Yes, sir."

"How's the madhouse?"

"Sir?"

"Our ship. You came to tell me something?"

"The Chief says the starboard pump can't be repaired. The line's broken at the hull fitting. All he can do is plug the hole to stop the water. The port pump is working but it can't keep ahead of the water at this speed."

"I see. What does Herr Navigator say about our chances if we go slower?"

"We'll miss the first tide, but that's in daylight. There's a chance we'd run onto a shoal too far off the beach near Touville, that's the closest place to land beyond Le Havre."

"If we land in daylight our war's finished. Tell Nav to steer southwest for the beach near Bayeux. It's the most open. We want to be in after midnight on a falling tide. We'll have to risk the destroyer catching us. We can still put up a fight, huh, Franz!?"

"Yes, sir! It would be an honour."

"Yes...I guess it would. Better than being pitch-forked in a haystack. Ask the Chief to dump the ballast tanks and hold our speed as long as he can." Franz nodded and started down the ladder. "What do you think of our new paint scheme?"

"Ah, very effective, sir," said Franz.

"Do you think the High Command would approve?"

"I doubt it, sir."

"No, they probably wouldn't. No imagination. That's the trouble with this damned war!"

"Would you like some breakfast, sir?"

"No, thank you. I was just thinking about two good boys who died in a trench while eating their breakfast. Brothers. Manfred and Axel. Dumb as oxen but good boys. Therefore, I deduce that eating breakfast is dangerous." Franz looked puzzled. Kurt continued: "Fishermen. What is the madness that kills two fishermen in a muddy trench at breakfast?"

"I, ah, better tell the Chief."

"Yes. And tell Eric I send my regards. Tell him to get some sleep. You get some too. That's an order. I'll take the watch and wake you before noon."

"Yes, sir. Thank you, sir."

Franz dropped back down the hatch. Seconds later the sound of compressed air blasting ballast water out of the main tanks reverberated through the boat. The boat rose to her light marks and picked up speed. The hull shivered with an out of sync vibration until the artificers adjusted the revolutions. The sound of the diesels seemed to retreat into a rhythmic, hypnotic beat. Kurt relaxed and listened to the familiar foamy *swish-splash* of the sea running along the casing. It was the sound he longed for most during his months at the Institute; soothing but dangerous. *What a lousy war,* thought Kurt. *Trenches! Mud! Gas, they say. Willie will be disappointed. He had such high hopes for this war. Too bad for those with high hopes. They should have been born a century earlier when war was less serious and more colourful.* Kurt decided that he was fortunate to have no expectations.

Kurt, satisfied that their ship was properly altered and confusing in profile, ordered the camouflage party below. He remained on the bridge, alone with his thoughts and his defiled ship. She looked like the aftermath of a drunken New Years Eve brawl; colourful but debauched. He checked the compass course. *A sailor can throw everything overboard except his compass. The compass tells him the one thing that really matters. If you know where north is you know where home lies.* He sunk down again and rested his head against the cold brass of the pedestal and smelled the verdigris. His dead first officer had been sitting in the same position when he died, a thousand years ago in a battle almost forgotten. The destroyer on the horizon continued on its harrier run. The British captain, enraged by the news of three damaged ships would try to hunt down the perpetrator. The Hun. The hated Bosch. Kurt wondered if it had always been that way. *Was hatred always the cause for war? History had many wars that were for practical reasons. Armies needed exercise. Kings needed something to do or just more land, or a wife, or to get rid of a wife or the wife's relatives. Or his own relatives. Sometimes wars were just misunderstandings, easily ended and forgiven. Then there were religious wars and Crusades. Hatred. Unforgivable!* Kurt was looking up at the face of Pius Humby. The face cursed him. Of all things in war it is saddest to be cursed by the enemy. But war was changing, and it was becoming more dangerous to treat the enemy as an equal and praise him if he fought well. German High Command had rescinded all the rules of engagement to do with submarines. Perhaps he should have torpedoed Hedley's ship and machine-gunned the survivors while they floundered in the water, arms raised in supplication. The survivors could be patched up and reequipped, sent out with a deeper hatred and a resolve to hunt him down. Then war would become killing for killing's sake, worse, for revenge. Kurt thought of his father and the Horse Guards in all their brass and flash and glitter, jingling as they pranced, music as they charged, bugles and drums and ribbons. *Poor Father.* His war was a thing of the past. The future of war was Kurt hugging a brass pedestal, tarnished green by salt water, unpolished or painted grey because it was necessary to remain hidden from view. *You must stay hidden to creep up to the enemy and slay him before he sees you.* Kurt felt bitter. Not for the killing but for the methods. A shell could come from over the horizon and blow him out of the water as easily as a lightning bolt from God. An enemy submarine might be stalking him at that very moment, the torpedo on its way. Romantics die in war also. He watched the destroyer racing for the sunrise and realized the enemy was not on the scent and felt very lonely on his barren, windy bridge. Life was going on around him and below him. The British. The

French. His own crew busy saving the ship. He was just sitting on his parade float watching the world go by. If he was plucked off the bridge by a wave Franz would take over. Eric would keep the engines running and Kurt would be only another entry in the log. He closed his eyes and drifted off thinking there were worse places to die.

At a Commander's meeting, before they left Emden, the talk had been about the trench war in France and Belgium. They all agreed that whatever terrors or discomforts the submarines had to offer it was nothing to the stupidity of the bloody trench war. The mud and disease and the constant shelling. They questioned the army's use of poison gas. Kurt wanted to remind them about their own methods of stealth and darkness, but kept silent. The question before the court of self worth was not what rank you should be when you die but the place and the circumstances. Kings and paupers. Kings and paupers...*On top of a mountain? With the world at your feet? No. To get to the top of the mountain you had to climb. There is a risk of falling and dying in a dark crevice, which would be the opposite of what was intended. Unacceptable risk of failure. In one of the new airplanes? No! To die in an airplane the device had to crash, unless you were shot in an air battle and died instantly. The odds were not good enough. The plane might crash in flames and death would be a painful failure. The only sure way would be suicide in your plane. Not a bad alternative; close to God and all that...*Kurt laughed at the absurd thought. Other possibilities? A farmer in a pig sty? A banker in his vault? A Lawyer under the weight of the law? A fisherman in his own net? No! A submarine was the best. The surest for maximum effect; using the tools of the trade. A submarine was meant to submerge so if you went deep enough the hull would collapse. No chance of failure.

When his submarine was based at Emden Kurt often went to Norderney to sit in the Fishermen's café or walk the North Beach. Sometimes he went out with Herr Glimpf for a day of fishing. Herr Glimpf's two young crewmen had been replaced by two old men from the village. He recognized one of them as the street sweeper and another the deck hand on the night boat from Norddeich. The two young fishermen, Manfred and Axel, had joined the infantry and died in a trench when a French mortar scored a direct hit while they were having breakfast. *Not a good end,* thought Kurt. The sun was warm. Seagulls circled overhead questioning everything. Kurt drifted off to sleep...

May 31, 1916: The daylight run to Bayeux was uneventful for Kurt's boat cruising south looking for a safe haven. A French patrol boat came out of Le Havre but didn't see the U-boat in its dazzle paint, gliding by under the pleasant May sun. To the north the sea battle off Jutland was beginning. It was the last time capital ships would meet in anything like Kurt's vision of multi-decked warships destroying each other in grand fashion, toe-to-toe as it were. But in Kurt's lonely corner of the war it was a nice day for a cruise. By midnight they were standing ten miles off the beach, below the hills near Bayeux on the Normandy Peninsula. Kurt directed the approach to the beach from his position beside the sighting compass. *The sky was overcast. The sea cooperative.* That was the last details for the log before the grounding.

The bow of the submarine touched the sand at 0114. The tide was falling. The hull settled on the edge of the bank with her stern in deep water. The crew abandoned their sinking ship in orderly fashion, destroying ammunition, torpedo mechanisms, books and documents according to their departments. The cook served a hot meal and made food packs of bread, sausage and cheese rolled up in blankets. Each man was allowed a bottle of beer. Small arms were issued. Maps checked and sketches made for each team leader. Kurt kept his journal, against regulations. He had nothing else of value to lug around.

No pictures of loved ones. No precious mementos of home. Just his memories. He would lead a large party of engineers that would move the injured. The other parties lead by Franz and the petty officers would be on their own to make it to the German lines. The parties abandoned their crippled submarine as they were ready. Kurt and the engineers were the last to leave.

Franz and his battered party fought their way to German lines near Saarbrucken. Franz went on to Hamburg and reported for duty, was made Oberleutnant zur See, given an Iron Cross and a new submarine and died with his boat when they were run down by a destroyer in the North Sea two days before the end of the war.

Eric insisted on overseeing the scuttle party pulling the plugs. When he had been laboriously passed up the ladder of the torpedo loading hatch and over the side, Kurt climbed down to the sand beside him. They watched from the beach as the shadow of their boat slipped off the bank in a pool of phosphorescence.

Their party had an interesting journey back to Germany. As far as Kurt could discover theirs was the only group to make it intact. The engineers weren't aggressive fighters, outside of a bistro, so they were more cautious, avoided contact with patrols and were inventive in methods of survival. They found the French more compassionate than expected. The wine was good and summer in the French countryside behind the lines was delightful. Kurt's group travelled southeast by night in good weather, away from the heavy fighting, and crossed the frontier into Switzerland in October. Kurt later wrote that, all things considered, he enjoyed the outing with Eric and his gang of thieves. He was reprimanded by High Command for scuttling his submarine on a French beach, but in deference to his family name he was awarded an Iron Cross of the Keiserliche Marine and the matter was shelved. He finished the war as an instructor at the submarine base in Wilhelmshaven, commuting back and forth to Berlin with side trips to Norderney. His only reference to Anna for that two year period was a small entry made concerning the landing near Bayeux: '...I sent the party ahead with the litters to get the injured off the beach and away from the damp sea breeze blowing in from the north east. We watched our valiant little ship slip under and were satisfied there was no trace of her for the English to find and conclude that we had come ashore. It was fortunate that we were allowed to become acquainted with the land and the hard lot of fugitives gradually, as we were all unaccustomed to that life. I had a sense of regret leaving the shore, not because I feared the hardships of the journey or the chance of being captured, but of being separated from the sea. I wanted to postpone the parting as long as possible so I stopped on the beach to say goodbye. The tide was out and the fore-shore smelled of iodine and rot. It may not sound pleasant but, to me, aside from the pure tang of salt spray over the bow, the low tide smell is most intoxicating. Unfortunately it reminded me of Norderney and the whole thing came flooding over me again. Perhaps it was the release of tensions or the fatigue, but I cried for something I couldn't explain. It was just as well the crew had gone on ahead. It wouldn't have instilled confidence in their leader to see him weeping like a baby. It's not unusual for a sailor to feel badly about losing his ship but it isn't necessary to cry about it. They wouldn't know of course that it wasn't the ship at all. It was an end to chaos and therefore an end to dreams of Anna. They wouldn't know either, that, when our sturdy boat was slipping under the waves I wasn't on the beach with them, I was on Norderney and it was raining. The Norddeich boat was leaving with my soul as a heavy cargo. When I was able to tear myself away from the beach I tripped over a weathered old tree half buried in the sand. The shape of the tree was human. Feminine. But withered and grey and dead. The spiky branches rose up out of the sand and grabbed at my legs. I stared at the grey, scaly crotch of the tree for a long time and thought I was seeing the end of her...'

INDIAN OCEAN

November 12, 1918: Lieutenant Pius Humby was seated at the small desk in his cabin aboard the light cruiser HMS *Paladin*. He had come off watch, taken tea in the wardroom and retired to his cabin to write a letter. A picture of Mary, holding Jeannie, with Roy, aged six and Harry, aged four, rested against a pile of sea books. Roy looked so much like his father and Harry had his eyes. Another picture was of a Grand Banks schooner, the *Sarah B*, his father's boat, when she was new. The Humby family, with the help of most of the men and boys of the village, had built her on the shore at Fogo Harbour. A few months earlier, driven by the need to have his own boat, Pius had made a contract with Rhulands Shipyard of Lunenburg, Nova Scotia, to build him a one hundred ton schooner. He longed to get clear of the endless patrols in the Indian Ocean while the real war played itself out in Europe...Pius heard urgent footsteps in the corridor. He knew the message was for him and was looking at the door when the knock came.

"Come in..."

A midshipman entered, grinning broadly. "Mr. Humby, sir. The Captain sends his respects, sir, and requests your presence in the wardroom, immediately!"

"Something wrong, Mr. Andrews?"

"No sir! He's standing drinks to the officers. Signal's just come through." Then the boy, unable to suppress his joy, shouted, "The bloody war's over!...Excuse me, sir."

Pius was stunned. So, it was finally at an end, but he was denied the chance for revenge on the Germans. They had spent two years chasing shadows and rumours from one typhoon to another. He should have been elated that the agony was ended. Pius looked at Mary's picture and felt guilty.

"Thank you, Andrews…I'll be along presently."

Pius' war ended slowly, and without a conclusion. A young man had left Newfoundland with a mission to fight the Germans. The mission had turned to hatred for the Germans, and burned to bitterness in the languid confines of the Indian Ocean. He would spend another two years with the Navy winding down the details when civil servants and bureaucrats would have been more at home dealing with the endless trivia of shutting down the machinery of war.

GERMANY

February 18, 1919: Kurt and Willie stood together in the Grand Hall of the Schulte mansion outside Berlin, watching from a distance as workers struggled to hang a large portrait in a heavy gilt frame. The portrait was of Kurt in full uniform with the German Iron Cross on a black ribbon around his neck even though his level of Cross was usually worn as a badge on the tunic and it amused Kurt. Kurt, in the portrait, didn't look amused. He looked annoyed, and ten years older. The rest of the family, friends and neighbours, were crowding into the Grand Hall to admire the portrait and celebrate the great event. Kurt didn't miss the irony. It was the portrait they flocked around when the real thing could have been had for walking across the room. Kurt was happy to be ignored but here was a certain amount of embarrassment on all sides. The comments that did reach him were quite neutral and proper to the occasion.

"A very good likeness," said a count who snubbed Kurt on most occasions.

"You must be so proud, Freidrich!"

"I knew the boy had it in him, Schulte. Chip off the old block, eh?"

Kurt watched his father take in the adulation. It was his day, not Kurt's.

'...Father never stopped smiling. You'd think it was his picture they were hanging. I wonder if it was his idea that the painter should do me as an older man. Perhaps that's the way Father wished I was, more severe. Matured. Well, they have their picture and their damned medal! They left me alone at least, although Father couldn't resist one last salvo. I had it coming and I couldn't hold it against the Old Man. Being the consummate strategist it wouldn't have surprised me if he had planned the whole affair just to be able to get even. I won't say he planned the war around it, not even Father could have thought up that one. Then maybe he did, and it just got away from him...'

The workman finished hanging the portrait and retired with their ladders and tools. Most families would have draped a portrait and simply pulled the covering off at the appropriate moment. There was something more dramatic about workers and equipment and noise. General Schulte signaled the servants to refill the brandy glasses. When the manoeuvre was nearing completion he cleared his throat loudly. The family and guests stopped talking and turned to the General. There was a high level of expectancy. A tension in the air. They weren't there to applaud as much as witness the blood letting.

'...Father almost choked on his opening words. I'll never forget it...'

"Ah, Kurt...I, that is we, your family and friends, want you to know how proud we are, for you, at this time...this honour. God knows Germany has little enough to be proud of in her hour of national shame. And, I'm afraid the humiliation will continue. Our perpetual enemies will not rest until Imperial Germany has been castigated and emasculated. It's to be expected when dealing with the French and the British. As I speak, Wilson and the Americans are betraying us to Clemenceau. The Russians, those damned Bolsheviks, are just waiting their chance. We are surrounded by fools and village idiots! We have been betrayed by Orlando! The treaty they propose to inflict upon us at Paris and Versailles will be a tragedy for us..."

"Dear...Freidrich!?" interjected Baroness von Schulte. "Please, this is for Kurt."

"Yes, of course, for Kurt. We Schultes have always fought with distinction, whenever the Fatherland has called on us..."

The Baroness warned the General off with a gesture. He changed tacks again.

"As you know, Kurt had been ill, before the war. When it was apparent that Germany was about to be set upon by our enemies once more, he rushed to join his brother Wilhelm in the defense of our great country. Unselfishly, knowing that he was in ill health from, the tuberculosis...we make no apologies for keeping it quiet at the time, Kurt chose to serve in the submarine corps. He did so with distinction and unflinching bravery. I'm told by his superiors that our brave little Kurt was a standout in training and one of the best leaders in our submarines, alongside the likes of Weddigen, Schwieger, Dönitz. You all know the story of how Kurt crippled three British destroyers in one valiant action..."

'...Father neglected to mention that while our insignificant little sideshow was taking place the High Seas Fleet was being battered and demoralized by the British off Jutland even though High Command claimed victory. But, since the grand battle was inconclusive it was best left in limbo...'

"...And so, to our brave, valiant little Kurt, I propose a toast. To Kurt and Schulte tradition!"

The assembly raised their glasses. Most saluted the portrait. Some remembered that Kurt was at the back of the room.

"And," continued the General, "in Kurt's own unique salute to his family..." The General suddenly threw the glass into the fireplace.

The guests were caught off guard. Flinging glasses about was a ritual for daredevil flyers and swashbucklers. But many recovered in time to follow suit. Some were disappointed that the event went off so smoothly and only a few glasses were smashed. The activity relieved the tension and distracted the guests long enough for Kurt to take Willie's arm and steer him out of the Grand Hall.

Safely outside the room with the heavy doors closed on his party, Kurt looked even more amused. Willie was angry with his father for the poor show but tried to make light of it.

"I do apologize for Father's behaviour," said Willie. "He's taking it hard you know."

"The war? Makes you wonder how we lost."

"He'll never admit to losing it."

"Marking time until the next one?" Kurt asked, with an ironic smile.

"Something like that."

They walked together through the study to the library. One of the Jewish maids who was dusting, lowered her eyes and curtsied. Willie didn't let on that he saw her. Kurt attempted to say something in response. Kurt had always been sensitive about having servants, it made him uncomfortable. He had vivid memories of the Jewish maid who gave him physical and spiritual nurturing when he was a child. It hung on him like an obligation, not as a debt that had to be repaid but a desire to give something back to a people who were looked down on by the families who treated their Jewish employees like children; unwanted children who had to be cared for. It would become much worse. Kurt had a heavy feeling about the Jewish people and their future in Europe.

"Father's right, you know," Kurt said, after the maid closed the door. "There will be trouble for Germany, but it won't be just about the Treaty. We haven't seen the end of this. During the war I amused myself on the long patrols studying the Roman Empire. The Romans were successful at conquering other countries but every time they succeeded it became more difficult to maintain control over their new territories."

"I have the horrible feeling you're going to tell me why," said Willie with a sigh.

"I'm going to tell you because there's a lesson we should learn. We both know we didn't go to war to redress grievances, it was to build an empire. The Romans were beaten in the end by their own success. They filled Rome with slaves from the hinterlands and did nothing for themselves. They became soft and fat and argued and plotted. When the real enemies were at the gate they had nothing to answer with. They died from lethargy and excess and corruption from within."

"I don't see what that has to do with anything. We lost the war before we had a chance to get fat."

"Yes, but don't you see? We need to conquer something, and we will someday. We already have slaves and we treat them badly. We'll die within from a corrupted soul."

"Dear, brother, I don't analyze why we do things. That's not my job. Or yours either," said Willie, with a finality that said the subject was closed. He tried to change the subject. "Kurt, tell me something. What will you do now that the war's over?"

"Haven't you heard?" Kurt asked, an edge of sarcasm overriding his smile. "I've been promoted. High Command's pushed me up to Intelligence. Isn't that funny? Me! They want me to travel. A job I'm at least good at. I'm to circulate. Make friends. Observe..."

"Spy!?"

"Spy. That's so vulgar," protested Kurt, half in jest.

"But that's it, isn't it?"

Kurt took a book from a high shelf, a history of the Roman Empire. He weighed the bulk of the thick volume as if assessing its weight against Willie's comment.

"The Romans used spies to weaken their enemies. It's an ancient occupation."

"So is prostitution."

"Let's keep the conversation on a higher plain, *dear* brother. I'm to be part of a goodwill mission. My job's to visit families of the good men we killed in naval combat. Holding out the olive branch to our enemies. A quaint Roman tradition they picked up from the Greeks.

"Now that's what I call vulgar. It would be better if you just went as an honest spy!"

"A contradiction, but yes, it does have a stench to it, I admit. But what else can I do?"

"You're famous. You could do whatever you like."

"I'm not a big hero to the Kriegsmarine. They're still mad at me for scuttling their precious submarine. If we'd sunk the damned thing in battle and gone down with her all standing we'd really be heroes. It's all right to get them shot up or lose them completely but the Brass have an aversion to leaving boats on beaches just to save the crew. That was my only concern. It was the least I could do after getting them into the mess. I lost five good men."

"You did account for three ships damaged. That's what they sent you out to do."

"Two destroyers and a light cruiser. Was it worth it? If we'd had five hundred submarines and the crews, like we were supposed to, maybe it would have been worth it. We would have driven the British off the lake."

"A moot point," said Willie. "What would you really like to do?"

"I'd like to teach literature or history."

"Father wouldn't hear of it!"

"I know. As Father's fond of saying, *'Schultes don't teach! We instruct by example!'*"

"You do a fair imitation of Father. He'd be amused."

"By example. I'll go to England for the Fatherland. There's talk of a trip to the Colonies. Seems we killed some of them too. It could be instructive."

Willie laughed. "You *are* a cynic!"

"It's a privilege of those who know more than they should about things they have no business knowing at all. And what will you do with your spare time?"

"Nothing as exciting as spying. The Horse Guards will remain intact, as a police force of sorts, and I've a small administrative role in the destruction of our glorious military machine, what's left of it."

"While I visit our former enemies to discover ways to build a better one?" asked Kurt, ironically.

"And all the while writing the Grand Novel?" countered Willie, sarcastically.

"Perhaps..." Kurt said, opening the door to the study. The important men were gathered around a table brilliant with candles and sparkling decanters of French brandy, liberated as the German army retreated from France in disarray. Smoke rose up in clouds with the conversation, as if nothing had happened to German society in the intervening five years. The power brokers were once again gathering to discuss Germany's fortunes and plot her future. The wake would be short. It was business as usual. Kurt had the sensation that it had all happened before and he and his family and the Jews and the country were on the continuous down side of the roller coaster ride. Hitler was still five years away from the scene but Kurt heard the familiar words and harsh denunciations of their enemies, without and within their borders. "Willie, why did I survive this war?"

Willie didn't have the answer.

LONDON

July 12, 1920: Kurt sat alone at a table by the window with a view to rain, umbrellas and taxi cabs. The lounge of the Colonial Cambridge Hotel was almost empty, except for the disturbing presence of a beautiful young woman in the white dress at another table. She was dark and sad and pretended not to be watching Kurt watching her. Kurt tried looking out the window with it's tiny, distorted panes of glass. Water rivulets ran down the glass and merged and changed direction. It made Kurt think of the Institute and that made him think of home and the casement windows of the library the night he and Willie sat up talking about Germany, their war and spying. It had started to rain then. A slashing rain that drove against the library windows, sounding sharp and harsh. The rivulets of rain on the panes were red-orange from the fire in the big fireplace and that made Kurt think of Norderney and Norderney made Kurt remember Anna. So he tried not to think about rain. Not to think about rain was difficult if he insisted on looking at it. When he looked away from the window to have a drink of brandy the young woman was standing beside his table. He could hear the silky swish of her dress which sounded like waves rushing off the bow of his submarine when it was all right to enjoy being alive on the ocean. But that would mean thinking about other pains, so he pretended he hadn't heard her approach. But there was her fragrance, fresh, like the sea, a fragrance dangerously close to something he remembered about the North Sea. He didn't want to allow her fragrance to distract him so pretended she wasn't there. But there was something about the feeling of her nearness, even if he were deaf and blind, with his nose shot off, and that's what made him look, not at the past, he had been dead for six years and dead men don't have feelings.

The woman was more than beautiful; she was stunningly handsome. Her dark hair and eyes and full red lips belonged to his idea of a romantic gypsy. Her skin had a natural healthy glow of the peasant families of Europe. Her white satin dress was plain but elegant and she wore just the right amount of expensive jewelry: sapphires that breathed a subtle fire of their own and complemented her colour and didn't dominate. Kurt had to look. The jewels were nothing in comparison. She stood there, it had only been a long moment, silently amused, while the sparks flowed back and forth until Kurt responded.

"Good day, Fräulein," Kurt said politely, to give nothing away.

"Hello." It was spoken with a smile and an invitation to life. Kurt's confused spirit wanted to run and hide. She let the *hello* hang in mid air for Kurt to deal with.

"Ah, very damp weather we're having," he said in his best English.

"Normal for this time of year."

"Some years, at home, it can be damp."

"You're German."

"I'm afraid...yes, of course, my accent," Kurt said, annoyed by the abrupt statement which sounded like an accusation.

"No need to apologize, darling. You're also lonely."

Her frankness put Kurt off. He tried to fight back, to hurt her before the damage was done.

"And you must be the 'Specialty of the House'. Well, I didn't order one."

It worked. She flashed anger and Kurt was immediately sorry. The woman recovered with grace and parried nicely with a sunshine smile.

"Mistaken identity...May I sit down?"

Kurt took a deep breath. It was like the moment before the order was spoken committing the submarine to battle, risking all on the toss and grimly accepting the consequences. He wanted to say *no*. It had been much easier to order the attack and face the depth charges of an enraged enemy after the torpedo had struck home and all hell broke loose. Kurt gestured to the chair beside him with a condescending nod. So far so good. She sat down and looked directly into Kurt's eyes as if she already knew everything about him. She knew the vital part. He was play acting and the part was painful.

"We might get on better if you dropped the superior attitude," she said with a smile. "You did lose the war by the way..." she added sweetly but with just the right amount of edge. Kurt got the message. He nodded again but this time in submission. "No fault of yours I'm sure, darling. I'm Lady Tifton. Bright Tifton."

Lady Bright Tifton, gracious in victory, held out her hand. Kurt took her hand as if to shake it like a man then held it to his lips. He meant it as a supreme compliment, for all the right reasons. Bright was impressed. Her heart skipped and the warm feeling rushed to her cheeks. Sparks jumped between their finger tips when she slowly, reluctantly, withdrew. Her breath came a little faster. She felt damp in interesting places. It's just as well the sparring was over because her own defenses were crumbling. There would be no more games and play acting.

"My friends call me Sunny. And you?..."

"Of course, I'll call you Sunny," Kurt said, unable to resist. "I'll call you anything you wish."

"You *are* human! I mean…" She almost giggled, "…what should I call you?"

"Kurt. Kurt Schulte, great grandson of Baron Freidrich von Schulte. My father is General Freidrich von Schulte the 3rd. My family has lots of money and titles. But I don't care about titles, to be honest. I don't need to work so I travel. There, that should just about cover the preliminaries."

"Touché," replied Bright with a trace of a pout. "To be *honest* I find titles come in handy sometimes. Especially when you're from a poor Liverpool family and your father's a dock worker and you're name is Steinman. Life is hard, but bearable."

"You certainly don't look downtrodden."

"Good! I intend to stay that way. May I have a whiskey? No ice."

"A preference? They have a good stock here."

"Yes, I know. The waiter will bring my usual." Kurt signaled for the idling waiter to bring them two. "I'm glad you decline ice. I believe it's an American thing, left over from the Yanks invading London." He settled back to wait for Bright to continue. He sensed that the lovely woman wanted to tell her story and be done with it. It was a day of truth, he hoped, and Kurt relaxed with it and didn't let the one doubt he had come to the surface before its time.

Bright held the glass of Irish whiskey and looked through the peaty amber at the candle flame. They gestured in an unspoken toast. The whiskey smoldered with a flame of its own and tasted as warm as it looked. Kurt had never seen a woman drink so sensuously. Bright's full lips made love to the edge of the glass. He received promising signals from his own body. It was possible, but the doubt still poked at the edges. He took another drink of whiskey, not his first choice, but the present company gave it an exotic glow the peat diggers never realized possible. The cold rain outside the windows made the warmth of their small, cozy space more important. Bright, her eyes slightly moist, continued when she was ready.

"My husband, Teddy, was killed in that beastly war you blokes organized," she said without accusing.

"Then I've come to the right place."

Bright was puzzled but waited for Kurt to explain. Kurt had a strong desire to tell this enchanting woman the whole sordid story of his spying and his cover. He wished he was either just spying or just visiting. The deception was distasteful. But a lingering suspicion of the woman's motives made him wonder who was dodging and weaving.

"Were you a flyer?" asked Bright, finally.

"No, why?"

"Then why is this the right place?"

"I'm visiting families of Englishmen we killed."

"My husband was a courageous flyer."

"Then I didn't kill him. I was in the German navy."

"Of course you didn't, darling. Teddy was brave but he wasn't a brilliant pilot. He crashed his plane in France showing off for the ladies. Just like Teddy, the clown..." said Bright, with an unexpected giggle. "He couldn't help himself. He couldn't help flirting either, but it wasn't serious, ever. It was just his way." She laughed at a memory. "Once we had some friends down to the country for a weekend. One of Teddy's chums brought this beautiful creature who could have been a marble sculpture. By the end of the weekend Teddy had her so in hysterics from teasing she came all undone and ended up drinking champagne from his riding boot in the fish pond." Bright was laughing too well. "She decided she was in love with Teddy...and challenged me to a duel with the boy's swords...I'm afraid she'd have cut my head off! I was in her way you see. Teddy managed to talk her out of it and sent her back into her boyfriend's arms." Bright settled down to giggles. "Teddy's chum was so grateful for the change that he promised to leave Teddy everything in his will…It was too funny! Teddy was wonderful. He was completely irresponsible. It drove his poor family to fits…He was such a nice boy you couldn't help love him." Bright was slowly winding down, but, instead of leveling off, her emotions plunged into the depths. Tears began to show, ready to fall if the memories continued. "Why did he have to die?" She said to keep from crying. "I'm well set up of course, but it doesn't count for anything does it? I don't get on with the family…" She tried to laugh again to mask the anguish but it didn't work. "His father disliked Jews intensely."

So there it is, Kurt thought. *It wasn't just in Germany. Why did it always come down to birthrights and privilege?* His own privilege had never sat comfortably on his sensitive shoulders. Perhaps it was why he couldn't come to terms with it. Still, he was boozing it up in posh surroundings, living well, on a journey for questionable ends, and all because he came from a certain class. And beside him was a wonderful creature who aspired to class, probably worked hard to get there, for the privileges it bought and suffered for it; deeply it would seem. Bright was crying. All he could think to say was: "I'm sorry…"

"I shouldn't do this to you, but…oh, he was such a lovely boy. I miss him badly. You're so like Teddy…"

Bright melted into Kurt's arm's and sobbed on his chest. He tried to soothe her, held her tightly and stroked the long shining hair that reminded him of gentle summer waves curling onto a smooth sandy shore. For the first time he felt as though he was truly giving something back, but it had nothing to do with obligations.

And then there was the other truth: the darkened room and the silence and two people who have nothing to hide, but the truth that Kurt feared was there also, stirring like residual fragments of emotions. It had been six years since Anna; six long years of wondering what she had left him. He felt badly for Bright and wanted to give her the only precious gift he thought he had to offer. Now they occupied a large bed in an expensive suite and the gift, offered, was empty.

Bright sat on the bed, knees drawn up, hugged by her long dusky arms. Her cheek rested on one knee, head turned so that she could see him. There was no resentment in her serene expression but the pout was unavoidable. Bright had lips that either smiled or pouted, as natural to her as breathing deeply or breathing lightly. She was expressive, open, unable to mask her feelings and she was feeling badly for both of them.

Kurt lay on his side of the bed, thinking of Norderney...*A land crab climbed over a body splayed out on the sand. A seagull left the circle of judges and approached the outstretched hand. Bright was sitting beside the body. He could feel her watching him, could hear laughter. Anna was laughing at him. He didn't turn to look but waited for the seagull...*

Bright didn't know they were in the dunes with the North Sea a distant drum beat. She didn't know the Frisian Islands existed, other than as obscure little sand bars in a school atlas. The island was going to have a significant effect on her future but at the moment her island was a tidy bed with fresh, unspoiled linens. Close by, like a pristine coral island in a dark sea, floated a white dress, carefully laid out on a love seat beside a dinner jacket and pants folded too neatly.

Bright shivered. *She was in a tomb staring at the body of a long dead saint whose dried remains were venerated for the questionable feat of lifelong celibacy.* She instantly regretted the thought as unfair. She had approached Kurt for reasons she didn't understand herself. She was Lady Bright Tifton, not the common, if high classed, prostitute Kurt had taken her for. He hadn't treated her like a prostitute. He had been tender and understanding, if a bit strange and she felt like a child in his care. Kurt had been circumspect about going to his room, as if he was afraid to insult her by suggesting it. She had been crying. Kurt asked if she would feel better if they went for a walk, but it was raining and they were too old for walking in a foggy London rain. Bright wasn't nearly finished crying so they walked to the lift. There was no reason to feel resentment about the failed love making, but the body has its own reaction to disappointment. She cried again, silently.

"Bright...I'm sorry."

"It's all right, darling."

"It's not that I don't want..."

"*Shhhh*. You don't have to explain."

"I do. I feel awful!"

Bright wanted to take him in her arms and soothe him. Intuition said no. Intuition was right. A few hours earlier, in the lounge, he had held her and stopped being a child himself. Bright wasn't the Jewish maid. She was the woman who gave him back his soul by needing him. She still needed him. She understood that as much as Kurt did. She cried inside while Kurt stared at the wall and let their spirits dance the dance of learning how to communicate. It had to happen on a much higher plain before the physical bodies could grope and pounce and play. But even spirits have to get acquainted when they have inhabited bodies damaged by turmoil. The chemistry was there, of that there was no question, but they came together from different contexts and the formulas were muddled by abuse. So they felt badly for each other and let the spirits get on with it. To fill in the time they talked and felt better just being together. "Did something happen? Were you wounded badly in love?"

"Savaged by a demon."

"Oh." Bright was silent again, wondering. It was easier to talk about war and tangible wounds but she experienced the hot flush of jealousy. An interesting sign, "A woman who spurned you?" she asked, finally.

"A devil! Sadist." Then Kurt was silent a long time, wondering if he should try to explain. Was he being unfair to Anna? It was easy to make her a devil, but he wasn't convinced she existed. He knew it was better to explain Anna as just a woman. Bright wouldn't be as charitable in her assessment of Anna once she knew the story. Bright was also a woman. Kurt was a man. Anna was a rival whose ghost she would have to live with and deal with if she wanted the man. "Six years ago I met a woman," he began. "It was a bad time in my life. The relationship was brief, intense." He wanted to say, destructive.

"I know. You're living with her ghost," said Bright softly.

"That obvious, *hein*?"

"Yes, darling, you're bleeding all over us."

"I can't apologize...yet."

"You don't have to. Do you want to talk about her?"

"No, but it's necessary. You should know everything."

"You don't have to tell me everything," Bright said, but she did want to know everything. It was the only way. "All right, tell me everything."

"Why do you want to know?"

"I'm a woman," she said. "Men are such babies when it comes to dealing with their guilt. You can be so cunning in politics and business and war but you can't hide the tiniest shred of guilt."

"I did nothing to feel guilty about. I was young, confused about life. She came out of my imagination and destroyed me with love because, the truth is, I wanted to be destroyed."

"You feel guilty, my darling, because something in your past prevents you from making passionate love to me, a casual stranger, when you owe me nothing and have nothing to apologize for. Making love is nice, but it isn't as nice as having a man take you in his arms when you're hysterical about your dead husband, and tries to understand. You were wonderful, darling. The love making will happen, in its time. Only my body feels unsatisfied. That means nothing. You make me feel like a woman because you let me cry and didn't feel ashamed. You are very brave, my German sailor."

"You're the wonderful one."

"Yes, I am, but only because you make me feel that way. Now tell me about the woman. Everything."

"Anna? I'm not even sure that was her name." *He wasn't sure if she had existed but Kurt focused on a day and date and realized it was time to tell his story, honestly.* "Anna happened in 1913. It was summer on Norderney Island. Anna came out of the mists on a day I almost succeeded doing the thing I had never been able to make myself do, but wished for all my life..."

Jimmy closed the journal. I was nodding over my notebook, and once awake had no idea what time it was, but it was too late to make the trip down the mountain.

"You may sleep there, sir," said Jimmy, pointing at the day bed.

"But, what will you do?"

"I'm going down to the village. We'll need a bit of food. This is going to take some time, I suppose."

"That's not right. I can go..."

"You'd have some fun in the dark, sir. I want to see Aunt Mary and get the news. You'll be all right here 'til I gets back. Just don't go off too far for your necessary."

By that I assumed he meant toilet. A false step and I wouldn't stop bouncing until I hit the harbour. I was too tired to protest and then I remembered Mrs. Penny. I explained the situation and my obligation.

"That's not a problem, sir. I'll ask Aunt Mary to watch for any guests. As to the cat and the plants, I'll see to those my own self."

Jimmy took a canvas pack with leather straps off a peg in the dark corner and turned down the lamp. I had a vision of Jimmy breaking into the General Store and stealing food, like Kurt's blonde sailor had done at Bremen. It was after midnight. "How will you shop at this hour? The store's closed," I said. It was a foolish statement. Jimmy had been living after midnight for years.

"That's not a problem either, Skipper," answered Jimmy. "Reg makes up my orders and leaves them in a box on the bridge, his porch, like. I gets a pension from the government, and mail goes to Aunt Mary, see, and she looks after what I owe Reg. I don't need aught else, sir. Uncle Pius says the government money adds up to a considerable amount. I can't remember how much, sir, but it'd scare you. I can only eat so much, see."

After Jimmy went out a profound silence fell over the shack. I sat at the table pondering the improbabilities of life that brought me to this barren hilltop, discussing piles of money with an old man who could get steady work in the movies as the person you'd least like to meet on a dark night. And what would Mrs. Penny say if she knew Jimmy White, the Phantom of Fogo Harbour, was slipping into her house at night to feed her cat and water her plants? Then I had a horrible thought. What if there *were* guests? It would be an experience, for them. Then I pondered Jimmy's future. He was a healthy old man and would live for many years. What would happen to him when Pius and Mary are gone? Well, it wasn't any of my business. I lay down on the cot, too tired to think about the stories.

It was an old cot, a daybed they call it, the kind found in every Newfoundland kitchen. Each one could tell a story of life, like a bedroom. This one felt crowded with stories. I would later learn some of its history and travels as it related to Jimmy's story. Thankfully the crowd was quiet that night and respectful and I soon fell asleep, dreaming about fog and smoky sea battles, waking to the wind picking up, dozing, and waking again when Jimmy returned before dawn. He set the loaded pack down quietly inside the door, went out again and returned with an armload of small splits of spruce and set to work to build up a fire in the tiny Shipmate stove. I was too groggy to get up and fell asleep again. When I awoke later the shack was cozy warm, smelled of fresh bread and the dawn was an orange patch on the wall above the cot.

"Morning, Skipper," said Jimmy cheerfully. "Tis a fine morning, sure."

"Good morning, Jim. Yes, it looks good so far, and so soon!" I said, as I staggered to the door to find the nearest scrub spruce. I wondered when Jimmy slept. Probably in the daytime, and, if so what would I do? We couldn't make much progress working opposite shifts.

Breakfast was a loaf of fresh bread with jam and tea. It was a big loaf and still warm from Aunt Mary's oven no doubt, and tasty but I missed heavy, whole grain breads and vegetables. I thought about our garden at home going to flower and the dark loaves of hand ground whole wheat bread that came out of our own woodstove. But that was a long road and another life style away. I decided to raise the subject of Jimmy's future since we were doing everybody's life.

"Well, sir," said Jimmy, in answer to my question. "Now that you've brought that up I'll allow as how it's been on my mind some. Aunt Mary mentioned the same thing. It worries her, see. She thinks she won't be far behind Pius, going off like."

"What would you like to do with the money?"

"The village needs a new school. The old one's been condemned but there hasn't been money enough to build a new one. Time was the whole gang of us would get together and build a one. Go onto the big island and cut the wood. Fine times they was, sir. Not no more. And those fellas in St. John's likes to ignore us as much as they can get away with. I guess that would be the place to put the money, sir, a fine new school. It'd be called after the Commander. He looked after the children as long as he could..."

Jimmy was alive to the idea. His sharp eyes flashed. I was still pondering the mention of the Commander looking after the children when he made the request that left me in a daze.

"And would you see to it, sir?"

"See to it? In what way?"

"Well, sir, as you can imagine, I can't walk into the meeting of the council and put it to them, like. And Aunt Mary wouldn't be up to it."

How had I gotten myself so deeply into the past, and the future affairs of the island? I was curious about an Iron Cross on a casket, that's all. Jimmy cleared the table and opened the journal. I opened my notebook. The present slipped away as the years reeled back. Below us, the village of Fogo was waking to the sunrise, unaware that the Stranger from Away and the Scourge were laying open the details of their past to the scrutiny of the sun.

FOGO ISLAND

July 21, 1920: Fogo Harbour. Pius finally came home from the war. Little had changed in the community in those six years other than the cemetery was larger and the old folks older than Pius remembered. The children born during the war were out and about. The fence around the cemetery was newly repaired, to keep out the wandering sheep. The tough grass, flailing at the weathered gravestones and wooden crosses, was plentiful but the living believed the dead wouldn't appreciate sheep grazing over their resting place. It was a difficult decision since everything was in short supply on the island, so the boys cut the long grass with hand sickles in the fall to feed the sheep over the winter. The small, ruggedly built Catholic church, with a fine view of the harbour, was open to ceremonies whenever the travelling priest arrived. There was also a Salvation Army hall and a Church of England. The villagers attended whichever place of worship was in session when they felt the need. Father Hennessy made a special trip over the trail from Seldom that month in honour of Pius' homecoming since he was the last of the Fogo Island men to come home.

The occasion was also a time to christen the current crop of babies conceived the previous October when the men returned from the Labrador fishery. There was a flurry of activity in the outports as the season ended. The dried fish were shipped and sold. The boats came ashore. The village was made ready for winter and the outport settled in to make the best of it. If the season had been a success there would be no hunger during the dark months and the men could repair their gear and heal their wounds, while getting ready for sealing time in March. Some would go off again to the Big Island and work in the forests. The old men would watch over the younger ones and dream of the old days, sailing down to Labrador. The women who had nurtured seed would be showing and their men would have another incentive to go on the ice in March and hope to come away with a few more pennies to tide them over until the fish could be caught and the merchants kept at bay for another year. It was a hard cycle of life but it was their own. It bred and fed the sturdy, proud people gathered in the church as a young Father Hennessy baptized three sleeping babies.

Pius Humby, in his navy dress uniform, stood with Mary, Harry, age eleven, and Jeannie age nine, watching the simple ceremony. Pius and Mary were godparents to Clara and George White's infant son, James White. Father Hennessy said the words and sprinkled the water and the fathers shifted their feet to be going. The children watched Pius, in awe of his smart uniform and the mystery of his time away, but longed to play in the warm but transient sunshine.

When the ceremony was over the villagers filed out of the church to squint in the light and gather around the three families to gossip and make silly noises over the babies. The babies were celebrated, but too small and inexperienced in life to hold a crowd of men for long and the gathering eventually formed around Pius. Mary gravitated to the women who never got bored with babies because they were soft and warm, innocent and full of life. Mary celebrated with the women but her eyes wandered to the ocean, unable to conceal her sadness and pain. She longed to have another baby of her own to hold and worry over.

Pius talked easily with the men but watched Mary's face, concealing his own regret. He wanted to hold young Harry very tight and protect him from the thing that worried at him, but could not.

Harry, torn between youth and manhood, stood with the men, listening to the talk of seals, fish and fishing. The other boys ran down to the harbour to get into some mischief. There were only so many things to do in the outports; they could just run around until they were exhausted or scramble up the scaly paths to their rocky castles and smoke illicit coarse tobacco until they were dizzy. They could push off in a Rodney skiff and race around the harbour and splash each other with oars. They could chase the sheep. They could fish for Tommy cod. They could tease the girls who pretended to baptize rag dolls on the steps of the church. Harry remained with Pius, ready to put away the simple joys of unfettered youth. His father wasn't as big as he remembered him before he left to go fishing on the Labrador that fall in

1914. He had grown up knowing his father only in stories, already legends. Mary had a picture on the dresser of Pius in his uniform, sent from a foreign port, and the navy pay that was used sparingly to fill the void. The few pounds sterling Mary received regularly was no compensation for a missing husband, and no more secure than the fishing. A shell from an enemy ship could be as final as a winter gale and a lee shore. A common enough worry in peace or war.

Clara left her group and presented her baby to Pius for his approval. She understood Pius' feelings about the loss of his son Roy. It was her way of sharing her own gift.

"He's as much yours, Pius. George and me would like for you and Mary to see to James if anything was to happen to us."

"Don't talk nonsense, sister. Nothing the like's going to happen. He's a fine wee babe is young Jimmy White." Pius held his leathery finger out for the baby who got a good grip and showed that wonderful toothless grin of the innocent. "And a strong one as well. I dare say he could hold the wheel of our new schooner in a gale o'wind."

"You'll let me wean the poor little thing afore you takes him to sea I hope?" she said.

"Then you best be quick about it, Clara," said Pius. "Can't start a good helmsman too young!"

The men laughed and nodded agreement, then turned their backs on the babies and left the women to their interests closer to home. The talk returned to the things of the men. Pius' brother-in-law, George White, captain of the *Sarah B,* looked at his old schooner waiting at the wharf. George knew she was well beyond her prime but must ask the old girl to hold canvas a few more seasons, or the outport would feel hard times.

"Will you go fishing with us, Pius?"

"I'm going fishing, old son, but on me own bottom. Got a letter from Rhulands' yard over to Nova Scotia."

"When's she ready then?"

"Quick as the Navy gives me my due and I make the final payment."

"Aye, that's good news, b'ye."

"Yes, sir," said Pius. "Mr. Rhulands says she's ready to launch off but it's cash on the barrel."

"Proper thing b'ye," said George White. The men nodded agreement. "You wants to start fair, brother. You gets behind them fellas and they'll never give you peace."

"They're just like the merchants," said Alf Pardy. "They wants to own you and everything you worked for."

"Tis killing we for sure!" declared Saul Humby, Pius' uncle and the elder statesman of the village. "You wouldn't believe what them as done since you been away. They own us, Pius."

"You keep clear of them fellas," counseled George White. "They's worse than a whole shoal of sunkers."

"No fear for that. Will you come along side of we next season then, George?"

"Thanks all the same, but the old *Sarah B's* still good for it. A few more trips down."

"You've always got a berth George, unless that new youngster of yours puts you out." George looked at his infant son, invisible under blankets. Then he appraised Pius' son Harry, tall and rangy, standing shyly behind Pius, absorbing the heady air of man talk. He liked what he saw. Harry was heir apparent to Pius' position as village leader. A position his family had traditionally held in the outport with never a speech or a vote. The system worked because no one thought to tamper with it.

"Best watch this youngster of yours," said George, with a grin. "He's apt to put you out of your own ship sooner than you think."

"Yes, and he means to put me out of my uniform and join the King's Navy."

"The Navy! Well now, he could do worse."

"Aye, so long as it's not in war," said Pius, thinking of the bloody night battle in the Channel. "No sir, I'd not wish that on any man under God's Heaven."

"Yis b'ye. Terrible thing, but we're all done with that foolishness sure," said George. The men nodded agreement again, hoping to God it was true.

"I'm done with it at least," said Pius, taking off his white officer's hat and flinging it into the air. It sailed on an up draught from the harbour and hung like a morning moon, then, with the children laughing and chasing after, it came down, bouncing and cart wheeling toward the harbour.

The mood changed abruptly and the men drifted away, following their women home for tea.

Pius left the next day, July 22nd, on the coastal boat for St. John's and Lunenburg, Nova Scotia, with Uncle Saul, Gus Froude, Alf Pardy and four other men, to take delivery of his new schooner.

LONDON

August 25, 1920: Two thousand three hundred and sixty miles due east of Fogo Island, Kurt von Schulte and Lady Bright Tifton were walking arm in arm along Regent Street window shopping. London's fashionable center had suffered from the deprivations of war but the dry goods that ladies of quality cherished were returning to the shops. Bright scrutinized the latest dresses while Kurt was preoccupied with a group of boys chasing a sheepdog that had run away from its master, a fat man in a bowler hat. Bright wasn't enjoying window shopping and neither looked very happy. The fat man in a bowler hat brandished his umbrella at the dog, the boys, or both. His antics were comical but Kurt and Bright weren't in a mood for comedy. The commotion rounded a corner leaving them with nothing new to say.

"Won't you take me with you, darling?" she asked again. The discussion had been going on for some time and had clouded an otherwise pleasant lunch. A last outing together before Kurt travelled down to Southampton on the evening train to catch his boat for Canada. "Please, darling. I'm so bored with London."

"Even more bored than you are with me?" asked Kurt rhetorically. He hadn't meant to say it. He was being unfair, and childish. Pouting because he was ordered to go by the High Command, unhappy because he was leaving Bright behind in England.

"You're not boring, darling," Bright said, with a smile that Kurt didn't deserve.

Bright understood his ways better than he imagined possible. She knew why he was pouting. She knew too well the story of Anna and what it had left Kurt and the only thing she could be guilty of was a nagging jealousy that she hoped was silly. But she was, above all, a woman with deep feelings and she allowed herself the luxury of feeling deeply. If Kurt could be a little boy and pout she could have the satisfaction of being jealous of the one thing, besides the German High Command, that stood in their way. Although the Kriegsmarine was no match for Bright, she was having the hardest time possible with the ghost of another woman, although she refused to let it show. It was a thing of pride, her need to be strong, and jealousy was the only emotion she worked hard at controlling. They both had reasons to go a long ways back into their childhoods for their emotions.

Kurt had enough reasons to pout and Bright had more than enough reasons to need to be strong. He had grown up suffering from over-privilege. She the opposite. It made them more interesting people when they met in the middle. Kurt wouldn't call it fate. Bright was far too romantic to think of it as anything else. It was in her stars, she said. Kurt understood stars as a tool to find his way around oceans. Bright found them useful to find her way around the seas of chaos. It was no wonder they fell in love, although they wouldn't admit to it; they fit together. The chemistry was right. There were some small problems to work out, but only surface problems. Small annoyances flung at them from higher authorities. But what of it? It had been a golden late summer in London. Peacetime. The problem was, Kurt was going on some mysterious mission and Bright was in love, curious and determined to go along.

"I'm afraid I'm not much fun for a woman like you," he said, guilty of being childish. It was his way of shifting the blame to himself.

"And what *kind* of a woman am I?" she asked. It was Bright's turn to pout.

"You English have a term...*vivacious*, I think. In German...*lebhaft*. It means lively, impulsive, and I think for you it also means sensuous, in a proper way though."

"Vivacious also means hard to kill, darling. I'm Jewish first. A woman second." Bright instantly regretted saying it. "At least you don't think I'm promiscuous."

"With me!? Hardly. I can't imagine why you'd want to tag along?"

Kurt was being playful again. It had been, if not perfect, at least the closest he had ever come to a relationship with a woman but he knew they were both feeling rotten and he wouldn't fight with Bright.

Bright was relieved. She didn't want anything except Kurt and if she was going to have to fight she would do it on a decent level, to be everything Anna wasn't, but she also had to be what Kurt needed. Intuition steered her course. It's a superior faculty men fail to use wisely.

She had enough for both of them.

"You have...promise," she said, with a sparkle in her eye that made Kurt chuckle. "You have immense possibilities, my darling."

Kurt responded as Bright intended, however evasively. "They tell me Canada's very cold, very new and very provincial. Hardly a place to get inspired."

"I wonder if they have decent cafés at least?" asked Bright, taking Kurt's hand. "Where would we hold hands over liqueurs?"

"I'll have to move about a great deal, meeting people..."

"I know the Governor General's wife," Bright responded. "We were at school together. She could introduce you to all the right people. I'm sure their capital must have at least one theatre, and even cold Canadians have to eat someplace!"

"Unfortunately, most of them are misplaced English."

"The Province of Quebec is just like France I'm told," offered Bright. "There will be good French restaurants or else the French wouldn't live there."

"The first stop *is* Quebec City," he countered, hedging.

"That's a *yes*, isn't it, darling?" Bright asked, glancing at Kurt's handsome profile to gauge his reaction. "Besides, it would be such fun to put on airs for the colonials."

Kurt would have laughed at Bright's enthusiasm if it weren't for the cloud that raced across their sun. He knew Bright was going to get her way and be on the ship when it left Southampton, but he was going as a spy and Bright his accomplice. His cover and her connections. It didn't feel right but it was too late to turn back. "You still haven't told me what this trip is all about."

"What?...oh, just goodwill. Germany needs help, with everything," he said evasively. He wasn't exactly lying but he was lying to Bright.

"That covers a lot of ground, darling. Could you be more specific?"

"No," he answered.

"Oh," said Bright, somewhat stung. She wasn't to ask. Intuition again. It told her not to ask because there was more to the story. She smiled coyly. "But you *will* take me with you."

Kurt was relieved. Spying or not, the trip would have been unbearable without her. Bright kissed his cheek and steered him into Liberty's of Regent Street. She would need a few nice things for the voyage, and a dinner dress for the Captain's Table.

Victoria station was stifling and crowded with families going south to Eastbourne, Brighton and Bournemouth for the last weekend of the summer season. The express train was late leaving. It almost never happened on the British Railway and the trainmen were apologetic. The passengers were very stoic and proper. Kurt and Bright had tea in a little shop near the station while they waited, she patiently, he, restless. It was after midnight when they slipped into their compartment feeling slightly mischievous, sharing a secret, and settled down to drink a bottle of chilled Pinot Chardonnay and watch the darkened South Downs out their window. The small towns were a sprinkle of light in the mist. Stations slipped by like blurred photos in a flip show.

"By the way," asked Kurt, "what were you doing in the lounge of the Cambridge that day?"

"Waiting for you, darling," she breathed, taking his hand.

"Oh, I see. Waiting long?"

"I was afraid you might not make it before my looks ran out."

"Never. I knew you were there."

"Oh, really?"

"Of course. Why else would I come?"

"The question is, what took *you* so long?"

"It was a long way across France and back. I walked the first time.

Some day I'll tell you about our adventure." Kurt wished the train could go on forever so nothing would have to be decided or revealed. Bright enjoyed the privileges of travelling first class and looked forward to more of the same on an ocean liner. They both daydreamed of the future, then they slept in each other's arms. The train arrived early in the morning and Kurt and Bright boarded the ship and went straight to their cabin.

Kurt was amused to discover that the compact liner, RMS *Express Packet,* belonged to the same small shipping company, British Atlantic Lines, that had so hastily abandoned their offices at Emden six years earlier for the convenience of the German Navy. It was an odd coincidence in a long line of coincidences that shuttled Kurt's life from one unlikely episode to another. *Not fate,* Kurt would say, *just coincidence.* Bright pronounced their stateroom on the main deck to be adequate, and changed into a smart sailing outfit from Liberty's. She didn't care much about the sea and the fog in the Channel, which obscured everything except Lizard Head, didn't bother her in the least. She settled down with Kurt and a good book. Kurt was happy to watch the waves and taste the salt spray.

GULF OF ST. LAWRENCE

September 3, 1920: The crossing was uneventful. The last tropical storm of the year veered eastward into mid Atlantic after it passed Bermuda and the sun shone two days out of seven. The food was good and the service excellent. War-damaged economies were recovering and wealthy travellers had shaken off the specter of German submarines. The world was entering the decade of excess, for those who had survived the war with the means, and for the next ten years Atlantic crossings would be made in lavish style.

When RMS *Express Packet* crossed the one hundred fathom line of the Grand Banks, the mist, which had been building for two days, settled down like a thick quilt. The comforting rhythm of the sea changed as the ship slowed. The irritating sequence of fog signals made the passengers tense with anticipation. There had been a tragedy, almost forgotten during the war, when another ocean liner sank somewhere nearby, they believed. There was talk of fog and giant icebergs. Unsinkable ships going too fast or German submarines testing their tactics and torpedoes ahead of planned hostilities. Kurt was tempted to enlighten his fellow passengers but preferred to remain the business traveller he professed to be.

To Bright it seemed the ship had plunged into nothingness and would sweep blindly along forever. Her means of battling the fog was to get into a deck chair out of the wet wind, with as many blankets as she could manage, order a whiskey from the attentive steward, slip into her book and pretend the sun was still shining. Kurt was content to lean on the rail and watch the waves come out of the swirling fog and foam along the hull to disappear in their wake. The images those waves carried of the hard times didn't escape him, but he didn't dwell, letting his mind idle, intent on enjoying the freedom of the ocean. Bright was in her bundle behind him, close enough to touch, if he needed to be reassured.

But even Bright couldn't cope with a Newfoundland fog for long. Her hair frizzed even under a scarf and her book became soggy and wrinkled and threatened to disintegrate. She put it aside, finished her whiskey and watched Kurt, hoping he wasn't some place else, like the Friesian Islands.

"Are you sure we've left England, darling?"

Kurt turned and looked at her rosy dark complexion and her full red lips. He wanted her at that moment and knew he was winning the battle. "The only sunshine on this coast is you my dearest, Sunny."

Bright beamed, uncoiled from her nest of blankets and snuggled against him. She kissed him full on the lips and shared the salt tang.

"You are sweet, if rather salty to the taste," she said.

"The spice of life and love," he said, breathing wetly in her ear. Something stirred deep down and she wanted him too, then and there. However, there were other passengers nearby to consider. For appearances she just snuggled, content in knowing their stateroom was a few steps away. They teased each other and the anticipation put a keener edge on the wanting.

"Where in Heaven's name are we?" asked Bright, peering into the murk that had become a black fog, giving up all pretense of being silvery and mysterious. "It seems we've been crossing this bloody ocean of yours for weeks."

"Seven days, twenty-two hours. We're over the Grand Banks, near Newfoundland, and soon entering the Gulf of St. Lawrence."

The names meant nothing to Bright who looked around the non existent horizon as if she expected to see a signboard announcing their arrival.

"How can you tell?"

"I could show you on a chart. I've been keeping track of our running time and approximate speed."

"Oh, my clever darling. Is it always this foggy?"

"Not always. But the Gulf is notorious for bad weather."

"How can you get around on boats without bumping something?"

"Sometimes even the best Kapitäns bump into things," said Kurt, envying the captain of *Express Packet* the challenge of navigating in the thick soup. To Kurt, the fog was just an element in which to immerse his senses. To hide from life.

"Don't tell me stories about the bumps."

"I promise."

"Not even one where they don't bump, if it's frightening."

"All right. No stories."

"But, do tell me why the fog happens."

"Here it's the elements. We're over the Grand Banks. They call them the fishing banks because..."

"I know! Because there's a lot of fish?"

"Your ancestors probably fished these waters."

"Not mine!" she said, with a chuckle.

"Of course. Yours would have fished the Sea of Galilee."

"They were smart. Warm water and sunshine."

"Do you want to hear about the fog?"

"Yes. But only the fog. No fish."

"No fish."

"I used to think English fogs very mysterious and romantic," Bright said, getting that far away look of memories not wanted but not rejected entirely.

"You don't like the fog now?"

"I travelled down to Dover to watch Teddy fly across to France with his squadron. It was all very romantic, at first. They took off together, made a dashing formation and flew into the silvery mist over the Channel." She hesitated, tearing up. "I never saw him again."

"I'm sorry. Maybe we shouldn't talk about it."

"It's all right."

"It doesn't seem so important now, the fog story," he said.

"Tell me, please. I'm all right."

"Well, fog on the water happens when cold water meets warm, moist air. The cold water comes down from Labrador. Warm air comes off the land. Warm water comes up from the Caribbean. That's the Gulf Stream. It's like a big river in the sea, and it flows all the way to England."

"It does?"

"Yes, that's why there are palm trees in Penzance."

"There are?"

"I've heard there are. If it wasn't for the Gulf Stream you English would freeze in winter."

"Rather than just being perishingly damp and cold."

"It's damp and cold here too."

"Not when you hold me."

"The fog's some use then," said Kurt, holding Bright tighter. "The fish seem to like it well enough."

"You promised, no fish!"

"I couldn't resist."

"You don't have to," she said, turning her dark eyes and full lips up to Kurt to be kissed. He kissed her and the feeling grew inside them.

"All right, I won't. Should we go in?" he asked.

"Not just yet. I like this. It makes it better."

"Yes, it does."

"Tell me what you did in the war."

"Not everything," he said, afraid to destroy the feeling. "Just the part where they made me Kapitänleutnant and sent me out to sink the British Navy."

"I forgive you, darling."

"If I tell you any more you wouldn't."

"Don't tell me then. It must have been terrible under water."

"I've been more frightened on land."

"Were you awfully brave?"

"Not very. I just didn't care if I was killed."

"Poor Kurt. I saw your Black Cross medal, in your bag. I wasn't snooping, darling. It wasn't exactly hidden."

"Careless of me," he said, with an edge to his voice.

"Don't be angry with me..." Kurt wasn't listening. "Did something awful happen? Darling, don't be angry if we talk about it."

...He was rolling in the surf. Anna was standing in a pool of sunshine. Lady Bright Tifton was beside her dressed in red. The dress clashed with Anna's hair. Bright was crying. Anna laughed at both of them. Kurt stood up, unsteady, wavering as if undecided which way to fall. He looked from Anna to Bright. Bright pointed to the water. Dead sailors, British and German, floated around him in wreckage from a ship. Bony arms reached out and skeleton fingers clutched at his legs. Kurt tried to run but couldn't move. He was wearing his father's full dress uniform. The gold braid weighed him down. He reached out for the women to help him. Bright extended her hand. Anna turned and ran up the beach laughing. Kurt broke free of the dead sailors and stumbled up the beach, after Anna...

"I won't ask about the beastly war, ever again."

Kurt hugged Bright tighter but felt guilty. Bright knew he had been away, probably with the woman.

"It's not the war," Kurt said, finally, wanting to explain. "Not even the men I killed. Thank God I never had to sink a merchant ship."

"I'm awfully glad you didn't...poor lamb."

"Why is it all right to kill a man because he's on one kind of ship? Because some admiral tells you to. What gives him the goddamned right?"

"I don't know, darling."

"Neither do I."

"Do you think war is awfully stupid?"

"No, not entirely. Unfortunately, war becomes necessary, stupidly."

"Don't tell me the reasons."

"I don't want to."

"It's too horrible. There couldn't be another. Not ever...!"

Kurt tried out a chuckle to relieve the bad mood sitting on them, heavier than the black fog. The sun was too weak to penetrate the layers.

"Are you laughing at me?"

"No, Sunny."

"You think I'm too melodramatic."

"I was thinking of Father and the war. He's already plotting the next one."

"I won't let you go."

"I'll be too old for the game. It'll take time for our great statesmen *to organize,* as you call it, another war."

"Do you think they do it on purpose?"

"Yes, of course. Old men love to plot battles, in the abstract. What else have they to do with their time and all those armies and navies?"

"It's horrid! Cynical at least."

"It's to do with economics. Very complicated stuff."

"This is too depressing. Let's go in and have a drink. Maybe we'll feel better. I must do something with myself before dinner."

Bright steered Kurt away from the rail, neither of them felt like love making, and walked the steady wood-planked deck that had been scrubbed in the morning but had never dried so that it looked fresh and new and dark. It would be silver-grey if the sun left the weathering teak and salt behind. They went to the lounge where they could talk and Kurt wouldn't have to wonder if he would fail to satisfy Bright because Anna was occupying their stateroom.

September 3, 1920: Pius wrote in his logbook: *The Gulf. Grand Banks. Lat. 45° 30' N Long. 54° 20' W 1115 hrs: Sighted steamer-Passenger. The Express Packet, Southampton. Passed close astern of us at 15-*

20knts. Visibility poor. ETA St. John's 4th, mid day.

The schooner *Liza & Mary Humby,* Skipper Pius Humby, was 450 miles east northeast of Halifax, Nova Scotia, bound for Newfoundland's south coast. The fog had set in while Cape Breton Island was still visible astern. Pius set his course for Cape Race with the prospect of a good breeze to fill the creamy white sails. He prayed they wouldn't get a blow before they reached Fogo Island. The new sails needed time to work in and take their shape before they were put to a severe test or they might end up as bags. He wasn't happy about the wet mist but he took what he was offered and gave thanks it wasn't worse.

They cleared Lunenburg Harbour on August 29th, for the short run to Halifax, satisfied that his new schooner was everything the Rhuland yard had promised. In Halifax Pius took on dry goods assigned to a merchant in St. John's. It was a gamble but the price Pius accepted to carry the goods was enough to cover the costs of their trip to Fogo. He would pick up salt and what cargo he could in St. John's, and some things Mary wanted for the winter. Goods were on the move again and merchants were eager to ship with a new hull skippered by a retired navy man. Pius was tempted to try his hand at running cargoes instead of returning to the heartaches of fishing. But he was a fisherman first and there were men at home with families to feed counting on the new schooner.

During the war Pius had seen more of the world and marveled at the numbers of ships plying the oceans in commerce. Every conceivable type of hull worked for its keep. Some did very well if the agents were clever and the captains were drivers. Even before the war he noticed the increasing numbers of engine-driven vessels. The balance had already shifted. Steam engines and diesel engines carried cargoes more efficiently. An engine could also carry fish. He was dreaming about a diesel engine for his new ship when Uncle Saul worked his way aft for his watch, coming out of the fog cloud that wrapped around the bows like a veil. Uncle Saul was already an old man, in appearance, which belied his fifty-odd years. He had worked hard since childhood and the toll was great. He limped and shuffled and coughed and had trouble filling his pipe with his gnarled, seal-fingers, a walking wreck with a chiseled face and bent body. But Uncle Saul was tough and keen and clever. He could catch cod as fast as the next man. He could read the sun and the moon and the clouds, and even the fog. He could smell land and tell a joke and dance a jig. Pius would not like to sail without him in any condition. Uncle Saul had been his mentor and his friend when his own father, Skipper John Humby, was away at sea. Pius had two good fathers and the only time he was without one of them was his time in the navy. There were days during the war when being an officer of His Majesty's ships taxed his native skills and patience. Navy regulations often defied logic but Uncle Saul would have found a way to get the most out of a situation. Pius was still learning.

Uncle Saul put his back to the wind and perched on the top of the main cabin facing southeast to smoke his pipe. His short, bandy legs dangled six inches above the deck so that they swung back and forth with the rhythm of the waves. There was no need to peer into the fog. It wouldn't be penetrated, so, as he put a match to the pipe he listened.

Pius and Saul exchanged nods. Pius had been listening also and Saul wouldn't interrupt until he had absorbed the scene himself, getting a sense of where they were on the water and in the universe. Pius waited for Uncle Saul to speak, if there was going to be a conversation. The two worked like a pair of seasoned vaudeville troopers. Saul succeeded in getting the damp tobacco to make the necessary amount of smoke. The moderate, almost mild, southwest breeze from the mainland blew the smoke away to starboard. They watched the smoke disappear into the larger haze. If danger lay to leeward it would be more difficult to detect so they listened harder in that direction.

"Believe I heard a ship's whistle just now."

"Some ways off yet," answered Saul.

"She steers easy enough with a nice breeze on her quarter." Pius' feel for sailing returned quickly after a six year separation. But having the feel for a sailing ship means many things. A hand on the wheel tells the tales of the elements. When the elements are working together the fingers grip the spokes lightly. All is well. The captain lying in his bunk below can read his ship by sounds that would alarm a landlubber but are music to a sailor; like separate voices in a symphony, accenting the joy, as if the hard hours of killing labour and adversity were worth the effort. A sailor might be unable to explain that moment. Uncle Saul looked at Pius who was relaxed, gazing around his new ship with the eyes of a proud parent.

"Fog's thicker if anything," Uncle Saul said, blowing out smoke at the same time as if to emphasize the thickness of the moist blanket.

"Aye," answered Pius.

"Nice breeze o'wind though."

"Aye. Holding up."

"Them Lunenburg b'yes ain't forgot how to stitch a sail."

"No, b'ye," said Pius, studying the pleasing shape of the new mainsail. There was hardly a wrinkle to spoil the dazzling expanse of creamy white canvas. He could smell the Stockholm tar in the bolt roping. The massive boom flexed its muscle. The stout hemp sheets creaked with the steady pull of the huge sail. It was a thing of beauty, a sail drawing sweetly with a good breeze on the quarter. But Pius was thinking about engines and working boats. There's nothing beautiful about an engine, other than its utility.

Uncle Saul smoked and smelled the new wood and studied the set of the sails, the strain of the sheets and the bend in the booms, the angle of heel and the slackness of the lee shrouds.

"Rigging wants set up again, first chance," he said, finally.

"Aye, a touch more," admitted Pius. "Some good job they done just the same."

"Aye," said Uncle Saul, in his turn.

It was a rare moment in the precarious history of a sailing ship, when the ship is new and well found and everything is in good order.

"The lads might have a go at the rigging before we leave St. John's," said Pius.

"We ain't there yet," cautioned Uncle Saul. He had no reason to think they wouldn't be safely tied to a wharf in St. John's harbour by the same time tomorrow, but, just the same.

"The Lord willing," corrected Pius. "And the boat be in one piece."

"She's a fine vessel, Pius," said Uncle Saul, to balance the assessment.

"Aye. As good as the mainland wood into'er."

"A smart carrier, or I don't know my schooners," said Uncle Saul, eying the set and draw of the huge mainsail and foresail as he slid off the cabin top for a better look. He meant carrier of sails and fish, not cargo.

It was Pius' turn to get one in on his mentor. "Aye, but sail's got to give way, Uncle Saul."

Saul's answer was a disparaging grunt. He limped to the lee rail and spit the foul juices from the bottom of his pipe over the side. He only used the diversion when necessary. The bitter spittle could be harboured in the bowl, and summoned to make a point. Saul listened to the air. Perhaps he had heard something also. Pius knew the trick and waited until Saul returned to take up his place on the cabin top.

"With engines a ship can do some wonderful things," Pius continued.

"Can't sail!" retorted Uncle Saul.

"No need to."

"Ain't natural."

"No more than flying but I seen aero planes that could take off and land on the water like a seagull."

"Suppose you wants one of those too!?" said Uncle Saul, sarcastically.

"Come to think of it, an aero plane could be handy to spotting a shoal of herring."

"You only got to watch the sea birds what already know how to fly. They'll tell you where to find the herring, and anything else you need to know…"

The booming voice of a steam whistle cut through the fog to leeward. The world stopped but the swishing sound of the waves leaving the bow carried over the deck. The nice turn of speed suddenly became a threat. Were they standing into danger? They waited for another signal, a sound, a sighting. There was no point in running about, changing course or speed until they knew what the whistle meant to their immediate future.

"Big fella," said Pius.

"Too big for a freighter."

They listened, waiting for the steam whistle to tell them how the invisible ship bore in relation to their own course. A new element intruding into their precarious space on the face of the ocean. It was still at a distance, but closing quickly. The whistle sounded again, ahead to starboard, but the heavy air and the breeze distorted its passage.

"Hear her, Uncle Saul?"

"Aye."

"You can hear her propellers."

Saul went to the lee rail again and spit more juice. An act of defiance as well as a ritual. "She's close," he said.

"Aye, we'll cross her track," said Pius.

"And if he's making that much racket he can't hear us neither."

"Should have been signaling all along." Pius motioned Uncle Saul to the wheel and jumped for the fog horn beside the cabin. He put the box on the cabin top, aimed it in the direction of the fog signal and began pumping furiously. A long, sonorous, ear splitting blast erupted from the horn. The sound of a schooner box horn is a sharp pitched wail, each with it's unique character, to signal other schooners on the fishing banks and a homing signal for the flocks of dories returning to mother ships.

All hands strained to listen. Seconds ticked away before the booming of the steam whistle shook the air. Had the steamer's lookouts heard the small schooner's signal? Pius repeated the pumping without waiting for the regulation interval. The wail went out as a plaintive cry for recognition. The power of the ship bearing down in the fog became a tangible feeling, thumping and thrashing at them from all directions. The air seemed to move as if buffeted by a wall of wind. Pius pumped again. The fog horn sounded pathetically weak, smothered by the speed and mass of the leviathan charging at them out of the dense black fog.

September 3, 1920: Rough log of the RMS Express Packet. Gulf of St. Lawrence. Lat 45° 32' N Long 54° 25' W Appx. 120mi south Cape Race. Course 265° C. Speed 12kn. 1123 heard weak fog signal and sighted sails of small fishing vessel ahead to port on collision course. Name unknown. Port of registry, Lunenburg Nova Scotia. Visibility less than one mile-took evasive action immediately-fishing boat maintained course and crossed our track to starboard-resumed course. ETA Pilot station, Escoumins 6th, 2030 hrs. Quebec 7th 1600 hrs.

Captain Clifton Wilkinson, tall, distinguished looking, forty-six and prematurely grey, was a veteran of passenger ships and Atlantic crossings. During the Great War he had interrupted his career with British Atlantic Lines to command troop ships. He had lost one ship, a luxury passenger liner pressed for the duration, to a German submarine and another, a smaller coastal ferry, to a collision with a friendly cruiser in the darkness of the English Channel, while returning from delivering an Expeditionary Force to Belgium at the beginning of WWI. Not much was made of the latter sinking due to the fact the troops had landed in secrecy. The War Department was embarrassed about the incident, hence there was no official inquiry. An inquiry might have noted that Captain Wilkinson's ship had been steaming at full speed back to England in reduced visibility. Compensation was paid to the shipping line and the incident was buried under the news of the war in Belgium. The former sinking was a fact of war. He had been commended for his actions in saving many of the crew and the troops. Captain Wilkinson served with distinction in two world wars and retired to the family farm in Kent to write a book about birds and their difficulties in the devastation of Belgium and France during the Great War. But in 1920 retirement was years and another war away.

The captain of RMS *Express Packet* gazed absently at the grey wall ahead of his ship. He was thinking of the home he had run away from at age fourteen, to be a cabin boy on a windjammer sailing to Australia. His great passion was birds and flowers. His first officer fancied birds. They held endless debates about flowers and birds. Neither was fond of the Atlantic fog that all but obscured the bow and the small figure of the bow lookout. The dense clouds opened up from time to time to give a quarter mile of visibility and just as quickly closed down to nothing. There were lookouts in the crows nest with a crank telephone to communicate with the bridge. Lookouts were poised on both bridge wings, their useless binoculars hanging on their chests, water droplets dripping to the deck. Two lookouts watched from the comfort of the wheelhouse and a lonely vigil was kept astern with only foaming wake boiling up from the two huge propellers to break the monotony.

The bow lookout suddenly stiffened and listened then signaled the bridge. All the lookouts strained to see into the mist. The ship's great steam whistle boomed out its regulation signal. The lookout in the bow shrugged his shoulders, then stiffened again and pointed in the direction of the repeated sound. Captain Wilkinson got out of his chair and the first officer took up his position beside the telegraph. A chalk board in front of the wheelsman, attached to the varnished, beaded woodwork showed the course, 265° C. and speed, eighteen knots. Well below its top speed but more than the official log recorded, and far too fast for the conditions. The first officer disliked flying through fog, but to Wilkinson fog was an enemy to be challenged.

"Ship!! Port bow!" yelled a lookout through the open door of the wheelhouse. The crank phone was also ringing.

"Where away!?"

The lookout pointed to a shadow emerging from the fog; the tall rig and dark lee hull of the *Liza & Mary Humby.* The schooner looked small and vulnerable under the bows of the big liner.

Pius and his crew could see only a black hull below their own great booms. There was no time for a schooner under sail to manoeuvre.

"Damn!! Hard-a-port!! I mean starboard, starboard your helm!! Full astern both!!" In the sudden emergency Captain Wilkinson committed the error not uncommon in postwar shipping. Merchant ships still used the old style helm commands; *put the helm down*, means opposite to the intended direction. The British Navy had converted during the war to the new style steering commands.

The experienced wheelsman, unphased by the contrary commands, threw the wheel to port, the first officer rang the engine room telegraph and the junior officer activated the emergency whistle. It would do nothing but add to the confusion.

The chief engineer answered immediately; the telegraph needles stopped on *Full Astern*. The pulse of the ship quieted momentarily as the engines were throttled down and the levers thrown to change the rotation of the shafts. The engineers worked as quickly as possible, it wasn't their department to know why, but it takes time to reverse a big ship or shafts could be wrenched out of line. In the brief interval a strange peace descended over the engine spaces as if the ship, like the spectators, held her breath and the only sound was from the big fans sucking air into the boiler rooms. Then, as the propellers reversed and the ship began to shudder, the citizens of the floating city, alerted to trouble, came pouring out on deck.

In the wheelhouse of the *Express Packet*, Wilkinson looked at his pocket watch, noted the exact time and stared impassively behind a mask of official calm as the hull of the schooner disappeared under his bow. He automatically braced for the collision as slowly, ponderously, the bow of his ship began to swing to port. Twenty-nine seconds had elapsed.

"Damn!!" he said again, under his breath. A collision would mean wasted time and endless forms and probably an inquiry. "Bloody fool!! What's he think he's doing playing about in this muck!?"

Kurt, understanding the endless, repeated fog signals, was alerted by the rapid booming of the ship's whistle. It meant trouble. Their ship was standing into danger. Bright had been startled, not by the whistle...ship's whistles meant nothing more than noise...but by Kurt's sudden movement. He dragged Bright to her feet and they were half way to the door when the engines went into reverse and the bottles and glasses on the bar began to dance and tinkle. Then Bright became frightened.

"Come on, Sunny!"

"What's happening!?"

"Another ship, I expect. Here, watch your step!"

Kurt held the heavy door and steadied Bright over the weather sill.

Other passengers followed them out, some with drinks in their hands.

Kurt and Bright hurried across the deck to the rail. Kurt instinctively looked ahead just as the bow of the liner plunged past the stern of the *Liza & Mary*. The schooner looked very small and vulnerable from Kurt's position on the main deck but as the stern of the schooner came level with Kurt he saw a pair of faces staring up at him. He and Pius locked eyes and in the instant of recognition both men were thrown back to a deadly night in the English Channel; Pius swore he'd never forget the face of the German Captain smiling up at him, waving like a lunatic. Then Kurt was lost in the crowd and Pius' face was blurred by fog and distance as the black schooner slipped into the mist and was gone from sight. Forty-seven seconds had elapsed from the first alarm until Kurt was left staring at painful memories.

The warning whistles stopped. The engines were disengaged and rested for several minutes as the engineers oiled bearings, tested shims and felt for hot spots while their ship glided smoothly and silently through the shroud; suspended in that odd peacefulness that descends over the aftermath of chaos.

On the bridge the incident was entered in the rough log. Memories were searched for a sequence, stories compared and questions asked about the name of the vessel. Only the port of registry had been determined. On deck the late arriving passengers questioned the witnesses at the rails for details of the most interesting thing to happen since the cruise began. The excited buzz died down and the passengers returned to their drinks or their staterooms to dress for lunch.

Kurt stared after the vanished schooner in a trance.

"Oh my, fancy those boys out yachting on a day like this," Bright said, innocently.

"That face."

"What face, darling?"

"That man…on the boat."

"He did look a bit miffed."

"He was looking right at me."

"Whatever for!? It wasn't your fault."

"During the war," Kurt began.

"You've seen him before?"

"Yes. He was on one of the destroyers…the story I wouldn't tell you? He tried to run me down, after I'd torpedoed their sistership. The battle was bloody and they were in flames when our two ships collided. Probably killed most of his mates on the bridge. He cursed me a thousand times as we came abreast. Such hate. Can't blame him, but I'll never forget that look." Kurt chuckled flatly at the absurdity. "Huh, remembering. That's probably one of the curses."

"Don't get depressed again, darling."

"My wonderful, Sunny. You keep things in balance, but can you keep off a thousand curses?"

"I'll try, one at time, but let's don't talk about it."

"All right, but how can you explain our meeting again, out here? The first time was war, and strange things can happen."

"We dine with the Captain tonight. You can ask him all about it."

"I'm sure he'd be delighted to discuss the war with a German spy."

"I mean, you can ask him why we almost ran down that poor little boat. Now, lets go in and have a drink, then I simply must do something with my hair before dinner." Bright put the incident in its proper perspective. Kurt added it to the puzzle of his life.

That evening, with Cape North, Nova Scotia, rising in the northwest, the RMS *Express Packet* steamed out of the fog. She exchanged light signals with a coaster crossing from North Sydney to Port aux Basques. The night was fine and clear. Captain Wilkinson ordered full speed ahead to make up for lost time, then bid the first officer good evening and took the outside staircase to the main deck. He wanted some air before going in to dinner; looking forward to dining with the charming Lady Tifton, who wasn't travelling with a husband according to the Purser. However, male companions were fair game. The Captain surveyed his ship with a critical eye, found everything including the weather in good shape, and spent a quiet moment at the rail straightening his formal dress uniform. Irresistible to the ladies. He noticed the annoying tightness around the middle and sucked it in, vowing to walk the decks more often, although he usually found himself arm in arm with a charming older woman who wanted to talk, too often about grandchildren.

Captain Clifton Wilkinson entered the Grand Salon and posed at the door until the assembled diners had sufficient time to notice. He then proceeded to his table where his guests for the evening waited, smiling on each and every face as he passed, at least he let them think so. It was all part of the ritual and Captain Wilkinson enjoyed the game, deserving every easy moment in the eyes of his subjects. Few of them were aware of the long days of manifests, details and politics, spiced with gut wrenching decisions in moments of crisis. Nor were they aware of the endless hours of tension when the world is a blind beast lashing out at his tiny ship plodding across the oceans, with miles of cold eternity outside the egg shell skin of the hull. Just as well. It's for the captain to worry and the passengers to enjoy their journey.

Captain Wilkinson approached the head table with an eye for Lady Bright Tifton. She looked different from the drippy-nosed, deck chair passenger with frizzed hair and soggy book the Purser had pointed out that morning, before the near incident with the fishing boat. Bright smiled sweetly as he took her hand.

"Lady Tifton, what a pleasure!" he said, kissing her fingers.

"Thank you, Captain. And mine," she replied, not immune to charm.

"What a pity we haven't had the pleasure of dining together before now. But, we make up for it tonight." He smiled around the table, to appear democratic at least.

"Captain Wilkinson, I'd like to introduce, Kurt, my companion," Bright said, proudly. A slight blush of colour rose in her already colourful cheeks.

"How do you do…Schulte, isn't it?" he said almost coldly, noting that the German features matched the name. He extended his hand when Kurt stood up. They shook hands behind Bright. "I'm delighted you could join us," he lied.

"Thank you, Captain Wilkinson. The pleasure is entirely mine." Kurt was not to be outdone with charm but the prolonged handshake was becoming awkward and they broke it off cleanly. Positions understood. But Kurt was not the least bit intimidated by the uniform or the man. His formal upbringing in the company of wealth and nobility hadn't been entirely wasted. He sized up his opponent and relaxed. Jealousy was another matter and it amused him to experience the sensation.

The Captain acknowledged the other guests again and he and Kurt sat down; the captain careful to hesitate long enough to be seated last. It was the signal to resume talk and the waiter's cue to begin serving the dinner. After a polite question about accommodations to the older woman on his left, Wilkinson zeroed in on Bright.

"Are you enjoying the cruise, Lady Tifton?" the Captain inquired.

"Well, yes, and no," she laughed, blushing nicely.

"May I take some credit for the *yes?*" he teased.

Bright looked at Kurt and blushed again. "I'm afraid not."

"I see," he said, with forced good humour. "Then I'm afraid I must accept the blame for the *no.*"

"Oh, heavens not at all! Everything has been just wonderful. Even the Captain can't do anything about the beastly weather."

"Easy to solve that problem, my dear. As the Captain I could simply order the ship south into warmer climes. Just say the word."

"Yes, that would be splendid, but, wouldn't it get you into an awful lot of trouble?"

"Undoubtedly," he said, with a nudge-nudge grin. "However, it would be worth it. I wouldn't mind a break from the North Atlantic myself, and with such charming company."

Bright sensed it was time to shift the conversation away from innuendo. The appetizers arrived to create a diversion and Bright held Kurt's hand under the table.

"Captain Wilkinson, Kurt would like to know what happened with that little boat in the fog today."

"Ah, yes, the small incident this morning," said the Captain, dismissing the incident. He would have to bide his time and play by the rules, "...the wayward fishing schooner. Common occurrence in these waters. The Channel too, I might add. Although, our own lads aren't as cheeky about it. They at least have the common courtesy to wave. Devil of a nuisance though. These little fishing boats go dashing willy-nilly about, no signals. The fellow was on us before my lookouts could hear his little foghorn. Toys, if they have them at all. Clumsy boats the old coasters. No engines, so they can't manoeuvre to save themselves. Some crossings we have to pick our way through whole schools of them in a calm. Add the ruddy fog hereabouts and, well...you saw what that fellow did today. Right across my bow. We clearly had the right of way. I doubt any of these skippers are even properly licensed masters!"

Kurt was thinking of the excellent seamen he knew who piloted humble working craft with skills honed in the best training school called experience.

"But they *are* generally good sailors," Kurt interjected.

The Captain lost his wind for the moment. "*Phuff*, perhaps, but with no Guild or Board of Trade papers to sit…or even competition for positions, how do we know?"

"Tradition, experience," said Kurt, sensing it would be a sore spot for a captain who obviously came up through the ranks in the Merchant Navy, or perhaps had retired out of the British Navy. The British Navy believed it had invented and held the patent on tradition. It wasn't to be wasted on common fishermen. "They seem to be born to it, as it were," added Kurt. And Kurt could have added, *conceived in a rolling skiff,* but deferred to the ladies present.

"Much too arbitrary in the real world," countered the Captain. "Some fishing captains came into the Navy during the Great War and were the very devils for mucking up. They just couldn't get it right, you know. Proper signals and ship handling etiquette. Too backward and unschooled. More nuisance than they were worth. Oh, let me not be uncharitable. On deck, in their milieu, so to speak, they were proper British seamen, good fighters, and all that. But in command? Not a bit of it. A proper muck up in a flotilla. However, we shouldn't bore the ladies with such talk of the war, should we?"

"Kurt was in the Navy," Bright said innocently. "He was a, what was it, darling? Kapitänleutnant, in one of those beastly submarines. They even gave him an Iron Cross for bravery." Bright looked around the table at blank faces.

The passengers in First Class had been whispering about the handsome German since Southampton, but it was their first close encounter. They received the news with stony silence. Kurt was amused by the effect of Bright's announcement on the British guests. The Captain, for his part, maintained an outwardly neutral expression. Kurt tried to warn her off but Bright plunged happily on: "That was the German Navy, of course," she said, and immediately realized she had dropped a bomb on the party. "But, the beastly war's over and he's such a sweet boy, as you can see..." Bright could tell they didn't see, but she had her hackles up, venting some spleen for her own rejections in life. And her women's intuition said she should at least try to deflate the Captain one notch. "Were you in the Navy, Captain? But, you must have been too old when the war started," she said with a disarming smile.

"Not too old, my dear, where experience counts," replied Wilkinson with good grace. "When the war started I was toiling for my present employers. I volunteered my services to God, King and country. The Navy was only too glad to use my humble skills. Even soldiers must be carried from place to place in safety. We couldn't guarantee caviar with all the meals, however," he said, and paused as the relieved laughter circled the table. "And the staterooms may have been a bit crowded. A platoon of young men could fit into your stateroom, my dear," he addressed an over-jeweled woman beside Kurt who flushed and hid behind her fan. "Oh my, that would be interesting, to see," she said, pretending to be a little scandalized. "And since you asked, Lady Tifton, I was Master of the *Colombian Prince,* a troopship, larger than the *Express Packet,* and beautifully appointed. She was a German liner, Mr. Schulte, Captain Schulte, if you prefer...seized in Montreal at the beginning of the war. I had four thousand young men on board, mostly Colonials, but good men. And a nursing corps, I might add." He addressed Kurt again. "One of your submarines torpedoed my ship out from under me, in the Irish Sea, in the darkness, without a proper warning or a chance to even clear the boats. Fortunately, and I'll give credit to your German builders, she sank slowly. We saved most of the troops but only half my crew. They were lost trying to get the nurses out, you see, because the nurses insisted on helping the injured boys."

Then he addressed Bright. "Bravery my dear? Men who hide from sight to kill then run away are not brave. Wouldn't you agree, Captain Schulte?"

"It was fortunate you were rescued and not allowed to suffer the same fate," Kurt said, and left the inference hang.

"Yes, it was a minor miracle." The Captain realized the dinner party was collapsing. He quickly changed tack. "But, as Lady Tifton said, the war is over. I'm sure Captain Schulte fought bravely for his country and a man can't always choose the side he must fight on. However, we are no longer enemies and such things must be forgotten if we're to get on with the business of trade, and all that. Don't you agree, Captain Schulte?"

Kurt smiled but thought to himself that the pompous bastard was pushing a bit too far, in the spirit of Mark Anthony at Caesar's funeral. Perhaps Captain Wilkinson assumed Germans did not read Shakespeare. Or perhaps he was sure Kurt did. Then it was a compliment.

"Yes, I fought for my country. I am German and proud of it, but I cared little for the reasons we went to war with Briton and I care less now that it's over," he said, taking in all the British faces glaring at him. He vowed to be on his best behaviour for Bright. "Therefore, I'd like to propose a toast." He raised his wine glass and the others followed, if reluctantly. "We have been friends before. We are friends again and, God willing, we shall remain so. To the new England and Germany!"

The toast was a great success if only to relieve the building tension. Bright was very proud of her Kurt and held his hand in her lap, much to the annoyance of the Captain. The meal was accomplished with strained good cheer and small talk about weather and fashions. "What is the nature of your trip to Canada, Lady Tifton?" asked the Captain after desert. "Oh, it's not *my* trip, really. I'm accompanying Kurt," she answered.

"Oh?" said the Captain. "May I inquire as to the nature of Mr. Schulte's business?"

"Not business as such," said Kurt. "A goodwill mission for my government, to the Colonies. England's colonies."

"Ahh, indeed! Goodwill," said the Captain with a sarcastic chuckle. "Germany will need plenty of that, old boy, *when* you decide who's going to run the country. Yes, and when the French are through with you?...." It wasn't a question. "We've no battle axe to grind. Live and let live I say!" The faces around the table nodded on cue. "And Lady Tifton, a word of caution." The Captain leaned in but made no effort to keep the others from overhearing. "I wouldn't announce your companion's prowess, in the matter of medals, in certain circles, if his mission is to succeed."

Bright flushed with anger. The Captain laughed and sat back, content in the belief he had put the capper on Kurt von Schulte, the arrogant Prussian hanger on. He decided to concentrate on the other well endowed woman opposite Kurt. The dinner broke up soon after with excuses. Bright and Kurt retired to their stateroom to salvage what they could of the evening.

QUEBEC CITY

September 7, 1920: The copper sun hung like a hot air balloon over the Citadel, turning the river into a cauldron of molten gold. RMS *Express Packet* nosed into the outgoing tide waiting for the Quebec City pilot boat. To starboard, the harvest farms and hardwood forests of Isle d'Orleans took that golden glow and flung it back at the watchers lining the rail. The summer homes along the banks were closed and the residents safely ashore in their urban enclaves, preparing for a another

Canadian winter. Ahead of the ship Quebec City shimmered in the heat and danced on the calm but ever moving river. The Chateau, the promenades and the jumble of stone houses climbing the slopes were already in purple shadow. The famous St. Lawrence Valley humidity haze was waiting for the cleansing winds of fall to sweep the valley clear. To port the city of Levis and the shipyards of Louzon were picked out with sunshine, the industrial sprawl heightened by shadows. Puffy white-grey clouds rode above the City of Stone to compact the scene and keep it from floating off into space.

Passengers with big box cameras, shutters clicking, were taking in their first close-up view of civilization since leaving Southampton, wondering what kind of a place was this French Canada. Many were going to live in the new country as displaced immigrants. Some were travelling for business: Canada had goods to sell, and Europe needed just about everything, including raw materials to rebuild. A few tourists, and wealthy entrepreneurs were idling around the globe to see what the war had left for them to pick over. Others were just curious. The Canadians had fought well in the war, making a name for themselves at Vimy Ridge, the Somme, Passhendaele and other infamous landmarks unknown before 1914, and they wanted to see the country that spawned such fighters.

Kurt steadied himself, focusing a small, precision made camera, discreetly taking photographs of the ship building yards below Levis. While others snapped away at the grand view of the Old City, Kurt framed shore installations, the fortress, docks, possible landing points, unaware that he was looking at the very cliffs the British Army had scaled that fateful night in September, seventeen fifty-nine, to attack the French in the skirmish that would define the raw colony's future. He was tense and felt conspicuous but he had to have something to show, so intent on his deception that he didn't notice Bright had joined him at the rail.

"What a charming little camera!" Bright said.

"Oh, hello, I didn't see you." Kurt, feeling guilty for ignoring her, tried to be nonchalant. Bright was puzzled by his odd behaviour.

"I didn't know you were a photographer, darling."

"A diversion. I, ah, forgot I had it, actually. I just remembered it this morning when I was looking for my shaving kit."

"It's not like you to forget."

"Oh, I'm a real dreamer, actually...especially when I see beautiful things, like a woman who smiles when it's raining...and, ah, nice scenery."

"Then why are you taking pictures of that?" She pointed to the jumble of derricks, ship's hulls and the general clutter of the Levis shipyards. Interesting, but not in the same league as the rest of the riverscape.

"Old habits. I like ships, and things."

"Is that why you spend so much time prowling the docks?"

"Yes, actually." He had said *actually* three times, a word he detested.

"You have an unusual eye for scenery, my darling. There's nothing beautiful about rusty old ships."

"In the eye of the beholder."

"What on earth must you think of me!?"

"No ship could match your graceful curves."

Kurt slipped the camera into his pocket and put his arms around Bright. She pretended to be annoyed and turned her back on him so he could hold her more closely.

"When you make your official visits to those, widows...is it just a coincidence that they all live in harbour towns?"

"A coincidence? Yes, I suppose it is. Sailors usually live near the sea."

"But not always?"

"Sunny...you're leading me."

"Sorry, darling. I'm just curious, because you're being curious."

"I see."

"Can I ask you just one more question?" Bright turned to look up at him. She already suspected she knew why and wanted to get it out and done with.

"You always study maps before you go on one of your excursions. Some of the maps are drawings of harbours."

"Peeking again?"

"You fell asleep over them one night, darling, that night in Portsmouth. I couldn't help notice. I'm sorry." She waited a moment for his reaction. Kurt looked away. "What *are* you doing, really?"

"Organizing sight seeing trips," he said, with a touch of annoyance. Bright turned to face him, pressing close. "You're such a gorgeous boy, and a promising lover, but, darling, you don't lie very well."

"No," he said flatly, looking beyond her searching eyes at the shore and the objects of his mission, "I suppose I don't." They held each other tighter. Bright didn't want to say anything or ask anything but she wanted to know everything. "I don't like lying to you," he said finally, letting go and turning aside.

"Then tell me what this trip is really about."

"You're a decent girl. You might not understand, the necessity."

"I'm also a big girl."

"Sunny..." Kurt couldn't continue.

"It's all right. I won't be shocked or faint on you."

"Sunny, I *was* sent by my government. Many of us in the Kriegsmarine have been. I'm supposed to get information, about ships, and things. I'm employed as a...spy."

Bright looked into Kurt's eyes. "We're friends, Germany and Britain, you said so yourself. Can't you just ask us what you want to know?"

"If it were that easy." Once in the open the topic was a mirage. "You've been awfully good. You may have saved my life."

"Splendid! And you mine. Now that you've leveled with me lets get on with *our* lives, shall we?"

Kurt sank into Bright's eyes in turn, trying to fathom his feelings. A weight lifted from his conscience and he felt his heart clearly for the first time.

"Sunny...I'm falling in love with you," he said, simply.

Bright did not look surprised or act coy. She looked doubtful. "No more Devil woman?" she asked obliquely.

"Almost gone."

"Good. There's hope."

"Let's chuck this spy business. Come back to Germany with me. We won't even get off the ship."

"Is this a proposal?"

"Proposal? You mean as in business?"

"Never mind, darling. We can sort out the details later."

"Then you'll come?"

"Is there anything to eat in Germany?"

"We manage."

Bright kissed Kurt passionately, to the amusement of the passengers. Kurt responded deeply and Bright was impressed.

"I'm sure you do," she breathed, taking Kurt by the hand and leading him away from the rail, the smiling passengers and the postcard view of Quebec.

GERMANY

The Mercedes touring car sped along the dry country roads escaping the outskirts of Berlin near Gosen, past the forests, canals, farms and farmers working in their fields. It was the end of September and the meager harvest was almost in. The peasant farmers should have been cheerful but they looked somber in their postwar uniforms of dark suits and dark peak caps. Some wore fedoras giving their work a classical severity. Others still wore the remnants of battle uniforms. The Socialists controlled the government. The confusion of the revolution spreading westward from Russia, hardships of the war fought and lost and the harsh demands of the Treaty plagued the countryside almost as much as it strangled the cities. Germans were not allowed to recover their dignity or their economy, and it showed.

Bright pointed out the gaunt, blank faces of the children playing near the narrow road. Kurt didn't like to think about them. His own guilt was a large burden as the big, smooth running car raced by, blowing dust over them. He translated the looks of the children as sneers and accusations. The Socialists taught them to suspect the aristocracy, Kurt's class, as traitors who had taken them to war and used up the peasant class in fruitless attempts at expansion, then sold their souls to the Devil at Versailles. Now the weakened government could barley feed the survivors. Germany felt the Great Depression a decade before the rest of the world would know what it was to be down and stepped on. The French said the Germans deserved the pain and humiliation, as well as the starvation. So the children suffered for Kurt's sins.

Bright tried to be cheerful and take in the scenery. Once clear of the poverty and the big-eyed children she applauded the mansions that seemed to grow out of the fertile forests, wondering what the Schulte estate would be like, and what would the parents be like? Kurt had made some references to his home life and it didn't sound promising so Bright was prepared to be disappointed but she was determined not to show it. Another grand manor took her mind off family.

"Oh my! That is lovely. Who lives there?"

"That's the von Holsen summer home. They have a bigger one in Berlin. Made his money importing arms for the Kaiser before the war. He plans to make another fortune before the next one."

"Oh," she said, frowning. "And who owns that charming little mansion?"

"They call it a hunting and fishing cottage. A blue blood. Another Prussian social climber, Count Wolfgang von Mielhausen. They only come to the country when the von Holsens are away. More Prussians, like us I'm afraid."

"You don't like your neighbours much do you, darling?"

"I try to avoid them and they ignore me. It works out very nicely."

"Be serious, Kurt."

"I am serious, Bah! *Bahhh!*"

"You call that being serious?"

"I'm a serious black sheep."

"You are the fool!" she laughed. "Still, it might be fun having a title in two different countries."

"The von Schulte Baronet? We might all disappear if the Socialists have their way."

"That's all right, darling. I'd much prefer being just Mrs. Schulte. Being a Baroness sounds so...unfulfilled somehow."

"Are you fulfilled, my Sunny?"

"Yes, very much, thank you," she said, with a mischievous laugh. She couldn't be happier, if a little apprehensive. She held Kurt's hand for the warmth, and the security. She felt like a little girl waiting in an anteroom to be introduced to her first important person. It was an odd feeling for her, being used to moving in the circles of British nobility, though at a lower level. She and Teddy had been invited to large events like Ascot and Wimbledon. The war changed all that for Bright. Kurt's war.

"Well, here we are, the autonomous State of Little Prussia!" announced Kurt, as the Mercedes slowed down for the turn into the Schulte estate. "It's not much, but it's home."

Bright wanted to add, *and very pink!* when she saw the huge edifice open up between the manicured linden trees. All she could venture to say was: "But, darling, it's so big!" Somehow the sight resolved her nervous anticipation. How could she take it seriously?

"Were you expecting a little hovel in the woods, or a cottage like Count Wolfgang's?" Kurt squeezed her hand and she squeezed back, sharing the joke. "It always reminds me of the Bastille. The French were clever enough to pull theirs down." Kurt laughed when he noticed the chauffeur glance at them in the rear view mirror. "Mother and Father are expecting us. Mother will love you. Father is, unpredictable."

Father was apoplectic. "…She's a Jew!!" shouted the General, spitting out the word.

"She's a Lady!" replied Kurt.

"*Phuff*! Scratch the gold leaf off a tin trinket and what do you have!?"

They were positioned on either side of a large, pedestal-mounted globe of the world in the dark-paneled drawing room, like warlords carving up the world between them. The fireplace beyond intensified the fierce rage on the General's face and the defiant glare in Kurt's eyes.

"I intend to marry Bright."

The General digested the news, his lips quivering but his cold grey eyes never wavered. Intimidation? Kurt wondered. A habit of command that usually worked but Kurt wouldn't flinch.

"I forbid it!!"

"Yes, I expected you might. But you can't order me not to love her."

"I can have your Superiors post you to South America!"

Kurt let the threat pass. He had another announcement to make and he wanted it delivered with a razor edge. To wound. It was his chance to redress all the years of doubt and misery.

"I resigned my commission." He said softly for effect.

"What!?"

"It was a sham from the beginning. I hated being a spy."

"Schultes never quit!" the General said evenly. Retreat was strategy. Quitting was a sin. The General's eyes remained ice cold but his voice came from a deep place where his heart should have been. "You disgrace the Schulte name!"

"I'm a Schulte in name only. I don't care about your traditions!"

"I want you and your English Jew trollop out of my house!"

"I won't come back."

"I don't want you back, until you come to your senses!..."

"*My* senses?"

"And not a single mark from the estate!"

"I don't want your damned money either!"

"Then go!"

There was nothing else to say. The antagonists glared at each other and lifetimes of conflict flashed by in the brief moment before the parting. Blood is only blood. It has no magical qualities to dissolve walls of stone, or hearts of steel. Kurt turned away and walked across the room. He didn't hesitate or turn back for a dramatic parting shot. He simply opened the door and closed it softly behind him.

General von Schulte, aristocrat and brilliant military tactician, watched his son leave, wishing Kurt had stormed out in a rage, slamming doors, he'd understand that. His face twitched as if he were in pain. Through the slits of his eyes a wetness appeared. Regret? If Kurt had turned back for a moment he would have known that he had been wrong about the Old Man. The General was a general first, incapable of showing the love he felt for his sons but there was no heart of steel. Only a stubborn old man imprisoned by his obsessions. He uttered one word, "Kurt…"

Lady Bright Tifton had been waiting in the anteroom to meet the General. She couldn't help over-hearing the harsh words and the denunciation of her race. It was as she had feared. But she was more fatalistic than Kurt.

"It's not the end of the world, darling," she said, holding his hand against her face.

"I'm sorry you had to hear all that."

"You become immune."

"It's unfair."

"I tried hiding my Jewishness to be accepted. It allowed me into certain social circles but it didn't protect me. It hurts worse when they include you in their nasty little conversations, but if they knew the truth they'd walk out of the room. And the really awful thing is, it's the ones with power. The ones we have to work through to get anywhere. It's always been the same. Unless we have money. Then they come with hands out, and it doesn't hurt to play the piano or the violin well. They let us entertain them. We can be very clever," she said, smiling to hold back the tears.

"Father thinks only of Germany."

"And because Jews don't have a country we're a threat to him?"

"That's part of it. But I think there's more."

"Of course there is! There has to be an excuse for treating us no better nor worse than animals."

"Let's not."

"No, let's not."

"You're awfully good," he said.

"Still love me?" she asked.

"More than ever. It seems you're all I have, now."

"What will you do?"

"I don't know," answered Kurt vaguely, but offering a grin. "I've never *done*, anything except play at war. I was absurdly good at that."

BERLIN

September 27, 1920; The prodigal son, cast out again, and his pariah mate, left the protection of the ancestral home for the streets of Berlin. Many Germans already knew the hardships of a depression and Bright had started out life in poverty, but for Kurt it was a new experience.

The chauffeur left them on the sidewalk at the entrance of the once magnificent Hotel Grand Imperial. The doorman, in tattered elegance, sizing up the expensive car and their good clothes, was quick to open the door and take care of the luggage. When the Mercedes drove away, their former way of life went with it and all that was left was the facade. It was important to keep it up. That night Kurt wrote:

'...Bright was awfully brave. Neither of us wanted to admit we were downhearted. I've never felt so low, but I think it was more for Bright than for myself. She's used to having the best. I don't care that much and if the truth were known I would have been happier in the hovel we talked about. Bright was determined to get out of that life and had, but by throwing in with me she has given up all that she worked for, and been insulted into the bargain. So here we are, pretending we're living the good life, knowing it's a sham too, like my brief, undistinguished career as a spy. I'll never forget the look on her face when we entered the suite...'

Kurt said the concierge reminded him of a weasel...He used the term *stoat*. A small, furry animal that darts about taking what it wants, too quick and cunning to get caught...On the way up to their suite Kurt had the feeling the Weasel would pick his pocket. There was a time when Kurt wouldn't have cared. He gave his money away if a drunken stranger hinted he was on hard times. The concierge lead the way from the lift along the gloomy corridor to their suite. Every other light in the long hallway had been extinguished to save money. They also saved by not hiring cleaners it seemed. Kurt went on:

'*...The large suite had floor to ceiling windows facing south. The light should have been good but the windows were covered with six winter's worth of grime. The living room was worn, dirty and tattered around the edges. The dirt was a legacy of careless boots and greasy hands. We found out later that officers of our once glorious Imperial Army were billeted in our hotel when in Berlin for staff meetings. I watched Bright circle her new home, fingering the frayed chintz furniture and heavy curtains and stained brocade wall coverings. It had once been an elegant suite, fit to entertain royalty, but now looks as though a gang of filthy boys played rough games for a year, then cleared out. Bright was very good though and never said a word. I blessed her. I don't think I could have kept up my end if she'd been a bitch about it. One of the many things about Bright I adore is the fact that she is incapable of being a bitch....*'

"It will do," said Kurt, to the Weasel who lingered for a tip. Kurt gave him a precious mark and sent him packing. "Have our things sent up." The Weasel smiled a toothy, black-penciled moustache smile. "Slimy little creature," Kurt said, after the concierge bowed his way out. "Must have Italian blood. I take that back."

"He gives me the shivers," said Bright, holding her arms around herself. The room was cold and musty.

"We don't have to stay," Kurt said, sweeping his finger through the dust on the writing desk.

"It *is* a bit tattered, darling."

"War and peace take their toll," he said, trying to make a joke.

"Poor Germany."

"Poor us," Kurt said, feeling sorry for Bright.

Bright threw the curtains wide. Dust clouds swirled in the sunlight. She pushed the French doors open to let in some fresh air and gazed at the suite's major asset; the balcony. A good view of the park and high enough above the Kaiserdamm Bismarkstrasse so as not to have to see the hungry children pestering the Berliners who still had money. She seemed to cheer up in the sunshine.

"I'll write my barrister," she said. "He can transfer some funds from Teddy's estate."

"I don't want to be kept!" Kurt said, too sharply. "It's not right."

"This suite may be antiquated and dowdy, darling, but the cost is certainly up to date."

"Damn my father! The stubborn old fool."

"Don't, Kurt. Don't make yourself hate him. You know you don't."

"I...no, I never have, God knows I tried. It's always been just as much my fault. But I can't let you keep us."

"That's noble of you, my dear brave boy, but we have to eat."

"I'm sorry, Sunny, it's just that I feel terrible dragging you into this."

"Nonsense, darling, I came willingly."

Bright went to Kurt and enfolded him in her arms. He was tempted to sink into her warmth for the protection she offered. They changed roles. Bright was happy to go either way if it would help. She did force the kiss. Kurt responded and held her tightly as if he was protecting her. They both knew who was doing what to whom, but it was all right because it worked and at the moment feeling better was more important than being right.

"You are awfully good," he said.

"You keep saying that."

"I mean it."

"I know, but I like it when you say it."

"You're more than awfully good."

"Don't make it too sweet," she said.

"Never as sweet as you."

"Shall we see if the bed's survived the war?"

He kissed her long and hard. They could have been in a ghetto flop house or in the Grand Hall of Westminster.

"It could be the Royal Palace," she continued, after the kiss.

"Would it matter if it was a hovel in the forest?" he asked.

"Not if you kiss me like this."

"Then I shall always kiss you like this."

They kissed again, the deep kiss of true passion, when nothing matters and time and place slip away. Bright forced Kurt down on the love seat. She smothered him with her warm kisses. The embrace went deeper. They were melting together, floating. Kurt slipped too far away...*on Norderney in the moonlight, a tiger mauling his body, ripping his flesh and the tide was rushing up and around them, cold and hot at the same time. Then there were bodies turning in the surf, bumping and clutching at him. Kurt tried to scream. The klaxon drowned out his scream and green water exploded into the submarine. Kurt was being crushed by the water, bodies piled on top of him and he tried to throw them off...*

Bright sat on the end of the love seat controlling her breathing. The sound of the crank bell ringing again and again jarred the room. Kurt pulled himself together and went to answer the door, waiting until Bright had straightened her clothes and pushed her hair into place. They assumed the pose for each other because it was easier than trying to explain and apologize and accept the apology as if nothing important had happened. Kurt opened the door. Two old porters looked from Kurt to Bright and smiled and waited to be invited to wheel in the luggage. They knew nothing of the struggle but they had overheard the sounds of passion and imagined what they wanted.

October 17, 1920: Kurt wrote: *'...When I returned from my walk today we had two letters waiting at the desk. One was for Bright, from her barrister in London, and the other from the University of Leipzig. I had written to the Headmaster of the Catholic College to inquire about a position in their history department. I was afraid to open it and decided to wait. I was also ambivalent about Bright's letter. I wanted her to have good news, she has been so down lately, but at the same time I chafe at the thought of living on her money. Sucking at the teats of the Schulte estate is one thing but I wanted to be my own man, for Bright. The British have a saying, 'It never rains but it pours.' Funny sort of saying. It took me a long time to get the right meaning of it. The British can twist things around so. They never like to come straight out and say what they mean. Not Bright of course, but then she's not truly British, is she?...'*

Kurt let himself into their suite to find Bright sitting in a big chair facing the window. The grey, dismal light of a wet fall day seemed reluctant to penetrate the dirty windows, but even so Bright looked unusually pale. She hadn't bothered with make up and was wearing her dullest dress. But it was her expression, or lack of it, that was the most difficult for Kurt to accept. He was sick at heart to see her so low.

It had taken only a few days for the reality of their situation to set in. They were without means to exist in the city and without the means to escape. And the city was not a friend, rocked as it was by revolution and chaos. Kurt hoped the letters were good news and his pride be damned. If it would cheer Bright up he would beg or steal, like his blonde sailor in Bremen. It wasn't so difficult, he knew, but feared desperation making decisions for them. He went to Bright and kissed her cheek. She made a small gesture of acceptance.

"Say, where's my Sunny Bright girl?" he asked, with forced good cheer.

"Hello, darling," said Bright, returning the kiss. "I'm sorry. I must look an awful drudge."

"I don't know what a drudge is, but if it's awful it can't be you."

"Your English lesson for the day. Me, and drudge...same thing."

"Cheer up, Sunny. We have letters."

Kurt handed Bright the legal envelope. She looked at the return address and let it rest in her lap. Kurt opened his and read the letter through to himself, letting Bright wonder. *Serve her right,* he thought. He'd make her curious. The news came early but he kept reading into the details. Finally he looked up and smiled.

"Now yours."

"Aren't you going to tell me?"

"No. Read yours first in case it's good news."

Bright broke the seal and opened the letter. '*Dear Miss Steinman,*' it began...*Miss Steinman!?*' "How can they...?" she asked, frowning, then continued reading. '*We regret to inform you that the family of your late husband, Lord Theodore Hamilton Tifton the Second, has uncovered evidence to support their claim that a proper marriage was not consummated between yourself and Lord Tifton under the civil laws of England.*' "What on earth!?..." Bright gathered herself and continued. '*The Court has ruled, therefore, the marriage null and void and, in consequence, the estate of the late Lord Tifton has been closed to you and the assets have been put in escrow.'* She read the last line over and over. "Oh Kurt! They've done it!"

"Is this true, Sunny? I mean, about the wedding night?"

"Well, yes and no," she said, in a daze. "You see, the day of the wedding Teddy got awfully intoxicated and the servants had to put him to bed. But I was already carrying his child. Don't you see, darling? Teddy and I had been seeing each other for over a year. His father wouldn't let him marry me, because I'm a Jew. Then when his father died..." Bright broke down and sobbed at the memory of the hurt and rejection. And the baby. There was no reason to be brave. Kurt took her hand.

"My poor, Sunny," he said sincerely. "Fathers seem to be overly protective when money and estates are concerned."

Bright sniffed. Kurt gave her his pocket handkerchief. She wiped her eyes and blew her nose and continued. "The next day, after the wedding, Teddy had to leave with his squadron for France. We didn't spend the night together, in that way," she said.

"The family has a legal loophole it seems," said Kurt. He understood only too well the politics of a powerful family.

"They shunned me of course. That's why I spent so much time pretending I was having a good time, in lounges, drowning my sorrows in expensive liquor."

"At least you chose your hotels well."

"But how long would it last before I ended up on the Isle of Dogs, like some slut out of Dickens!?"

"Never!"

"The family were horrid after Teddy died. They hounded me, but there was nothing they could do, I thought. When the hounding didn't work they went after my family. They tried to connect my father with the unions and the Bolsheviks. He's lost his job. I gave my mother some of the jewelry that the family didn't confiscate. I kept my birth stone set from Teddy...the sapphires you like so much. Father wouldn't touch the jewelry so mother sells them as they need the money. I couldn't give her money from the estate directly because the barrister..." Bright had another spell of sobbing.

"How did they find out, that you and, your husband didn't consummate...that night?"

"The servants! None of the family came to the wedding of course. Just some of Teddy's chums who got intoxicated too and rode horses through the Grand Hall declaring chivalry was alive and they'd have a joust." Bright stopped again, but this time instead of sobbing she had to stifle a giggle. Kurt was confused but happy to see the old spark in Bright's eyes. Her sense of humour was refreshing even if it came to the fore at unusual times. "The horses couldn't stand up on the marble floors, let alone run, so they decided to ride off to the aerodrome and go for a spin. It was a near thing though," she said, giggling at the memory. "Teddy had to talk them out of getting into their airplanes. You see, they had all flown down for the wedding. Teddy was always talking somebody out of foolish things. He knew they were going to do something so he suggested they have a hunt instead. Which was all well and good except it was dark. You can imagine where they held the hunt."

"In the Grand Hall?"

"Yes. Minus the horses at least, but it was hysterical! Imagine grown men riding on each other's shoulders, swords drawn. The poor Siamese cats will never be the same."

Bright was laughing well and Kurt couldn't help laughing with her. He could picture the scene in the Grand Hall. Drunken flyers in full dress uniforms, crashing about after a brace of terrified cats. Bright stopped laughing. The cloud returned.

"When Teddy was killed I miscarried. The poor wee thing, hardly looked human, but it was, mine...I spent the rest of the war as a nurse volunteer, almost penniless, fighting with the family through the barrister. But all the while he was on their side, just waiting for his chance. He wasn't above making rude propositions and fondling me...and worse, even in the hospital, after the baby...Those awful people!"

"Let's not talk about it."

"I don't care about the estate, darling. I just want to be respected, as a person, not hated because I was born Jewish. My father works hard. He's a good man. Mother tried to raise me to be a good girl but I wanted more. I thought being Lady Tifton was the answer...but I did love Teddy. Oh, what a mess!"

"It's not such a tragedy, Sunny. We have each other."

"I have you, but what have you got? I'm not even a wealthy widow. And I've caused you to be disowned as well."

"Just by Father. It would have happened, sooner or later...but look here, Sunny! I have good news, from the University at Leipzig. I've been accepted as a teaching assistant."

"Oh, that's wonderful, darling."

"I had to use what's left of the family's influence with the Catholic Church, before they discovered I've been disowned. I'm afraid the rewards will be slight. But, in these hard times I'm lucky to get a position."

"We'll be all right. I don't eat much," Bright said, attempting a joke.

Kurt smiled. "There's the part at the end you must know about." He read from the letter. '...*But I regret to tell you, Herr Schulte, that the residence usually available to teaching assistants was destroyed by fire during the Communist riots at the end of the war. There are, unfortunately, no funds available to provide alternate accommodations. If you still wish to take the position you will have to see to your own living*

'...etcetera. It won't be easy, Sunny, but if you're willing to see it through I know things will get better. Shall we try?" Bright's answer was a brave smile and faraway look.

LEIPZIG

October 19, 1920: *'...It was raining this morning when we boarded the train for Leipzig. It's still raining, in sympathy with how we both feel. Bright is down again, although she tries not to show it, because she had to sell her clothes and jewelry. We got little enough for the really good things and were lucky to sell anything. Even the pawn brokers are cautious. I sold what I could and don't miss the rings and pins, but the miserable pawn broker wouldn't even take my Iron Cross. Says he already has too many. I always had too much and feel cleansed. But I worry about Bright. Her clothes meant so much and our future looked so bleak when we got to Leipzig. On the positive side, we have less luggage to haul about. The trip was tiring, the train crowded and we couldn't sleep so I told Bright the story of the Blonde sailor and Bremen and suggested we could live on the lam. She pretended to be disgusted. It was fun to watch the children play in the aisles. Nothing seems to bother them. What a blessing to be a child. Not my childhood though. I asked Bright what hers was like and she said it was very nice, as she remembered it. They had very little but there was much warmth and love. I envy her.*

Waiting in the train station for it to stop raining. The people come and go. Many look depressed and hungry. There's too much poverty and too much politics in Germany. We will make some inquiries then try to find a flat or a pension for the night...'

It was still raining when Kurt and Bright left the train station to look for a place to spend the night. The station keeper gave them directions to the Lower Town. It was a long walk and Bright seemed more tired and downhearted than usual. Kurt could only carry the extra luggage, he couldn't carry her spirit as well, though he tried because he knew she would do the same for him. They passed through the deserted central square and entered a narrow street of shops. The streets and the gutters were running with dirty water. Their feet were already soaked when a big touring car sped by, splashing their legs and stopped in front of a butcher's shop. The chauffeur, holding a large black umbrella, blocked the sidewalk as he waited for his mistress to disembark. It involved getting her ample self, her purse and her dachshund out of the back seat. Kurt was angry. Bright was fascinated, remembering scenes from her childhood, watching the privileged being handed down from ornate carriages, wishing someday to travel in style. She laughed at herself as she eyed the shop window and the trays of meat. Kurt took her arm and steered her around the touring car.

They turned the corner of Papiermühlstrasse into a block of run-down flats near the university. Kurt thought there was something significant about the name. The buildings seemed to lean in, cutting off the light, threatening to fall on them. Kurt consulted a sodden piece of paper and pointed to a shabby looking walkup on the other side of the narrow street. It looked like all the other building fronts that were once elegant but fallen into disrepair during the lean years. A broken water spout allowed rainwater to splash over them even as Kurt knocked on the door, knowing their life was about to change.

"I usually have students," said Frau Schnarr, breathing heavily, leading Kurt and Bright up the dark stairs to the top floor. Frau Schnarr was middle aged, overweight and breathless. "They don't deserve a nice place. Swine most of them! Now there's not so many. If you stay...no noise!" She opened the attic door at the top of the stairs.

Bright, exhausted from the climb, rested against the bannister looking back down the stairwell. If she hadn't been so tired she might have appreciated the irony. She was nine years old again in Liverpool, living in the worker's ghetto, simple housing at the low end of the scale, even the smells of cooking and poverty were familiar. Kurt gently urged her into the room.

The room was only a little brighter than the stairwell but it had been whitewashed at some time in its history and made the most of the light from a small dormer window that looked north and west over the city and the university. Sitting in a chair one could only see the sky. Bare beams decorated a plastered ceiling stained by leaks. There was a table, three battered chairs, a coal stove, a bed, and a sideboard with cracked glass front and some heavy plates and cups on top. It would be cold and damp and hard to heat in the winter. Hot and stuffy in the summer. But it was cheap, even for a university town.

"It will have to do," said Kurt of their garret. He was thinking of freezing artists and writers. He felt like neither. Only poor. He handed her some marks from his folder.

"No singing, no music, no dancing. The toilet is one floor down until the plumbing's repaired. Share with the old woman below. Clean up after yourselves. Coal's in the cellar. One scuttle for each day, extra. Pay in advance."

She held out a pudgy, red hand, cracked and rough from washing in cold water. Kurt opened his leather folder again. He thought of Eric. Physically they would have made a good match, Eric and Frau Schnarr, but she didn't have his temperament. Kurt was glad Eric had been Eric. He missed his engineer and the rough talk and the danger.

"Two marks each month for coal. Ashes go in the bin in the cellar. No mess!"

Kurt removed two marks from the folder. Frau Schnarr eyed the remaining marks. Kurt closed the folder and put it back into his jacket pocket.

"One mark each month for the electric light," she said.

Kurt looked up at the single bare bulb hanging from a cross beam above their heads. The small bulb couldn't burn a mark's worth of electricity in a year; if it worked. He took out the folder and gave her another mark. It was stuffed into an apron pocket with the coal and rent money.

"Water's provided but you carry it from the tap on the first floor, until the plumbing's repaired. If you spill, clean it up!"

Bright had been silently surveying the room trying not to betray what she was thinking, too proud to give the matron a hint that she was repulsed, not because she wasn't used to humble surroundings, but for the opposite reason. Kurt thought she was being very brave until he noticed the tears in her eyes that the matron couldn't see. Then Kurt realized the matron was staring at her.

"If you have Jewish friends at the university, do not bring them home. No Jews!"

The Matron, satisfied that she had extracted all the money she could and imparted all the wisdom necessary to assure harmonious relations, departed, slamming the door for emphasis.

"I like her better than the little stoat of a concierge at the Grand," said Kurt.

"You can't be serious, darling. The woman's a...tyrant!"

"At least she didn't hang about groveling for a tip."

Kurt tried on a smile to see what her reaction would be. Bright was about to smile but the tears flowed instead. Bright's emotions could shift very quickly. Kurt seldom knew what she was thinking or feeling and it was hard to keep up. Bright was still holding her bags as if ready to flee. Kurt took the bags, set them down and held her close. Bright buried her head in his chest and had a private cry for her race.

"Sunny, I'm sorry, what she said."

"She wasn't speaking to me."

"She's just a mean old woman with a rotten heart."

"Are you apologizing for her *and* your father?"

"It will change. There has to be a home for you...for us."

"A home?"

"Yes, a place where people don't care who you are or where you were born or how many titles you have."

"America," she said, not as if it were a fantasy land, but a fact believed strongly. "We should have stayed in Canada."

"All right then, we'll go to Canada."

"You're forgetting one thing, darling. We've cut our options to this!"

"Our very own hovel?" asked Kurt.

"Oh, darling, you must think me a spoiled brat. I grew up in a place like this. It's just such a shock coming back."

Bright broke away from Kurt's arms and confronted the room. She opened one of her bags and took out a fine linen towel with her initials on the corner and began to dust the table and sideboard.

"My sister and I helped Momma clean and bake. She insisted because she said it was necessary to be a good housekeeper, to get a good man. I always wanted a big house with servants so I wouldn't have to do it." She laughed, a small tight laugh, very unlike Bright. "Good thing Momma insisted."

Bright dug into her bag again and came up with a colourful scarf that she tied around her hair so that she looked like a gypsy. Kurt picked up their bags and put them on the bed, watching Bright take a broom from behind the stove and begin sweeping the floor, humming a Jewish folk song. He recognized the tune. Kurt wrote of the occasion:

'...Bright put on a head cloth and became my romantic gypsy princess. I remembered the tune instantly of course. The maids used to hum it and do a little dance while they dusted and cleaned. I thought it added the missing colour and life to the mausoleum Father liked to call his little country house, to impress his friends. The Jewish maids never hummed and danced while Father was around. Once a new maid tried to, the one who cared for me so well, and Father went into a rage and said that if she was having such a good time she didn't need to be paid for working. The maids were careful to be happy only when Father was away planning a war, or something equally joyous. I'm being facetious. But Bright had put me into a gay mood, despite the awful come down. I believe I loved her more that day than I thought possible, even before she gave me the wonderful news...'

"That's my Sunny Bright girl! I'll go up to the University and introduce myself to my new masters. Here's the rest of our marks." Kurt put his leather folder on the table, took Bright in his arms and kissed her. "Buy the things you need and I'll be back as soon as I've had a look around to see what we've gotten ourselves into."

"Still love me?"

"More than ever! You're, as you English say, a real trooper."

"No, I think I was born to be a simple working girl. I can't make much of a mess of this. Besides, it's better than spending the rest of my life behind a loom in one of those dreadful textile mills, like my mother."

"We'll make a proper home of this yet."

"And an honest woman of me?"

Kurt looked at her for a moment. Bright was serious and Kurt saw something more in her eyes than determination to make the best of a bad deal. They were dark and sensuous as usual but there was also a new light he hadn't seen before.

"Is it important to you, Sunny?"

"It will be important to our baby."

Kurt was wide eyed. "Baby?..."

"He'll need a good name as well as a good home," she said.

"We're having a baby!?"

"Yes, I'm pretty sure. Are you pleased, darling?"

Kurt laughed to keep from shouting. "God! I'm ecstatic! A baby! We'll be a real family! Oh, Sunny, of course we'll get married. When?...the baby, I mean."

"A few months yet. Seven I think. You didn't waste time, my lover."

"I'll get another job, anything. Oh, God! I'm so pleased! You've no idea. But, you've got to take it easy!" Kurt said, fussing and trying to make her sit down.

"Darling, I'm a big strong girl. I'm not ill. I'm just having a baby. Momma worked in the mill until an hour before I was born. And, she went back to work the next day. Don't worry about me, I come from good peasant stock. Now, off you go to your university and get out of my way."

"A baby! Oh, Sunny, this is the happiest day of my life!"

Kurt took Bright in his arms again and hugged her as though he would crush her then remembered the baby and put his hand on her tummy. He wanted her. He was confused about what he should do in her condition. He kissed her passionately. Bright understood and laughed and pushed him out the door.

"Out with you!"

"I'll steal a bicycle so I can get home quicker."

The door closed on Kurt still grinning like an idiot. She stood for a long time with her back to the door, a smile on her beautiful lips, glowing with happiness, touching her tummy. Then she took up the broom and swept the floor and hummed the happy peasant folk song and wondered about life.

The University of Leipzig's Catholic College was not what Kurt had expected. The students were distracted by the revolutions sweeping across Europe. The war had upset traditions and Germany was poor. The war had killed so many; in the millions the authorities said, accusing the French and English of genocide. Defeat is always hard to accept but defeat and poverty are the hardest when treaties are purposely written by the French to punish Germany and prevent her from recovering. Germany was ripe for the Communists. The students either argued constantly about the revolution or, just the opposite, saw no point in preparing for an uncertain future. To many it was more important to have fun. The fun was self destructive. The wild, low-class cabarets did well and the students came to classes when it suited them. Kurt went to the University every day on his bicycle to teach the ones who showed up and tried not to be boring in his lectures but had to keep the students from fighting when he lectured on politics. It was a confusing time. Kurt longed for the simplicity of his submarine. He would have left the University had it not been for Bright and when classes were finished each day he flew home to be with her, and her growing belly, to find some peace and sanity.

Bright was happy at first. She had the baby in her swelling womb during the day and Kurt when he came home, red in the face from riding in the cold winter air. She made the flat clean and cozy but she only put the stove on just before Kurt was to arrive so the flat would be warm and they wouldn't have to scrimp on the coal. When he found out he was a little angry but Bright said it was better to work cool and she only had to put on more clothes and usually she had to take some off because she got so hot sweeping and scrubbing everything clean.

She bought some whitewash and painted the ceiling so the little light coming in made the room brighter. He told her to use the electric light but she said it wasn't necessary and he said they were paying for it and there was no use doing the greedy matron a favour. Then Bright would tell him about her day and he would tell her about his day and all their days were shared.

On Saturdays Kurt tutored students of wealthy families for extra money or did research in the library. Sundays they went for a walk and looked at the city but it usually made them sad because the children were hungry and the people didn't smile and those who had possessions held them close. Kurt said Leipzig wasn't always like that and things would be better in the summer. On the dull days, when the snow fell in the park or it rained and everything looked shiny but cold, they talked about sunshine. Kurt told her about Norderney. Not about Anna and Norderney, just the beaches and Herr Glimpf and the café and the galliots and swimming and laying in the hot sand. They would save some money and when the holidays came they could take the train to Norddeich and the ferry to Norderney and stay at the inn.

"Are you sure you want to go?" she had asked one day as they walked in the park.

"Yes, of course! How can I show you the island if we don't?" But he didn't say that he could only go because Bright would be there to protect him.

They talked about the children they would raise but Kurt only talked mentioned marriage in vague terms, in the future. But the baby was getting bigger inside her and they both felt that soon it had to be done. But winter isn't a good time. It's a new life so spring would be best. Bright said that she and Teddy had married in the fall and it was already cold and then he went away and all she had was winter and no baby to fill the empty, cold spaces. But she and Kurt had the baby and that seemed to be enough. Talk of a wedding was less and less interesting as the winter became bleaker and the news about the failing economy of Europe and England was more depressing.

Kurt worried that he might be let go by the College because his classes were smaller and the students more difficult. The ones who remained were the political activists who liked to argue and make trouble or the louts who were too lazy to look for work. When they learned Kurt was from the old aristocracy they became hostile when he tried to reason with them, using his upper class experience as an instructive example.

The new Socialists and the old military establishment had a tenuous symbiotic relationship. Germany needed the military to keep the reins on the Communists and the military was still controlled by powerful generals like Kurt's father so the students were content to argue. Kurt was unhappy about the situation but there was nothing else to be done. He tried never to complain and each day he escaped from the classroom and returned to Bright.

One day Bright passed an old lady on the dark stairs. They were both filling their water buckets at the tap on the first floor. The old lady had never spoken to Bright before and Bright was shy about speaking German, so they usually nodded and the old woman seemed content. But that day Bright had to pass the old woman to get up the stairs unless she wanted to wait behind as the old woman struggled with the heavy pail. Bright herself was having some trouble because of her swelling belly.

"Oma," she said. "May I help you with that bucket?"

"Oh, my dear!" said the woman. "You are an angel from God."

Bright took the bucket, careful not to spill too much water, and carried it, along with her own, to the old woman's door. She couldn't see her feet properly on the dark stairs but the balance made the carrying easier.

"This bucket is too heavy for you, Oma."

"Yes, I know it is, dear. There used to be a student here who carried the bucket for me. He was such a nice, polite boy. The others? *Phuff*! just ruffians. They'd push me out of the way."

"What happened to the nice boy who helped you?" Bright asked.

"Oh, he was Jewish. Frau Schnarr put him out."

"That's too bad," Bright said. The *too bad* had many implications.

"I don't care for the Jews myself," said the old lady. "They're dirty people and can't be trusted."

Bright didn't bother to question the logic of her statement. She excused herself and went up the last flight of stairs to her flat, vowing not to tell Kurt about the old woman.

But Bright needed a friend to talk to about the baby and share the experience. She didn't complain to Kurt about being lonely, nor did Bright complain about the long days in the flat. At first she didn't go out unless Kurt went with her but she knew she had to try. She made Kurt speak German until she felt comfortable shopping. Shopping was the best part of the day even though she had little money to spend and what she did buy was rationed or expensive.

That night Kurt entered the flat wet and cold from his ride as usual. The heat and the smell of cabbage soup with garlic sausage met him at the door. It was almost dark and Bright had switched on the electric light. He went to Bright and kissed her and touched her belly then stood at the stove to warm his hands. The stove didn't draw as well as it should because there were bird's nests around the chimney pots but Frau Schnarr wouldn't have them cleaned until spring. Kurt sniffed the steam rising from the pot, then peeked in and burnt his finger.

"Serves you right," she scolded him, gently.

"And I've been punished for it," he said, sucking his finger. "Smells delicious. I could eat my books I'm so hungry."

"Should I make you more lunch?"

"No, no! They're splendid. It sharpens my awareness of life to be on the edge of hunger."

"That's called sarcasm, darling," she said, sarcastically.

"No, I didn't mean it that way at all. It's good for me to have some understanding of what the poor souls on our streets are feeling. And they don't have you to come home to."

"That's called flattery, and it's perfectly all right to do it."

"Good, then I shall. You're very beautiful."

"Even with my big belly?"

"Even more so."

"Some women still look this way after they've had the baby."

"Then I would have to reconsider."

"I promise I won't," she said.

"Good. It's settled then."

"Would you still love me even if I got fat?"

"Forever!"

"Don't say forever, darling, if you know you can't."

"I don't know about forever until I experience it. I don't know anything, except that I love you now."

"That will have to do. Come, sit down. Were the students quarrelsome today?"

"Just the usual," said Kurt. He took off his coat and hung it behind the door and pulled a chair up to the table. "The only reason they come to my lectures is to argue politics or fight. Frankly I hate the constant rancor, but the only things that keeps me going are you and the baby."

"I could never understand why men like to argue about politics," she said, as she served out the cabbage soup.

"Something to do between wars. And usually it's what starts them. I wonder if this nightmare will ever end?"

"Let's talk about the baby. Or lying on the hot sand."

"I'm sorry, Sunny. It's so much a part of my day. No wonder I'd rather think about you all the time. And how was your day?"

"Oh, the usual, I wasn't sick. I mended your good coat, again. Really Kurt, you must be more careful on that silly bicycle. You're not a little boy you know!"

"Nor a dashing flyer?..." Bright stiffened. "Sorry, that was uncalled for."

"It wasn't, but I forgive you," she said, noticing that Kurt looked contrite. "I went to the shop to get your favourite sausage. Loads of garlic. I put some in the cabbage."

"Oh, really, I hadn't noticed!"

Bright laughed. She always felt better when Kurt came home and she didn't feel lonely or afraid. "Honestly, I don't know how you can eat it. Your students must rebel."

"They do enough of that, but not because of the sausage," Kurt said, teasing. "All I can do to keep the buggers from snitching it. Snitching? Is that the word? And I certainly can't hide it."

"Can you guess who I ran into at the butcher's shop today?"

"Honestly, I couldn't," he teased in return.

"Remember that awful woman with the dachshund? She was buying a leg of mutton...for the dog! She said she wasn't a meat eater herself but the poor poochums, or whatever she called it, needed the best. That made me mad so I asked her if she had any idea how many children are hungry in this city. And do you know what she said? '*You should mind your own business and go back to Latvia or wherever you came from*'," mimicked Bright, laughing.

"Latvia?"

"Yes, I think my accent must have thrown her off."

"Your accent is charming, Sunny, but I would say it's more, *East Lithuanian*."

"Oh, you!" she said, in mock disgust and slapped his hand. "You are the fool. I must tell you, I went a wee bit over the budget today." Bright got up from the table to get the coffee pot. "I bought you some South American coffee beans. Just a handful," she said pouring the black steaming brew into Kurt's chipped mug.

"Excellent!" Kurt inhaled deeply as the aroma floated up. He had a brief flash of drinking dark coffee at his sidewalk table in the sun of Norderney, before the troubles, when all he had to think about was his disease, his failures, suicide and not being able to write. "You are the best wife I've ever had."

"You don't have me yet." She opened the cupboard. "Coffee's nothing without cake, so I also bought you a sliver of Black Forest cake."

"Oh, extravagant!"

Bright set the piece of Black Forest cake on the table and took his empty bowl away as if serving royalty.

"Say, I'm not the Chancellor of the University, yet. I think I'll leave that to our son." Bright sat down beside Kurt to watch him eat. Kurt broke the cake in two pieces and fed Bright from his fingers. She kissed his fingers and put his hand on her tummy and lower. "How is my little scholar today?"

"Lively, to say the least. Less a chancellor I'd say, than a rugby player."

"Rugby! Yes, I've heard of it. A typically British game. Barbarous behaviour! None of the finesse of football."

"Teddy had his nose broken playing rugby. I think he did it to spite his father because he thought it was a game fit only for commoners, ruffians and criminals."

"I can see why," Kurt said.

"Why what, darling?"

"Why Teddy played it."

"I know."

"I did the same thing to my father. Got beat up pretty badly some times, not playing football, but playing rough. In cabarets mostly. Had I bloodied my face at football Father would have been proud of me. No, I had to do it with drinking and whoring, pardon me for saying it."

"That's all right, darling. Might as well call it by name, if that's what it was."

"It was. But who did I really hurt in the end?"

"Yourself."

"I was still hurting myself in the Cambridge when you saved me."

"I know you were," she said.

"You said I was just lonely."

"That too."

"How is it you know so much?"

"I know from pain."

"I'm sorry, Sunny."

"Not much of an accomplishment in life, is it?"

"Let's don't."

"All right," she said.

"It's already done, isn't it?"

"Yes, I guess it is."

"That's why it was so easy to say."

"I don't want to spoil it for you."

"Should I keep my hand there?"

"If you like," she said.

"And what about you?"

"Me? Does it matter?"

"Of course it matters."

"Then, yes, please keep your hand there. I like it."

Kurt put his hand under Bright's long skirt. She smiled and relaxed. He was still giving something back, but it still wasn't an obligation. He kissed her forehead, her eyes, her nose, her mouth. And they gave something to each other. Then after a while Bright sighed and quivered a little and Kurt just kept his hand there and it felt warm and wet and nice. When Bright opened her eyes Kurt thought she was far away.

"Do you miss England very much, Sunny?"

"No, darling," she answered, honestly. "This is my home. With you and the baby. I could ask for nothing more."

Bright closed her eyes again and rested her head on Kurt's shoulder so that her warm, moist breath came slowly on his bare neck. It felt good. Then she burrowed in closer to the warm place so Kurt couldn't see her silent, happy tears. It was the moment of peace they both had been waiting a lifetime to share. Bright drifted off to a dream sleep of whiteness and softness and the feeling of her own small baby in her arms with its face pressed against her breasts and she gave it life from herself, and their world, for a moment, was perfect.

Jimmy said that Kurt Schulte wrote the next entry in the journal although it didn't look like Kurt's strong hand. The writing was different, as if the German had been under great stress or in a great deal of pain or drunk, or all of the above. I now know why it was so very difficult for Kurt and wished we could have skipped the next part.

It was late and Jimmy advised that we stop for the night. He made ready to go down to tend to my chores at Mrs. Penny's. I crawled onto the cot and pulled the thin blanket over my shoulders. It had turned cold after supper and the fire would be out before Jimmy returned.

But, as tired as I was, sleep wouldn't come. Maybe it was the strong tea we'd been drinking all day. Maybe it was the strain, not of the work, but of living the lives of these people I was coming to know, and like. I thought about a book I'd read, a novel my wife brought home from the library because it seemed to do with boats, a long, and in the beginning, difficult story called *Tidewater Tales.* The story is an epic journey through the myths and legends of gods and goddesses and literary heroes, Don Quixote and Scheherazade and Arabian nights and corrupt politicians, told by two fascinating people during the course of a final summer cruise on Chesapeake Bay. I grew to love the two people, Peter and Katherine. Katherine was pregnant and due at any moment. I wanted them to be real, especially Katherine, and I didn't want the book to end because it would mean they would cease to exist and I had to force myself to go on because I knew the end was coming.

When I did doze off I had disturbing dreams that night on Jimmy's day bed. And the bed seemed more crowded than the night before and there were spirits lurking outside the shack. They didn't move about and make noise, they just whispered about my people. Jimmy returned before dawn, built a fire and lay down on the floor with his head on the food pack. I finally fell into a troubled sleep and tried not to dream about what was coming.

The smell of fresh brewed coffee brought me around. I wasn't dreaming. Jimmy remembered a comment I had made about Kurt's special coffee gift from Bright. He understood about the coffee. While Jimmy was preparing our simple breakfast of fresh bread and jam I went outside to do my necessary, as Jimmy called it. I walked a distance from the shack and in the process I made three interesting discoveries.

In the middle of a small thicket of stunted spruce I found the remains of an officer's cap; the kind worn by British merchant sea captains. And German submarine captains. Only a scrap of the white canvas top remained, enough to identify it, but there on the band above the crumbling peak was the tarnished badge of an Imperial Navy, but which one? It had a royal crown and cockade that resembled the British roundel but also the German Navy. The cap had a tree growing up through it. The spirits were still whispering and I had a feeling the cap was there for a reason. Then, with that puzzle fresh in my mind, I discovered the Luger resting on a rock. I could make out the initials F.V.S., even though the gun was rusted and almost invisible. I searched the scrub for more clues and had the feeling of being watched.

A bald eagle perched on a rock outcrop above Jimmy's ledge seemed to be looking through me. The eagle, like the Luger, obviously belonged there but it would be a while before I was told the significance of the magnificent bird. I didn't touch the gun nor did I tell Jimmy about my conclusions when I went back to the shack. If he had found the hat and gun and left them, he did so for a reason.

Jimmy had breakfast organized when I returned, still puzzling over my discoveries; the cap I assumed was the Commander's and the gun his father's Luger. The cap and the gun fit into the story somewhere, but where? The eagle could be explained as a coincidence. Perhaps Jimmy already knew what I had found but he didn't mention it either, although he must have known I would eventually stumble over the site. The site of what event? We lingered over my coffee and Jimmy's tea, neither of us anxious to begin the next part that Jimmy knew too well, and by his mood, I suspected.

December 23, 1920: Kurt's journal entry began: '...*I was supervising the students writing an end of term paper before the Christmas break. I don't know how I knew. I just knew. The clock on the wall of the examination room said 1045. Bright called out to me. I left immediately and hurried home...'*

That morning Bright kissed Kurt goodbye at the door, tucked the canvas bag with his lunch under his arm and sent him on his way. If Bright didn't push him out, Kurt would linger at the door kissing her neck, ears and lips and touching her swelling belly until he was late for classes. She was flattered but also practical. They needed the little stipend he received from the College to survive.

"Be careful on that silly bicycle, darling. I love you," she said, and closed the door.

Bright drew down the fire and started her housework. She cleared the table and washed up using the water which had been heating on the stove while she made porridge of oats or wheat grains with pork fat, their inevitable breakfast. It was hot and filling, nutritious and cheap. Kurt liked it with a little butter floated on top and a dash of salt. Butter was hard to get and salt was also rationed out carefully but Bright felt Kurt needed a small reward each day. When the bowls and the porridge pot were cleaned out and dried and the few vegetable scraps from the evening meal put into the bucket, she set the bucket beside the door to take down to dump and refill with water. She dusted and swept their room. She cleaned the window everyday, remembering the neglected windows in the Grand Imperial Hotel. Her mother kept the windows clean, telling her little girls that they must give every bit of God's light a chance to get in.

The bed was already made. That was Kurt's job in the morning while Bright made breakfast and put up his lunch, a simple affair. A chunk of garlic sausage and a piece of dark rye bread or heavy pumpernickel wrapped in cotton. An onion, if there was one held back from the soup. A bottle of tea or coffee measured out from the breakfast ration that Kurt would drink cold with his lunch. He ate lunch secretly in the stacks at the library so he could read history books or dream about submarines. He didn't like to eat with the professors in the faculty lounge because they argued about politics and complained about the students and life in general. His fellow faculty members were old men who would die in their classrooms, if they weren't already dead in the brains.

Each morning Kurt got up two hours early to stoke the fire and make the trip to the cellar for their scuttle of coal. He would hide a lump of coal in each pocket just to spite Frau Schnarr, who waited at the landing eying each scuttle of coal as if it were gold dug from a mine. Perhaps it was. It would be more precious than gold if the winter was long and hard. Kurt felt a little guilty about the purloined coal but he had been saving pieces as a present for Bright because he suspected she was putting out the fire each day to save coal. Then Kurt would make the climb to their room, build up the fire, put on the water to heat, undress again and get back into the big bed.

Bright liked the quiet mornings best. Kurt would be cold when he returned to bed and they would snuggle down in their one luxury, the feather duvet, and she'd warm his hands and feet. Sometimes they just talked or dozed. Sometimes they made love in their special way and slept again; that deep sleep that only comes after making love when it means something. But Bright would wake up first, concerned that Kurt would be late for his class. Then she'd have to prod him out of bed and they would wrestle and usually end up in a heap on the floor laughing and giggling like children. When Bright got bigger Kurt was careful to fall out first so Bright ended up on top.

That morning, Bright, satisfied that her house was in order, dressed for going to the shops, picked up her bucket and went down the stairs. She dumped the waste water and vegetable scraps in the hole in the floor; Frau Schnarr proudly referred to the hole as her indoor toilet, cleaned out the bucket with a harsh disinfectant and started down the next flight of stairs. She would leave the bucket by the tap and fill it when she returned from shopping. She was getting big and it was harder each day to make the climb with water and her meager shopping. *I'm not as strong as mother*, she said to herself, because Bright had been pampered and she was ten years older than her mother when her mother worked in the mill and gave birth to her in the coal dust of the furnace room because she couldn't get to a hospital. The mill manager had been angry and, as soon as she could walk, sent her away with her baby wrapped in the rough sacking from cotton bales shipped from America. The kind woman who left her machine to help Bright's mother had been fired as a result. Bright was bitter about the story but her mother never was. She said she had named her baby Bright because the only rays of God's light in that black room was her baby in the glow from the fire and she thanked God for the warmth of the furnace and for her healthy baby.

Bright savoured the bitter image of her mother holding her wet baby close to the furnace for warmth, but the image of the blackness and the coal dust made Bright shiver.

Bright felt her way carefully for each step. On the second flight of stairs she met the old woman coming up with her bucket of water.

"Good morning, Oma. Can I help you with that bucket?"

"Thank you, my dear, but as I get older I get wiser. I now carry a smaller bucket and use less water."

"Are you sure I can't help?"

"You could get me an onion if you're going to the shop."

"I can do that for you. I'm just going now."

"I'd appreciate that so much. It's so very cold out today. I couldn't make it without freezing in my tracks."

"The fresh air might do you good. I can walk with you if you like."

"Oh, no, no! I'd perish. You run along."

Bright swallowed the bad taste she still carried for the old woman's comments about the Jewish student. She wanted to share their happiness. "Would you like to have dinner with us on Christmas Day?"

"Oh, my dear, I would love that so much! Christmas is lonely without my husband. Bless you, dear."

"Good. I'll be back with your onion," said Bright, cheerfully, feeling better about forgiveness.

Bright continued down the steps and didn't see the puddle of water left by the old woman's slop. She was happy again. Her life was simple and full of good feeling. She could speak some German and be comfortable and she forgave the old woman. The baby was lively and Kurt would be home early. She was thinking about the goose she had ordered from the butcher. She would buy it today and make a stuffing with onions and dried bread from the ends of the loaves she had been saving and a bread pudding and they would be happy and warm. She had accidentally found the small bottle of cognac Kurt stashed in his old sea boots. It had a red bow and a little tag with her name on it. She would put a drop in the goose and they would drink some after dinner and when the old woman had gone back to her flat they would make the coal fire hot and sit in front of the stove with the door open and pretend. No, they wouldn't have to pretend. It would be real and it would be nice...

'...*The doctor and Frau Schnarr were leaning over Bright on the first floor landing. Bright was dead. I knew before I opened the door but I'll never erase the sight. The old woman from the flat below ours waited for me further up the stairs. I believe she was in shock. Later she told me what happened. The doctor covered Bright with a heavy, coarse wool blanket, like those on the U-boats. I wondered how Frau Schnarr came into the possession of that blanket. What a stupid thing to think about* at a time like that. I asked the doctor about the baby. He shook his head. How easily a professional can shake a man's life away. It was just as well. The baby would have been too small to survive but it was a boy...'

Some time later Kurt wrote: '...Bright was dead. My baby boy was dead. I was dead from that moment because there was no reason to be alive. It wasn't a difficult thing to do after all. It's absurd really. I'd worked at it so hard all those years, but that day I just stopped being and entered another world where all the same players existed as ghosts, whose only purpose in death is to torment me more than they had in life. But they didn't know I couldn't be touched. Bright's gone and that's all I know, or care to know. How I function day by day is, to me, a mystery...'

Kurt didn't date the last entry. Dates were no longer important. He continued teaching and moved to another lodging. There were no further entries in the journal and several blank pages. The next book, the blue journal, began with an entry for 1933. A gap of thirteen years.

Pius' scribbler log had only a few entries during that same time period to do with fishing and the new schooner. One entry for 1929 was significant but didn't give details. I had to fill those in later. Another entry for 1931 was the beginning of a story Jimmy told me in detail and I wrote it down. Then we discussed Kurt's last entry in his journal and the time gap. Jimmy said that Kurt mentioned some things about life in Germany between 1920 and 1933 but he said it was mostly things to do with their governments and the problems about money. Jimmy didn't understand much about recessions and depressions. Even though it was still early in the day, neither of us felt like going on with the blue ledger. Bright's death had affected me more than I realized. Later, alone in the hills, looking out at the ocean, I found myself wondering about life and losing.

FOGO HARBOUR

July 6, 1929: Pius' log entry for that date: '...*The coastal boat come today with the engine we'd ordered. We got her aboard and opened her up and isn't she a dandy. Red painted and shines like a new penny. We'll put her down below tomorrow. Gus has some understanding of engines. He's the lad to get her going...*'

Pius had been planning for that day since he took possession of the *Liza & Mary Humby* from Rhulands of Lunenburg in 1920. Uncle Saul and Pius had many heated discussions about the engine but Pius was steadfast, determined to have an engine, looking forward to the arrival like a child waiting for Christmas morning. There was a great deal of excitement in Fogo, the event had been anticipated by all the villagers, except Uncle Saul of course, and they came streaming down to the wharf when the whistle sounded in the offing. More arrived when the church bell rang. The heavy packing crate was swung from the coastal boat across the wharf to the deck of the schooner. Then came the crates of parts and spares, exhaust pipes and fuel tanks and even drums of diesel fuel.

Jimmy White, nine years old and already fighting to be the leader of his playmates, lead the assault on the packing crates. There were no injuries or mishaps even though the children did their best to get in the way and cause the usual chaos. It was an occasion for a 'time' with dancing and a drop of rum and much speculation about hull speed and power, noise and fish to be caught. Only Uncle Saul remained aloof.

In preparation, weeks in advance, the tall spars had been cut down and a wheelhouse built on the stern. The engine beds were bolted home to the massive timbers, so when the engine arrived it had only to be set in place, connected to the shaft coupling through the hole they would bore, and the vital parts and accessories installed.

The next morning the schooner was put broadside to the shore on a high tide. When the tide went down the men bored the shaft log hole through her deadwood at the stern. It was a difficult and arduous task but there were many hands to take a turn on the boring tool and many eyes to sight the line up and as many opinions. When the shaft hole was bored and the log set, the shaft and propeller were run in before the tide returned.

The following morning Gus was down in the engine room getting ready before Pius had his morning tea. Gus was a natural with engines. He tinkered happily with the small but mighty 'make'n'break' engines that powered the dories and trap skiffs. They were simple enough to operate but could be cranky if drowned by salt water too often. Gus had a way with recalcitrant engines but the big four cylinder Lathrop diesel would become his passion. His wife said Gus was never clean again from the day the blessed thing arrived. Gus said she was only jealous. Perhaps she had good reason.

Uncle Saul stayed away while the installation took place. Sulking, biding his time, watching from the kitchen window. He drank two pots of tea before his curiosity got the better of him. Finally he put on his coat and hat and strolled to the wharf to have a pipe and visit with some of the old boys supervising the operation.

When the moment came for the initial test firing Uncle Saul was the first face over the hatch combing. Pius looked up, grease smeared, and grinned at him. Uncle Saul grunted and puffed his pipe trying to make more smoke than the diesel did as it caught and sputtered to life, shaking the schooner and sending great gouts of white smoke up the stack. When the engine settled down to a slow rumble and the exhaust cleared, the effect wasn't unpleasant. But Uncle Saul wouldn't relent. He set his jaw and hollered down at Pius: "You've spoilt your boat, Pius!"

"Ah, now Saul, engines' got to come!" Pius shouted back.

"You'll not catch a fish racketing about like that!"

"My son, we can chase them fish all over creation now!"

Pius climbed up to the deck to get away from the racket and leave Gus to his tinkering with the settings.

"Shameful 'tis!" persisted Uncle Saul. "You've cut down your sticks so she can't sail proper and put a house onto'er besides, as if we're a bunch of old ladies!"

"Then you'll come down the Labrador with me this season just the same?"

"Yis b'ye," Uncle Saul said, grudgingly. "I'll come…to keep you from more foolishness!"

"Then you'll see I'm right about the engine."

"And what in creation will we do when that infernal machine breaks down?…and us without a proper rig to see'er home!?"

"She'll still sail b'ye," said Pius. "Not as handy perhaps," he admitted, "but she'll sail if she's got to. Besides she's a diesel girl now. Nothing in the world can hurt one o'them."

"Hold your tongue, Pius Humby!" Uncle Saul cautioned.

"I didn't mean to say…"

"Don't tempt Him to show you who's Master over all. You mind that big ship what drove onto iceberg not two hundred leagues from here before the war?"

"All right, Saul…"

"And another thing!" Uncle Saul continued, "Buddy on the radio said England's got herself into an awful fix. Starving some is. Can you imagine that!? And they says if it happens here the price of fish is going to fall so we won't even bother to catch a one."

"People got to eat. The fish has always seen us through."

"'Tis different this time. Buddy says the merchants are too busy looking after they selves to worry about the rest of us. And according to anything I know, if we don't sell our fish how in Jasus we going to pay Buddy for that engine!?"

"Won't happen, Saul."

"Never say never, Pius. And another thing!...." Uncle Saul was determined to get it all said. "Buddy on radio says them Germans is still mad with us, and stirring up trouble and it looks like the world's going to hell in a hand basket, again."

"Another war," said Pius, glancing to the east.

"Them Germans has a score to settle is my guess."

"I won't say you're wrong, but I'll not be a part of it." Pius watched the engine heat rolling out of the stack. He didn't want to think about the troubles over the horizon. Their rock of an island was harsh and cruel enough but it seemed remote and safe from the turmoil in Europe.

The diesel worked as Pius hoped and they were able to make good runs to Labrador in the late summer and fall, though the price was always lower when the times were good. They were also able to try a hand at catching herring with a big seine net. Gus rigged up a derrick and powered it from the new engine so they could lift the big nets aboard. It appeared Pius had been right and prosperity was theirs for the taking.

Even Uncle Saul had to admit that fishing was easier, although he missed the satisfying and often thrilling runs from Labrador under sail with the holds full and the lee scuppers running green water, the sails taut and the wheel alive. Most of all they missed the silence when the only smoke blowing about was from the men's pipes as they sat on the high side of the cabin to talk about their season and home. All that changed. But if it meant more food on the table and a better life for their families, then it was a good thing. And it was a good thing for a year or so. In the winter of 1931 the Depression caught up with Fogo Harbour.

January 15, 1931: Outside the snugged-down houses, a bitter northwest wind drove the first real snow in wind devils and whirling eddies, fingers of frost finding every gap and crack. The coastal boat had been hove-to off the harbour, the skipper jogging his small steam boat into the seas since dawn waiting for a chance to run in. A heavy swell was running into the harbour and a cross wind threatened to push him ashore. The wind dropped off a little before noon and Captain Perkins nosed in past the Head, lined up the entrance and put his hard pressed ship alongside the wharf; 'a nice piece'o work', Saul and the cronies would say. More prudent skippers would have refused but it was only a routine landing for the coastal boat Skipper. If he shied away from every difficult landing half the outports on the northeast coast would never see the coastal boat from early fall until late spring.

Pius, the study of a troubled man, was sitting at the kitchen table with his own ship's documents in front of him when the church bell began to toll. He was placed so he could see the harbour, the wharf and the entrance. A plume of steam rose up from the ship's whistle on the black stack, to be blown down wind in shreds before he could hear the muted blast. He looked at the documents again and seemed resigned.

"Coastal boat's comin' in, finally," he said to Mary, who was stirring a single pot on the cook stove.

"And none too soon, my dear," she said.

The fishing had been good that summer but when they tried to sell their season in St. John's the buyers offered next to nothing for prime salt because they couldn't sell what they already had to Europe. Pius brought the dried fish home and divided it among the families of the village. There was no money to buy supplies and the men were hoping Pius could arrange another extension of credit with the merchant Ashcroft in Twillingate. The same thing was happening all over the world. It was heartbreaking to see the fish coming over the side knowing it was work in vain, but it was more heartbreaking to see the faces of the women on the wharf when they turned away, loaded down with salt fish, but no flour, sugar, molasses or the dry goods they needed to make clothes for their families. The men would get used to a ration on tobacco and only the odd bottle of sprits to get through the winter.

The Depression caused panic in the markets and the flow of goods stopped unless cash was on the table. Payments for the engine made Pius' problem more acute. He couldn't turn to the land as the other men did when times were hard. He was beholden to a different master; the faceless counting house ledger. The ledger had a bottom line that had to be covered to satisfy a supplier in England. Pius Humby was just a name on the wrong side of the ledger.

"The flour's almost gone, and the molasses is used up. Don't know what we'd do if they was late sure," sighed Mary.

It was time to tell his wife. "Mary, dear...Ashcroft's cut off our credit. Won't be a thing on the coastal boat for we this time."

Mary was silent for a long while staring out the back window that looked over the long grass and tottering fences to the hill were they picked berries in season. She needed sugar to make their winter jam but she had known, by intuition, and the way the men avoided talk of a future, that there were hard times ahead if they could not sell their fish. "And how can that be, my dear? He knows we got to eat on this island."

"That's not his concern now is it?"

"We can't perform miracles."

"He wants cash. He wouldn't take next year's catch against the bill."

"If you'd listened to Uncle Saul…" Mary began. She didn't need to finish the statement.

"He's a bit of a nuisance sometimes, with his cranky ways, still."

"But, he's usually right."

"Aye, I give him that." Pius noticed a familiar figure jump down to the wharf before the ship was tied up. The tall, lean figure, carrying a sea bag and wearing a navy duffel coat, doubled up the path toward the house. "Hello!" said Pius. "It's Harry home!"

"Oh, and I've not a decent thing to feed him."

"He'll have to shift the same as we."

The front door burst open with Harry's usual enthusiasm. Harry, handsome with Pius' strong features, but looking younger than his twenty-two years, put down his duffel bag and gave his mother a hug.

"Welcome home, son! You're a grand surprise!"

"Hello, Harry, lad! Surprised we are," began Pius.

Harry's grin faded quickly. "Hello, Father. I wanted to surprise you, but…" Harry seemed troubled as he scanned the faces of his parents. "There's some men come along on coastal boat. I heard them talking about the schooner. Father?" Pius turned to the window.

Mary searched Pius' profile for an explanation. "Pius? What's Harry saying?"

"Can they do it?" asked Harry.

Pius sighed and sagged visibly. He didn't have to pretend any longer. "Aye, they've a right to'er."

"You can't let them have'er, Father! How will you fish?"

"Huh, it's no good to fish, son. Can't sell a one."

"How will we eat?" asked Mary, her concerns more immediate.

Pius looked out the window. His crewmen's houses, barely visible in the blowing snow, seemed to be huddled for mutual security around the harbour. Each kitchen held a stove burning rationed wood and a family gathered near it with a bleak winter to face. "I thought the engine was the right thing. The modem way..." he said, to the window. The lace curtains moved with the wind as if to answer. A loose pane rattled. He'd meant to put a run of putty on that pane before winter. A one pound gub of putty cost two pennies. "We'd done better to leave the blessed thing ashore!"

"Then give them back the engine!" said Mary.

"They don't claim the engine, Mary. The ship was the guarantee we'd pay."

"Surely a schooner's worth more!" said Harry.

"I was too clever b'ye. Too clever by half. That wonderful big engine, and all that fancy gear, cost twice what we paid Rhulands for the hull eleven years ago..."

Pius walked over to Harry who was still standing by the door.

"I'm sorry to bring you bad news, Father."

Pius took his hand and shook it the way he should have been able to shake it when Harry first came through the door.

"Nonsense. We're glad to see you. You didn't bring the bad news son. It came in the box with the engine when the cursed thing arrived. We might as well have spat on'er and called'er names. Now we're for it."

"What are we going to do?" wondered Mary.

Pius returned to the window and looked down at the wharf where his ship moved against her lines as a gust of wind caught her rigging. He could see a knot of strangers on the wharf talking to Uncle Saul.

"A deal's a deal," he said, looking for his ship again. She wasn't there. A stronger gust whirled a cloud of snow between them and for a moment the ship vanished. He would have to get used to not seeing her first thing in the morning and last thing at night. In that moment he felt the stab of pain and realized how much he loved the boat. "We got to pay up. Harry...best go down and ask those men up for tea. They'll be perishing on the wharf in this wind. Mother, we'll serve out what we can."

"We've little enough for ourselves," Mary protested.

"All the same, those men have come a long ways."

"I'll go to Clara," said Mary.

"Clara will understand."

Mary moved the big kettle to the hot spot on the stove. She gave the pot a stir and took her shawl from the peg behind the door. Pius watched her go out and the pain increased.

"It's hardest on the women, son. They have to wait by while we men prove ourselves foolish, and then they got to make out of it what they can."

"Is there nothing to be done?" asked Harry.

"Yes, go down and ask those men to tea."

"Are you sure, Father?"

"Go on, son," he said, gently. "'Tis no fault of theirs."

Harry left his sea bag beside the door and went out. Uncle Saul came in before he could close the door. He and Pius looked at each other. Uncle Saul wasn't saying, *I told you so*. It was time for supporting a friend.

Pius took down the bottle of rum from the top shelf of the pantry and set it on the table with a thump of defiance. Uncle Saul sat down at the table, fired up his pipe with a brand from the stove, folded his hands and watched out the window with Pius as Harry approached the knot of strangers huddled near the schooner.

The coastal boat finished unloading the few supplies for the independent fishermen and was already backing away from the wharf. Harry spoke to the men and led them up the wharf to the path. The wind was easing off. *They'll want to be away before dark*, thought Pius, watching the small procession.

Later, when the schooner rounded the headland and disappeared from sight into the evening gloom, Pius stood alone for a long time holding the Humby flag and his sextant, all that remained to him of his beloved schooner. When he trudged up the path toward home curtains moved in the houses as he passed. The village was watching but there were no kind words to ease the growing pain. He had let their schooner sail away. The old *Sarah B.* had gone down in the Strait with five of her crew two years before. Now the *Liza & Mary* was gone as well. The loss was heavy on Pius' shoulders and he hunched over, drawing further into himself.

LEIPZIG

February 7, 1933: '...*Willie came down on the train to today. It has been a long time and I was glad to see him. I hadn't realized what a recluse I have become until he prodded me to go out to a cabaret and have some fun. Later, after Willie left, I went out, for Willie's sake. I was shocked at what I saw on the streets of Leipzig. I had only read in the papers about the youth gangs and the fanaticism. I can imagine it is ten times worse in Berlin. Still, it was good to get out. I even brought home a souvenir. She's asleep on the sofa as I write this. I blame it on the bad brandy and too much Bock. Time to make some notes about myself. I have been so involved with the novel. No, that's not true. I didn't want to know what I did from day to day because I couldn't face knowing I was only living through the story. Someone else's life. It is almost finished...*'

Kurt and Willie set up the chess board close to the fireplace. They talked about the weather and the crisis in German politics. The winter was as cold as the political turmoil in Germany was hot. Willie gave his opinion of their future; the National Socialists had seized power and the Depression was deepening. Adolf Hitler was using Germany's economic chaos and resentment of the Treaty to stir up the rabble. And of his own brother? He said Kurt was an island of self denial. *'And look at this place!'* The small flat was decorated with untidy heaps of books and the manuscript laid out on the table. What furniture there was existed to hold books. What couldn't be stacked on the furniture collected on the floor with aisles for passage. Kurt ate, when he cooked, from an ottoman in front of the fire most evenings, unless he went out to drink cheap beer with some ruffians in a local pub. It was obvious to Willie that Kurt entertained himself at home with books and brandy. The empty brandy bottles were gathered up only when they began to crowd the manuscript for space on the table.

Willie still looked trim in his uniform...He was a major now...but the cane was always close at hand. He was concerned about Kurt's slovenly appearance, his greying unkempt hair and his thickening middle. Kurt had aged, but not well. He looked ten years older than Willie. They sat close to the fire and listened to the wind and drank their brandy and played a distracted game of chess, piecing together their lives.

"I can't remember when it was so cold," said Willie, holding his hands to the fire, but declining a rug for his legs.

"They say it's bad everywhere this year," replied Kurt.

"It's your move," said Willie. "I can feel it in my leg, when it's cold. It's worse when it's cold and damp. Germany's too damp."

"Hmm, shall I build up the fire?" Kurt asked, and moved his queen's knight.

"Sure you want to do that?"

"Build up the fire?"

"Move your knight. I take your queen, and...check."

"Oh! Foolish!" said Kurt. "I'm not concentrating."

"Then I won't take your queen."

"Where's your killer instinct? You never let me get away with stupid moves."

"You seldom made stupid moves."

"Willie, dear brother, Willie, when have you ever known me to make a good move, in life?" He returned the knight to block for the queen and pretended to ponder another move.

"Don't let yourself get depressed. In times like these we need all the inner strength we can muster."

"Willie, you're becoming a philosopher."

"It's just a simple idea, strength. Armies thrive on it. But an army is only as strong as its weakest soldiers. They must have inner strength. You get your strength from bottles."

"Not when I had Bright. She was my strength. I was nothing before and have been nothing since."

"Kurt..."

"She's not here anymore, you know," Kurt said absently, gazing at the fire.

"You shouldn't."

"I look for her, sometimes. I look very hard but she's not here."

Kurt finally made a move and Willie immediately took a pawn. Kurt shrugged and stared at the fire. "If she was here the place wouldn't look like this," he said gesturing around the chaotic room. "Anna was chaos."

"It's still your move."

"I look for Sunny and find Anna...Funny, huh? But I never see her, just a feeling, old boy. Sunny's dead but Anna's the ghost. Never Bright. Only Anna."

"Kurt, did Anna really exist?"

"I don't know. I don't know...but what does it matter? She torments me. That's real. She seldom gives me rest, even though I never see her." Kurt picked up a chess piece. "Anna got me through the war. Did you know that? How could I be concerned about dying when she tore my spirit apart every moment? Bright picked up the pieces and put me back together. But, like old Humpty Dumpty, I fell apart again." He dropped the chess piece, scattering the pawns as if a bomb had been dropped in their midst.

"Humpty Dumpty?" quizzed Willie. "That infernal British nursery rhyme," he said, hoping to get Kurt on a different track.

"Old German nursery rhyme. Humpelken-Pumpleken. Eggs and kings, horses and men. Fantasy. Give me the harsh realities of Grimm!"

"You hated Grimm," said Willie, remembering their childhood stories.

Kurt wasn't listening. "The Brits are a puzzle I shall never fathom. They're so tradition bound and sentimental. It's a wonder their little island survives at all."

"Because they're too stubborn to know when they're beaten," said Willie.

"Father must be part English then," said Kurt, finally broaching the subject they had both avoided. "He's like a huge rock in the road. Won't be moved, so you have to go around."

"Father's not as hard and unmoving as you might think. Proud, yes, to a fault. But I tell you, his hardness is just a shield."

"Which nothing can crack," said Kurt, replaying the argument.

"Don't be too sure. You should go back."

"He threw me out! And Bright! She'd be alive! I had a son!" *Was it that long ago?*

"You left because of your own stupid pride!"

"His prejudice!!"

"His love for Germany!"

"His hatred for people he knows only as servants and peddlers!"

"I'm truly sorry about, Bright, but you can't change history," said Willie, trying to soften the tone.

"You can learn from it! You learn chess by not making the same stupid moves. But we're not talking about dumb figures on a board!" Kurt swept the board clear of pieces.

Willie sat back and looked at the classic figures scattered across the floor. Kurt's queen lay in the glowing embers of the fire but Kurt made no move to save her. His queen burst into flames. Willie sensed a crisis and tried to change the course of the discussion again. "Kurt, please, let's not argue. I understand how you feel about Bright, and the baby."

"No! You don't understand. You have a wife and children, someone real to hold and to love. I have a nightmare in which two women battle to possess me...and always the wrong one wins."

"Anna?"

"How should I know!?" shouted Kurt.

Willie watched Kurt's face for a sign; an answer to his question. There was none. He was worried about Kurt. Bright's death was a tragedy but Kurt had seemed numb to it. Willie thought Anna was imaginary, but she had been a disease to be treated. Now Willie wasn't sure. He watched Kurt pour brandy into their glasses.

"Herr Hitler's taking Germany on a dangerous course," said Kurt, as if the previous conversation hadn't taken place.

Willie, alerted to a new danger, cautioned, "Don't come out against the National Socialists if you value your position at the University. Father thinks the Chancellor can be managed because he needs us. He only needs us because he needs our money, and the generals' influence with the Army, but he's no fool."

"Father was wrong, you are a diplomat."

"Fair warning, Kurt. Hitler could just as easily call himself a pure Socialist, emulate the Bolsheviks and seize what he needs. And the Brownshirts won't tolerate intellectuals getting in the way of their social programs. He has a vision for Germany, regardless of what we think of him, and he might be right, for the times...the Devil we know? Who else is going to resist the Communists?"

"Willie, not you too?"

"I'm a realist. You've been buried in these books and your own misery too long. Look around you. Germany was dying from a cancer inside before Hitler arrived in Munich. Listen to his damned speeches! He gives the masses a sense of their own worth."

"Hysteria," said Kurt.

"Yes, I admit he's dangerous, but the people love him."

"He'll lead us into another war."

"Probably," admitted Willie.

"And you approve?"

"Of course not. But Father thinks it's inevitable."

"Then it's unavoidable," reasoned Kurt. "The old boys get together and say the right things, rattle their sabers, and another spark sends us marching across Belgium, again."

"Poor Belgium. But this time it'll be bigger than the trenches of Western Europe or the colonial skirmishes in Africa."

"Germany can't afford another war. The world can't afford another war!"

"Once a tree is cut it has to fall," said Willie.

"And when all the trees are gone?"

"Don't write against Hitler." Willie watched Kurt's expression trying to fathom which way Kurt would fall. Kurt turned to the fire.

"I'm writing fiction, that's all."

"Come home and make peace with Father, for Mother's sake. She misses you terribly." Kurt made a sound like a fart. Willie ignored the comment. "Father won't let her mention your name. His pride, not his real feelings. I'm sure of it," Willie said. He looked when Kurt turned for a moment, watching his eyes, looking for a sign that Kurt would relent but he turned away. "He's dying inside, Kurt..."

Kurt stopped staring into the fire. There was some expression in his eyes finally, but Willie couldn't read it. After a long moment Kurt drank off his brandy and smashed the glass on the hearth. Willie knew the stone wall was still standing.

"I must be going. I have an appointment at the Ministry in the morning. I can get the last train if I hurry." Willie put on his coat and hat, muffler and gloves and took his cane from the table by the fire. He looked around Kurt's dusty, book covered room. "You should get out more. This room is stifling."

"I'm sorry it offends you, but I'm used to humble surroundings."

"I didn't mean that. I mean, go out. Have some fun. Your soul is stifled. Have an adventure. Have a woman for, God's sake!"

"The whores? Even whores won't stay long with a dead man."

Willie realized further discussion was pointless. He kissed Kurt on both cheeks and opened the door. Kurt just stared at the fire. He saluted Kurt with his cane and closed the door softly.

Kurt surveyed his room, really seeing it for the first time. He poured brandy into Willie's glass and drank it off. Later he put on his coat and slipped into the dangerous night.

In the square a few blocks from Kurt's section, a Hitler Youth squad marched to a ragged brass band, brandishing torches and red and black swastika flags. Another of the endless torchlight parades. Kurt held back in the shadows to watch them march by stepping high in the peculiar exaggerated step intended to instill fear in the opposition. Another demonstration of blind acceptance of Hitler's speeches shouted in spasms of indignation. Another declaration of his venomous hysteria repeated to the faithful in Leipzig by a young zealot; a disciple with blue eyes and pimples, a student in his class. Kurt shivered but not from the cold wind blowing the flags and the torches dangerously close to the people on the sidewalks. How could it have happened? *How did the man get this far?* he asked himself.

A student rushed from the crowd and grabbed a Nazi flag, a ragged agitator, but at least it was a protest. Other Communist students came to his aid. The Hitler Youths beat the young men with their flags and fists and boots. One boy was left near death and no one went to his aid for fear of being attacked. Germans attacking Germans. *What will it come to?* he wondered. He knew about the problems of the Jews, and understood the hatred, intellectually, but he experienced real fear in the callous way the Hitler Youths beat the students and left them bleeding in the gutter. Although they showed the hatred in their blue eyes their faces were impassive. There was no logic to explain the beating. They tried to kill the boy who, but for an ideology, could have been one of them. Helpless to intervene, Kurt turned away in disgust.

In another section of the square a large, noisy crowd circled a blazing fire. Kurt pushed his way through the press, looking into faces and eyes. The people on the periphery weren't cheering or shouting, only watching. The cheering came from the inner circle. A shouting mob encouraged students wearing swastika arm bands, heaping cartloads of books onto the bonfire. Killing their history. Burning their culture. Hitler demanded a New Germany and the children were delivering it to the Chancellor with fire. A youth glared at Kurt, accusing him for not cheering. The boy was no more than sixteen but in that face, those eyes, Kurt saw the future. He turned away again and melted into the crowd fearing the persecutions would soon begin.

On a back street, away from the bands and the fires, the flags and the cheering, he stopped beside a lamp post to light a cigarette. The band could still be heard, and the glare of the flames could be seen on the low clouds above the roof tops of the old city. The wind blew the cigarette smoke away before he could savour the effect. He wished a wind could blow the growing fear away as easily. Willie was right, it was going to be bigger than tribal resentment or boarder issues, Europe in flux, realigning it's ethnic origins. No, this was going to be Germany's rage against the world to disguise a desire to control and punish a larger enemy. Bigger than anything the world had seen. How could it happen? How could it be stopped? He knew it wouldn't stop until the several torments left from the last indecisive war were erased and the powerful men who order nations to war had died out. He crushed the half smoked cigarette under his foot and walked on.

A terrified boy ran out of the darkness toward him. Other boys were throwing rocks. Kurt could see the terror in the dark eyes but the eyes didn't look to Kurt for help. They didn't expect help from an Aryan. The pursuers rushed by Kurt intent upon their game. They weren't ruffians or hooligans. They were school boys in uniforms from good Christian families who might have caught the boy if they hadn't stopped to pick up more rocks. The Jewish boy hurled himself over a high stone wall and escaped.

"Jew boy!!"

"Kill the Kike!!" yelled another.

"Pig shit eater!!" screamed a third.

"Get away from here you little swine!!" Kurt yelled without thinking. The boys stopped, startled by Kurt's outburst. They eyed Kurt with suspicion but backed away when he advanced on them, then turned and fled.

"Jew lover!! We'll get you!!" a boy yelled over his shoulder.

And they were gone into the darkness, around a corner, running toward the square and the fires. Kurt pulled up his collar and faded into the shadows. There was danger for him in the side streets. The boys might return with a gang of Hitler Youths so Kurt became a fugitive in his own city. He would stay away from the fires and the rallies, heeding Willie's advice. He turned another comer and walked toward the part of town where the other students congregated in drinking halls and didn't throw stones or wave flags or burn books. They didn't care about flags or books. They were anarchists without a cause.

The cabaret was crowded and hot and dense with smoke. The music was brassy and decadent. American jazz blasted out by a brassy orchestra, the song sung badly by a brassy transvestite singer. The dancers bumped together in the middle of the room, a lurching gyration that looked tribal and ancient and anarchistic, and somehow innocent compared to the scene in the square a few blocks away. The transvestite was too obvious to be taken seriously and the music too loud to be enjoyed. The drinks were watered down but Kurt was looking for sanctuary, not satisfaction and the chaos was reassuring. It was like a constant depth charge attack, always dangerous but not yet deadly.

He recognized a few of the faces twisted into painfully silly grins by too much booze. The irregulars in class were regulars at the cabarets when they should be home preparing for their exams. And why not? What was there to prepare for in a Germany intent on self destruction? These young people, staggering about in a frenzy, probably understood the situation. They were too young for the Great War and therefore survived. But now the world was on a downhill slide to another war and they were in the path of the Juggernaut, a ritual of India. The trick was to jump out of the way at the last moment. It was more dangerous that way. More exciting. They were, after all, Germans, not Hindus. Living on the brink and not caring was all they had to prove that they were alive.

Kurt remained in the safety of the shadows sipping a stale, warm beer. On the balcony above he could hear the laughter and the rude talk, jarring and disjointed, youthful energy wasted. He was no one to judge the follies of the young. He smoked another cigarette, content to be assaulted by the sights and sounds, until he saw her.

She was too young, but she had the same hair. He stopped beside her table and stared. She was too made up and cheaply flashy, like her friends, but there was a familiar look about her, in spite of the latest fashion. They called themselves 'flappers', an artless American invention imported to make life look different from the reality of Germany and it was very effective, if not very attractive. She wasn't the only woman who assumed the *look*, but she was the only one with a henna halo around her fragile, pale features.

The girl smoked a cigarette in a holder, holding the device in that peculiar way at the ends of her painted fingers so that the smoke rose up as an extension of her bare arm until a gyration from a nearby dancer disrupted the column. The girl's male companions stopped talking when the girl turned to look up at Kurt. She smiled at Kurt as if recognizing an old friend. Kurt's vision blurred when his heart contracted, *or was it his stomach?* and his body didn't know how to react and he felt faint but he'd been in action before and the danger was acceptable.

"Hello, Opa," she said sweetly but it was intended as an insult. "Out rather late aren't you...Opa?" She drew out the word for emphasis, casting her eyes upwards, coy or innocent.

Her companions laughed and cheered. Two dancers came over and then other friends and soon a crowd formed a wall of bodies around Kurt.

"Isn't it past your bedtime, Opa?" she asked, and this time the *Opa* was a challenge not an insult. "Or are you looking for something to help you sleep?"

The Wall laughed and surged and he heard *Opa* repeated and carried around as if it was the newest thing that week and they wanted more. Anna would have taunted him that way. Her eyes drew him closer and he could feel the sweat...*The depth charges were coming closer. He had to keep up appearances for the crew so they wouldn't lose heart. He tried to appear calm and then Anna put fear to flight and he laughed at death...*

"I seldom sleep, but I am looking for nourishment."

"You see something, tasty?" she asked, and stood up to show Kurt the figure, which was still young and firm and not yet spoiled by drinking the bad beer and not enough food.

If the Wall was laughing he could hear only his own heart and the waves pounding in the distance when the North Sea retreated beyond the sands. Kurt became light headed and wavered and the girl looked concerned.

"Give Opa a chair and something to drink."

Someone guided Kurt to a chair and a glass was in his hand, then the harsh liquor was going down his throat. The Wall curved in to watch and hear.

"What's happening to our beautiful blue-eyed children?" asked Kurt, when the fog cleared, watching the tribe dancing beyond the Wall and hearing the depth charges.

"Life," she said, and mussed Kurt's hair, letting her hand rest on the inside of his thigh as she leaned closer so he could hear her over the crashing of the cymbals and the machine guns. "What else is there?"

Kurt took another drink of the burning liquor. "I knew you once. Still wild and dangerous."

"Not me, Opa," she said, laughing and smoking but not inhaling. "I've just been born. And tonight we might all die." She took a drink of Kurt's liquor and held the glass up for the blessing of the Wall. "To our imminent deaths!" she shouted. "To die laughing, singing, fucking...!!"

The Wall cheered and undulated and drank anything available and dissolved onto the dance floor to gyrate and grind against whatever moving body was close. They didn't care if their beautiful companion picked up a handsome old man. He was a nice old man and she needed experience and so did they, so they tried to pull the dress off the transvestite singer.

"Don't try to shock me child. I've seen too much," Kurt said over the screams of the singer, although he knew he hadn't seen anything very interesting except death. Some of it by his own hand and that gave him license.

"We don't care," she laughed. "We don't want to see anything!"

"You're absolutely right!" Kurt understood but he thought her use of *we* was interesting. She had no identity of her own and if they were going down they were going down together. It was a strange but reassuring type of loyalty. Maybe there was still hope. Maybe, when the ardent, fanatical, burning Youth squads outside were killing themselves off, these anarchists, these nihilist survivors, like rats and cockroaches, would still be around to sort out the pieces. Maybe they were more clever than they imagined. They would not want to know about this new responsibility to set the world right in the aftermath. The girl pulled Kurt to his feet and onto the dance floor and the anarchists cheered their new leader.

"There's nothing," she said in his ear. "So let's dance and have fun and maybe we'll fuck...if you live. Okay!?"

Kurt had never heard the American slang expression, 'okay' but he got the message and laughed and they danced into the centre of their tribe and Kurt was initiated, accepted as if swallowed up by a raging sea. He had always been a Nihilist at heart.

Later that night, with the storm tearing at the casement windows, Kurt worked over his manuscript, writing with an intensity he seldom experienced. Their wild lovemaking, though fierce for different reasons, had left Kurt on an emotional plateau fuelled by intellectual energy. The fire had gone out some time in the night but he didn't notice. Pages of the manuscript grew in an untidy pile, while in the background, the girl slept peacefully, in a world of her own.

FOGO ISLAND

January 3, 1933: By the miracle of radio the people of Fogo Harbour were aware of the events unfolding in Europe, still safely at a distance, the wide ocean a temporary defense, but the weather was just as bad and they were just as desperate. Hitler had not yet come to power but the legions of his followers were on the move as the rhetoric heated up. It was only a matter of time before the cauldron boiled over. Pius and Uncle Saul discussed the implications but in the face of their own problems, Herr Hitler and his Storm Troopers and their consequences for the world would have to wait. The Atlantic was in full gale and mountainous waves crashed on the guardian rocks. The swell carried into the harbour and surged around the wharf, but there was no schooner tied in for the winter. The schooner was gone, not lost to the wild seas, but a victim of the Great Depression. The village huddled down, put its back to the wind and the hungry families gathered near their dying radios and rationed wood fires to dream of better days.

Several homes around the harbour were missing a man that night. Pius had called a meeting in the big net shed near the wharf. A light burned in the window and sooty black smoke from crackling, tar-soaked hemp raced up the chimney and vanished downwind.

Pius, Uncle Saul, Harry, Alf and Gus, and twenty other fishermen gathered around the big stove discussing the latest news from the BBC about events in Europe and the grinding Depression. Gus opened the door of the stove and threw in more tarred hemp. It was all that remained of the *Liza & Mary* from her last refit before she was taken away. The roaring fire cast a reddish hue on sullen wind-burned faces. The storm raging against their stronghold piped up another notch. The old store shook to a higher gust and the mood deepened. Gus kicked the stove door closed.

It had been two lean years since the schooner was taken. The fishermen fished with their small boats and tended gardens, but both fish and gardens failed to keep their families from the pinch of living on the margins. They were wearing out. Bodies could be replaced by having babies but the goods from the outside world had stopped flowing and along with the deprivation came the self doubt. Pius held up a rationed bottle of rum. Most looked away and Pius knew the gulf was wide. He was their leader, and he had failed them.

"Well, b'yes," Pius said, searching familiar faces for an ally, "we've been shipmates these many years and you won't share a bottle with me!?"

A fisherman spoke up. "'Tis not a time for celebrating, Pius."

"Oh, aye," said Pius, "I've not asked you here for that. Now come on…what about you, Alf? Have a drink with me?"

"We don't mean to spite you, Pius. You've been a good friend, and a good Skipper," replied Alf. The unspoken was implied.

Pius held the bottle out again. "Aye, I know what you're thinking. It's the schooner we've got to talk about."

Alf accepted the bottle because Pius was still their leader as well as the Skipper. He took a small sip and passed the bottle to the fisherman beside him.

"We know you meant well, Pius," said the fisherman, "but my dear man, we've fallen on hard times because of this foolishness about engines and the like." He took a small drink and passed the bottle to Gus.

"How are we to feed our babies?" asked Gus, whose missus was pregnant again. Gus took a drink and passed the bottle to the next man.

"Hard work, Gus," answered Pius. "Hard work and more hard work. Harder work than ever you've done on God's earth."

The fourth fisherman nodded agreement and took a drink, wiped a calloused hand across his mouth and passed the bottle. "We're not a feared for that, Lord knows, but what's to be done about the schooner?" he asked, looking around the circle, encouraged by the nods and murmurs. "We can't make a go of it with the dories other than to get a few fish, and we can't jig our flour and molasses."

"I know..." Pius began, but was interrupted by the next man with the bottle.

"And the women needs cloth. We'll be in rags come sealing time!" he said with passion, and passed the bottle.

"The price of fish's that low," continued Pius, "that I doubts we'd make a penny more than we owe Ashcroft in any case."

"So we lay down and die?" asked the next holder of the bottle. He didn't take a drink.

"No b'yes," said Pius. "We don't lay down. Things got to get better. We got to be ready."

"Aye, we're ready," said Alf. "We'd be overhauling those traps," Alf pointed to a large pile of tarred trap nets hulking in their bin like mounds of coal, "if there was a chance we'd be setting down the Labrador come spring."

"My dear man, what are we going to do without a boat!?" asked Gus. There was a loud murmur from the assembly. The bottle had stopped circulating.

Pius scanned the faces of his fishermen. "We can't expect help from England. They don't want to know about us. We got to look out for ourselves." Pius waited for reactions. They listened to the wind and could feel the waves thunder through the rocks and up the pilings to their feet in black sea boots. Some of those boots, old leather or the new rubber kind, had rags and gunny sacks tied around them to keep out the cold. But the fishermen had one thought. They needed a boat to fish because it was all they knew. All most of them cared to know. They didn't ask for anything except a chance to work. "The *Liza and*

Mary ain't coming back to us until we can make up what we owe those fellas in St. John's."

Pius caught Uncle Saul's eye. Saul knew what Pius was getting at. The men were waiting for Pius to get to the point.

"We'll build ourselves a schooner," said Pius. He paused until the statement had sunk in. There were a few raised eyebrows. "A small one. A 'jack', thirty-five tons or thereabouts, big enough to make the Labrador. Some of we'll live ashore to dry fish and the rest'll carry fish up to Ashcroft with the schooner. We won't make that much but we'll get fish onto the wharves before the bigger boats come in, and make enough to get our needs at least."

"Oh, aye, I grant it can be done," said Alf. "But, my dear man, we can't feed our families, never mind outfit a new vessel. And we can't wait a season or two 'til a boat's proper built."

"That's right, Alf. She's got to be done now. Turn out your stores, b'yes. We've all laid gear by. We'll put a ship together with trunnels, like in the old days. Gather up all the old sails and we'll stitch a suit she won't be ashamed of." Pius looked from face to face. There was a new spark of hope in some eyes and skepticism in others. A few heads nodded. Anything, even dreaming, is better than doing nothing and dying of hunger and shame. "I need seven good men who'll come along with me to Exploits before the ice sets in?"

"You mean to go now!?" asked Gus.

"Exploits in winter?"

"Aye, and back in the spring with a new ship. B'yes has done it before. Uncle Saul can tell you."

Uncle Saul nodded. It was not unusual for a gang of experienced men to build a small schooner between seasons, but they were usually on their own beach within sight of their kitchen windows. There was a low murmur as the men debated the thing Pius was asking. A winter built schooner was a difficult task even in good conditions. Murmurs of indecision bubbled over to crowd out the new spirit of hope.

Uncle Saul spoke up. "I'd go along with you, Pius, but with these?" Saul held up his gnarled hands. "I'd not be much help."

"That's all right, Saul. I know you'd go if you could. Who then?"

"I'll go with you, Father," said Harry.

"You'll wish you was back in the Navy, son," said Pius, unable to refuse Harry in front of the men.

"I'd like to help, just the same."

"Thank you, son." Pius tried to ignore the sensations running through him, knowing the dangers, and Mary's objections. "Who else then?"

"I'll go, Pius," said Alf without hesitation.

"You don't go to Exploits without me," said Gus.

"Me too," said Lloyd Legge, a young man who'd lost his wife to tuberculosis. They had two children who were living with Lloyd's sister. They needed a future.

"Anything's better than dying in me own bed," said Uncle George.

Other fishermen raised their hands. Pius counted out seven including Harry, Alf Pardy, Gus Froude, Lloyd Legge, Seth White, Andrew Rogers and Uncle George White. "Good, then. We leave in the morning. We'll ask you other men to see to our families best you're able while we're gone."

This time the murmurs were of agreement. The bottle moved on again, the contract sealed.

January 4, 1933: Mary was up before dawn baking bread. Seven loaves cooled on the sideboard. Pius came down the stairs wearing his heavy canvas coat that was waterproof from cod oil and tar after years of fishing. Mary laid out the tobacco and personal items Pius would cram into the old sea bag that had been around the world with his father. Pius sat down to bread and jam with a mug of steaming tea to listen to the marine weather report while Mary fussed over him. He sensed she was feeling uneasy.

"He'll be all right, Mary."

"He's our only son…"

"Don't say it in the dark of the morning. 'Twill curse us sure." Pius counted the loaves of bread. "Seven. There's eight of us going."

"I'd have made more, my dear, but that's the last of the flour."

"Keep one aside then."

"You take the bread. We can make do."

"It's not the bread, woman! It's the number." Pius saw the hurt in Mary's eyes, and knew there was an apology due. "All right. I'll take them," he said, not wanting to explain superstitions. "We'll stop at Ashcroft's with Father's gold watch and his old cane."

"Pius, you can't trade off your heritage to that man."

"What good's a fine watch when the only time you need to know is when we'll die on this rock for want of some flour. And the cane? I memorized all those places when I was a lad."

Pius was referring to the hawthorn branch his father carried with him around the world, carving the names of ports of call until the cane was covered with exotic places like Singapore, Shanghai, Bangkok and San Francisco. A record of a man's life at sea. Ashcroft had always coveted the cane but old John Humby would never part with it.

"It's not right," said Mary.

"Ashcroft's got to have something besides promises. It'll be a miracle if he agrees."

"We'll only be in deeper to that man and never get out from under," Mary almost whispered, not wanting to upset Pius. She knew he carried the burden of the whole community on his narrow shoulders and felt responsible for their predicament.

Pius knew the system as well as any fisherman on the coast. The merchants set the price low for fish they buy and sell the fisherman what he needs to live at inflated prices. It was a system guaranteed to keep the merchants rich and the people of the outports slaves, in good times. In good times the system almost worked. It worked for the merchants who made a good profit but the fishermen were never out of debt. In bad times the families with nothing to sell or trade went hungry. Starvation was no stranger to the outports.

"That's the way of it, but don't make me feel worse. Give us a kiss now, I've got to meet the lads."

Mary did her best and gave him a hug besides and hung on just a little longer. "Look after young Harry," she said, with an edge that said more.

Pius' heart was already heavy with the memory of a lost son. In the bedroom above, Harry was stomping his large feet into sea boots, over thick woolen socks Mary had knit for young Roy, to be a gift when he was ready to take his place with Pius on the schooner. But it was Harry that had grown into them. Pius had objected to the legacy and wouldn't wear them himself, but it was about economy in hard times. Mary broke away and finished wrapping the loves of bread in flour bags, stowing them in oiled canvas. Pius put on his cap and took up his sea bag, tucked the bread under his arm and was gone. Harry clattered down the stairs with his coat and sea bag, took a slice of bread and jam, and with a kiss for his mother, was out the door after Pius, eager to get on with the adventure.

The storm of the previous evening turned to freezing rain after midnight, just as the men finished gathering the supplies at the skidway, blowing itself out before dawn. The morning was overcast and ominously still. Harry, slipping and sliding on the icy path, hurried to catch up to his father. They walked together down to the wharf. Pius stopped to watch the seas crashing on the outer rocks knowing there would be a long swell out on the open sea, left over from the storm, but that was nothing for the dories. It was the smell of more wind after the calm that worried him. Marine weather reports were seldom wrong. The wind would come from the southwest with wet snow but there was no point waiting for good weather on the coast in winter. They would go if they could get out of the back harbour on the tide.

The others were assembled at the skidway with the two power dories loaded and waiting, bumping the landing planks fitfully. Some fishermen and young boys had come down to help load the mounds of gear and see them off. A young girl, Margaret, with red ringlets blowing free and wind-blushed cheeks, stood apart wrapped in her father's large coat. She shyly watched Harry laugh and joke with the men and refused to let the tears show.

The wet snow that Pius expected was already trailing down, deceptively benign, almost cozy; the kind of soft flakes that make one think of Christmas and warm fires. The newest system would have wind in it later and they would have it on their beam as they pulled for Twillingate on New World Island. Change Island in between would make a brief lee and the smaller islands some protection, but not much. He knew that the waves coming out of Hamilton Sound would be short and dangerous with the dories so loaded down. The four men in each dory would have to pull hard the entire way without a chance to rest. All these elements Pius had to consider. But there was no turning back. The men knew the risks. Only Mary had sounded a warning.

"Nasty bit o' weather before this lot's done," said Alf, by way of a greeting. Alf and Gus had the only other radios in the harbour still operating. As the batteries failed the few radios on Fogo Island fell silent.

"We'd expect aught else. I'd be concerned if it was too civil," Pius said, with a forced grin. "Harry, you go along with Alf."

Harry lashed his sea bag to the load in Alf's dory and nimbly jumped over the gunnel. He took his place on the forward thwart, hefted a sweep and fitted the hemp grommet over the stout thole-pin. The peculiar but powerful 'make 'n' break' engines had long since been taken out of the power dories because there was no spare petrol to be had on Fogo, nor batteries with enough life left to provide the spark.

"See that Harry puts his back into it, Alf. The navy's made him soft."

Harry winked at Margaret, almost invisible in the folds of her father's coat that hung down to the tops of her rubber boots. She ran up the skidway to the wharf to watch the boats leave. Jimmy White, age thirteen, hung about trying to help, getting wet to the knees. He longed to be going with the men and kept his distance from Margaret who stayed on the wharf watching the dories pull for the back harbour outlet until the damp cold drove her to the warmth of her kitchen and the long, hard waiting time for Harry to come home.

The twenty mile pull to Twillingate in a rising southwest wind, with a beam sea, stinging spray and ice pellets mixed with wet snow, the gunnels rolling down and the water coming in so that the men had to bail turn about, was no worse than Pius and his crew expected.

Six hours of constant effort brought them inside the protection of Twillingate Harbour by noon. A long wharf ran out from Ashcroft's empire; an imposing collection of out buildings, stores, warehouses, rope walks, and blubber trying works. A dozen big schooners and as many smaller schooners lay at anchor, all owned by Ashcroft and operated by local skippers. The Ashcroft family ruled the commercial life of Notre Dame Bay and Hamilton Sound. It would take another war and road travel, competition and the collapse of sealing to release the strangle-hold they held on the outports. But it was the only system the outporters knew and fishermen who failed to pay homage to their masters did so at their peril.

Like many before them, Pius and Harry walked up the wharf to present themselves to Ashcroft while his crew tended the heavy dories. Pius carried his father's cane, the gold watch heavy in his coat pocket, feeling the questioning eyes among the gang of Ashcroft's men working in the cold air stripping spars or laying out rolls of sail canvas on the hard packed snow. They sensed this winter visit by Fogo men was an event. Pius knew most of them and nodded greetings as they walked through the yards toward the main store.

Ashcroft's was an emporium of exotic goods and necessities; foodstuffs and marine gear arranged on shelves, in bins and barrels or in heaps and coils on the floor. The heady smell of Stockholm tar, pitch, turpentine and oiled hemp and above all, the tang of dried salt fish, floated on the overheated air. The big stove in the centre of the room roared its defiance at winter. Ashcroft, it was said, burned enough fuel in a winter to heat half the homes in Twillingate. But his schooners carried wood and coal back from the mainland so he and his family, at least, always had enough.

Pius pushed open the big glass paneled door, a rare commodity on the Island, imported, like most goods of quality, from England by way of Boston, to be met by a wave of heated air and the scent of plenty. The stock boy, a smaller version of his father, ran to get Ashcroft and lingered in a back room to hear the news. Pius and Harry stood in the centre of abundance and tried not to gape at the canned goods crowding the shelves waiting for times to get better and the fishermen to be tempted to buy luxuries again.

Ashcroft appeared wiping his mouth from a greasy lunch. He was short and big around the middle, with a fleshy face and jowls set off by mutton chops, a pasty complexion and soft hands. He was no fisherman but he was the best merchant on the coast, with the largest fleet of ships and was known to be reasonably fair in dealing with his fishermen. He needed them as much as they needed him. But he was above all a businessman.

"Pius Humby!" he said, pleasantly, coming forward to shake Pius' hand. "We didn't expect to see you 'til spring. And this must be young Harry grown up. And the family?"

"Mr. Ashcroft..." Pius began hesitantly, unused to begging for basic needs, "things have been hard with us, this while."

"Yes, sir, it's the same all over," said Ashcroft, condescendingly.

"You see, with nary schooner a man can't get down to Labrador."

"That's a fact, Mr. Humby."

"Well, sir, we mean to build us a 'jack' over to Exploits."

"A 'jack'?" said Ashcroft, with raised eyebrows.

"Aye, 'tis all we can manage. We'll need supplies...flour, salt beef, tea and molasses for eight men, and our families are in need."

"Pius, the price of fish is that bad!"

"We need a boat, Mr. Ashcroft."

"Aye, and you'll want gear to outfit her as well."

"We pay our dues, sir, always have."

"What do I put on my books in exchange?"

"I've Father's gold watch, and his cane," said Pius, holding them out like an offering.

"Not much against the balance." Ashcroft pretended to be looking through his ledger. "I didn't charge interest on the balance owing from the last fit out, in deference to John Humby's good name."

"I appreciate that, Mr. Ashcroft, but your price for our goods was high enough."

"And then you try to sell your best fish to St. John's."

"Truth of it is, sir, you weren't buying the last season and we had a prime lot of dried."

Ashcroft grunted in ascent. "You realize, man, I run a great risk of losing everything if things get much worse in Europe. Spain wants nothing. Portugal ordered less. The English houses have cut back. Italy? The Caribbean?..." He shrugged. "I have to sell my fish for nothing as it is."

"Yes, sir, I understand that."

Ashcroft tapped his pencil on the ledger. "You're going to build a 'jack' boat."

"Thirty-five tons, thereabouts, yes," said Pius.

"And I get all your catch?"

"I would agree to that, sir."

"All Portuguese dried?" Pius nodded. "Prime, mind, and none to St. John's?"

"Aye, sir. You have my word."

"That's only if there's a price at all. The market may drop again."

"It'll be another hard winter for us."

"For all of us, Pius," he said, looking at the piles of goods. "I'll have the watch and cane."

Pius handed over the gold watch and the carved cane. Ashcroft slipped the watch into his pocket and laid the cane across his stand-up writing desk. He burrowed into his ledger and waited for Pius to begin. Pius scanned his list of supplies knowing that he was about to commit the outport to another heavy burden of debt. Harry felt sorry for his father, a beggar in a bazaar. Dignity and indebtedness lay uneasily side by side.

January 5, 1933: Pius and his crew spent a cold but dry night in Ashcroft's net shed, but considering the options they were comfortable enough. Breakfast was what each had brought in a pocket wrapped in cotton waste; a piece of cod, a chunk of dry bread, with a gub of lard if available, or a hard biscuit with only memories of fish'n'bruise with scrunchions. They didn't wait to brew tea on the shore.

The heavily laden dories pushed off before dawn, cut for the tickle, heading west and were well out of Twillingate Harbour before weak sunlight smeared the dull eastern horizon. Once clear of New World Island the rowers settled in for the difficult eighteen mile pull across the Bay of Exploits. The wind, which had laid off during the night, got up quickly and veered stubbornly into the north, then northeast, sending a regular sea into Exploits Bay. Pius had hoped the wind would stay in the westerly, off the land, but he wasn't surprised by the contrariness of nature. The dories, loaded down with more goods from Ashcroft's stores, took what they were given and sat lower in the water, their motion more sluggish and the wave tops slopped over the cap rails when the boats were caught leaning into a sea. The men pulled and bailed their turn.

The sky was leaden and the atmosphere heavy with another winter storm brewing. The wind increased to a good blow from the northeast and blew steady just short of a gale by nine o'clock. The now following seas made steering harder but at least the men could see the waves coming. They pulled and eased up as necessary as each wave lifted the stern and tried to turn the boat sideways. The big dories were built for the conditions and the men on the sweeps knew what to expect. But Pius still worried about the landing on the open, uninhabited beach he had chosen for their building site. He knew it to be a fine timber area but the shallow cove had no protection from a northeast gale.

The crossing took another six hours in the building sea and Pius was a mile ahead of Alf's dory when he was ready to make his run in.

A hundred yards out the bigger waves were breaking on the shoaling bottom and the stony beach was a mass of foam.

His approach was slow and deliberate, the three other oarsmen waiting for his signal. Pius talked them up to the beach and between two large waves they pulled with a will, bumping hard on the pebbles, jumping over the side to hold the dory from being swept back out by the wash. They were almost home free when the next large wave slammed the boat, turned it sideways and water poured over the rails. The four men strained against the backwash and in a clear patch carried their sodden gear above the tide line, bailed her out and finally ran the boat above the tide line.

Exhausted, the men sat on the stones wet and shivering, but a pipe came out and another, and a dry match was found. They smoked and watched the speck of Alf's boat grow until it too was less than a hundred yards off. There was nothing they could do for their mates except watch and pray.

Alf eased up to the beach until he found the rhythm of the breakers and at the right moment urged his men to pull for it. Fifty feet from shore a rogue wave reared, lifted the dory up and passed under. The aft two sweeps caught air, the dory slipped sideways down the back of the wave and stalled. The men were unable to regain control before the next wave towered above them and came crashing down. The dory was thrown on its side, spilling the men into the cold water. Shouting and struggling, they grabbed at the loose gear but the dory was smashed on the bottom.

Pius cursed the frigid Atlantic when he saw Harry go under, his son's big coat and heavy sea boots dragging him down. One moment he was on the top of a wave surrounded by floating gear, then the huge wave collapsed of its own weight, tumbling, burying everything in a welter of foam. As Pius plunged into the surf Harry appeared on top of the next wave without his coat and sea boots. Pius threw himself at the waves, calling for his men. The sodden crew splashed back into the foam and when Harry was flung off the top of a wave Lloyd got an arm and Seth some hair. Pius and Alf grabbed a leg. Harry was dragged clear and dropped a choking heap on the stones. Gus rescued his coat and one boot; they were as important as food. The other boot came ashore later with more precious gear. The rescuers ran about collecting items washed up, or searched with their feet for the heavy gear, all the while laughing and panting with the effort but counting their blessings.

Lloyd and Seth, the youngsters, headed up the beach looking for dead wood. It took time to find dry kindling and a dry match to set it going. The others captured the wrecked dory and sorted their gear, hauling it up the beach to the pile of precious supplies, lamenting only the loss of the keg of boat nails and some iron fittings. They rigged canvas tarps as a windbreak and huddled around a blazing fire, drinking hot tea, joking about the landing. Pius found the canvas roll with the seven loaves of bread. Two loaves had survived.

"There's a blessing at least," he said. "But Mary'd be heartbroken to see what's become of her wonderful loaves."

"Aye, and what would she say more," asked Alf, innocently, "if she seen her Harry all beat up and looking like a near drowned bilge rat?"

Pius handed Alf a thick chunk of bread. "A little salt water never hurt a good sailor, sure..." he said. Pius chewed a crust and looked beyond the fire to the dense stand of spruce trees, thinking about a time, before the war and the troubles, when he was a boy in awe of his father and Uncle Sam who could create miracles with a few hand tools. "Some wonderful trees up there, brother. We'll put the saw over on that rise," Pius said, pointing to a natural clearing on the edge of the tree line. There were hard hours ahead felling distant trees and hauling them to the site and working the long pit saw. There were trees nearer the building site but they were the guardians; the ones that took the full brunt of the Atlantic gales. Timbers cut from the guardians would be *shawley*; weak and splintery in the hearts, from the constant bending forces of the wind. Pius wanted the spruce trees on the level ground further in, before the slope climbed again to the hills. "...And we'll lay her keel down there," he continued, indicating the building site on the wave-washed pebble beach above the high tide line. The grade of the beach was a smooth run into the high tide foam. "She's just about right." He nodded with satisfaction. "Yes, sir. She'll do fine. Wish Father and Uncle Sam was here. They'd enjoy this b'ye."

The men nodded, each remembering someone who would have relished the adventure. The first ordeal was already forgotten. They were safely ashore with a fire going and hot tea and the prospect of nothing but a winter of cold, punishing labour ahead. Most Newfoundlanders live their whole lives within sight of the sea. Dying in it is a constant danger but the danger had to be put in proper context. Seth found his harmonica, blew out the salt water and started a reel. The men huddled around the fire, moving their feet, keeping the spirits of the forest at bay. The sun fell out of a bank of clouds on the western horizon and went down in a blaze and a promise. Long shadows crept out from the tall, dark trees that would become their hope for the future.

January 6, 1933: At dawn the sound of broadaxes rang through the dense forest. Two men rigged a cumbersome six-part block and tackle, that would become the main sheet tackle of the new schooner, to handle the fallen spruce tree. When the giant came down in a long slow arc, ending in a ground shaking thud that silenced the ravens for miles, the crew gathered to limb and skid the chosen one to the beach.

Pius supervised the critical setting of the keel blocks. Beach stones were dug out by hand and small trees cut to make three cribs of short spruce logs filled with stones. The angle had to be just right because once the keel was set up, the angle dictated the placement of the timbers for her frames and in the end, the success of the ship. Skidder poles were laid on each crib and the big spruce tree was rolled into place with ropes and levers to be rough squared with the broadaxes. The gang, still fresh and eager to be about the task, worked away, getting a rhythm finally and the squaring went well.

The keel was squared up by late afternoon. A major achievement in itself but the day was not over. Pius, Alf and Uncle George began the exacting task of shaping the forty-foot log to its finished dimensions of ten inches by fourteen inches, using only adz, string and eye. The others set to work cutting guardian trees for the pit saw frame. The first full day on the beach was a great success. The weather held. The wind was moderate and not too cold. The little rain squalls became only a fine drizzle then a heavy mist by evening. That night they huddled under the tarps again over hot tea and salt beef and shared the last damp loaf of Mary's bread.

January 8, 1933: In Russia the peasants were being forced onto collective farms and those who resisted were shipped to the interior of Siberia to starve. Joseph Stalin's unique brand of rule by terror drove the peasants to increase production while the rest of the world slid deeper into the Depression. In Germany, Adolf Hitler and the National Socialists were on the verge of taking control of the government. On a small island off the North Coast of Newfoundland, Pius and his crew toiled on the shore of Exploits Bay to build their ship. It was their answer to a world gone mad.

Alf finished smoothing the golden yellow keel timber, the razor sharp adz hissing through the fresh wood like a milling machine. Beyond the work site, sounds of chopping echoed through the forest. Voices called out and a tree crashed to the ground interrupting the chopping and the chattering ravens. Then the chopping would start up again and soon the ravens would be commenting on the work.

A rhythmical *swish-swish*, came from the pit saw where Pius and Harry sweated to slice thick planks from a huge log. Pius worked above, guiding the cut, pulling the long saw on the up stroke. Harry worked below pulling with all his might on the down stroke. Every stroke sent a shower of sawdust over him to mix with his sweat. Harry prayed for a chill wind to cool his body and keep the cursed sawdust out of his eyes. Halfway through a plank Harry hesitated on the down stroke to wipe his face. The saw skipped free.

"Thundering Jasus, b'ye!! Have you left me!?" yelled Pius, nearly tumbling from the pit saw frame.

Harry wiped his swollen hands on his coat and groped blindly for the handle. "No, sir. I can't see is all!"

"You don't need to see, Harry! I can see where the blessed thing's got to go," Pius said angrily. "You only have to put your back into it and not throw me on the ground!"

"I'm sorry, Father." Harry willed his swelling fingers to curl around the grip. "I'm ready," he said, through clenched teeth.

Pius pulled the upstroke then stopped. "Harry," he said, "you're doing fine, son. It's a miserable task. I know, I had to do it for me own father."

"I'm all right," said Harry.

"By'n'by I'll tell you about the time your Grandfather and Uncle Sam and me built us a 'jack'. Just the three of us."

"How old were you then, Old Man?"

"Half your age," answered Pius, allowing Harry more time to recover. "My son! Your Grandfather was a devil to work. Good as three men. Trouble is he expected us to work like four!" Pius grinned at the memory. "Uncle Sam was master builder then. He laid down the keel and frames then let Father tie into'er. You never seen a man work like that, my son. That boat flew together like all the demons in hell was on the end of the maul. We had to run just to keep up. And when she was finished she was as fine a boat as ever man could build, of this old spruce, mind. We wasn't building no rich man's yacht, see."

Another tree crashed down, sending shock waves through the ground. Pius and Harry were brought back to the present.

"Best get on with it, I suppose," said Pius. "She'll not build herself."

January 12, 1933: The keel shape was finished and ready for the frames. Pius and Alf ventured inland again to find and mark the crooked trees for the frame timbers. Their objective was to cruise the juniper stand on the other side of the hill while the men fashioned a crude shack with slabs cut from the stack of planks growing beside the pit saw.

The hastily built shack, less than twenty feet on a side, dictated by the supply of slabs, was cramped and dark. The single window facing the sea was covered with the skin of a washed up flatfish stretched across the opening. Gus had found the dead fish tangled their rescued gear and knew it would come in handy for something. The low door, covered by a flap of heavy canvas, was little proof against the cold, but the double walls were at least insulated with damp sawdust. A crude log chimney let out some of the smoke from a stone fire pit in the middle of the space where they could sit at night out of the wind and dry their clothes and share a pot of strong tea. Gus turned his hand to fashioning a type of unleavened bread in their big frying pan with mealy flour cooked in rancid pork fat. The scraps of meat had long been picked out. Much of their supply of salt cod had been soaked when Alf's boat capsized so they dried what they could over the fire and endured the resinous flavour of spruce-smoked fish. For vitamins they had a tub of seal blubber that got added to just about anything except the tea. The livers were left behind for the folks at home to nourish the young and old.

The next day the gang trooped to the juniper stands to cut and haul the crooks marked by Pius for the stem and stern. The men adzed the crooks flat and Pius marked out the lines from eye and Grandfather's half model he'd tucked safely in his sea bag. It was a masterful job of lining and cutting the long sweeping curve that would give the schooner her shapely bow. The stern and horn timbers were more straightforward. Alf worked on those and had the stern timber in place in two days. By January 15th, they had the backbone up and were placing the last of the leveling braces.

It was cold and raining in ugly, ragged squalls. The wind veered to the north and then the northeast and was working up to a gale, the rain changing to sleet and ice pellets as Pius hammered home the last brace. Spray from waves crashing on the beach blew horizontally over the site and froze where it landed, glazing the site and anything stationary. Pius and Alf stood back to check the line up of the stem and the stern members once more. Pius nodded his approval.

"That's enough for this foul day," said Pius, giving one of the trunnels holding the juniper knee a final whack with his mallet. "You've done well lads. Let's go up for a mug."

The men gladly picked up their tool bags and followed Pius to the shack with the freezing wind urging them along.

"A drop o' rum wouldn't go amiss," said Alf. The other men agreed.

"I've put a bottle by for just such a time," said Pius. "A right straight backbone in a new baby or boat is a time for celebration, b'yes!"

Harry and Gus sheered off for the forest to check the snares. Pius looked back at the golden yellow backbone of his new boat and was pleased with the way she stood out against the dark clouds rolling in from the east. She had a good start, he thought, and didn't want to know about the future any more than he knew that day.

January 17, 1933: The storm blew itself out in a long day of howling winds, backing to the southerly driving a slashing rain that at least melted the ice of the day before. The shack-bound men made the most of the time, repairing clothing or working away at the never ending chore of whittling treenails out of juniper branches by the light of the fire. The ship would need thousands of trunnels to hold her together. Set properly in bored holes they would hold planks to frames and frames to keel, deck beams to shelves and deck planks to deck beams, as well as any iron fastener, and do it longer if the boat was salt-soaked and looked after.

Juniper trunnels were free for the effort. Each night the men talked and whittled trunnels until the pile threatened to force them outside. And there were iron fittings to forge and canvas to cut and stitch, new rope to plait and oakum to pull from old rope, pitch to boil and on and on until the thousands of pieces necessary to the creation of a ship had been fashioned by hand, drawing on the ancient skills, stacked in the corners waiting to be added to the elemental mix called a schooner. It was no mystery of alchemy, just a progression of age old methods that resulted in a thing of utility. That's not to say the rough-built schooners lacked grace or beauty. If the builder was also an artist the thing could be the most pleasing sight in the world, or almost. Not to be compared with a shining bride, a new born baby or an elder with a face creased by experience. The new schooner still had to acquire experience.

Sunday: Pius entered this note for Sunday: '...*This being the Lord's day I had the lads lay by as though we was at sea. I always believed His day should be kept as much for the men's sake. We always kept His day on the grounds as much as possible. Some of the skippers didn't like to stop when the fishing was good. I never went home with any less fish than they. Was like my father said, "Fish like Billy Jasus for six days but don't forget Who makes the fish on the seventh." A good rule. I couldn't find fault. After prayers and a clean up I left the lads to their chores and idled down to the site to peck away at the keel rabbet. Harry come along later. The sun come out and we had a nice gam for a spell...*'

Pius was sitting on a block of wood beside the keel cutting in the rabbet with a mallet and a big chisel, working carefully to a line drawn the length of the keel, sweeping up the curved stem. The line also ran up the deadwood at the stern. Pius cut with a slow rhythm, savouring the smell of the resinous spruce, working forward from amidships on the starboard side facing the sun. He had to squint when the sun shone between the ragged clouds riding over the trees from the west. He didn't consider the task work. For him it was a meditation on wood and God's reward for perseverance.

Harry didn't speak to his father but walked down to the shore and stood looking out across the water, thinking about his last vision of Margaret in her father's coat. Most young men his age were married with babies of their own and it was time to make up for the four years away in the navy. He skipped a few stones, settled his mind to speak to Margaret's father when they returned home in the spring, then walked up to the building site.

"Morning, Father."

"Harry. Fine day, what?"

"Good enough, I suppose."

"It's a long time away, son. She'll be waiting."

Harry, grinning at his father's prescience, watched the chisel set and gouge, set and gouge, and with each tap of the mallet, clean, sweet smelling chips flicked away. Pius eyed the half model his grandfather had carved years ago, compared the lines of her garboard to the line he had drawn and chipped again. He moved a block of wood along and repeated the chipping until he was satisfied with the angle of the groove. Harry squinted along the groove, also savouring the resinous wood. It was a spicy, intoxicating smell that all boys grew up with playing in their father's store or under the frames of a new boat. It wasn't always a boat they were building. It could be a cradle or a coffin. All are necessary in the outports.

"Old man, how do you know?"

"Know what, son?" asked Pius, concentrating on the groove.

"You've naught to go by, only a line and that toy boat I used to play with, and then I wondered why granddad only made a half a one."

Pius chuckled remembering the look on Harry's face when he found the half model in his store and tried to sail it. "'Tis enough."

"I mean how do you know the angle? I've not seen you gauge her once."

"I just know is all," said Pius, cutting into fresh wood and eying a troublesome knot. "Father taught me how to cut a rabbet, and his father taught him. Look, she comes full here," said Pius, sweeping his arms out in a wide curve to show Harry the shape of the hull amidships. "So, the rabbet's just so here for angle, then she goes fine to the stem and the angle gets steeper, like. And she does the same going to the stern. But she changes in between, here, look..." Pius used the block of wood the thickness of the planks, to run along the groove. It followed the angle Pius cut by eye. "...just a thing I know. I could use a gauge I suppose, but the way Father showed me I don't bother. I can read the angle, see?"

"Oh," said Harry, still puzzled. "How is it you never showed me?"

"We've only built one boat since you was a baby. And that was only a *bummer* for getting around and having a bit of fun."

"Did you show Roy?"

"Yes, son, I did..." Pius let a memory wash over him, eyes following an invisible form of his lost son, and looked up at the sky. There was a halo around the sun. No gulls or ravens circled but the ever-moving sea worked up the beach stones as an old swell rolled in against the light wind and died in the wash. "If you'd needed to know I'd have taught you," Pius said, resuming tapping and chipping. "But times are changing, Harry. You've an education and no need to build a boat." Pius took longer to eye the groove but he wasn't seeing an angle, he was looking into the future. "She'll come out well enough, I suppose," he said. He was more certain about the groove he was cutting into her keel than the course she would keep. He didn't know why. He looked into the forest again. There was no answer there, only a longer sigh when the west wind piped up.

"Another front coming, what?" said Harry, looking up at the halo.

"Dare say, we'll get some weather out o'this one."

"I dare say," agreed Harry. "Sun dogs too, Old Man. Could be a hard one."

"The Lord doesn't give us too many breaks in this old world."

"Only a hard life, Father."

"Hard? No more than we make of it, son."

"You could have stayed in the Navy after the war. You'd have a nice pension by now. You wouldn't have to do this."

"What, build this old boat? 'Tis no harder than getting out of bed on a cold morning at home. I'm a fisherman, son. All I ever wanted to be."

"But look here, Old Man, you're working away on this God forsaken beach because the bloody Brits took your schooner, and a fine thank you for joining their war to save them from the Germans."

"I hated the Germans! I should have joined up because I loved my country ad the freedom to fish. A man shouldn't do anything out of hatred. I don't hate the fish, see."

Pius looked to the east, beyond Harry's gaze. He didn't know what was happening in Germany. He was going further back, to the Great War. Harry guessed what he was thinking.

"You've never talked much about that day," said Harry.

"No...not a thing I like to remember. It makes my guts turn! That man, grinning up at me, and him just killed every soul on the bridge of our ship, except me. Why was that? My fine young Skipper spoke to me...and then he was gone. He and the Mate too, and another boy, like they never was. Then we hit the German and that man was looking up at me, grinning like his war was just some kind of wonderful entertainment. What kind of heathen...?" Pius absently tested the edge of the chisel with his calloused thumb, shaving off a fine sliver of skin, watching it fall to the stones to disappear in the chips of wood. As easy as that, he thought. No more than a piece of wood or a fish. All the same. But fish don't hate other fish. "Best left alone. It's done with. Those good men are gone. But my son!...I'll never forget the blood, and the sweet awful stink of it, worse than in the thick of a pan of fresh killed swiles, no son, never forget that day, nor that man's evil face."

Pius, not wanting to make Harry dwell on a bad day, resumed chipping with more good cheer than he felt. He was responsible for the morale of his men. They had to rely on each other and work together, be friends and build a boat, most of all he had to keep his son safe and deliver him home. The sooner they got the blessed boat built the better. The mallet rang on the chisel. The chips flew away and Harry was walking up the beach toward the shack. Pius felt a cold chill run down his back. It wasn't just the wind.

The storm arrived as predicted and their world changed over night as if the hand of God had struck the land with a challenging bolt of frost. At dawn on January 19th Pius and his crew crept out of the shack to find the beach building site, the keel and the forest trees white with new snow. It had turned cold finally, as Harry and Pius predicted, but it was no more than the challenge they expected so they trooped into the forest and made their way to the juniper stands to cut the crooked trees for the frames.

The job of cutting and hauling the juniper crooks was a test of perseverance. The distance from the juniper stands to the beach site was more than half a mile of broken ground and dense bush. The first part was uphill. Each crooked log had to be skidded over deadfalls and through thickets. It took three days of hard work to get the one hundred trees to the beach. It took another two days for Pius and Alf to sort them for quality and match the curves to the half model while the crew used broad axe and adze to flatten the sides of each log so the lines could be drawn in. When the cutters and the framers got into their stride the work went ahead quickly despite the working conditions. In all it took twelve long, exhausting days of struggle against the elements to get the ship framed out.

January 30, 1933: Hitler was proclaimed Chancellor. The bottom of the cycle of the Great Depression was near but the world continued to slide into an abyss of human degradation. Some time after the war Kurt wrote in the margin of his journal for that date: '*...It was a dangerous time. It was the beginning of the greatest evil ever visited on mankind. The clouds that gathered over Europe like a plague should have unleashed fire and brimstone, if justice had been done. If God had been paying attention. If I had known then what I know now I would* *have taken Father's gun and shot the fucking Führer myself...'*

Pius' entry for January 30th, 1933, was more optimistic: '...*We put the finish to her frames today and she looks all right. But the weather is closing in again. This time it looks like a proper gagger and I doubt we'll see the sky for a few days. She commenced to blow out of the nor'east and is black with snow. The frames is going to set in with frost...'*

In the late afternoon those black clouds gathered on the northeastern horizon and built up quickly, moving on the land as if all nature was in sympathy with the political chaos about to descend on the world. At first the storm teased. Wet flakes of slobby snow drifted down thick and fat; so heavy with moisture the men could hear them sizzle through the air to splat on the wet frames they were handling. They looked at the sky frequently, gauging their time before the full fury of the storm broke over the building site. It was coming as it was expected so they hurried to finish the last sets of frames at the bow and the stern. Pius and his crew worked forward. Alf and his crew worked aft. Pius finished first and went to help Alf and they worked together to stand the last frame pair. They marked the ends where they were to land on the horn timber, took them down and trimmed the feet, bored the holes for the trunnels and stood them up again. Finally they drove home the trunnels, all the while glancing at the horizon.

The nuisance slobby snow turned to sleet and the sleet was followed by the first puffs of wind ruffling cats paws over the greasy swells rolling into the beach. Soon those easy swells would be racing waves crashing down with a roar shaking the earth like thunder. Pius was thankful high tide had passed and they were in the cycle of the neap tides. He didn't want his ship launched before her time. The inevitable ice buildup, the barrier ice, as the leading edge of the Labrador pack moved south, would be a benefit and a Godsend.

Then, as if on a cue, the blow came in earnest. The snow driving horizontally against the frames turned their windward sides crusty white. At a word from Pius the men left off dubbing the high spots and put up more battens and braces. They were wet through and freezing cold and eager to run for shelter but the frames had to be secured against wind and ice. Those working without mittens, handling hammers and iron nails, suffered the most. Finally Pius hollered over the blast that they were finished. The men gathered their tools and scrambled up the beach, urged and pushed by the wind, and dove into their shelter. And so ended January 30th for Pius and his crew, and the world; and none of them would be the same again.

January 31, 1930: Cowering supplicants huddled around a smoking pit fire, canvas shawls pulled across their shoulders like ceremonial robes, hunched forward to find the elusive heat, repelled by the acrid smoke. With their soot-blackened faces and tear-red eyes and ceremonial robes, they looked like a tribe of ancients huddling together in an ice-bound cave; a prayer circle asking for deliverance from the wrath of the elements roaring and searching for a way in. Their Chief hammered a tattoo on a glowing iron bar and the sparks flew out like star showers in the smoky gloom, the Wizard under the mountain and his gang of worker trolls forging weapons in the fires of damnation where all men are punished for their sins. Their sins were obstinacy and vanity to think they could rip a vessel from the raw earth. Outside, the forces were gathering to crush the tribe and if they couldn't be driven back into the sea the furies would send the sea to devour the lot in their lair where they huddled. The wind shook their hiding place and ripped the door aside, covering the cringing men with snow. An ancient rose to subdue the flogging canvas, drove more nails into the fraying, bulging cloth. Another ancient heaped damp wood onto the blaze and the smoke curled up and filled the room with pungent, sooty clouds before it found its way out through chimney, chinks and cracks.

Gus pumped the bellows and Pius hammered on a white hot iron bar. The others worked at stitching canvas sails or whittling cleats or tending the pitch pots filling slowly with the resin bubbling from the ends of green spruce logs. While Gus rested Harry worked the crude bellows for Pius and ignored the cold penetrating the shack. He looked slightly demented with his blackened face and red-rimmed eyes, but at least he was somewhat warmed by the activity.

On the third day of the storm Pius wrote: '...*Seems God has forgot we on this blessed shore. The wind hasn't softened a wit since the 31st. We can only imagine what the snow has done to us since we crept into this awful place and shut ourselves up. Seems the world has come to an end and nobody come to deliver us. It can't last much longer. No blow, no matter how bad, lasts forever, but the lads are getting anxious. Lloyd and Seth had a row last night over the slightest thing. We all need to get back to work...*'

February 3, 1933: Gus was up before dawn tending the fire, mixing his fat and dough, and making tea. At the first diffused light through the translucent fish skin the men woke to an unusual silence. They dressed and drank their tea and ate the bread cakes, made their small preparations and crept out of their tomb into waist-deep snow. The sun was already above the horizon and the sight dazzled them and filled them with awe. Spray driven by hurricane winds encased everything in sparkling ice. Their world had become a crystal chaos of twisted, ice-caked trees and encrusted mounds of materials. Most amazing of all were the skeletal ribs of the ship, sweeping gracefully up from a white desert, bony fingers silhouetted by the rising sun. A

Gothic temple turned upside down. But it wasn't a scene of beauty to the men who had to build a ship before they could go home.

"My son!' said Gus in awe. "There's a day just to find our job of work!"

"She looks like a beached whale!" said Harry.

Pius surveyed the site and the future of his ship. "Aye, and what foreign beach will she leave her bones bleaching on when her time's done?" He hadn't meant to say it out loud.

"She'll last forever, Father," said Harry, in all innocence.

Pius shot Harry a harsh look. The lines of his face, picked out by the low sun, were etched even deeper. "Don't say that, Harry! You'll curse her sure!"

Harry looked at his father with surprise. Pius seldom raised his voice and the day on the pit saw frame was a rare occasion. Harry was stung. "I meant only that she's strong..."

"Nothing lasts forever!" said Pius, determined to pass his judgment for Harry's sake. "Especially what the hand of man has wrought."

It was hard to guess what father and son were thinking. Pius couldn't weaken in front of the men who watched closely, hardly breathing, hoping for a word to break the spell. It had been said, and if something happened to the boat as a result of the boast, the blame would be cast on Harry's young shoulders. Pius had said a similar thing about the new engine that cursed the *Liza* & *Mary*. Many had heard him say it and the ship was lost to the English bankers.

Pius turned to look at the buried hull. "She'll not shake herself free o'that lot." He broke his way through the hip deep snow capped by a crust of ice, forcing against the hard-packed drifts, breaking through and stumbling forward again. The men followed silently.

Gus patted Harry on the arm as he passed. "Take no mind, son," said Gus.

"I shouldn't have said it," Harry answered.

"Once said, a man can wear himself out trying to fight it. In the end it happens anyway. Pius has a load to carry. If we fail, it'll go hard on us, but the skipper takes it hardest of all."

The men hammered at the ice crust with their hands, casting aside the large chunks, digging into the softer snow beneath, flinging it aside in clouds. Harry watched, remembering when he was a boy and the first real snowfalls were always a wonderful time. The children romped and slid and dove and threw snow and went indoors to crowd around the stove and dry out and have hot tea with molasses...He wasn't a boy and throwing snow was now a man's job. He waded after Gus. It would be another long day.

BERLIN

February 13, 1933: Kurt's journal entry for that day was a short note: *'...It was no surprise and there are no expectations. I wish I could mourn...'*

The General had died on the 1st of February after a long, unspecified illness, Kurt was told. There were a few blank lines as if Kurt intended to fill in the spaces at some future time. The spaces remained as a mute testimony to his feelings for his father or his own inability to come to terms with his death. Willie said he believed their father's death was a reaction to Hitler's dramatic rise to power and what it meant for the aristocracy, and Germany. Kurt had no opinion about what had killed his father in the end.

Kurt later wrote of an interesting day spent with Willie after they left the lawyer's office. It was his only journal entry concerning the death of his father until he wrote down the details of the reading of the will.

The Schulte brothers stepped out of the lawyer's office and trudged along the snow lined street with the wind at their backs. Willie was in uniform, a heavy cape over his shoulders. Kurt was dressed in a soiled dark suit with a tattered greatcoat from the First War pulled on but not buttoned. Willie limped noticeably and seemed to be in pain, alternately holding his leg and holding his cape from blowing away. Kurt took his arm when his cane slipped on the ice. "Thank you. I'm all right," said Willie. "Let's go to the club and have a drink."

They walked in silence for another block, deep in thoughts of their own. They stopped at the comer of the Kurfüstendamm to wait for a line of army trucks, piled high with expensive furniture and paintings in heavy guilt frames. Soldiers held the furniture so it wouldn't bounce out. The soldiers were young, wore swastika arm bands and looked grim in the cold. The people on the streets watched the trucks with little interest. Kurt knew what it meant and what it would mean. "Kurt...I hope there are no hard feelings."

"What?..." said Kurt, distracted. "I'm sorry?..."

"About the will..."

They started across the Kurfüstendamm before another convoy reached their corner. Kurt noticed an old man with a dark beard and plaited hair, dressed in the peculiar long dark coat and wide brimmed hat. The long coat was thin and patched. Kurt wondered how they kept warm in the middle of a German winter. The old Jew looked out of place, yet he was a German, a Berliner, by birth. The old man also watched the trucks.

"Oh, yes...the will," said Kurt, absently. He had turned to look back at the old man. "It's not as if it was a surprise, Dear Willie. Father was always true to his word."

They walked another block. Willie hesitated to pursue the subject. "It isn't...wasn't his true feelings," he said finally.

"Yes, I know. It was his damned pride!"

"And yours!" said Willie defensively.

"And mine," admitted Kurt. Kurt didn't want to pursue the subject either. His father was dead. The subject was dead. Everything was dead except Kurt's mind and it worked hard at writing ideas that he had to understand and put into words on a page. "I'm used to living the life of a pauper. I practiced for this when I was young."

"It was play acting, Kurt. You only had to come home when you and your friends got hungry or tired of playing at Bohemians."

"Still, it was good practice. Character building and all that."

"Some character! You learned to live like a hermit, crawling out long enough to go to the University to teach that rabble you call students."

"They keep me on my toes. They love to argue. Arguing makes the blood flow. When I get home I can write with passion."

"Writing! My warning still stands."

"I'm writing fiction, Willie. I'm an insignificant romantic working in anonymity. Who would notice?"

"You were a spy. Your name's recorded, as a resister."

"I wasn't very good at spying so I quit."

"Well, the best of your bunch were amateurs compared to Herr Hitler's organization."

"Then I'll continue being an insignificant recluse, if only to keep you from worrying. It's not so bad being impoverished. You tend to concentrate on the really important things...like bread and sausage, and a good wine now and then, and there's my books. The University has a wonderful library, for the asking. Why should I care about the estate!?" said Kurt, unable to hide the sarcasm.

"Please, don't be bitter, Kurt. It's not like you...and it makes my position harder to tolerate."

"I'm not crushed. I told you, I expected it."

"An allowance perhaps? I could arrange…"

"No! No, thank you, Willie. I won't be the family's charity case!"

"If you need anything…Kurt," Willie said, but let it drop.

They arrived at the Rosenstrasse and turned right. Willie apologized again but was drowned out by another column of trucks, filled this time with young boys, dressed in school uniforms, wearing swastika arm bands, singing the new Nazi anthem, cheering Hitler and exhorting pedestrians to get on the trucks or get out of the way. The trucks and the earnest youths and the noise careened down the street and out of sight, but not out of Kurt's thoughts. It was a common occurrence in Berlin.

"Nothing, Willie dear. My needs are simple. My life fits neatly into compartments…small ones, where there's no room for frivolous acquisitions."

"Or people?"

"The door's always open, you know that."

"You never come home," said Willie,

"I'm not welcome."

"Mother wants to see you. She needs more than ever to have the family together."

"Yes, it would be nice to be with the children again…but it only makes my heart ache."

"You have to face it sometime."

"Huh, I face it every day, and the dreams. I wake up sweating. If I go further than the University I'm vulnerable."

"So, you live with your writing and your memories."

"And my cognac."

"Very dangerous, this living with memories. More dangerous than writing."

"And the cognac?"

"Come, I'll buy you a drink," said Willie, motioning to a door. They had stopped outside an officer's club on the Rosenstrasse.

"No! I'll buy you a drink," countered Kurt. "Then I can propose the toast. To Father and to death!"

Willie gave Kurt a pained look. He didn't like to hear Kurt talk about death.

The well appointed club was smoky and crowded with officers of Germany's secret army, forbidden by the Treaty. The walls were paneled and richly dark, hung with pictures of famous generals and regiments and divisions and graduating classes from the academy. There were the usual regimental plaques and flags and the place stunk of cigars and men who rode horses and talked of war and women. A male bastion with the rich, heady smell of power.

The several polished tables supported young officers with heaps of braid and ambitions and families with money. It was a stronghold of the fading military aristocracy, no Nazis need apply. They would fight for Hitler but the Nazis hadn't yet broken down the social barrier. It was in the club that some of the attempts on the Führer's life would be plotted when things got bad and the young aristocrats knew the war was going to be lost. But on that day the talk was optimistic and the language harsh and the future bright because Hitler was their only hope against the Communists. Kurt looked like a Communist.

Kurt felt out of place immediately. He looked for submarine officers but there were none. He would have felt more comfortable with his own kind, if only to ask about the new submarines that Germany was planning, also in defiance of the Treaty, and talk about the old days and tell irreverent jokes about their admirals and swap lies about how deep they dove and how many depth charges they had endured, drinking endless toasts to the many who went out and didn't return. But the club wasn't for irreverent submarine commanders, it was for plotting to blow up the Chancellor because the Wehrmacht couldn't take a joke.

A few older officers said hello to Willie, who guided Kurt to a table near the fireplace, out of the way so they could talk. They took off their coats and sat down in comfortable arm chairs. Willie ordered a bottle of cognac from the uniformed waiter who eyed Kurt with unveiled distaste. Kurt was the only one in the room not wearing a uniform and Willie realized it was a mistake to bring his brother to such a place. Kurt smiled and looked at the pictures and thought about his father and held himself aloof from the earnest looking men around him.

An officer about Willie's age, tall, once good looking but gone to boozy-red in the face, with a big moustache and a thickening middle, approached their table and gave Willie an exaggerated Nazi salute.

"Heil Wilhelm!" he said loudly, drawing looks from officers at nearby tables. A few smiled.

Willie just grinned and offered his hand to the officer. "How are you, Ziggy?"

"I'm fine, Wilhelm! I was just saying to the boys, *We haven't seen Wilhelm for months*. Where have you been hiding?"

"I've been in the country…" he said, about to introduce Kurt but was forestalled.

"You haven't joined the Party I hope?"

"There was Father's funeral and family affairs," answered Willie.

"Yes, I heard. I'm sorry. The General was a good soldier. My respects to your family, especially your sister. I'll never forgive her for marrying that fat Rhinelander."

"Your castle wasn't big enough," said Willie, trying to make a joke.

"Huh, I could show her what's big enough that counts!" said the officer so his friends could hear. He got the laugh he expected. They all knew the story.

Kurt bristled. The officer noticed and played to Kurt's reaction. Willie realized it was more than a mistake to bring Kurt to the club. It could be a disaster.

"You had to know the girl," the officer said to Kurt. "She's beautiful, with tits out to here!" He held his big, soft hands in front of his medals.

"Ziggy! would you like to sit down and have a cognac with us? We're drinking to Father..."

The officer smiled and sat down. Kurt resisted the urge to go for his throat with a broken bottle. He had learned the trick during a riotous trip to Spain before the war. Before Norderney.

"This is my brother, Kurt," Willie continued quickly to deflect further damage. "He's a professor at the University, in Leipzig. Kurt, this is Major Siegfried Siegwald."

Neither made a move to exchange a handshake. Willie was becoming desperate to find common ground. A trait Kurt appreciated in his diplomatic brother.

"Ah, Ziggy's determined to be a general. But the Wehrmacht's top heavy with out-of-work generals. Isn't that right, Ziggy?"

"Yes, curse the French!" said Ziggy, then laughed. "The generals step on each other's toes at the postings board."

"They'd shoot each other if they thought it would help," joked Willie.

"We're lucky to be only majors, huh, Schulte?"

"I don't plan to retire as one..."

"Listen, Wilhelm," Ziggy almost whispered, leaning in, "Herr Hitler's shaking up the service. Putting in his own men. A big game to see who can be in Herr Hitler's pocket without being caught up his pedestrian ass..."

The red-faced, swollen-nosed officer leaned back and laughed. Hitler's rude beginnings was one of Ziggy's favourite subjects. Like most of his brother officers, the old school, he also hated Hitler and his fanatics but lectured that they would have to play the game. The alternative for the wealthy families was a pauper's prison, their property confiscated and their children without a heritage other than the Nazi creed of violence and intolerance. Ziggy downed his cognac but kept his narrow eyes on Kurt. He lowered the glass slowly then let it fall the last inch with a thump to emphasize what he had to say further on the subject.

"I'll tell you, Wilhelm, the High Command's in turmoil. You'd best stay out of it for now and only jump in when things get hot!"

"Hot?" queried Kurt.

"Hot!" emphasized Ziggy, watching Kurt's reaction. "They say Herr Hitler has a master plan to control Europe. The French won't like it of course." He grinned and refilled his glass and drank off the cognac. His eyes sparkled. "It means war. Then the promotions will come thick and fast. You be a good boy, Wilhelm, and don't step on sensitive toes. You'll see. Hitler's going to build us the biggest goddamned army the world has ever seen!"

Ziggy helped himself to another glass of the good cognac, drank it off and sat back with satisfaction, grinning stupidly because he was getting very drunk with the idea of being a general.

"You're looking forward to it of course," said Kurt. "The war, I mean. The killing and another generation of our best boys blasted to bits in the mud of France, so you can retire as a general."

Ziggy looked at Kurt myopically. He seemed to have trouble focusing on Kurt but when he did the look was full of contempt. Willie was about to step in when Ziggy smiled benevolently. Willie relaxed. He should have known better.

"You were in submarines in the war? Willie might have mentioned you."

"Kurt was decorated, by the Kaiser himself," Willie said quickly. "The Iron Cross."

"*Phuff*...many were," said Ziggy, shrugging his sloped shoulders causing his medals to jingle. "The Kaiser gave them out like candy to children. No doubt you deserved yours, Schulte, but submarines!" Ziggy tossed off the whole notion of U-boats, the Kriegsmarine and the Iron Cross with a derisive grunt. "I can understand your distaste for a fight."

"Just like Father," said Kurt. "Don't you think Major Siegwald reminds you of Father? You should have been his son. You'd have gotten on famously!"

Willie tried to warn Kurt off. It was hopeless so he plunged into the one topic he knew would get the conversation away from dangerous ground.

"So, Ziggy, you're certain we'll go to war?"

The one thing Major Siegwald liked almost as much as going to war was talking about war. He cleared his throat with another dollop of cognac.

"We must!" he said, banging his fist on the table causing the glasses to jump. Some officers nearby looked over and nodded. "The Führer," he whispered, "is a cunning little rat of a corporal but he can move the masses to riot. He talks big." Then he spoke louder, fully into his subject. "He screams at us! He makes the weaklings want to kill for the Fatherland! He can whip up rallies all he wants but eventually he'll have to tweak the noses of our enemies. Huh? Frenchie has a big nose and doesn't like to have it tweaked too often." Ziggy laughed and poured another drink. He seemed to be ignoring Kurt and talking to the whole room. "The French only get out of bed to fight when they have no choice, so we really want to get them where it hurts." He waited for the chuckles to circulate. "Hitler will get them by the balls and twist until Frenchie screams for mercy!"

Ziggy laughed and punched Kurt on the shoulder. Kurt grinned and nodded. Ziggy laughed more. Willie knew Kurt was just waiting his time. Neither man was finished. When the laughter subsided Kurt leaned close to Ziggy as if they were old friends.

"Well said, Ziggy old man! You are a man of erudite insight. Strike first. Strike hard! No mercy! Rip Frenchie's balls right off and his women will come running to us. Then substitute the Deutsch mark for the franc and Hitler for Napoleon and make the French send us their best cognac and their best Impressionists, dead or alive, and we'll be in Valhalla!" Ziggy smiled and nodded as if satisfied that Kurt finally saw things his way. Then he wasn't so sure. The smile became a puzzled frown. Willie returned to the alert, knowing Ziggy hated to be made the fool. Kurt saw the effect he was having on the blowhard and waded in again. It was dangerous and he was enjoying it. Circling for the attack but keeping low, out of sight until the last moment.

"But, Ziggy my old friend," said Kurt, as if talking to an idiot, "if Herr Hitler wants to be Napoleon, and who doesn't, then he, your same cunning little Austrian rat, had better have plenty of submarines because it won't be just the French he'll have to deal with. I have that on good authority from my brother."

"*Acht*! Submarines! An aberration! Lurking around in the muck. No wonder they call them pig boats!"

"But he wants hundreds of the little water wieners. That would make Herr Hitler the head swineherd," offered Kurt.

"Because they both stink, huh!?" said Ziggy, with a great loud laugh, getting the joke. "But Herr Hitler will at least be of some use to us!"

"The U-boats did their share in the last war."

"Bah! They ran and hid at the first sign of trouble!"

"We didn't run!"

"You didn't stop the British in the North Sea!"

"High Command never understood how to use our U-boats until it was too late!" retorted Kurt, angry again.

"Gentlemen…" pleaded Willie. "Please, let's not fight the war before it starts."

"Or make accusations about the last one," said Kurt, glaring at Ziggy.

"We could have been victorious, with an effort!" said Ziggy.

"The U-boats certainly didn't lose your damned war!" said Kurt.

Several of the officers were watching and a few rose, circling the trio like spectators at a cock fight. They knew their man. A duel of honour in some secret place with the inevitable results, at least a show of blood. A diversion from the annoying peace. Officers do not fight in the club like common soldiers. A forest clearing on the outskirts of Berlin with pistols in the old style. Carriages. Seconds. One or two shots. A man bleeding and something else to talk about over brandy and cigars back at the club.

Ziggy looked around at the grinning faces of his comrades. They wanted a show. But there was something about the eyes of Kurt Schulte that gave him pause. The eyes weren't wild, nor did they show the slightest fear. They were indifferent and therefore dangerous. Ziggy had gone up against a man like that during the war. The argument had been over a young woman. The other officer had survived two years in the trenches of Belgium. The eyes of the veteran were cold, as if he didn't care if he died and Ziggy should have known better. He was lucky to come away with only a wound to the arm. The only wound he received, despite being called out twice, being safely employed at the War Department in Berlin for the duration.

"Who would you blame then, Herr Submariner?" taunted Ziggy, determined to approach the edge, hoping Willie would intercede in time.

"Overfed officers sitting on their butts at High Command!" replied Kurt, not realizing he had hit too close to the mark. Ziggy gave no sign but the other officers looked at each other and made faces. Kurt plunged on. "Drinking and whoring at the Hotel Grand Imperial while Germany's best wasted away in the trenches!"

"Is that so, Herr Submariner of the Candy Cross!?"

"That's so, Herr General-in-Waiting!"

"And if the little sailors hiding in their toy boats had been making the decisions? What then!?"

"We would have fought the goddamned sea battles properly and won, before the Americans got mad at us!"

Willie watched the debate as if it were a football match of free kicks, waiting for his chance to jump in.

"I see," drawled Ziggy, backing down a touch, but not giving up the game. "That simple, huh? And was it not a stupid submarine commander who got the Americans mad by sinking a British ocean liner full of them? What was his name, Willie? Schwieger, wasn't it? A big fat ocean liner that any idiot could identify was not a British freighter! How could this happen!? How do you explain that, Herr Submariner Schulte!?"

"Because orders from the High Command were never direct!" said Kurt, leaning over the table close to Ziggy's reddening face. "Misleading orders can be denied if something goes wrong! Just a bunch of military bureaucrats! They take the laurels for victory but save their fat behinds and dodge the blame if something does go wrong!!"

Willie knew Kurt was hopeless with a pistol. He loved his brother too much to care about the honour. However, as heated as the insults were no challenge had been flung and he was surprised at Ziggy's restraint.

"Enough!" said Willie. "Kurt, please, no scenes. Let's go…"

Willie inserted himself between the two men and almost dragged Kurt to his feet. Kurt didn't resist.

"I'm sorry, Ziggy," Willie said. "Kurt was very brave in his beloved submarine…"

"Don't apologize for me," said Kurt, unable to resist a parting shot. "If I think your friend is an overstuffed hypocrite I'll say so!"

"Hey, Herr Submarine man, how is it you couldn't get into your father's Horse Guards!?"

"Come on, Kurt, Ziggy's just baiting you, Don't go for it!" Willie picked up their coats and steered Kurt away from the table.

"Go back to your university and play with the children!" chided Ziggy, relieved that Kurt was moving out of the danger zone.

The noise and jeers filled in behind them like the wake of a ship as they passed through the room and reached the door.

On the street the cold wind blew red and black swastika flags and banners around, and snow and posters of Hitler whirled in wind devils. They struggled to pull their coats on with fingers already chilled, but Kurt didn't feel the wind. He was still seething inside. Willie already had the cold chill of fear for his brother before they left the overheated atmosphere of the club.

"Are you all right?" Willie asked, as they pulled up their collars, gathered their coats around them and hunched forward into the wind.

"That man's a first rate boar!"

"He's also a deadly shot with a dueling pistol."

"Now you tell me!" Kurt said, with a tight laugh.

"You're lucky you didn't find out the hard way."

"He's still a boar!"

"He's shot two men in duels, that I know of."

"All good German gentlemen no doubt?"

"Yes, his family's very well placed so Ziggy spent the war in Berlin. You guessed right and hit his sore spot. He has nothing to do but play soldier and he's bored."

"At least Father never tried to buy us out of harm's way."

"Of course. Father was always willing to make sacrifices for the Fatherland," Willie said, with some irony.

"Poor Father," said Kurt, and meant it. "He'd be crushed to see what's happening to his country. Your friend Major Siegwald is the worst type. The only thing that stops him from disappearing up Hitler's asshole is his shoulders!"

Willie laughed. Kurt laughed also and they walked down the Rosenstrasse, arm in arm and turned the corner out of the wind.

February 20, 1933: Kurt returned to Leipzig after his day with Willie and the lawyers and the incident in the club with a need to finish his manuscript. Kurt's entry for the 20th was brief but significant:

'...When I returned from Berlin I threw myself into the manuscript. I risk being expelled from the University for being absent but I don't care. I'll tell them I was sick; it isn't far from the truth. I'm sick at heart for my beloved Germany. In five days I have revised certain chapters and added the finishing chapters. I haven't written with such intensity since that night at the cabaret and my young lady. Too bad she was so young and I was just an experience. I think the manuscript is quite good. Now to find a publisher. I must return to Berlin immediately...'

February 21, 1933: Kurt took the morning train to Berlin, elated about completing the manuscript and then depressed having to part with a finished major work that had occupied his heart and soul for so long.

Perhaps it was like giving birth, he thought. Bright had said that women often feel depressed when the baby is no longer inside. A sense of loss, letting go? He didn't know but he knew Bright was very clever about such things because she listened to her mother and she was a good woman. He also had anxiety about the manuscript. Maybe it wasn't as good as he hoped. Maybe it was very bad.

Kurt sat beside the window on the train and watched the children playing war games in the aisles and giving Nazi salutes in earnest little voices. He went over the manuscript, scanning the good parts, experiencing the fear and the elation and the doubt that rose and fell like the gentle contours of the snow-whitened countryside. He also watched the parents of the boisterous children. Unhappy, stony faces. Before the war there would have been talk and singing and food and wine. Not over the top ebullient like the Italians or the Spanish, but happy in their way. He hadn't slept more than a few hours in the past week and the monotonous *click, clack, click* of the iron trucks on the contracting rails, the swaying of the rail car and the drone of voices made Kurt drowsy. The tension slipped away and he let himself fall asleep with his head against the cold glass of the window, the precious briefcase clutched closely at his side.

Kurt was jolted awake by the crash of a sliding door. For a moment he was back in his submarine and had just slammed the main hatch and was waiting for the dive klaxon. But the sound he heard was the strident voices of a group of Hitler Youth who forced themselves aboard at Jüterbog station. More propaganda, thought Kurt, as a young boy with a swastika arm band held a pamphlet in front of his face. Kurt shook his head but the boy pressed it on him with a look. The look was menacing. The look said, *If you don't take this pamphlet bestowed upon you by the Führer I'll call my mates and we'll beat some sense into you, old man!* Kurt took the pamphlet. It was an anti-Semitic tirade written in hysterical language with terrible grammar and bad spelling, but it got the point across. Kurt read a few lines, looked up at the clean cut, handsome youth with perfect, angelic, Aryan features and felt nausea. The youth's face faded before his eyes and became the smiling face of Bright Tifton in the family touring car on their way to Berlin, to meet the General and be cast into exile. They killed her, they all had a hand.

Late that afternoon Kurt stood in front of the Deutsch Redefreiheit Verlagsgesellschaft. *The German Free Speech Publishing Company.* It sounded optimistic but in his worn-down condition he was not optimistic. He hesitated to enter the building, tempted to flee back to Leipzig and his books and his bottles. He turned away again, the second time and again the Nazi flags waved at him from all the buildings. He watched the flags, mesmerized by the colour and the meaning, then he watched two smartly dressed Gestapo officers talking to an old man and woman in an alley. The old people were very frightened, producing papers with shaking hands. The woman was about to cry. The Gestapo officers handed back the papers and walked confidently on to have a drink before dinner. The old man and old woman returned to their business of searching through the waste bins of an apartment building, looking for scraps of clothing or food. Kurt, resolved, pushed the door open and entered the building.

February 28, 1933: One week later Kurt returned to Berlin for a meeting with the publisher of Deutsch Redefreiheit Verlagsgesellschaft. Frank Heppelmann was a small man with small hands and quick movements, like a sparrow. Heppelmann used the English name Frank rather than the German Franz. Kurt thought it odd. Heppelmann motioned for Kurt to take a comfortable chair beside the desk. A good sign. Heppelmann ordered coffee for both of them. An even better sign. He wasn't going to throw Kurt out of the office immediately.

The manuscript was stacked neatly on the desk. There was a notation scribbled on the cover page in a strong cursive hand. Heppelmann put on his glasses and turned the pages slowly, nodding his head like a bird drinking water. Blue pencil marks chopped across the pages. Many marks, slashes and arrows. Kurt began to fidget. He glanced around the office at the richly paneled walls and the good paintings and the heavy curtains. Heppelmann was a man of culture who had done well in the business but Kurt wondered if he had come to the right place. He wondered what Heppelmann's views were on the Jews. Heppelmann stopped turning pages and took off his glasses. That was where the man's strength lay. His eyes were dark and clear and piercing and his thin face was fringed with iron grey hair. Heppelmann shook his head quickly from side to side and put his glasses back on and turned more pages. Finally he spoke to the pages as if addressing an errant child.

"Badly overwritten, Herr Schulte. Badly overwritten!"

Kurt nodded in agreement. "Yes, but the story."

"A common problem for the novice. You don't know when to stop," said Heppelmann. "It comes with practice. It helps to be less excited and more lazy. Intelligent but lazy. Think more, write less."

Kurt nodded again, feeling like a schoolboy being lectured by the headmaster for one of his ridiculous pranks. Then there was the time his Uncle Arthur Schulte had too much brandy at a Christmas party. Kurt was twelve and in love with the maid and wanted to be anywhere but under the breath of Uncle Arthur. Uncle had been lecturing Kurt for an hour about choosing a discipline. *Do one thing and do it right*, he had repeated over and over until Kurt was in a trance. Kurt decided then and there to do everything harmful, and to excess.

"Think more, write less," Heppelmann was saying, "then tear up half of what you've written until it is a story about a good person with a flawed personality doing something interesting. The villains and treachery will find their own way in."

"You don't like the manuscript," Kurt heard himself say aloud.

"I didn't say that! I said it was badly overwritten. There's too much! But that's better than not enough. Too many of you come in here with nothing to say."

"Then you like the manuscript?" asked Kurt hopefully, his heart doing leaps and dives as if it were a submarine harried by a relentless destroyer.

"I said it's badly overwritten. But that can be fixed."

"Then you'll print it?"

"You must understand, Schulte, this is not a good time for publishing private works. The new government keeps us busy with information printings. And, well, there are restrictions on what we are permitted to print."

"Censorship? The official version that I wrote about, in there, chapter…"

"The Reich has made, well, suggestions, huh?"

"But this is fiction. Names changed. Details altered. Pure fiction!"

"Very thin fiction. To be quite honest, Herr Schulte, this work is inflammatory!" Heppelmann smiled and Kurt saw something else in his eyes and his face. The eyes weren't so piercing and his teeth weren't perfect and his coat was open to reveal a slick pin with a small gold Star of David that could be hidden easily by doing up the buttons. "But, yes, I do like the story. And so will thousands of other Germans who fear the Führer and that gang of anti-intellectuals too busy creating the New Republic."

"So you will print it!?"

"I am also Jewish. Half Jewish at least. My mother's a shiksa, pardon the expression, it's one the American love, as they say. I was born not a block from this office. We were a large family. All the children worked hard and made something of themselves. My older brother is a concert violinist. If he was not Jewish he would hold the principal chair in the Berlin Philharmonic. My younger brother was a professor at the University. If he was not Jewish he would be headmaster of his college. Now he doesn't even have a job. My older sister married a young officer during the war. He's now with the Gestapo. My sister lives in fear that he'll choose Hitler over her!" Frank Heppelmann paused to light a cigarette, offering one to Kurt. "The Gestapo have been putting the pressure on me to sell the business. My father started this printing house because he loved freedom of speech. You would not believe how little they want to pay me for years of work. They wait. I hold out, hoping for a miracle. There won't be any miracles. Not while the National Socialists are around. You know what I don't understand, Schulte? During the war I was in the army. Many of us were. Enlisted. Many were decorated by the Kaiser. I am German and proud of my country and my city, yet they treat us badly. It'll get worse. You have been very observant, Herr Schulte. And I fear your predictions will come true."

"I hope they don't, but I share your fear, Herr Heppelmann."

"You're an interesting man, Herr Schulte. May I call you, Kurt? You are the epitome of the Aryan this man Hitler holds up as the ideal, the foil against which my people are judged. You have the heritage of the German aristocracy to back you up, and, but for the ranting's of the Chancellor, your class could have all the privileges in the world, yet, you seem to understand us, your Jewish maids for instance, almost better than we understand ourselves. Why is that?"

"I've had a good teacher."

"Yes, she comes out clearly in the story. And I sense there was a strong relationship between you and she, yet you don't put yourself in the story with her. Why?"

"I didn't belong. It's her story. I wanted her to succeed on her own without the help of gentiles. It would be patronizing and self serving. I wasn't making any apologies for us, just telling the story as I see it."

"I understand then, the story is true. You tell it very strongly. But, the story suffers from too much emotion. You can't tell her story without distancing yourself even more from her and her ordeal. The story needs also to have some good gentiles. You describe all the horrors of the past and to come, but don't forget there is more goodness than there is evil in this world."

"I wish I could believe that."

"Writers don't see everything, Kurt, only what they want to see. And what they need, they make up. I know things are going to get bad in Berlin but I have friends, non-Jewish friends, who I can turn to. My life rafts? All my Jewish friends have their life rafts. We'll survive Hitler and his Nazis. Your book is a good warning, however, so yes, I will publish it."

Heppelmann smoked and waited for the implications to sink in. Kurt seemed dazed, finally hearing the words, as if the doctor had announced he had a son after years of painful gestation; but Bright was gone, and the baby, and he had only a book to fill the void.

"But, I want you to put in some good gentiles. My editors will take care of the rest. They have very clever blue pencils that do magic tricks. However, they won't be able to disguise the intent of the book so we'll probably all end up in jail." Heppelmann smiled and stubbed out his cigarette in the big brass ashtray with a miniature Gutenberg press for a holder. The platen could move up and down by pulling the handle to flatten butts. It fascinated Kurt, as it would a child. As it would have fascinated his child, the clever brass toy.

When his senses returned to the present Kurt could see the fighter in Heppelmann. He wished he had had him in his submarine. When they finished discussing the details Kurt promised to seek out Heppelmann's good gentiles and have the manuscript back in two weeks.

"Where will you work?" Heppelmann asked.

"I'll go back to Leipzig, to my flat."

"No! Leipzig is not Berlin. You'll see nothing there. Berlin is the centre of the world. You can see all you need to see in a half hour's walk from this office. You will stay with me and my family. Finish the manuscript and I promise I'll have it published in a month or so. Perhaps three for unforeseen problems."

Kurt developed a non life-threatening ailment that would satisfy the College, with a doctor's report, supplied by Heppelmann. He walked the streets of Berlin by day and really looked at his city and its people. He saw all the things on the street he knew were obvious but he began to see the other things. Berliners accepted the new regime and obeyed the laws because Germans had their traditional respect for authority intact. Hitler had been appointed Chancellor by the President of the Weimar Republic, Hindenburg himself. Germans were pragmatic about their duties and their future. It was Hitler or Communism. But not all Berliners loved him. They only seemed to when it was necessary, when the great man made his infrequent visits to the city. And many were simply caught up in the hysteria of feeling good after fifteen years of living like third class citizens of the world. If he could restore their pride they would follow him. And even though Hitler screamed out his intentions in his endless tirades from Munich, the people didn't realize what atrocities the Nazis were capable of because they were too captivated by the slogans to read the small print. *During the war there were rumours. Poland was just a place the Jews and enemies of the Third Reich were sent for internment. The Germans didn't know the whole truth until it was almost over and by then Germany was fighting for its life. The Jews were one issue. Survival was another.*

Kurt could only speculate about the coming war and the fate of the Jews. He and Heppelmann spent the mornings over coffee discussing what they knew. Heppelmann was fatalistic as well as realistic. He gave Kurt information and names. Kurt had to see the people and draw his own conclusions. Two weeks became four weeks. The College threatened to put him out. Kurt found his good gentiles and finished the story and turned it over to Heppelmann on March 28th, 1933, five days after Hitler demanded and was given the power to rule Germany by decree.

Heppelmann was true to his word, his setters and pressmen worked feverishly, day and night. On May 12 the first copy of the book came from the bindery and was sent by messenger to Kurt at the College in Leipzig, with a dedication by Frank Heppelmann on the frontispiece.

Two days before Kurt's book came out students at the University in Berlin had burned books by Jewish scholars and Storm Troopers began beating civilians. The Labour Union had been broken in February. Hitler and the National Socialists seized complete control. What opposition remained, caved in to Nazi terror, and the leaders of the opposition found out what life in a concentration camp was like. The long slide had begun.

May 20, 1933: Kurt began the entry for May 20th in late July as follows: '...*Fame is fleeting and dame fortune never arrives. If you stand at the crossroads waiting for one or the other you had better cast yourself in bronze and be prepared to be a repository for pigeon shit...*'

The euphoria of having the book published faded quickly. The Gestapo had an agent working in Heppelmann's shop. Unbound copies of the book reached the Gestapo almost the moment the press run had begun. Kurt's Nazi Party students had read the book within two days of his receiving his own copy. They were the students who argued the most and caused the disorder. They were more hostile than usual that morning, taking exception with everything Kurt said. He saw the tattered copy of the book circulating in the class and knew what was behind the hostility. Nazis feed on fear but Kurt was determined to face them down and defend himself if necessary. He had taken precautions before he left his flat and the remains of the bottle were in his briefcase. He could drink the rest. If that failed he had the bottle itself.

"No single country or political system," he began unsteadily, "has ever succeeded in controlling another country or changing the philosophy of a country after the conquest. So, can you call it conquest?" Kurt leaned on the desk for support and looked around the lecture hall with its tiers of seats and banks of young, intense faces. Half the faces that stared back at him were devotees of National Socialism, or professed to be. Kurt doubted most of them actually knew what it meant other than grand parades and colourful pageants and hysteria. The deadly fantasies, Kurt called them. "It's no trick to conquer countries by the use of superior force or cunning in battle or subversion, but once conquered the people have to be subdued. They must submit to the new rulers and do it willingly. This is where totalitarian regimes fail. Consider the Bolsheviks. They rule but still do not control without force and unless they do they will ultimately fail in Russia...even though they rose from within the country. Simply occupying the borders of a country does not mean you control the people..."

The students became restless. Some made remarks. Some clowns pretended to be drunk and lolled about and giggled. Kurt had a reputation. He had been seen in the cabarets.

"The Romans, the Macedonians, the Mongolian hoards...even the Norse raiders...all were very efficient at invading, conquering, or whatever you want to call the insinuation of one people into the homeland of another. But!..." he said too loudly, "...but, they were never able to subdue the will of the people for long. Resistance was endless and the resources of the conquerors were severely taxed to maintain some kind of control..."

"What is your point, Herr Schulte!!?" shouted one of the boys, a ring leader and known malcontent in class. Kurt stared at the boy. "My point, Herr Kohl...is this: If you want to know what I'm getting at now, instead of waiting for a clear interpretation, which by the way, is not the intention of my book, the one you all seem to be reading with enthusiasm. I'm flattered, but." Kurt forgot what he was going to say. He searched his mind for a clue but got only blurred visions of chaos and waves and horses and distorted messages from the past. The students began to snicker. He could see pages from his book and he scanned them for a hint. The book suggested the danger of Germany's present course in the story of a young German Jew and her family and their struggle to survive in Berlin even before Hitler became Chancellor, and all the dangers that it implied for Jews, or anybody the Nazis didn't like. He foretold, through the young girl, the systematic persecution of the Jews, which only years later he was to learn became true, but his fictional scenario could not even come close to the magnitude of the real horror. No civilized nation in modern times had so systematically set out to obliterate an entire race of people. There were historical records and anecdotal evidence, the catalyst for Nazi purges, but Europeans had forgotten the ancient narratives that should have been the warning signs.

The students thumped on their desks until the thumping sounded to Kurt like the boot-falls of a hundred thousand troops marching through the Brandenburg Gate following German boys dressed as Roman soldiers, riding the new Caesar's wave to power. Then he remembered the point he was trying to make. "...Imperialism! Imperialism is only another form of conquest by expansion. It failed. It shall always fail. The Kaiser's attempt at Imperialism...which by the way, was just envy of the British and the French...only gave us a war that ruined our wonderful country. The British are taxed to the limit trying to maintain the empire they've carved out and wish they could divest themselves of...Spain, for all her plundering of the riches of the Americas, is still a poor country..."

"That's not your point, Herr Schulte!" the student with the arm band shouted. "Your meaning is as transparent as the plot of your trash book. You're trying to retard the work of the Führer!!"

"You flatter me again, Herr Kohl. To think that my humble story could stop the National Socialist movement in its tracks..."

"Old men like you are an anchor to our cause! You refuse to see the benefits!"

"Are you blind young man!? You should wear that arm band over your eyes! You're all blind! Hitler's a tyrant! The Nazis are the real enemy!!..." Kurt was losing control. The students began thumping their desks again and Kurt had to shout over the noise. "Hitler's a maniac who'll lead Germany to another war and thousands of you will die for your stupid cause!!"

"Then I would die gladly for the Führer!!" shouted the youth. "Heil Hitler!!" The boys wearing the arm bands jumped to their feet and gave the Nazi salute and yelled out their leader's name again and again. The other students tried to shout them down and thumped their desks and threw books. They weren't on anybody's side. They just wanted to make noise. A scuffle broke out near the top of the bank of seats. A student was punched by some boys wearing arm bands. The rest of the students were too disorganized to help. They continued to shout and thump their desks, enjoying the commotion they were creating. Suddenly the door opened with a bang and the headmaster of the college entered.

Another man, dressed in a black fedora and long black leather coat, entered and stood to one side of the headmaster so that he had a full view of his quarry, Kurt. He was tall and wore a belt done up so that he was at once slim and broad shouldered and he wore the wide brimmed hat pulled low, putting his eyes in shadow above a sharp nose. Even in shadow the eyes were cold and capable of being cruel.

"Herr Schulte!" said the headmaster. "What is the meaning of this outburst!? This is a lecture room, not a gymnasium!"

The headmaster was addressing Kurt but his look of disgust took in the students. Kurt watched the man in the black trench coat. He was uncomfortable in the man's gaze and his senses warned him of a new danger.

"Herr Schulte," continued the headmaster, "Kapitän Kliner wishes to speak with you...in private."

Kliner bowed slightly to the headmaster and made a barely perceptible gesture with his head. The subtle gesture was more menacing than a gun. Kurt took his coat from the rack, picked up his briefcase and walked to the door. Two uniformed Gestapo officers were waiting in the hallway. Kliner lead the way along the empty hallway to the rotunda. The wooden-faced officers fell in close behind Kurt as if they expected him to bolt and run. Kurt was tempted but it meant bullets in the back from the deadly looking machine-pistols they carried. He thought of Bremen station and the trick the blond sailor had played on him and almost laughed. The students poured into the hallway to watch Kurt being led away. He ignored the jeers and wondered if the class would ever be resumed.

"May I ask where we're going?"

"Berlin," said Kliner.

"Are we returning soon?"

"That's up to you," answered Kliner.

BERLIN

May 21, 1933: For that date Kurt wrote in July of '33: *'...Years of training under my father's guns were not wasted after all. Kliner tried to intimidate me but he was a rank amateur compared to Father. Even the ice-cold baths helped because I learned to take the discomfort like a stoic. In my later childhood I refused to show emotion or hurt when Father was around because I wouldn't give him the satisfaction of seeing me in pain or begging for his cold mercy...'*

Captain Kliner posed in front of his desk, below the stern picture of Adolf Hitler in a cheap black frame. The desk was flanked by red and black Nazi flags, like the flags in the parades, with the black swastika in a white circle on a red ground. Kurt wondered if the Nazis knew the swastika had originated as a mystic symbol of peace and plenty in such diverse cultures as ancient Japan, Persia, India and North America. Now it would be forever remembered as the symbol of evil in the hands of the Nazis. *What's in a symbol?* wondered Kurt.

Kliner smoked and waited for Kurt to squirm. Kurt was uncomfortable on the straight backed chair but refused to show any emotion. There was a comfortable chair beside the desk but this wasn't the office of Commander Müller in Emden or Frank Heppelmann's office. He was experiencing the Gestapo's early attempts at intimidation. Kurt would have preferred to look out the window but the heavy, wine coloured drapes were closed allowing only a small shaft of light that knifed in and cut a line across the black and white tiled floor. Kurt watched the sunbeams rise and fall and the cigarette smoke blow across the shaft of light like a thin lace curtain. Outside the windows children played in the park while nannies of the Gestapo watched over them from the shade of the late blooming linden trees and gossiped about their mistresses.

"Suppose you just tell me now, Herr Schulte," said Captain Kliner. Kliner was agitated because Kurt had refused to talk during the train ride back to Berlin, preferring to look out the window or watch the people nervously watching Kliner and the armed guards. They weren't concerned about the German prisoner who looked too self possessed and arrogant.

"Tell you what?"

Kliner walked around the big desk, took the book out of a drawer and tossed it on the desk. It skidded across the polished mahogany surface and stopped in front of Kurt as if Kliner had practiced the manoeuvre. Kurt didn't look at the book, he watched Kliner's eyes for signs but the man didn't give anything away. Kliner walked back around the desk and leaned against it so that the book was partially obscured. Then he offered Kurt a cigarette from a silver inlaid box on the desk. Kurt shook his head but thought of Willie. This was Willie's army, although the Gestapo and the Storm Troopers were Hitler's private police, they were technically on the same side. He wondered if Willie could be like Kliner, or like the other self important Gestapo officers strutting the streets of Berlin, intimidating old people and looking the other way when gangs of Hitler Youth beat up Jews and stole their property. No, Willie was a soldier. Willie could never be one of them. But how did senior officers like Willie tolerate Hitler and what he stood for? His own father, for all his pompous nonsense and stiff militarism, would not agree with the tactics used increasingly by Hitler against his own people.

The SS, *the Schutzstaffel,* formed by Heinrich Himmler in 1931, would raise institutional terror to new levels but Kurt was spared the experience. The SS would concentrate on the Jewish problem and the battle fronts. For the time being he would have to survive Kliner and the Gestapo. "You won't be simple enough to deny you wrote it?"

"Of course not, it has my name on it."

"Good. We'll get along fine, Herr Schulte. Now tell me about it."

"You've read my book?"

"Not worth a thorough read," said Kliner.

"You at least know it's fiction."

"I know it's worse than fiction! It's a pack of lies!"

"The definition's relative. Fiction is truth by another name but born of the same mother."

"Don't play word games with me, Herr Schulte! It's a gross lie! Propaganda of the worst sort! A blatant attempt to discredit the Reich and the Führer…!"

"It never mentions the Reich or the sainted Führer, perhaps that's why you're upset, because I left you all out. I'll remember you in my next…"

"Silence!!"

"Do you want me to talk or be silent, Kapitän Kliner? I'm a simple man and easily confused."

"You're an intellectual snob, Schulte! One of the small minority of intellectual snobs and elitists and misfits who seek to weaken us in the eyes of our enemies, by spreading lies about the Führer's plans for the future of Germany!"

"Germany has no future…" Kurt began, and stopped. He drew back. Imprisonment was one thing Kurt could not survive, or so he thought.

"Yes, Herr Schulte? You were about to say?"

"I was about to say, that even if there were a small grain of intention in my book, the little truths that creep through should be of no concern to the powerful Reich."

"You *are* clever with words, Herr Schulte. You write well, for a misguided fool. But you're also a disease and even a small disease can spread and affect the otherwise healthy body."

"Is Germany healthy when people are persecuted for their birthright and writers can't print the truth!? Surely the principles of free speech and the laws of Germany...?"

"Laws!? Don't talk about laws! Laws are to protect us from people like your Jew friend, Heppelmann. We have tried to be fair with him. They're greedy, those Jews. They think only of themselves, never Germany. We offered to buy his printing house. Does he think of Germany? No! Only money. More money! That's Jews, Schulte! They'd sell out the Fatherland like it was an auction, if we let them."

"He's German. Born and raised in Berlin. He fought for his country."

"To protect their money! The fathers sent their sons to the army to protect their money!" He wondered about Heppelmann and if Kliner was right but it was foolish to argue and Kurt wasn't thinking straight. He was angry again and anger is a sign of weakness. He let his temper subside while Kliner watched for a chink in the armour. Kurt automatically reached into his inside coat pocket for a cigarette, but the guards had stripped him of his cigarettes and papers. He felt naked and vulnerable. They could strip away his freedom as easily. There was nothing to be gained by being difficult.

Kliner opened the cigarette box just out of Kurt's reach, again precisely as though the spot was marked out on the wide, bare desk. Everything calculated. The large high-ceilinged office was sparse and cold so a prisoner couldn't get comfortable. Even the lighting was cold and harsh. Kurt thought about the spring sunshine and the waves on sand beaches and the terns soaring...

"Cigarette, Schulte?"

"Yes, thank you," said Kurt, politely. He wanted a cigarette and there was nothing to be gained by refusing once more. He didn't reach for the box.

"Help yourself."

"In my father's house the guests were always served."

Kliner smiled. "Your father's house was known for genteel courtesies. You were born well. What would the General have said about his son plotting with the enemy to undermine the Reich?"

"Father was a purist. I'm afraid he'd object to some of your new... tactics!"

"You have a brother, a Major Wilhelm von Schulte. He has ambitions to become a general, no? It would be a shame if your involvement with the Jews compromised his chances."

"My involvement? I wrote a book. I needed a publisher."

"The family estate is large," Kliner continued. "Not my idea of elegance but well situated and the family holdings are valuable. Much of your income is derived from your land, is it not? We're looking for a suitable place for our officers to escape the pressures of the city." Kliner let the statement hang and handed Kurt the cigarette box.

Kurt selected a cigarette and noted they were French. Kliner lit Kurt's cigarette with an American Zippo lighter. Gold plated. Monogrammed. If Kurt refused to go along with the Gestapo it could ruin his family. A word from Kliner and two hundred years of Schulte history would be wiped out and his family homeless. It would be that easy. And what of the families who worked on the estate farms? They represented generations of tenant farmers dependent on the Schultes for their living. Weren't they a part of the family? And the domestics? They also had families. And the caretakers had families. Kurt could displace a hundred people into poverty by being stubborn and Kliner knew it.

"What would you like me to do?" asked Kurt, blowing a cloud of smoke toward Kliner. If he was giving in he didn't have to appear servile.

"That's better, Herr Schulte. You are not a stupid man."

"Really?"

"But, you're right, Schulte, your little book is inconsequential to the Reich. However, you show a certain flare for language, despite the things you say in the book; the veiled references, the innuendoes. All lies of course. If you were to denounce the lies and dedicate yourself to helping the Reich I would consider releasing the book to the sellers, with certain alterations, minor corrections." Kliner's smile was ingenuous.

"Release!?..."

Kliner crossed the room and drew back the curtains. On the far side of the room was a stack of shipping crates. The name of Heppelmann's publishing house was stenciled across the crates. Kurt was stunned. Kliner reached into a crate and held up a copy of *Der Republik des Teufel*.

"All of them?" Kurt's voice was barely audible. The cigarette slipped from his fingers and rolled across the tile floor toward Kliner. Kliner crushed the cigarette with his polished shoe and returned to his desk.

"A few copies slipped out...to party members, for their amusement. Congratulations. You're in demand. Unfortunately, the plates were destroyed in a tragic fire." Kliner let that information sink in before he continued. "Your Jew friend, Herr Heppelmann, is missing and presumed dead. An unfortunate accident."

"An accident!? You don't expect me to believe that!?"

"What you believe is immaterial. What you say and do is something else. You have considerable talents, if you chose to use them for a positive end..."

"I won't be a propagandist for a gang of criminals and thugs!!"

"I'd be careful, Herr Schulte. Your father is no longer here to protect you or your brother. The Reich is for the common people and therefore families of the privileged class are...suspect."

"Suspect of what!? Being loyal to an old idea...a more decent and noble Germany?" asked Kurt rhetorically, barely able to control his anger. He felt strange defending his family. Since he was a boy he had rebelled against the stiff discipline, the militarism and the facade of the life he lived. He regretted mocking his heritage and realized it was suddenly very important to him and to Germany. He saw them all on the brink of destruction at the hands of the vulgar gang who beat Germans to death in the streets and burned books and threatened to wipe out a whole race of people. The Nazis were committed to destroying the old order and replacing it with their peculiar brand of fanaticism for the Führer. Hitler wanted to be Caesar. He wanted to be a god. He said as much in his writings and in his speeches. Wasn't anybody listening? Kurt was cold with fear, but not fear for himself; fear of the death of a part of Germany he had once despised.

Kliner doggedly followed the party line. "No," he said, with patience, as if Kurt were a misguided child, "suspect of being self serving opportunists, collaborating with the American Zionists who control the foreign money markets."

Kurt seethed inside. "In other words, you think my family and all the families who kept Germany's industry grinding through the war, and provided the officers and the money to fight the war, and who tried to get Germany going again after the war...you suspect they're collaborating with the Jewish bankers."

"An interesting theory, Schulte. Perhaps you'd like to develop your theory for the Ministry?"

"Never!" said Kurt.

"Never?"

Kliner let the question lie there, like the book on the desk. The two men watched each other; both sure the other wasn't about to budge from their ideological positions. Kliner didn't realize how far around Kurt had come in his thinking and Kurt was surprised at himself. He didn't know what it meant. He felt old and tired and too demoralized to fight or lash out for principles he didn't understand. Kliner was also tiring of the game but he couldn't hold Kurt on any substantial grounds.

"All right, Schulte, I'll give you time. Go back to your University and think about the future. You are forbidden to write, by the Führer's decree! And remember, you will be watched."

Kurt stood up to leave and as if on a cue from Kliner a small side door opened and a clerk entered with Kurt's coat and briefcase. Kurt checked the pockets for his personal belonging, dragging out the process to annoy Kliner. Satisfied, he put on his coat and hefted his briefcase which seemed lighter. The Gestapo had confiscated his lecture notes and a garlic sausage and bread and a bottle of coffee. Kurt laughed and went out the door where the two guards waited. Kurt nodded to them but they pretended not to notice. *Proper little wooden soldiers,* thought Kurt, as he walked across the main lobby of the police building to the big brass and glass doors. The Reich loved a good show. The façade was important. "Not unlike home," said Kurt, to the guard outside. The guard made no sign. *At least it's spring,* Kurt said to himself. He turned toward the sunset and crossed the Prinzalbrechtstrasse and the River Spree to the solace of the green Tiergarten.

Berlin looked more alive than he remembered it after the Great War. Uniformed men and boys, some patrolling, others off duty, strolled in groups or with young women. Berlin usually came to life in the evening when the theatres and the opera and concerts drew the wealthy Berliners into the streets. Now it seemed as if everybody was on the move and there was a new spirit. Berlin was beginning to look prosperous again, if one looked beyond the lingering poverty, the legacy of war and depression. He had noticed it during the weeks spent searching for Heppelmann's good gentiles. Poor Heppelmann. If he hadn't walked into his office that day Heppelmann would still be alive and the family business intact. Kurt felt badly about what happened but knew it would have happened sooner or later. His book predicted it. Heppelmann printed the book and the prophecy became self fulfilling. *God, what irony!* He sat on a bench, feeling depressed, and watched the people traffic. Heppelmann the Jew was dead. It was no accident and Berlin moved to a new beat. The Jews would die so Germany could live.

It turned cold when the sun went down behind the government buildings. Kurt left the park and bought some overpriced sausages and bread and wine from a small grocery shop. The ancient owner of the shop looked Jewish. He also looked German. Kurt thanked the defenseless, vulnerable old man, wanting to say more. He took the S-Bahn to the railway station and boarded the night train for Leipzig.

The night air was cold. The second class car wasn't heated and the rowdy group of young farm workers travelling to the south insisted on keeping the windows open. The young woman in the seat opposite to Kurt had sad brown eyes. She was poorly dressed, as were her three children; a boy about five and two girls, younger. The children were cold and hungry; their mother tried to comfort them and put her thin arms around them. Kurt was sorry for the children but felt nothing for the woman, who wouldn't look at him. She would have been very pretty with her straggly blonde hair under control and the sad look on her face turned into a smile. Kurt guessed she'd had problems because of a man rather than because of the government.

"A cold night," Kurt said, finally, feeling silly for saying the obvious.

The woman looked at him for the first time. She had nice eyes but they only increased her sadness. The boy, shy in Kurt's gaze, tucked himself under her right arm, peering out like a small animal. *The problem is definitely a man,* Kurt thought. The little girls ignored Kurt and argued about a bedraggled doll with a cracked head and the body stuffing coming out. Kurt wondered what their story was but hoped she didn't tell him if it was sad. He knew it was sad. He guessed the young couple started out life optimistically after the war but were trampled by the crumbling political and economic situation in Germany even before the Nazis came to power. Out of work, the man drank too much cheap bock in the beer halls and got drunk and took out his frustration on the young woman who would have been so beautiful when they were married, expecting a life of bliss and beautiful children. She had the beautiful children, behind the hunger and the tears. He didn't want to know the story. His imagined story was bad enough. If it was worse...

"Do you have anything for the children to eat?" asked Kurt. It was also an obvious question but he didn't know what else to say. She shook her head and looked out the window. It was dark and there was nothing to see except dim points of light in the distance and her own reflection and the reflection of the man opposite who was being a nuisance.

"No," she said quietly, not looking at him. "I spent our last marks on the tickets."

"Oh," said Kurt, remembering the pain he and Bright had experienced having to sell their things to buy tickets for the train to Leipzig in 1920. So long ago. So much had happened and nothing had happened, and here he was thirteen years on and he had nothing but a little wine and bread and a warm coat. "Where are you going?"

"Near Augsburg," she answered vaguely.

Going home to mother after the last argument? Had the man beat her? He hoped she'd never go back. The bastard didn't deserve a wife and beautiful children.

"A long journey," he said. Kurt offered the woman the bag and the bottle of wine. "Please, I'm only going as far as Leipzig. I don't need it."

The woman hesitated. Kurt knew what she was thinking. Her children were staring at the bag and up at their mother. She accepted it for them. For herself she would have refused. She hadn't been alone long enough to take gifts from strangers, especially unshaven, sad looking men in tattered old greatcoats who looked like beggars.

When the children had eaten, the woman had some bread and a sip of wine and gave her children some wine so they would sleep.

"Keep the rest," he said. "I'm not hungry."

She knew Kurt wasn't telling the truth. Her perfect mouth twitched into a small smile and her eyes said *thank you*. The children were sleepy. Kurt took off his coat and put it over the four of them. She didn't look at him again but she trusted him and closed her eyes and went to sleep with her arms around her children who somehow managed to get all their arms and legs tucked up on the seat under Kurt's coat. Kurt watched them sleeping. His heart ached and his eyes betrayed him, and he felt the tears beginning to trickle down. When he tried to wipe them away he felt the stubble of his scruffy beard and understood.

LEIPZIG

The night train stopped at Leipzig station a little after two in the morning. The woman and her children didn't wake up. Kurt took only his briefcase and left the train and walked to his apartment building through deserted streets. The air was cold and damp but he didn't mind. When he reached his flat the door was already open.

The small apartment had been torn apart and all his possessions turned over or broken and scattered. Books, furniture, his few clothes, brandy bottles smashed and ink splashed across the books. A crude Star of David was scrawled on the wall, the ink running down like tears. Kurt was stunned, numbed to explanation, but went to the table, righted it and pulled back the two halves. The manuscript was still hidden between the leaves of the table along with the first copy of the edition in its heavy brown wrapper, sent to him by Frank Heppelmann. Kurt left the manuscript and the book, put the briefcase on the table and went out, slamming the door behind him.

It was nearly three in the morning, colder and raining when he pounded on the door of the wine merchant, shivering uncontrollably and wishing he had his greatcoat. The merchant, in his night shirt, grumpy with sleep, opened the door. He didn't recognize Kurt at first and was about to shut the door in his face.

"Wait! Herr Mustner!" said Kurt, in a horse whisper, as if afraid of being discovered by Gestapo agents. "It's Kurt Schulte."

"Schulte!" he said gruffly, opening the door again. "Are you too drunk already to know what time it is?"

"I need a bottle."

"I suppose you won't let me sleep. Wait here."

"Three bottles," he said, as Herr Mustner closed the door.

Kurt watched the street while he waited and thought about how the cheap brandy would taste. The first drink would be harsh and rough going down. He drank too much to afford good cognac but he didn't care. He needed the hard warmth, and then the distance it would put between himself and reality. Why were they persecuting him? It was just a small story and the Reich was so big. He vowed not to be held prisoner in his spirit by the Reich. Then he thought about what he was doing; standing in a doorway in the middle of the night to buy brandy so he could get drunk enough to forget.

Two policemen, carrying rifles casually over their shoulders, came down the street slowly, talking. Kurt pressed himself back into the shadow of the doorway. There was a time when policemen didn't carry rifles as though they were an occupation force. He was on the run whether he liked it or not.

The merchant opened the door and handed Kurt three bottles wrapped in paper. He handed Mustner a few crumpled marks and the merchant gave Kurt the change and shut the door. Kurt waited until the patrol had turned a corner before he returned to his desecrated lodgings.

May 22, 1933: '...*I remember the day very well, although I shouldn't have been able to remember anything. I returned to my flat after buying brandy from Herr Mustner, straightened the furniture and drank some brandy, lay down on my bed and went to sleep thinking about Bright. I awoke a few hours later, unable to sleep, got up, drank more brandy and tried to salvage my books. I was shocked to see how thoroughly the books had been attacked. Pages torn out and the covers ripped off. Someone had stabbed the books over and over as if the books were the real enemy. It must have been the pointless destruction of my books that caused the fit, or whatever it was. I began ripping apart the books myself. I drank more brandy and became more angry and began burning them in the fireplace. They were my only companions and somehow books had betrayed me, or so my unbalanced mind believed. I must have made a lot of noise because the concierge pounded on the door. I told him to go away. Willie came down from Berlin that evening...'*

When Willie arrived Kurt had used up his rage and was talking to himself, leafing through the few remaining books, tossing them into the fire while drinking the second bottle of brandy.

"What rubbish! What bloody good are books if civilization's crumbling around our ears!? Philosophers!...Jung! What good has he done us!?" Kurt tossed the book into the blaze. "Kant! For God's sake!" Kant followed Jung on the pile. The fire retreated momentarily then caught on the dry pages and flared again. "Nietzsche!! He warned us at least!" Nietzsche, one of Kurt's favourites, followed the others, "Plato! For the love of God!! We couldn't be further from Plato! What good are they then!? What possible good? All goddamned lies! Bunch of intellectuals like us, talking, talking, talking, while gangs of hooligans roam the streets and beat us up and the Communists and the National Socialists all saying the same thing...*My way or die.*" He tossed the last book into the fire and picked up the manuscript. "And this pitiful effort! Where did I get the gall to think I could change their minds? Rubbish!" Kurt tossed the manuscript into the fire and watched the pages curl, turn black and crumble away one by one, in orderly fashion, like good Germans; like dead leaves in a fall parkland. He drank more brandy. Time passed, he wasn't aware, day or night and then someone knocked on the door. "Go away, you sons-a-bitches!"

"Kurt?" It was Willie's voice, muffled but unmistakable. "Kurt! Open the door!"

"Not locked."

Willie, weighted down by his heavy dress uniform, was out of breath from the climb. "Kurt, I came as soon as I heard."

"Why should it be locked? They come in anyway." Kurt stared at the fire, watching the last pages of the manuscript turning black. He didn't have any feelings about the book and he wasn't curious about why Willie was standing in the doorway. "My life's an open door, Dear Brother. I have nothing more to hide. Just want little peace."

"You're drunk," said Willie, closing the door and taking off his coat.

"No, knifed in the back. Bleeding ink."

"I took the first train. The Concierge telephoned and said you were smashing the place up. He said you wouldn't answer the door."

"He let them in, the bastard!"

"Who!?"

"Gestapo. Hitler's gangs. Storm troopers! My students! What does it matter? I've been violated. Life ends. Anarchy reigns. They were looking for that." Kurt pointed to the burning manuscript.

"I warned you not to come out against the Reich."

"They have no sense of humour, those Gestapo bastards. No imagination either." He laughed.

"Kurt, grow up."

"And you're with them, Willie!"

"You're just stupid drunk to say that."

"You've sold your soul for more gold braid. Know what Kapitän Kliner said?..."

"That's not fair. It's my career. Just because you choose to live like a beggar, don't expect me to. I have responsibilities."

"He said if I don't cooperate you'll get the sack. That's the kind of good boys we're dealing with. Regular German gentlemen. And know what else? Mother gets the sack too and the estate is turned into a big pink whorehouse for Gestapo flunkeys. At least it's the right colour...that's what the good old Führer will do for us."

"Kurt, I have a family to think of!" Willie was instantly sorry. "I shouldn't have said that."

"Please, just leave me alone."

"What will you do?"

Kurt watched the fire consume the last of the manuscript pages. The black ash moved with the heat and pieces rose up the chimney. Kurt thought there was something symbolic about that but he didn't pursue the thought. "I have two choices don't I? To live or to die."

"You mustn't think that way again. You have your students."

"Tell me then, what should I do about them?"

Willie couldn't answer the question. He thought it was obvious but perhaps Kurt was right. What *would* he do? What *could* he do if it was his own students who attacked his flat? He suddenly realized Kurt was in danger from forces other than his own depression.

"Well?" asked Kurt. "I know you have the answer, Dear Brother. You've always had the answers."

"Come home with me."

"No, thank you."

"You're in danger if you stay here."

"Danger? What's more dangerous than a family?"

"From the gangs, whoever." He meant to say from Kurt himself. He could see the signs, but he also knew whoever wrecked the flat could come back.

"I'm to be watched because I won't do dirty things for them. Kliner said so."

"What did he ask you to do?"

"Write lies for the new Ministry of Propaganda."

"He's offering you a way out."

"I refused."

"Couldn't you pretend to go along?" Willie knew it was the wrong thing to ask. He expected at least a withering look. It didn't come. That was even worse because it meant Kurt was giving up. "I've been a lot of lousy things in my time, Willie, but I can't lie to save myself."

Willie unbuckled the belt and holster with the Luger nestled inside and laid it on the table near Kurt's elbow. "I want you to have this." The firelight danced on the polished leather. Kurt looked at the holster and then at Willie.

"What am I supposed to do with that?"

"Protect yourself, if you insist on staying here."

"One weapon against them?"

"What else can I do for you?"

"Nothing. Thank you for the offer, but it's your only weapon."

"It was Father's."

"He'd be annoyed with you for giving it to me, the prodigal, malcontent, bastard son!"

Willie took a deep breath. "Kurt, Father shot himself with that gun."

Kurt flushed with guilt. It was the first real emotion Willie was allowed to see. "You said Father died in his sleep...causes unknown."

"You weren't around to see the end. He suffered, but not from an illness. You could have prevented it. I'm sorry to be so blunt but you might as well know the truth, and deal with that too." Willie opened the holster and drew out the gleaming, blue-black pistol, held it by the grip and pointed it at the fireplace. "He asked for his Luger that night. I brought it to him and he took it out like this and pointed it at the fireplace in his bed chamber. He shot three of Mother's favourite vases off the mantel and then picked off the figurines. It was quite funny, actually. Mother was disgusted of course. I think it was the most fun Father had for years." Willie sighted the weapon at a brandy bottle on the mantle. "The domestics refused to go near the room after he shot the figurines. I think the old bugger had it planned because later, when he shot himself, no one paid any attention. We found him in the morning. There was a short note beside the pillow and lots of blood. He mentioned you. His last request was for me to have this gun and do something useful with it. That's why I'm giving it to you, to protect yourself."

Willie put the gun down on the table and waited for a reaction or even a sign that Kurt understood. Kurt was absorbed in thoughts of his own so Willie put on his coat, crossed to the door and looked at Kurt slumped in the chair staring at the dying fire.

"Kurt?...Come to us when you're ready."

Kurt didn't look up so Willie closed the door softly.

Later Kurt got up to stir the unburned pages. Satisfied the fire was going well he returned to the chair, touched the Luger as if reading it's power, watched the fire and thought about a night of fire and chaos in the English Channel. What had happened to the angry young British sailor who cursed him from the shattered bridge of his dying destroyer and remembered the same face in fog when he still had Bright? He was certain it was the same man, not a nightmare. The man had cursed him the first time they met, but only accused him with a look the second time. The curse must be working. His life was reduced to burning books and putting out the flames of memories with brandy. He was forty-five years old, looked sixty-five and felt as though he had lived forever. He picked up the Luger, pointed it at the fireplace and squeezed the trigger. The red flames jumped at the sound of the explosion. Sparks flew up the chimney and pieces of hot stone showered the room. Kurt laughed and fired again. It *was* fun. He squeezed the trigger again and again until there was one bullet left in the clip.

I woke up after midnight, cold and stiff, sprawled across my notebook. Jimmy was gone and the cabin was shaking. Vicious freezing rain pellets drove against the window and drummed the thin walls like thrown gravel. The Atlantic was in the full fury of an early fall storm and the wind shrieked and moaned through the cracks in the cabin as though angry with the earth, intent on destroying something.

Kurt would dismiss my personification of the elements as a silly affectation but we had left Kurt to an uncertain future and I was feeling set upon by the elements as well as the events threatening my Germans. Also I was concerned about Pius and his crew left on the exposed beach that winter of 1933, building their schooner. If the conditions in their tilt were more extreme than Jimmy's primitive shack their winter ordeal must have been very hard. Reading the accounts of Sir Ernest Shackleton's failed Antarctic Expedition, his party surviving in stone huts, without heat, living a long winter in rotting sleeping bags, eating rancid blubber with frostbite and gangrene for companions, I marveled at man's ability to survive extreme conditions and remain sane. But Pius and his crew had to get up every morning and crawl out through the snow to work on their exposed beach site. And their objective was to build a small ship seaworthy enough to cope with conditions like the gale screaming at me around Jimmy's shack. I could feel the tremors as the waves crashed into the rocks outside the harbour and the cold was creeping across the floor, glittering on the window pane.

A new fear crept in with the cold. How would Jimmy make the trip back up the hill and what would I do if something happened to my interpreter? Opening the stove to light the fire, the wind sucked grey ash up the chimney. The kindling was still outside the shack. But where? Jimmy brought it in each morning when he returned from the village. Giving up the notion of a fire I crawled under my blankets, curled into a ball, shivering, listening to the wind until I was hearing voices; choirs singing, cellos, violins, triangles, and whole orchestras playing, sending the shivers racing up and down my spine. It had happened before, on a camping trip to Algonquin Park late one fall. Storm stayed on a small island, I huddled in a tiny tent with my faithful Brown Dog at my side, hearing all the strange sounds; voices, the music, the symphony orchestra, but doing alright until I realized Brown Dog, her neck hairs standing up and big brown eyes wide, was hearing them too. I tried to ignore the voices filtering through Jimmy's shack but there were too many narrators and the cot became crowded with musicians and story tellers and characters from the past and the present and I didn't have my Brown Dog.

Suddenly the door burst open with a gust of wind and Jimmy was back, arms loaded with wood, jamming his shoulder into the door to force it closed. His face twisted in fear and loathing of the elements. Needless to say I was glad to see him.

"Not a civil night," Jimmy said, in a triumph of understatement as he began prodding the cold stove to life.

"You've been to the village and back already?"

"My son! 'tis gone dawn but the sky's that black. Everything's fine at Mrs. Penny's, but the news isn't good. A trawler's gone down, they think, coming in the Strait for Raleigh Harbour. That's down around Cape Bauld way. We heard it on the news at Aunt Mary's. One of the men's from Fogo. Young fella, Gary White, a cousin of mine, see. He'd come back 'cause he wanted to work at home. Lucky to get a job right off but he's a good boy and knows how to work. It was Mrs. Penny's husband got him the job, see."

"Maybe they had a life boat or something?"

Jimmy looked at the window. Rain and sleet splattered against the glass and ran down in nervous little rivulets, blown this way and that by the wind. Few reached the bottom of the pane before being torn away to join the scud. Dawn was barely showing through the black storm wrack and the low, wind-driven clouds seemed to be driving straight at us. Jimmy shook his head.

"My dear man, the Strait's no place to be adrift in a small boat.

You're on the rocks that fast, see, or the wicked tide lop puts you under. Only God Himself can save you. No sir, if their boat went down they're resting peaceful with God."

"That's some consolation, I guess." It felt inadequate even commenting.

"Gary has a young wife, Lindy, and a baby girl, Sarah. A lot of the babies get called Sarah now. She's a pretty thing. I saw her one night when Gary asked me to come along at a certain time, and he brought the baby to the window. His woman said it was all right if I came in but I didn't want to do it. It would have been something to hold that little one though. I never held a baby…not even young Thomas, Rosie's son?"

That name again. *Rosie.*

"Lindy's from away, like, and finds it strange here, but she's a good heart and tries her best to get on with us. It wasn't that way with Rosie, see. She never tried to get on with us. By'n'by I got to tell you about Rosie, I suppose."

Rosie, the picture in the album in the trunk in the Commander's house was clear in my mind but Jimmy seemed reluctant to tell the story. Why? She's *Rosie* to him, not Rose as she was to Pius and Aunt Mary.

"Don't know what Lindy and the baby's going to do, sure, now Gary's gone."

Jimmy sounded certain that Gary White was gone. Maybe he did know. Maybe the voices I heard in the wind were the spirits reporting the news. *Don't be foolish!*

"What if I was to give some of that money to Gary's woman?" He sat down at the table and stared out the window. The Coast Guard hadn't begun the search for the trawler and already I was mentally preparing myself to go down to the village and introduce myself to a fisherman's widow, with an offer of money from a crazy, distorted man on the hill.

The immediacy of life on the rugged coast came in a rush. We weren't talking about history, old shipwreck tales or the romance of sail. This was Newfoundland of the present, where men still went to sea and it didn't matter if the boats were wood or steel, it was the same ocean with the same dangers. And Jimmy lived on the top of his mountain for the same reason.

The eastern sky lightened as the storm showed signs of blowing itself out. Jimmy brought in more firewood, put water on to boil and cut thick slices of fresh bread sent up by Aunt Mary. I went out to do the morning ritual. It was more than a ritual in the wind. I was a long time coming back to the shack because I couldn't take my eyes off the wild scene below, as fifty foot waves smashed themselves to foam and fury on the jagged coastline. Spume blew over the rocks and made the village a blur. Never had I witnessed an ocean in such turmoil. When I returned from battling the elements the coffee was brewing and the bread laid out, spread with a thick coating of Aunt Mary's partridgeberry jam.

I sat in my chair near the window, sipping a scalding cup of coffee, and opened Pius' scribbler to a date in April, 1933. With a slice of jambread in one hand and a pen in the other, I was ready to begin another day. Jimmy watched the ocean for a long time. I wondered what he was thinking and where we were going that April day in 1933. At least winter had been endured and my boat builders were still at work, but I had a bad feeling about the outcome. There was a large gap in the writing and imagined why.

EXPLOITS BEACH

April 15, 1933: Pius wrote: '...We've made some good progress and the boys are glad of a spell of fine weather. March was bitter with cold and I didn't have the desire to write. Today we put in her last ceiling planks and tomorrow the last of the deck planks will be fit where we left some out to run the long ceiling pieces down below. The boys made a nice job of it. She looks all right. They worked hard all February and March month and had her planked up in good time. They were glad enough to get some work down below out of the weather. It was no worse a season than usual I suppose, but on the beach, exposed like we are, every breeze of wind cuts right through. Andrew got a foot nipped by the frost and still feels it. Poor Uncle George let his left hand get nipped and didn't say anything 'til the gangrene got hold. We had to cut his hand off before it spread. He never complained and worked as hard as the rest of us with one good arm. Time to get at her spars and fit out the cabin and maybe we can move aboard soon and have a better place to lay down. This shack is a filthy black hole and I hope I never have to spend another winter in the likes. It's better for sleeping now at least. The fire can go out and we can breath almost normal. The lads have been very good and put up with their lot and done everything I asked them to do. I seen a whale carcass lying around the cape there when we came in and the bones would make a good black paint for her hull. We see an end to it now. Another month or so and we'll be ready to put her off. Right now I need to get my head down for a spell. Tomorrow we'll go up an cut the trees we marked in January month for her spars. Labrador pack has moved in tight to the shore and runs to the horizon and beyond...'

April 16, 1933: The new ship's planks shone golden in the morning sun, fresh and clean like a newborn child. She looked complete but Pius knew exactly how many pieces were still to be added to the puzzle. Every morning he stood for a few moments organizing the day's work, matching his men to their jobs. Today he and Harry, Gus and Alf would go back into the forest and drop the big spruce trees they had marked in January for the spars while the others finish the deck planking and begin the tedious but exacting job of driving in the caulking. All winter they had been separating and pulling out strands of old hemp and soaking them with a mixture of cod oil and pine tar, preparing the strings of oakum and hanging them from the rafters. The excess oil dripped back into the pots so as not to waste a drop.

Pius scanned the ragged ice field pressed tight to the shore. The pack showed no signs of moving off, but it was early. He wouldn't begin to worry until May. Some years the ice didn't move until June and the outports were imprisoned by the packs which jammed into the bays and harbours, pushed hard by the currents and the wind and more new ice from Labrador. But at any time the wind could come off the land and one morning the ice would be a sliver of white on the horizon and the ocean would be so blue it would make your eyes burn.

The men came out of the shack one at a time and Pius knew what most of them were thinking as they took in the scene. Somewhere out there the seals were gathering, the late arrivals having their pups. The adults would laze about on the ice and nurse their fat pups and gossip in the sun. In the spring the seals called the Newfoundlanders to the ice as surely as the Sirens called Ulysses almost to his doom. Pius wasn't Ulysses. He wouldn't venture out on the ice. Some of the men knew his feelings and didn't press the point although they would have trooped off gladly with a rifle for a day of hunting and the promise of seal flipper pie or a fresh heart.

Later, in the dark forest above the beach, Pius, Gus and Alf stood aside and watched Harry taking his turn with the broad axe, cutting big chunks of sweet smelling wood out of a giant spruce tree, the sap beginning to run free and the resin boiling out of old scars.

All the wood used in her construction was green but the ship would be in the water before the weather warmed up. The masts and spars would shrink and split lengthwise of course, but that didn't affect their strength. As the masts shrink the wedges at the deck partners are driven in further; accepted procedure for a working schooner living in a damp climate, wet most of the time with sea water and salt fish. If, after twenty years, the spruce gives out another ship can be built to take her place.

The chips of wood from Harry's axe fell on corn snow lying in the deep shadows. The satisfying *thunk* echoed through the forest until it sounded as if a dozen other men were at work. The morning wind sighed through the tops and the first ravens of the year returning to claim their territory called from high up, complaining about the intrusion into their forest.

Harry, shirtless in the chill air, had filled out over the winter months, despite the hard labour and poor food. His strong young muscles rippled with each swing of the axe. He enjoyed the task that required maximum effort and worked out his frustrations on the tree.

"A hard winter hasn't hurt that one," Alf observed.

"My son, he'll have that tree down before us gets another go at her," said Gus.

"There's a good enough one for you beyond," said Pius. "She'll do for the foremast, if there's no rot into her."

"She looks too young for rot."

"Aye, even then you've a job to tell," offered Alf.

"I'll be some glad to get her done and on the way home," said Gus.

"If the ice has left," Alf reminded him.

"There was scattered seals on the ice this morning. We could have us a couple killed by tea time, sure," said Gus looking at Pius in a curious way.

"No! I'll not allow it," answered Pius, sharply, walking away from the group. He took the axe from Harry and began chopping at the tree.

"Pius' still afeared of the ice."

"Old man, he's that vexed," said Alf. "You'll never get Pius going out after seals. But he ain't afeared. It was his son, Roy."

Harry had put on his shirt and joined Gus and Alf as they continued their conversation about the seals.

"But we need them seals for the fat," said Gus.

Harry perked up at the mention of seal fat. "Here now, we eats nary fat old man! We're not Esquimeaux, what?"

"That old hull wants a couple hundred weight with lime and the seals ain't going to walk ashore," said Alf. "And if the ice ain't going to go it's soon time we was walking home ourselves."

"Home is it?" replied Harry. "And leave Pius with his boat on the beach!?"

"We'll bide with Pius 'til we got to go," said Gus.

"We've had no news the while," answered Alf, in his own defense.

"No one wants to go more than myself," Harry said.

The splitting sound crackled through the forest interrupting the discussion. Pius stood well back, ready to flee if the butt kicked back. The big tree shuddered and leaned away from the master cut, picking up speed as it headed for the ground, snapping branches and sending a shower of needles drifting down like rain. What began as a graceful arc ended in an earth shaking crash, the air filled with flying bark and twigs and a dust of snow hovered over the site like mist. The silence deepened while the ravens assessed the situation.

Pius studied the cut to see if there was any sign of rot or weakness in the heart. He moved along the butt to where the first limbs stuck out like supplicant arms begging for mercy.

From the beach, where the rest of the crew had paused as if to honour the fallen giant, came the rhythmic tattoo of the caulker's hammers, picking up again. There was always apprehension when a big tree came down and the men would pause and pray there was no alarm.

The next morning two groups worked on their trees set up on blocks parallel to the hull. The first task was to square the logs before the exacting job of tapering and rounding the masts could begin. Four broad axes and four adzes rose and fell and the men concentrated on the lines and the cuts and still found time to make small talk. Harry was learning to handle the broad axe deftly and Uncle George worked the adz with one hand as if he had done it all his life. The work went quickly. By evening the two trees had been reduced to long, square and surprisingly smooth sticks of aromatic, golden wood, thirteen inches on a side. Beside the sticks the hull sat gleaming in the sunset looking clean and fresh and still a part of the forest. In the sunset sky the ravens called down to the men finishing their long day, but at least one man noted that the black birds looked like vultures circling a kill.

The next morning, after a hurried breakfast of black tea, bannock and dried rabbit, the exacting task of cutting the tapers and rounding off began; Pius' favourite part of building process even though it seemed contradictory to square a log only to chip it all away again. A jig was used to mark off converging lines from one end of the stick to the other. Adzes then cut to these lines and the stick magically had eight sides. The lines were run again, and the men cut and planed and the stick had sixteen sides. If the mast maker wanted to be very exact the lines could be run again to produce thirty-two sides, but Pius pronounced the sticks ready at sixteen sides and the men set to with draw knives and planes to complete the rounding. The formula for rounding a spar varied on the coast but the results were the same. The main mast finished out to fifty-six feet from heel to truck. The foremast finished six feet less. In three days two beautiful oiled spars were lying side by side, waiting for their fittings.

April 21, 1933: '...*This morning was fine for weather again but it was cold with not a breath of air. A warm front on the horizon is moving in slow so the wind would hold off a spell. It was a good time to set her spars. We got a good start. Days are longer now and the lads are in better spirits. Setting spars is always a time to be happy when the day's done and the job's behind...*'

Pius made a final check of the preparations for raising the main mast. A set of sheer legs made out of two thirty-foot trees stood in a tall 'A' leaning over the mast with their feet lashed to the rails abaft the mast hole. A tackle ran from the top of the 'A' to the stern and another tackle ran from the top of the 'A' to a point half way up the mast. The new mast, fitted out with her shrouds and running rigging, was lying on the deck with its heel resting on blocks and the top of the mast protruding over the stem like a bow sprit. Pius took his place on the end of the tackle line and nodded for the strain to begin. There was no hurry. Haste is an enemy waiting to catch a foot or a line slack or too tight. The men on the ground with iron-tipped poles steadied the mast, alert in case the mast shifted or went off line; then a ton of wood and fittings could come crashing down. Pius orchestrated the lift, quietly encouraging, but the men knew what had to be done and no strong-arm foreman would accomplish the task any better.

"All right, lads, heave now," he said. Inch by inch the head of the mast rose into the air. "That's it. Tie off and hold'er. Alf, she wants to come to the left." Alf pushed on his pole to bring the heal of the mast in line with the hole in the deck. "Heave again, together."

They counted off, and on three the men on the tackle heaved on their line and the massive six-part tackle creaked, the sheaves turned and the line took up a few inches at a time. The men on the poles strained to push upwards and the mast rose slowly until the push-poles were almost vertical and the mast was on an angle poised to slide into the hole. Uncle George, his good arm wrapped with line, and Seth took a strain on the tackle leading to the stern.

"Ready then, b'yes," said Pius, when the men were in position. "Heave now!"

The mast and the 'A' frame moved together and the heel of the mast crept toward the hole. "Heave again, lads." The men on the ground steadied their poles. Suddenly the blocks kicked out from the heel of the mast. "Hold'er now!" said Pius. They all took a deep breath. The critical part had been reached. The mast was poised at a steep angle and if it slipped and jammed they might not free it without cutting the mast down. "Tie off, b'yes," said Pius. The men on the lines snubbed the hauling part of the tackles to grumps on the rails and took a breather while Pius went to the heel of the mast and studied the situation, resting a hand on the key as if taking her pulse. Pius signaled to the men on the poles to leave them and come on deck. They scrambled up and stood ready at the lines. Seven ravens circled high above the ship and the wind sighed over the forest and a small gust swept down to the beach; a precursor of the wind waiting over the horizon. Pius scanned the sky and the men looked at each other waiting for the order. Pius nodded and they untied their lines.

"Heave again now!" The 'A' frame creaked with the weight of the mast and continued its arc upward until Pius was satisfied. "Tie off, b'yes," he said to Seth and Uncle George. "Ease tackle and God show her the way."

"Wait!" shouted Gus, suddenly. Everyone froze, wondering what had gone wrong. "We've forgot a coin in her step," he said. There was a sigh of relief and then some consternation. It was a tradition to place a coin under the mainmast for luck. A ship that went to sea without this important piece of equipment was considered to go unprotected.

"You're right, Gus. Who of us has a coin?"

"I've got a half crown!" said Harry, fishing in the lining of his coat. "The one I carried with me in the Navy."

"Uncle Saul gave you that half crown," said Pius, reluctant to accept Harry's good luck coin.

"Old Man, I can't think of a better place to put it, and she needs it most, for all of us." Harry found the coin and handed it to Pius.

"Thank you, son. Saul would understand."

Pius climbed down the main hatch and placed the half crown in the notch in the keelson where the heel key would sit, then signaled to lower away. The mast started down and he rotated the mast so the key lined up with the notch. "All right b'yes. She knows where to find a home now. Ease off, easy."

The mast dropped through the deck, swelling out until it was almost as big as the hole. With two inches to go Pius stopped the decent again to check the fit of the heel key with the notch. "Time now! Set'er," said Pius quietly. They let the line run until it went slack and the mast was down. The key fit perfectly and it only required a strain on the 'A' frame tackle to pull the mast to its proper angle. Pius drove in the keel wedges while thin wedges were driven around the mast at the deck.

The men sent up a cheer when Pius emerged from the hold. Pius looked up the main mast critically. He could already see the canvas taught and the little schooner heeled down to a good breeze. How many times had he summoned that vision during the long winter when the ship seemed so far from completion?

The fore mast was easier to raise using the tackles from the main mast's head to the sheer legs of the 'A' frame. They accomplished the task after lunch, without a hitch. By nightfall the rigging had been set up, and the booms and gaffs were brought aboard and made ready to bend on the sails. Spirits were high and Pius promised rum in their tea. That night they had a big meal of the last of the salt beef, rabbit stew, Gus's flat bread and the strips of the smoky salt cod eaten raw, a delicacy like candy, sitting around a fire outside the shack before it started to rain.

When the first drops splattered down they moved aboard the ship and settled back to drink scalding tea with rum and molasses. They talked about the ice and going home and it didn't matter if the weather had closed down and they were in for a day of rain. The decks were tight, the cabin snug, if a bit crowded, and they no longer suffered the choking air of the shack. Gus suggested putting a torch to it, which they all cheered, but no one felt like going out in the rain to do the deed, instead they shared stories and the good feeling of having the worst behind them.

April 22, 1933: A day of rain with a strong wind out of the southwest but still the ice showed no sign of breaking up. Pius and the men remained below decks for the day, finishing bulkheads and fitting out a galley and marking any leaks that showed up in the covering board wedges around the stanchions, and otherwise getting in each other's way. Without a stove it was chilly, even with all the bodies under deck, but at least it was dry and out of the wind. Best of all was the smell of new planking, slightly resinous with a hint of fermentation from the wet sap and warmer weather, but the combination of wood and oakum and pine tar and cod oil and honest sweat was perfume to tired boat builders.

The rain let up by nightfall and the storm blew itself out, and, with the wind still off the land, the night was warm compared to other nights spent in the old shack. The forest creatures were already taking over the abandoned shack looking for what they could scavenge among the hundreds of interesting smells left behind by the humans.

April 23, 1933: Pius' log entry: '...*The day come on fine and warm and the lads set to work to finish up. We still need to paint her hull and get some fat on her bottom before she's ready to go off. I sent young Harry over the Cape today to burn the whale bones to make her black paint. He'll be gone about three days but we're down to the finish work and Harry isn't so handy to the fine cutting. Don't know what's in store for him, or any of the young ones coming along these days. More and more of them talk about going away to find work, up to Canada they say and who knows where else. Hard times ahead most likely. I just don't know what it's coming to...*'

The day was sunny, warm and optimistic but the pack ice was still jammed tight against the shore. Gus thought there might be an open lead a few miles out. Harry climbed the rigging to have a look and confirmed that there was a narrow lead, but beyond that was broken white ice to the horizon. Harry also said that he was sure he could see a few seals on the ice near the lead. Pius didn't say anything when Alf looked at him for permission to go.

Pius walked to the edge of the beach where the restless, slobby, honeycombed ice fractured, tinkling like breaking glass as the tide lifted the pans over the rocks. He was lost in thought when Harry approached from behind carrying the ship's brass bell. Harry held the bell close to his father's ear and gave it a good clang.

Pius jumped and turned on Harry. "My Saints b'ye! You'll have my heart found yet!"

"Where would you like'er to?" asked Harry, holding the bell up for Pius' inspection.

"Handy to for'ard doghouse, I suppose," Pius answered and turned back to the ice. "She's got to go sometime."

"Takes'er sweet time, what?"

"Aye."

"Ever see the ice so stubborn, Old Man?"

Pius wondered if he should answer. He had never told Harry the whole story of losing his first born son. The details were locked in the memories of the elders and seldom mentioned. He decided it was time. "Yes," said Pius, finally, "the year your brother Roy drowned. We was too impatient to get at the seals. Didn't wait for open water to take the boats and the bunch of us went out on the ice. By'n'by the wind went off the land and broke'er up. There was Alf, Uncle Sam, Uncle Saul, young Roy and myself, all ended up copying to get to a small island before the ice drove too far off." Pius looked at Harry, appealing for understanding. "Roy slipped, son. Just as we reached the rocks. I saw him go under. I tried to get down, under the ice. I couldn't do it. I could see him there, on the bottom...curled up like a baby. I couldn't get down. My boy was dying but I couldn't save him."

Pius kicked at the beach stones. One shot out on the ice, skidded a few feet and disappeared into a gap in the slobby ice. All along the shore the ice was rotten where the sun warmed the darker stones below.

"As quick as that the ice closed again. Nothing to mark his place on God's earth...nothing but ice." Pius regarded the enemy with a look Harry had seldom seen. "The wind changed, the ice tightened up again and we walked home, as easy as that. It was some hard to tell your mother. You were just young then and didn't know the torment, but you missed him just the same." Pius could have stopped. "My fault you know. I shouldn't have let him on the ice so young. But he was headstrong, see. He wanted to be a man too soon. Now there's just you and

Jeannie. Mother never wanted no more babies after that. Said she couldn't stand to raise'em up for me to lose on the ice. Terrible cruel thing to say. Just the same, I couldn't blame your mother."

"Is that why you're afeared o'the ice?"

"Who said I was afeared!?"

Harry studied the bell. It was making his hand cold. Then he looked at the ship, the one constant in their lives. "She's almost done, Father."

Pius kicked at the stones again, regretting his bad humour.

"A fine vessel. Pretty lines," continued Harry.

"I'm pleased you like her, son. She's only a poor spruce-built thing, but then she wasn't meant to be a yacht."

"She wants a bit of colour, what?"

"Black," said Pius, as if Harry had asked what colour.

"The boats are always black, Old Man," said Harry, in mild protest.

"And so she'll be!"

"If we had the paint I could turn a hand."

"There's some whale bones round the head. You might burn them for the black."

"Aye, in the navy we did enough painting, but we never had to make the paint ourselves."

Pius' face crinkled into a rare grin. "Three days should do it."

"I'll take the gun. Might be scattered moose up over," said Harry, excited by the prospect of a change from endless days working on the ship.

"Mind you take care o'that gun. 'T'was Grandfather's."

"I'll guard'er with my life, Father."

Later, Pius sat on the cabin-top splicing lines. Nearby Alf and Gus were fitting the last section of cap rail while Lloyd trimmed a section fitted that morning. The spring sun was warm on their backs, the mood relaxed and optimistic. The end was in sight and the weather in sympathy; a nearly perfect day, despite the dazzling expanse of ice from shore to horizon. The only breaks in the monochrome sameness were the dark line of islands to the southeast and the specter of a giant iceberg on the northeastern horizon; the first of the spring migration from Greenland travelling with the Labrador Current to perish in the Gulf Stream.

Harry, in the shadow of the hull, hefted his pack, picked up the rifle and emerged into the glare of the sunlight. He waved at Pius but the sun was a brilliant jewel that blinded him to all but the dark outlines.

Pius was absorbed in the eye splice and didn't notice Harry until he was hopping over stranded ice flows along the high tide line. Pius rested the splice in his lap and watched his son's boyish progress along the beach.

"Young Harry's off on a bit of fun you'd think," Gus said.

"Those rocks'll take the wind out of his sails, b'ye, they will," said Alf.

"Aye, I wouldn't care to make that climb myself now, but there was a time," said Gus, shaking his head at a memory of their youth.

"Too true, old man!" interjected Uncle George, climbing from the cabin with a load of fresh off cuts to add to the pile on the beach.

"Do you mind the time we was lads," began Gus, "the summer the *Gladys and Hazel* went ashore and was wrecked and we climbed up to the Eagle's rock to see'er?"

"I mind. And the old eagle took a dislike to you. I never seen a soul hop to it like you did," said Uncle George, with a wide grin.

"Aye, my son! That old lady was some mad with us," agreed Alf, remembering a good time without worries or responsibilities.

Pius watched Harry who had reached the top of the rocks and rested, staring out over the ice toward Fogo Island. "Harry's got more on his mind than whale bones. 'Twouldn't be surprising if there was a wedding when we get home, God willing," he added, quickly.

"Proper thing!" said Gus. "I've a bottle of wedding rum by just gathering dust."

"Dust on the outside never hurt the rum inside," said Uncle George, "but it's well to dust them off now and then."

"Aye, Alf's woman caught him dusting off her wedding rum that time and dusted him off good with her broom!" said Gus, loud enough for the crew to hear. There was laughter from various locations on the deck.

Alf winked at Pius. "And who was it went to bed with'is boots on after young Robert Manuels' wedding, the year last?" said Alf, indicating Gus with a motion of his head.

"My feet were that cold from dragging your carcass out of a snowdrift!" retaliated Gus. Gus got a big laugh even though the story had been told a dozen times.

"And wasn't it you, Gus Froude, who danced up such a lather your woman had to pour a puncheon o'cold water over you?"

"That water was no colder than your miserable body going stiff in the snow..."

Pius tuned out the dialogue. The next part of the story would relate a hilarious scene when Gus dragged Alf out of the snow but took a wrong turn and they both went off the wharf into the water. It had been a near thing but fortunately witnessed by enough clear thinking fishermen to pull them out before they perished. Pius shut his ears to the words but the laughter punctuated the tale thrown back and forth and Pius knew the exact moment when Alf had slipped under the ice and Seth dove into the harbour, hauled him up so others could get grappling hooks and save them both. Pius could see Harry look back at the ship before he started down the other side of the headland; he might have waved. Then Harry was gone from his sight.

Pius chastised himself for the number of times he had been short with his son and regretted being away for six years during the war. The times had been difficult in between, then Harry had been away in his turn. He would make it up when the ship was finished, he vowed. Perhaps he would name their new ship after Harry. The *Harry Humby,* or the *Harry J. Humby,* after Harry's grandfather, John. It would give Harry good standing in the village if he took up the fishing game. But Harry didn't seem inclined toward fishing, or had Pius read his son wrong? A shipbuilding job was one thing, an adventure for a young man. Harry would soon have to decide, Pius said to himself, picking up the eye splice and absently rolling the line between his rough hands.

From the headland Harry could see several leads in the slackening ice and the seals scattered over a wide area. The seals followed open water, cruising among the flows, lounging in the sun, whelping when due. A man travelling on the ice would have to pick his way around the open water but Newfoundlanders were masters at travelling on the broken ice, at play or at work; called it *copying* or *tippy-panning.* The children made a game of it in the spring, leaping from flow to flow, timing their leap so that as one small flow began to sink they were already springing across the gap to the next. It taught the children many things they would have to know when they became adults. Harry, like most outport children growing up, had no fear of broken ice.

He scanned the sweeping curve of the whale cove for his first objective. Below, where the beach ended and the rocks began, the ribs of the whale carcass Pius had noted in January protruded from the pebbles.

"A humpback," said Harry out loud to hear his own voice. The cove was as quiet as a tomb. There had always been the sound of voices at work or snoring at night and the constant sound of hammering or chopping or sawing. And when they weren't working it was because there was such a storm raging that the roar of the wind drowned out everything.

A raven answered Harry's voice from a tree top. Other ravens wheeled around, dark against the sun-splashed sky, investigating the new presence on their beach.

"She was big enough!" Harry said of the whale, using the female gender. Further up the beach he discovered a much smaller skeleton, jammed between rocks. "And there's her wee one, I suppose." The baby may have been injured and the mother washed ashore with her young one. "Funny what creatures can do sometimes. Well, old girl, you and the little one can be some use to us."

Harry dug out a pit in the beach stones, collected driftwood and covered the floor of the fire pit with several layers of dry wood. Then he hacked apart the baby whale; the ribs and back bones came away without too much trouble, and placed them in the pit. He put a layer of wood over the bones, gathered dry moss, started the fire then set about to break up the mother. She proved more difficult. Harry beat down the skeleton and layered bones and driftwood. He waited an hour, heaped on more bones and wood, and, satisfied that he had a good burn going, picked up his rifle and headed out on the ice.

Pius, about to go below for a mug of tea, looked up at the headland and noted the plume of grey smoke boiling into the clear sky. Harry was burning bones. Pius dropped down to the cabin to join the other men satisfied with their progress but ill at ease.

Harry had at least five hours of good daylight to get his seals. And if he was unlucky the whiteness of the ice would extend the evening light or the half moon would be bright enough that he could make it back before two in the morning. But the moon couldn't be counted on. Low clouds were massing on the western horizon. The ice would become dangerous if a warm wind came off the shore. Snow was a remote possibility but fog was as dangerous as snow.

Harry made the leap across the broken shore ice considering his options. The seals were only two miles off. If he hadn't reached the patch in two hours he would turn back, Harry said to himself. He wondered if he should drag them straight in to the building site, place them at Pius' feet and have a hot mug of tea with the boys. The sun was warm on Harry's right cheek. He was young and strong and full of adventure. The first open lead was short and the detour took only a few minutes. He sighted between the two headlands and a tall stand of trees in the centre of the Whale Cove to put him back on course. He noted that the wind seemed shifty and undecided but he was determined to get his seals.

Ice hummocks and open leads put Harry off schedule but the seals were close. He kept low and worked ahead, ignoring his plan to turn back after two hours and about the third hour of slow going he spotted the first black shapes beyond a jagged pressure ridge. Too close to turn back now, he decided, and the warm sun still seemed comfortably high above the hills. He crept to the pressure ridge, positioned himself behind a large upturned block of blue-green ice, and sighted the rifle on one of the smallest adult seals. No point killing a seal he couldn't drag. He would kill three, if he could get off the shots before the seals dove for safety in the black water. He would skin two for the fat and take the third for the meat; a good plan but the seals lolled in the late afternoon sun too far away for a sure kill.

Harry lowered the rifle. He was panting from the effort and the anticipation of the kill. His hands trembled and when he took off his mittens for a better grip they quickly chilled down in the breeze. And now that he was laying still he was aware of a new movement in the ice; a restless motion, as if the pans were anxious to get free of the land. He could hear the ice floes grinding together, the massive expanse eating itself up faster than the cold nights could replace it. For the first time Harry felt a rush of fear but fought the urge to retreat. The harp seals stirred as if they sensed something. Harry stayed still, waiting for them to settle down again, knowing that soon they would bestir themselves to feed. The fat pups were content to sleep but the mothers grunted and sniffed the air. Harry slipped around the ice block and over the pressure ridge. The seals became nervous, sensing something upwind. He should have noticed the wind shift. There was another small pressure ridge between himself and the seals so he crept forward, determined to get at least one. It would have to be a big one.

Harry was over the pressure ridge and onto flat ice before he realized the new pan was moving parallel to the ice he had just left. The new wind from the westerly had loosened the offshore ice and the pack was free to manoeuvre in the currents, and below his feet the rotten ice changed colour from white to dark. It was nothing, Harry said to himself. The ice moved apart and would close up again, there or at another location. The concern was getting the seal across the gaps. He crept forward on hands and knees, careful to keep the rifle out of the slush. His pants and mittens were sodden in moments, but what of it? The boys would soon fix him up as they roasted fresh seal meat over a fire on the beach. He reached the far side of the pan and crept toward a ridge. He might still get off two shots.

The seals had his scent and were moving toward the black leads. Harry stood up to take the shot but a sudden gust of wind made him look back. The lead was opening fast. There was no longer a thought of shooting a seal.

Harry began to run, slipped on the watery slush and fell heavily on his left knee. A sharp pain ripped through his body and made him gasp. He got up and ran again, hobbled by the broken knee cap. Blood flowed from a gash below his knee and left speckles of bright red on the ice. He reached the edge of the pan on the run but the gap was too wide to jump. To the north the lead was wider. To the south there was a finger of ice close to the shoreward pack. Harry ran along the edge of the pan, ignoring the pain. His only thought was the gap. He had to get across because he knew the wind was going to open the ice and may not close again for hours. The lead narrowed as he approached the southern end of the pan but the rotting ice became more treacherous. He splashed through the watery slush, using the rifle as a crutch, hobbling and hopping. A picture flashed through his mind of Uncle Saul's rambling gate and remembered that Uncle Saul had hurt his leg in a similar accident. Harry pictured himself as an old man limping across the ice, chasing a fat seal that refused to fall no matter how many times he put a bullet into her fat hide. Harry reached the end of the pan still running. The gap was only a few feet wide and without stopping he threw the rifle ahead of him and gathered himself for the jump.

A boy would laugh and make the leap for fun. An old man would have to make a supreme effort to bridge the gap. Harry, an athletic young man, who should have made the gap easily, weighted the broken knee for the leap. The knee collapsed. Only momentum carried him across the black water but his landing on the slippery, jagged edge of the pan was short. His legs splashed into the frigid water. As his stomach crunched against the edge of the ice his head came down with a sickening thud, smashing his face open and gouging out his right eye. The survival instinct was still strong and Harry shook off the wool gunning mittens that Mary had knitted for Roy, desperately clawing at the slush, but he was slipping under, his lean, muscular body already numbed by the freezing water. He no longer felt the pain. He didn't call out. The last thing he saw in the distance was the Humby family flag at the masthead of the schooner and he felt badly about letting Pius down.

Pius was sitting on the cabin top with the men, doing the endless jobs of rigging and splicing, noting that the wind was warm and had finally shifted off shore, as his son's body drifted slowly down through the silent green depths. He was thinking how lovely the ice could be against a clear blue sky, as long as it didn't have to be crossed. The sweet smell of resinous wood and tarry oakum wafted up from the sun-warmed deck. The troubles of the last three years floated away with the exotic scents given off by his new boat. Pius tried to relax, if only for a moment. He looked at the headland where the plume of smoke still rose above the tree tops but now it was blown seaward. The wind would be off shore for a day then would switch to the east and drive the ice hard against the shore again; and bring a cold rain, he predicted. He still felt uneasy about something. Maybe it was just the approaching weather. He organized the next day's work. No need to push the men. There wasn't much they could do on the exterior of the hull until Harry returned with the bone ash for the black paint but he would do the name boards while Harry was away.

That night he had the recurring nightmare about Roy drowning under the ice.

April 24, 1933: The rain Pius predicted was only a drizzle that cleared off by noon but the wind did come from the east, cold and damp, driving the pack tight again. The world had a grey, dismal aspect and the work site was engulfed in a pall of heavy depression that even the proximity of the new schooner could not dispel. The men worked at their jobs above and below decks and hardly spoke. Those above cast glances across the ice toward Fogo. It had been a hard winter for the outports and the men were anxious about their families.

Pius double checked the rigging to make sure that everything would function properly in a hard chance. In the afternoon he paused in the positioning of the main sheet blocks to note that the plume of smoke from the headland had trailed down to a wisp. Something was wrong. Gus, working nearby on the cap band of the rudder stock, noticed Pius' expression.

"What's at you, old son?" asked Gus.

"Oh..." said Pius, as if returning from a day dream, "Harry's let his fire die."

"Probably up over chasing a big moose, and forgot."

"I suppose."

"Just like him to. Always was a bit of a dreamer, that one. You'll hear a shot by'n'by and Harry'll come over the head dragging a bloody haunch for our supper." Gus waited for a response. None came so he filled in the silence with optimism. "A thinker, young Harry is. He'll go someplace, mark my word."

"Aye," said Pius, unconvinced and less than optimistic. He didn't see a future for Harry in the outports, perhaps on the mainland. He was distracted by the ravens chattering in the trees, gossiping about the latest news.

"Noisy devils, those," said Gus. "What's got them so riled I wonder? Grandfather used to say the ravens was the smartest birds in the world and if they were noisy it meant something was going to happen, a great change like. I hope it means the ice's going off soon."

"Still a fortnight to spring tide," said Pius, only saying what they all knew to be a fact of nature, the one thing they could depend on in life, the tides. "If this wind keeps up from the easterly we'll not make that tide neither."

"She's got to go sometime, by the Lord!" said Gus with more conviction than he felt. "Aye, but never mind, Old Son, when young Harry gets back we'll tart'er up pretty like she was going to a dance. She'll look the proper lady then. Sooner or later, ice's got to go."

"Sooner's better," said Pius. He wished Gus would stop talking. He had a vague picture of his son under the ice and mistook it for the recurring vision of Roy. Gus was still talking…

"...I've got this cap set, but I don't like the looks of this swing arm, here. I'll allow she'll get home fine but that wants changing first thing we can set up a proper forge or get one down the shore from that old wreck washed up...when was that, Pius?"

Pius didn't know, or care. He went below to find a shackle pin in the box of spare parts, leaving Gus wondering.

Pius had trouble falling asleep that night. Around him the men breathed easily or talked in low tones about home and their prospects, comfortable enough in their snug cabin but anxious to make an end. Pius lay awake in the dark, listening to the grinding ice working up the beach with the tide. When he did doze off he had the same terrible dream about his son under the ice and woke in a sweat. Nothing had changed. The men breathed and shifted positions and slept on. The ice was dropped on the beach by the falling tide, grinding and cracking and there was no wind to soften the ice sounds. The sound he feared as much as the sound of a drowning man was ice around the hull of his ship. But his schooner was safe on her cradle, ready to be launched when she was painted properly and the tide right.

He dozed again and dreamed the ice had gone and a pale moon shone over a restless sea rolling into the cove. The schooner was afloat, at anchor ready to cut for home but an errant, malevolent spear of green ice suddenly crashed though the hull and pierced his heart. Pius woke up grasping at his chest. He was soaked with sweat. He tried to stay awake to avoid the next part of the dream, the part where he was under the ice, and it was silent and beautiful and he could see a white shape drifting down toward him. The white shape was a body and when the body turned slowly toward him it was Harry. Pius, choking for air, stepped over arms and legs making his way to the deck and was sick over the rail. The eastern sky was a blood-red canvas where the sun would paint itself brilliant below the bank of clouds. Then the rain would come again.

Pius looked down on the whale cove from the rocky headland for a sign of Harry. The pile of charred wood and bone still smouldered and the thin veil of smoke rising against the green of the forest was all that moved. He was tired from the climb but only paused long enough to scan the ice. Black shapes were scattered over the field around the leads. None of them walked upright. He knew they wouldn't. He climbed down, his spirit ebbing like the tide when he found the axe, the blanket and the canvas bag near the fire pit. The food was not touched. The rifle was missing.

"Harry!!?"

The echo from the forest mocked him. A raven lifted from the top of a tree and climbed into the grey sky soaring gracefully over the ice. It called out a single, long piercing *caaawh*. Pius crossed himself and scanned the forest fringe for a sign but there were no tracks in the old snowdrifts banked in the shelter of the tree line. There was no sign of Harry along the shore of the cove. Pius turned toward the ice, hoping he was wrong but realized the dream was a sign.

"Oh, please, God, not Harry too!?"

Pius sat beside the cooling fire pit watching the ice, finally admitting what he had known for two days. He dumped the food on the rocks and began scooping the ashes into the canvas bag, wiping away silent tears. He collected the axe and the blanket and climbed back over the rocks to tell his crew the awful truth.

Seven ravens circled high above the cove. The drizzle of rain that had threatened all day began soon after the men left for the ice. Pius stood on the beach beside the schooner and watched them, ashamed that he couldn't go out on the ice to look for his own son. And he was still there, too numb to be cold, when they returned; a dark line of men against the bleak, white desert of ice. The look on their faces said everything. Alf held the gun and the woolen mitts out to Pius.

"I'm sorry, Pius...'Tis all we found." Alf didn't mention the traces of blood at the edge of the ice.

Pius nodded. "Thank you for going."

The crew drew away and left Pius to mourn alone standing on the beach stones staring over the ice field. The men, sitting on the rise near the saw pit talking in low tones, came to their decision and went separately to the few remaining chores. A meal was prepared, and their tea, and Pius was invited to join the circle around a fire. A tangible wall of silence rose between them. Pius could sense something else in their manner. Their eyes spoke sorrow for his loss, but they were unable to say the words until Alf, their spokesman, began to relate what Pius already knew. "Pius, it's hard to say...but...some of us want to go." He looked at his Skipper and friend, asking for understanding. "It's been a hard winter and our families may be in need." It wasn't the whole truth. A raven called down with a shrill accusation.

"Aye, we knew that before we come away," said Pius, searching the eyes of his friend. "What more else?"

Alf's resolve collapsed, he cast his eyes down and shifted his feet on the stones. Gus took up the explanation. "Well, Skipper, we're deeply sorry, but with young Harry gone, we're only seven souls, like, and with the black birds about…" Gus let his eyes flick up to the sky. The ravens circled easily on the dead air.

Alf took up the dialogue again. "The schooner's mostly done, Pius, else we wouldn't conscience leaving you. There's aught for a gang to do now but wait out the ice, that might never go for a fortnight or more, and we're that concerned about home. Lloyd and Seth'll bide along with you and help you put'er off and carry'er home. But my dear man…" Alf trailed off, embarrassed by his own inadequate words.

"We got to go while the ice's still fit to cross," added Gus, casting his eyes to the sky as if appealing for divine understanding. The ravens cried out and flew into the trees on a mission of their own.

He knew their reasoning was sound. "You'll tell Mary gentle as you can?"

Alf and Gus nodded. The others got up and went aboard the schooner to gather their few belongings. They wanted to start immediately for Exploits Island, a six mile walk over broken, shifting ice. They would stay with a fisherman overnight, and continue on to Black Island, then to Morton's Harbour, hike across the island to Twillingate and, if the ice had moved off, get a dory from Ashcroft for the long row to Fogo. A journey of only thirty-seven nautical miles, as the raven flies, but they weren't ravens. It would take them a long week of hardships to reach home but to the men it was no more a hardship than spending another day waiting for the ice to move and the tide to rise.

Pius walked along the beach, turned his back on his crew as they set off across the ice, and slipped into another state of being, the one he inhabited for two years after the battle in the English Channel.

April 26, 1933: Pius continued to make entries in his log: *'...I ground up the bone ashes today and mixed it with cod oil and set to work to paint her black. She looks all right. I'll get another coat onto her when the first coat soaks in. The weather was fine today but the ice is still with me. I seen some men on the ice today and wondered who they was and where they were going. They seemed to be lost or just laying around. I think it was some of the boys from home out on the ice. I'd go out to meet them but I can't leave the ship until she's painted proper. Maybe I'll go out tomorrow...'*

Pius rose early to prepare the charcoal and bone ash with pungent cod oil and old kerosene. He never mentioned the men who had left to walk over the ice nor did he acknowledge the presence of Lloyd and Seth, although they tried their best to work alongside Pius, anticipating his needs. If they spoke or handed him a tool he looked through them as though they were spirits. But all the while Pius talked to himself or addressed his conversations to the ravens who were gathering in greater numbers around the work site.

The second day was sunny and hot working close to the hull, now blackened with the coarse paint they applied with brushes made of dried grass lashed in tight bundles. The method was crude but the work went quickly. Pius, eyes glazed and sunken, concentrating like a man possessed, splashed on paint, heedless of Lloyd and Seth working nearby; painting over their sections and splattering them until they retreated to the other side of the hull. Pius continued to talk to the ravens, his words coming from a man on the edge of reality. The paint dripping over him, competing with the sweat running down his thin face, only heightened the haunted visage.

The ever-present ice was painfully white. In defiance Pius slapped more black paint on his schooner and stood back to note the stark contrast. There was something important about the blackness of the hull against their prison of ice. But it was never black enough and Pius became frustrated when the coarse pigment wouldn't stay put on the light wood. The oil ran down the planks and dripped on the stones, "Like black blood, b'yes," he repeated over and over. He wasn't talking to the boys.

"Stay on there you!" he said, defying the paint to run. "Black's the thing, b'yes. What's wanted now. A nice black box to carry us home, eh, b'yes?" he said to a pair of ravens sitting on the cap rail above his head. "Dead b'yes, and not a fit marker. Just this black box to carry us over. Be cold out there. Yis my son! Cold. She's just cold...and dark. Black!" growled Pius, flailing the hull with his brush, beating the ship more than painting it. Lashing out at the thing that brought them to the beach. "Black, like this cursed ship!"

Lloyd and Seth were still young men. Lloyd had lost a wife and knew something of grief. Seth knew about grief just by growing up in an outport where death can come quickly and cruelly, but neither were prepared for Pius' kind of grief. They were distraught hearing Pius carry on and not able to help him. They silently cursed the ice also and wanted desperately to launch the ship and go home if only to escape the growing madness. The adventure was over. There would be no triumphant return to Fogo with the new ship. Both young men were seized, as the land was held fast, by the ice, and by a foreboding they couldn't name. And as the days of madness grew Pius continued to talk to the ravens, lecturing them, as if they were his sons and he had to teach them the ways of the world to survive. Lloyd and Seth watched, and despaired.

"A little fire to forge the iron, eh? Make her fittings strong. Hot! To burn the bones...a little frost then to set her frames and your heart, eh? She wants salt into'er frames as well, if you want her to last. And she wants tar into'er rigging. Lots o'tar, lads, and you got to renew it every chance and not fail'er by being lazy about it. Get up there and lay it on. She'll thank you for it! Don't forget, she has to have some blood into her colour..." Pius took out his rigging knife and slashed at his left arm. A trickle of bright red blood ran down his arm, coursing through the rivers of blackened cod oil. Pius uttered an oath from ancient times as if imparting power to the blood. The blood and the oily paint didn't mix. He walked to the bow, absently wiping his bleeding arm against his filthy shirt, and looked critically at the lines of his ship. "The elements got to come together just right to make a ship, yes. She's not so bad for all that," said Pius, to a glaring raven. "Uncle Sam you should be right proud of her, and Father too." Another raven landed on the rail. "What say you, Father? Is she good enough to put over and not be ashamed of?..." Pius regarded the raven as if listening to something it said. "She's only a poor spruce-built thing, but she's as good as we can make'er. She'll have to do 'til we drives her on the rocks or she rots out from under..." Pius laughed and the ravens flew away.

May 4-9, 1933: Pius' log entry covered five days and was the first mention of his crew. '...*Shy a fortnight gone, I suppose. We got at the cradle the other day. Seth said that he felt the weather and the ice going off. A shore lead is promising...'* It was the last log entry during their time on the beach. The tale was pieced together from stories Jimmie had heard from Pius or the crew and Kurt Schulte had written. Fact or fantasy?

By the first week in May the shore ice was melting back from the beach each day but the pressure of the offshore ice kept pushing in and each morning new pans of rotting slob ice filled in the space. At dawn on May 4th, the three men emerged from the cabin to check the ice which was undulating from the remains of a distant storm out on the Atlantic. It was the first time they had heard the swishing sound of surf, although the minuscule ripples could hardly be called waves. The restless ice pans, wearing themselves into round cakes like giant flagstones, grumbled and gyrated, slivers falling away to join the melting slush, but refused to move off.

The sky was a leaden pall and the heavy air felt dead and deadly. The ravens commented on the approaching storm from the safety of the forest as Pius scanned the sky for other signs. The sun remained shrouded by low clouds on the eastern horizon and to the west the clouds looked black and full of wind and rain. Seth rubbed his knee, a slight twinge that meant a change, a reminder of a slip in his own youth. They didn't need a barometer to read the changes. Fishermen could read the sky and the water or their own peculiar signs. Change was certain. If it was fine, it was certain the weather would change. How bad it would get was known by intuition. Intuition would tell the fisherman it was either time to get home or if ashore, stay home.

Pius, buttoning his coat against the damp, chill air flowing over the stubborn pans, scowled at the leaden sky. "High tide in two days," he said, by way of greeting to his enemy.

"Me knee's all a tingle," said Seth, climbing over the rail to reach the beach. "Last night it come onto aching fearful. I think we'll get a blow by tonight sure, Old Man."

"Aye," said Pius.

"She looks like making up some weather in the west," said Lloyd, relieved that their Skipper seemed his old self. "Sure to blow the ice out with it."

"Dare say..." said Pius, distracted by the ravens. He searched the tree tops as if looking for a familiar bird. "Best put the wedges to'er then."

Wedging up is a special time. It means the hull is finally ready for launching. Wedges are driven under the keel to lift the ship clear of the blocks. Spacers are driven in to hold the hull on the cradle and cross members are placed under the keel and the wedges driven out to leave the boat supported by the cradle resting on a skidway. When the time is right, the cradle is encouraged to slide down the skidway into the water.

Pius, Seth and Lloyd worked quickly but carefully to drive in the wedges under the keel. The ship vibrated and trembled as if coming alive, eager to be gone from the awful place. The cribs were knocked apart and the stones scattered. She was ready to go, except for the seal fat and lime mixture on her bottom, but that could be remedied another time at low tide, in a safe harbour.

The men-in-waiting bent on the sails and finished up small jobs and watched the sky for the inevitable spell of bad weather. The front moved in slowly from the southwest. The breeze held off all day and it was almost pleasant working in the open. Pius seemed cheerful and spoke to them frequently about little things that needed attention. Lloyd and Seth used up the remains of the cod oil and kerosene on the deck planking. Pius spent the day carving name boards. That evening they had a hot supper of roasted hare cooked on the beach and then sat on the main hatch in silence, smoking, watching the sky and the ice and the ever present ravens who seemed content to mutter amongst themselves in their forest.

Before dusk the wind came over the trees in hesitant puffs with some rain. Then it turned cold and the wind blew in gusts and couldn't make up its mind. The men went below and shut the hatch. Seth and Lloyd slept. At ten o'clock Pius laid down but didn't sleep. He surveyed their sparse refuge in the light of the lantern hanging from the deck head, turned down to cast just enough light to give the cabin a soft, warm glow. Pius may have dozed but the first sharp sound of the wind in the trees brought him to the alert. It was the southwest wind they wanted and it blew hard. The little schooner, hanging as she was in the cradle, moved with the wind. It was a gentle motion at first; just enough to make the flickering lantern light dance on the unpainted cabin sides. Pius watched the lantern swaying, entranced by the motion and the sound of the wind. After awhile he slept.

Before dawn Pius was jolted from a fitful, dream-plagued sleep by a jarring crash, a shuddering motion and a new and terrifying sound. The wind was the first recognizable element Pius could put in place. It was a *real gagger,* as Uncle Saul would have described the gale. An early hurricane. While they slept the wind had backed into the east and was hurling loose pans of ice against the shore.

"The cradle!!" shouted Pius, at a pair of dazed faces, grotesquely distorted by the wildly swinging lantern. Seth and Lloyd followed Pius up the ladder.

When Pius opened the gangway the wind tore the doors from his hands. The starboard door was stripped from its hinges and flew over the rail. Pius was staggered by the force of the blast. He lurched to the rail and went over the side on the ladder. Seth and Lloyd followed and huddled with Pius in the lee of the hull as the flood tide surged around their legs. The air was thick with spray blown off the tops of the breakers. Large blocks of rotten ice drove ashore and jammed against the cradle which was in danger of collapsing under the pressure; one upright already broken by the ice. If another let go the ship would be driven onto her starboard side.

"Get shores under!!"

Seth and Lloyd attacked the pile of scrap wood looking for stout timbers. Pius climbed back up the ladder and made his way forward to the heavy anchor line coiled down beside the kingpost. He slipped the lashings and cast the coil over the bow. The ship lurched and tilted to starboard throwing him off his feet. He crawled on his hands and knees to the rail and climbed down to the beach where Seth and Lloyd were jamming supports under the turn of the bilge. Pius left them and splashed through the remains of a large breaker, struggling to keep his footing in the wash that carried loose timbers and tools. The coil of anchor line was caught up in the flood, wrapping itself around the cradle. Pius struggled to free it, knee deep in the freezing water. He found the end and dragged it up the beach making flat turns and loose overhand hitches around a solid stump, jamming small timbers in the hitches to prevent them from tightening up, ever the sailor with instincts for survival and the future. The precious anchor rode was too valuable to have to cut. And he was damned if the sea was going to claim his ship before she was launched.

Pius started back down the beach to help Seth and Lloyd as a rogue wave reared above the others, curled onto the beach and broke, hurling a large block of ice at the ship, taking out more supports. The schooner staggered and the cradle started to give way on the lee side. The backwash surged down the beach sucking anything loose out to sea. Seth and Lloyd scrambled in the darkness to grab supports that had come adrift, frantically jamming them under the hull. Pius saw what was about to happen and yelled but the warning was blown back in his face and he could only watch, helpless, as the next big wave reared up on the top of the flood and crashed down, exploding around the cradle. The remaining support timbers snapped and jumped away. The schooner collapsed on her side, rolling in the foaming chaos.

Seth and Lloyd vanished under the hull in the tumult of white water and debris. Pius fought his way to the fallen ship and grabbed at Lloyd's arm. The young man was torn free, flushed out from under the hull by the third wave, still calling to Pius.

Seth was crushed by the weight of the thing he helped to build and Pius was tangled in the rigging he fashioned so carefully with an eye to chaos. Only the stout hawser kept the hull from joining Seth and Harry in the ocean. He could only rage at the waves and surrender to the feeling of helplessness...*on the deck of a burning destroyer in the English Channel with explosions and machine gun bullets ripping into the bridge as if searching for him. He cursed the grinning face of the German...*

"Damn you!! Damn you to hell!!"

Then Pius disappeared in the welter of foam and became one with the elements, hanging in the rigging of his ship as if on watch, dreaming of sinking under the ice, seeing the bodies of his sons and friends and crew, drifting down from the ice above, turning slowly in a cold whiteness.

Another day: The ice was moving away and the narrow lead of blue water between the white ice ribbons was ruffled by the offshore breeze. The sun was already high in a perfect sky and ravens wheeled and complained because the presence, though diminished, had not yet removed itself from their beach.

The little schooner lay on her side like a mortally wounded beast, or asleep or resting from a long journey. The flood tide, the tide that should have carried her triumphantly to her new life, lapped gently at her keel almost buried in the stones. She looked strangely peaceful, debauched and battered, resting in the sun as though she had resided on the beach for decades, having returned, tired and worn out from a hard life at sea with voyages made and battles fought, to bleach her bones and decay gracefully.

A delegation of ravens circled down and lined up on the port rail, curious about the stones being cast out from the shadow of the hull. Several snow-white gulls with black wing tips drifted in and idled on the breeze, wings spread in easy insolence, and called the ravens names. The ravens rose up in a black fury to engage the intruders. The gulls were driven off and gave up in favour of more interesting carrion further out to sea, leaving the ravens in control of the beach. The stones flew out from the shadows.

Pius backed out from under the hull into the sun, hunched over, pulling Seth's body by the feet. The ravens, disturbed by the sight, commented in low tones. Pius dragged the body up the beach without looking at the bulging eyes, surprised in death. What were Seth's last thoughts as the hull crushed out his life? Perhaps he drowned slowly, wave by wave, realizing that Lloyd was gone and Pius couldn't help him. It would have been lonely and dark in the cold water. The eyes said terror.

Pius didn't see the eyes, didn't look at Seth as he dug into the moss covered stones at the edge of the forest. He didn't see the body as he covered it with the stones. He stared down at the crippled hull and out at the distant ribbons of ice, wondering why his ship was lying on her side. It had something to do with the ice.

And another day: The weather remained fair. The ice was gone as though it never existed. Pius, looking gaunt and shrunken, his bristling beard turned grey, sat on the beach near the water's edge watching three dead seals rolling in the surf. The tide lifted the bloated carcasses until the seals bumped at his feet; the sea presenting him with an offering to atone for what it had taken away.

"Come home finally, have you lads? I've waited for you this last while. These old stones are hard and cold, b'yes!" Pius got to his feet, slowly, older, unsteady and weak. "Come back to be buried proper? Come along then, Roy, you've been dead the longest..." He waded into the water and seized the hind flippers of the smallest seal. Roy was only a boy when he died. "You wait there, Harry. I'll be back as soon as I've seen to Roy." He dragged the carcass up the slippery stones and rested. "You'll be anxious to get to a nice warm bed, Roy. I've got just the place, up by the trees. Terrible cold in that water, son. Terrible cold...then you know that don't you, Roy. Yes, b'ye." He gripped the flippers again and then looked back at the seals in the water. "And don't you worry, Lloyd. I'll be back for you too. We'll see you're proper buried..." He dragged the seal further up the beach to the mound of stones where he had buried Seth's body, a simple wooden cross marking Seth's mound.

Pius buried the three bloated seals in separate shallow graves like Seth's. He piled the moss-covered stones carefully. The mounds could have been there for a hundred years. He rummaged in the pile of slabs that used to be the shack and made three more crosses and on each he penciled a name. On Seth's cross was the name of his mother, Liza, and on the seal's markers were the names George John Humby, John Humby, and Uncle Sam Pardy. Pius read the markers off and seemed satisfied with his work.

Pius found the name boards he had carved so carefully wedged in the scuppers and sat down on the slanting side of the main cabin to finish chiseling out the name of his vessel. He thought of her as a wounded bird. A raven landed on the rail a few feet away, shuffling sideways to get a better view. Pius looked at the black bird and went on with his work. The raven called off a curious seagull that cruised in too close. The black beast seemed inclined to just watch Pius tapping away at the name board, cocking its head in a critical way.

"It's good you're back," said Pius, to the raven, finally. "Too fine a day to be drowned, Harry, me son."

"A fine day for sure, Father," agreed the raven.

Pius tapped on and the raven hopped closer. "No use to mourn now. By'n'by I'll join you and Roy."

"No use to mourn for sure. We'll wait for you…the whole crowd of us."

Pius, troubled by the news, put the name board aside and retreated to the mast. The raven followed, perched on the pin rail and supervised while Pius absently sorted the tangle of lines and halyards.

"Glad you're not under the ice no more…Not under the ice. I'd as soon go to hell."

"And join the merchants, Old Man?"

"No, my dear. I'd not care for the company of the Water Street crowd."

"They're all there for sure."

"That's certain, and if they aren't there's no justice in this world. Still, it'd be better than the frost."

"It's not so bad, Father, under the ice. You don't really feels it you know. Sort of peaceful, like. And pretty too."

Pius picked at the snarl, studying the lines as if seeing them for the first time, trying to avoid looking at the raven. "We've missed the tide…"

"Another'll come along. Always has, Old Man."

"Yes, but she's not ready to go, is she."

"She's a wonderful fine ship, Father, just the same."

"I suppose she is, but my son we've paid a terrible price for her...a terrible price!"

"I only wanted to make you proud."

Pius pretended to be occupied with a halyard. He tugged on it but the main gaff was jammed somewhere under the ship. He belayed the line to a pin and coiled the rest of the halyard, dropped a turn and threw the spoiled coil down in disgust. It slid down the deck to fetch up in a heap in the scuppers. The raven, startled by the sudden movement, flew away and circled the site. Pius called after the bird, "Harry!"

The raven returned to the rail. "Yes, Father?"

"Oh, I thought you'd gone."

"I'm still here."

"It's good of you to stay."

"There's much to be done."

"On this blessed ship? Oh, aye. She's had her day, and her toll. She'd want an axe or a torch to put her out of her misery."

"Then t'would all be in vain."

Pius regarded his crippled ship with a jaundiced eye. She reminded him of the old fin whale that beached herself near the village when he was young. The whale wasn't dead. The boys of the village, some of whom as grown men had come to the beach with him that winter, climbed up on the whale and sat on her head near the blow hole, listening to the slow rhythm of the whale's breathing, and smelled the stench of the bloody breath bubbling out of her collapsing lungs. He put his hand on the tough, thick skin and felt the shock waves of the heartbeat as the great organ laboured to sustain life. He looked into her eye and he was certain the eye looked back at him. She was asking him to ease her suffering. He couldn't and it made Pius sad that she was dying alone far from her family and in agony.

"In vain?" Pius asked, putting his hand against the warm deck planks of his dying schooner. The pulse of the surf curling up the beach trembled through the keel, and through the frames and beams and planks to his hand. "I suppose you're right, son." He scanned the wreckage for other signs of life. The ship was disheveled but otherwise intact. But he was one man against the laws of physics. "She's a tough one, just the same."

"The fore mast has some rot into'er heart. We'll have to cut another," said the bird.

"Uncle Sam would have spotted it straight away," Pius said, testily.

"And there's a bad spot in the forefoot knee, hard along by the scarf. It'll do for now but she'll devil you for leaking at the stopwater."

"Aye, we'll keep an eye on that lot, too."

Pius made his way along the slanting deck to the hatch and climbed down into the dark hold. He returned with an axe and braced himself against the rail at the deck. He eyed the long taper and thought of the labour invested to shape the beautiful spar and the hours it would take to cut and shape a new one. He patted the smooth, oiled mast, as if saying goodbye to a friend. "Is Uncle Sam along with you then?" he asked, delaying the first cut.

"Yes, Father, Uncle Sam's here. He's been with us the while, and a whole gang of the old b'yes come along with him. Uncle Sam says you did a fine job, but only because you're a bullheaded Humby."

Pius chuckled and took a grip on the axe. "Uncle Sam always said that about your grandfather too, if I remember."

"He says she wanted less tuck in her after frames to ease the run some, but says she's not so bad for all that, and she'll probably sail almost as well as if he'd built'er himself."

Pius was a little stung by the criticism. "Why didn't he tell me then!?"

"He says he tried, but you was being stubborn and wouldn't move your hand."

"Oh...thought it was only the wind."

"And Grandfather's here as well. He says to tell you her garboard run's just the way he showed you. He's some proud!"

Pius laughed at that, but was relieved to hear the accolade. Three ravens wheeled around the ship and landed on the port rail. He raised the axe and brought it down hard on the foremast just above the deck. The ship shuddered at the violent blow like a living thing taken by surprise. The ravens rose up again and dispersed to the quiet of the forest. The second blow of the axe sent a large wedge of wood spiraling over the lee rail.

When the mast was cut through, the shrouds could no longer take the weight. The hemp shrouds parted one by one and the mast crashed to the beach. The butt end hit the rail, leaving a deep, half moon depression that only Pius could explain.

A day in mid May: Pius was up at dawn and made tea over the small fire on the beach beside the ship. He drank a mug of strong tea with molasses, chewed a fatty chunk of salt beef, dredged from the scum off the bottom of the barrel, and washed it down with more scalding, sweet tea. He only wished there was a chunk of Gus' pan bread. Then he hefted his axe and strode up the beach to the forest.

Pius took his time selecting a proper tree. He studied a giant and seemed to have a conversation with the air about its merits. Pius cut the fall notch and took up a position on the opposite side. His axe bit deep into the sap wood. He withdrew the axe with difficulty and stood back. There was a sound of another axe failing on wood. Then Pius swung and the chips flew, and then the other sound, and Pius swung again and more chips flew. The wind sighed in the trees and more sounds of axes rang through the forest. The ravens called and the big tree trembled, swayed as if undecided, and after a long pause and a helpful push by the wind, crashed to the ground with the usual big show of twigs and needles and dust. Then there was the silence.

The big tree was set up on trestles, this time at right angles to the fallen schooner. Pius balanced on top of the log and with the broad axe cut into the side of the log at short intervals. Other axes joined the chorus and low voices murmured about things to do with a hard life and home. He eyed the line and deftly cut the wood away between the scored marks, repeating the sequence until one side of the log was flattened. A brief discussion followed and Pius counted three and the log rolled so that the flattened side was down. He walked on the tree to slab off the next side and so on until the tree became a four sided timber. His adz sliced and shaved the rough cuts and for each strike of Pius' adz there were three more. By evening the timber was smooth and tapered. The next evening the timber was a beautiful, round, oiled mast ready to be set in place.

The third morning the 'A' frame was set up beside the ship and the butt end of the mast was hoisted first and guided to the hole in the deck. Then the 'A' frame was moved further out beyond the balance point and the mast was hoisted to the angle of the fallen ship and pulled into position by ropes and pulleys with indistinct voices and grunts and mild curses as feet slipped on the stones. The mast was bedded into the step, new shrouds set up and the ship was ready to stand on her feet.

And still another day: The ravens watched intently from the high-side rail as Pius worked a long day beneath the keel. Stones flew and voices murmured and whispered adding encouragement. By midday the pit was the length of the ship and four feet deep. The pile of stones grew rapidly. For every stone that Pius threw up the bank it seemed there were a dozen stones added to the pile. At dusk the trench was six feet deep and extended to the waterline at low tide. The keel hung over the trench and the hull balanced precariously on the turn of her bilge.

All night, as Pius slept, there was a sound coming from the pit saw, although it might have been just the *swish-swish* of small waves on the stones. By dawn there was a pile of planks stacked beside the trench. When Pius awoke he immediately set to work laying short timbers across the bottom of the trench and crossing those with longer planks the length of the trench until he had a reasonably good platform sloping to the sea. He hammered together a half cradle on the far side of the trench. That accomplished, he jammed the largest timber he could manage under the starboard side of the ship and constructed a fulcrum crib. Several voices assessed the situation and one voice rose above all.

"Now, b'yes, heave like the Devil himself was on the brink of damnation an' all we got to do is give He a nudge!"

"Over she goes, lads," said another. Pius thought he recognized Uncle Sam's voice.

Pius made a sling for stones on the end of his lever, added weight and strained until his guts nearly burst; heaved beyond his mortal strength. The hull moved and rocked and the grunts and voices mingled with the calls of the ravens who were dislodged from their perch and the wind and the waves joined in until the beach was a chaos of sounds. Equilibrium was overcome and the schooner slipped into the trench.

For the rest of the day Pius laboured, hammering wedges between the hull braces and the trench timbers until, inch by hard won inch, the ship stood on her keel. The following day he assembled the matching side of the cradle and wedged the hull up and hung it on the cradle, then lay down on the deck, falling into an exhausted sleep, dreaming of voices and noises and bodies buried under mossy stone mounds and smiling faces telling tales around a fire. The faces were all from the past, long gone but remembered for their goodness.

Pius drifted through two days of delirium, passing in and out of sleep until he regained strength; enough to make a fire and cook gobs of rancid flour dough on sticks and brew strong tea with the dregs of the molasses. He couldn't remember when he had eaten last. He couldn't remember standing up his schooner. He sat beside the fire roasting the dough and eating the bread and washing down the flatbread with hot tea, all the while gazing at the ship in wonder.

That night Pius slept on deck again. The night sky was full of stars and the voices were soft murmurs from up forward, near the hatch. Pius imagined he could smell the smoke from their pipes and recognize some of the voices when a good tale was told or a time remembered and all concerned were comfortable in the knowledge that the job was done and the losses counted on one side of the ledger and the gains on the other and the imbalance accepted as part of life. The final reckoning would come soon enough and the balance sheet marked finished. For that one night at least, Pius could rest easy and not think of his losses.

May 23, 1933: Pius reckoned the launch date by counting back from the time he arrived at the merchant's wharf with his new ship. It was a sad day and didn't deserve a name: *'...Never was there an unhappier launch day. Or a harder loss at the end of it. If I'd been taught a lesson then I don't know what it was. We needed a ship and we built one. Then when she was ready to be launched off my heart was breaking. I'd give anything to hold my sons again, and I wish I'd never seen the tree that could make the keel of that cursed hull...'*

Pius waited for high tide with some concern. He wasn't sure of the day but the tide had been making higher every day and the day before it had come near enough to the highest tide in the cycle before. It would have to do. The ship was dug in, so to speak, and handier to the water, so the launch would be easier. His other concern was the gravel bar beyond the end of the skidway. Momentum would have to do the trick. He skidded the dory down to the water, gathered up anything useful and loaded it aboard. Anything not useful he added to the fire until the blaze was a roaring inferno of resinous wood, snapping and crackling and sending sparks as high as the trees. As high as the masts of his ship with the Humby family flag, a green 'H' in a white oval on a sea-blue ground, blowing out in the offshore breeze. At least the conditions were in her favour.

It had been a good spring for weather, when the ice finally left, he recalled. Pius thought about home. The lads would be getting ready to go fishing, waiting for Pius and the boys to sail into the harbour with their new ship. And then he thought of the merchant, Ashcroft. He would present himself to Ashcroft and negotiate for the gear, the supplies for his men and their families for the season they'd be away; and be deeper in debt. And if the season failed? He tried not to think about the season to come, or the ones gone, the accounts still to be tallied.

Pius finished his preparations and went up the beach to the grave mounds. Confronted with them in a clearer state of mind he wasn't sure why the names had been penciled on the crosses, although he had a strong feeling about Seth's marker. He knew Seth and Lloyd were gone but he couldn't remember how or when. There was a familiar stench of rotting seal coming from under the rocks and some animals scrabbling around had dug up what looked like the bones of a flipper, it could have been a hand. Pius didn't have the stomach to dig it up to find out. He piled on more stones and walked away from the place.

The tide was near top flood, playing around the rudder in busy little waves that seemed impatient for Pius to do something. He tossed pebbles as he stood near the water's edge watching the ocean creep up the stones to his tattered sea boots until the water stopped rising.

"Time to go, I suppose." He looked along the length of his schooner and found her pleasing to the eye but his eyes were tired and sunken and without life. "I couldn't have gotten this blessed hull out alone. Harry!? Father!? Uncle Sam!? Any of you b'yes going to dodge along now and help me put her off?"

The warm west wind came sighing over the trees and through the rigging. A raven called from the forest as an answer. "Roy!?..."

Pius walked to the bow and picked up the axe lying beside a wooden block. A mooring line was stretched taut across the block, the only element holding the cradle from sliding down the skidway. At some time during his delirium, although he couldn't remember doing it, Pius had greased the planks and the skids of the cradle with the fat of fish washed up on the beach...*while the remains of three fat seals putrefied in the stones above the beach*...and the rest of the tallow and anything else he could find in their meager stores that would grease the skidway.

Without ceremony he raised the axe and cut the line cleanly. The ship sat ponderously still. No telltale creaks came from the skids. The wind sighed and the small waves curled in against the wind and the ripples played around the keel. The tide neither rose nor fell. When it was time for the tide to go it would go, with or without the new schooner. Pius placed his hand on the shapely curve of the stem, the way a father puts a weathered hand on his newborn baby, to feel the life forces. Pius looked up the long, sensuous curve to the eyes of the ship and the board upon which he had carved the name, *Raven*. The chiseled letters were black to match the colour of the hull and his sentiments and his spirit. The hawse pipes, the almond shaped eyes of the ship cut into the bulwarks, reminded him of the stories his father told about the exotic Far East, and the women with almond coloured skin and almond shaped eyes, who gave lonely sailors memories for their old age when voyages and storms and wondrous sights had been forgotten. They were his father's memories. His own days in the Indian Ocean after the war were spent longing for Mary, the children and Fogo, and a schooner of his own. He remembered the day the delivery crew took the *Liza & Mary* away. And there was the reality of this cursed ship, reluctant to be launched, but already beaten down and bloodied. He considered her heritage and the voyages she still had to make, but he felt as if she were a waif, a bastard in the true sense, unwanted and unloved.

"You'll get no fine words from me by way of a christening. You've been baptized enough to suit any damned hull!"

Pius glared at the dumb wooden thing, defying it to remain static. The ravens were gathering again, circling above the ship, calling loudly; exhorting the thing to move, to leave their beach.

"Get off with you now, and be smart about it!"

The schooner sat stubbornly solid and unflinching. A bold raven swooped low and made a pass at the bow, shrieking ominously. Pius crossed himself and wished Godspeed to the latest soul on its way to Heaven.

"Go on then! I've no time for foolishness! You're no blushing bride to hang back from your wedding bed. Get in there you whore, and get your fanny wet!"

Whether it was the strength of the exhortation or just physics overcoming metaphysics, the cradle creaked and shuddered. A moan came down the wind from the forest. The hull came alive and the cradle moved, picked up momentum and smoke curled up from the greased skidway and the hull foamed into the water, over the gravel bar, to freedom.

The schooner bobbed back on her restraining line and rocked from side to side, testing the new element. Pieces of cradle and wedges and blocks popped to the surface, bumping at the shapely hull sitting nicely to her light marks. Pius eyed her set and had to admit that she looked as good as he had dreamed in the freezing cold and choking smoke of the shack. He had to love her in spite of himself even though she broke his heart. He had to love the thing or it would all be in vain.

"You did that well enough. We'll soon see how handy you are for an old man and a gang of ghosts to sail home."

He skidded the dory into the water and sculled out to his new schooner, unable to avoid a chuckle and a humorous postscript: "At least the fo'c'sle crowd'll not cost over much to keep."

Then he laughed with relief and the ravens joined in, shrieking and calling as they circled the ship. The unwanted presence was finally leaving.

Pius secured the deck gear, hoisted sail and shaped a course from the deadly Exploits beach across the Bay of Exploits to the Long Point Rocks. Exhausted by the months of labour, the tragedy and the lost days, he was near collapse. Once under way, with halyards belayed and lines coiled down, he sat wearily beside the old teak wheel, another legacy from John Humby, a hand resting lightly on a spoke. There was a story behind the ornately carved wheel but it was too involved for Pius to dredge up or his battered senses to appreciate, so he rubbed his hand on the smooth spoke and closed his eyes, feeling the power of the breeze filling the sails. The sun warmed his right cheek as a steering guide and the gulls drifted on the wind, keeping pace near the schooner's quarter, an escort on her maiden voyage.

Pius was in a deep sleep before the schooner passed Exploits Island. He couldn't remember watching for the eye of the gut between the islands to open up, a favourite bearing for a line of position. He remembered little about the sail, only the never ending parade of visions in his daydream. He imagined the voices again and movement on deck and orders given by the old pilot at the wheel. The way the ship flew, the pilot must have spent many years under sail and crossed many seas. He had the touch. When Pius awoke he was lying beside the wheel, covered by a piece of canvas, rested and hungry.

The little ship passed unnoticed well off the Long Point Rocks with the familiar lighthouse in full view on the starboard beam. Time to make the approach to the Burnt Island Run and the harbour. He was about to jump to the sheets to harden up when he realized the sheets had been hauled and set up and the sails flattened and drawing and the wind was throwing a fine spray over the starboard rail, slightly ahead of her beam. He silently thanked the pilot, put a hand on the top spoke to signal he had the con, and took the helm.

May 24, 1933: The jack schooner *Raven* worked up the long reach of Twillingate Harbour in graceful tacks on the top of the tide, rounding into the failing breeze off Ashcroft's wharf. Beyond the wharf Ashcroft's empire glowed like burnished gold in the low sun; the golden palace of the King and Pius was an indentured serf approaching his master's gate to pay homage.

The rusty kedge anchor was cast over the bow with a resonant splash that bounded off the buildings. The little ship ranged back on the turning tide and the strain came on the rode. The first voyage of the schooner *Raven* was over. Pius drew the dory alongside and sculled across the anchorage to the wharf.

Several schooners lay at anchor further up the harbour preparing for the fishing season down the Labrador Coast. Most belonged to Ashcroft. The rough little *Raven* didn't stand out among them but the people of Twillingate knew about the loss of young Harry Humby on the ice and the crowd of men and boys on the wharf had come down to pay their respects. Rough, strong hands reached to help Pius climb to the deck of the wharf. Many offered condolences as Pius passed among them, staring in awe at Pius' haunted eyes and weathered condition. Something more had happened during the long winter. The older ones, old sealing hands, had seen the look on the ice in a bad spring when sealing ships couldn't find their men or a bad winter when starvation claimed the outport people one by one. They could only speculate and stand aside to let him pass.

The crowd followed Pius at a respectful distance to the merchant's store, filled in around the doorway and looked in the dusty windows as Pius presented himself to Ashcroft.

Ashcroft, shaken by the specter of the gaunt man standing before him, the sunken eyes staring through him as if he wasn't there, almost lost his resolve to press his advantage.

"Pius...we're sorry to hear about young Harry. Alf Pardy and the others were here a few weeks back."

"Was Lloyd Legge and Seth White with'em?"

"Why, no...Alf said Lloyd and Seth stayed by with you, over to Exploits."

"Then I think I know where I left them. Seth, at least. Only the Lord knows what's become of young Lloyd."

"My God man! You don't mean...them two boys as well!?"

"Aye," said Pius, dismissing the incident.

"My son! I can't say enough."

"We've built us a schooner, Mr. Ashcroft. We'll need stores and gear for the Labrador."

Ashcroft retreated to the protection of the big ledger on the writing stand. He opened the book, slowly flipping pages, looking for Pius' account. It gave him time to phrase his reply. Finding the Humby page he stabbed at the figures as if seeing them for the first time. "Pius, 'tis hard for me to say this...what with your grievous loss and all. God knows, my son. The debt's that high, and the price of fish is down again. I can't take a chance."

Pius fixed Ashcroft with a look the merchant would never forget. "You've always taken a chance, sir."

"There's last year's stake, with nary a cent paid, and there's this winter's supplies. I seen to your families like they was my own."

"I thank you for that, but you was well paid with Father's watch."

"Another bad season could break me," whined Ashcroft, ignoring Pius' logic.

"Break you!? Yes, b'ye, break you, but my son if us don't fish it will kill we for sure."

"I'm sorry, my poor man...I need security."

"Security!?"

"Be realistic, Pius. These are hard times. We've all felt it. The price of fish isn't your fault, I know. You've had bad luck, what with, young Harry, and the *Liza and Mary* gone..."

"'Tis kind of you to call it bad luck, sir. A curse more like!"

"The more reason to have security," said the merchant firmly, feeling he was back on secure ground.

"As to security, sir?...I've none but my word, as always."

Ashcroft avoided Pius' eyes. He walked to the window and looked beyond the jumble of marine gear and canned goods, through the dusty, sun-brushed windows to the little schooner in the harbour below, tugging at the anchor rode as if impatient to be sailing. There was a stir among the older fishermen who saw the object of Ashcroft's gaze. They had known Ashcroft too long, had grown up in the shadow of the family. Went to school with him, before his family sent him off to the better schools in England. They sensed the businessman doing what he knows best; working up a deal. A trade off. The kill.

"That's a fine new schooner. You did yourself proud," said Ashcroft, without looking at Pius.

"Father and Uncle Sam think so."

Ashcroft turned to see if he was joking. The look in Pius' eyes said that he wasn't. "Uncle John Humby's been dead these many years..." said Ashcroft.

"Not so dead as you might think, sir. He had a hand into'er. And Uncle Sam, and all the old b'yes what could build a ship."

Ashcroft smiled, relieved. "Yes, I see what you mean. Your family were good builders and I'm sure the vessel attests to her heritage."

"Maybe so, but I didn't build that ship alone, sir. And I wasn't alone after the lads left me. The ship was cast off her cradle in a storm. Lloyd and Seth was killed is my guess. I couldn't have stood'er up alone. Neither was I alone when we put'er off. And it wasn't me who sailed'er home, Mr. Ashcroft, that's what I mean!"

Ashcroft went white. "John Humby was there? And the others?"

"Aye, I'll swear. And they're still into'er, I suppose."

Ashcroft crossed himself. So did one or two of the men at the door when the word made the rounds. Some of the older men just nodded as if having spirits on board was as common as building a small schooner on a winter beach. Ashcroft looked doubtful but he wasn't the one who had to sail the thing if she was bewitched. And what if she was? Others had been so cursed and some of them had long, prosperous careers. It depended on the pedigree of the spirits. The Humby's were a good lot and good builders.

"Nevertheless," he said, looking Pius in the eye, "I'll take her against the balance."

"My ship!?..."

Ashcroft was more sure of his ground; and he had the upper hand. Pius could accept or refuse, but either way Ashcroft had control. If Pius refused he could legally impound the vessel against the bill. "The schooner, to clear the debt."

"That's a hard bargain, sir. No, more than hard, 'tis cruel!"

"The best I can do."

"How would we fish?"

"You can buy her back anytime you can better the sum."

"You know that's not possible."

"Then you can sign on as skipper, for a share."

"No! I couldn't work for you, Mr. Ashcroft. Not sail me ship and know she's not me own."

"Then I'll have her, clear."

"There's more than wood and oakum into'er. To take'er away..." Pius could see the Humby family flag over the heads of the onlookers and considered his situation. Ashcroft was within his rights. Adversity was a way of life and it wasn't the first ship Pius had lost to the merchants. He would pay up his debt and not count the losses. "If you take'er then we're all clear of you?...me, my family, and my men and their families?"

"Well, I hadn't calculated all."

"You know she's worth more tied to a broker's wharf in St. John's!" Pius said, barely controlling his anger.

Ashcroft decided to take the deal. He hadn't lost, only accepted less than he had counted on. But he hadn't reckoned with Pius' wild eyes and he was almost ashamed to have presumed upon his only weakness, the Humby good nature.

"All right, Captain Humby. As you wish."

"Write that in your big book, Mr. Ashcroft. Fogo's debt is cleared as of this moment. You write that, sir!"

"Fogo's debt!? That's more than the bargain..."

"Not a bit of it, sir," Pius said evenly. "I said, me and my men and their families. There's not a man sails for me who isn't related to enough of us that we aren't all family, Mr. Ashcroft, and that's the deal you agreed to. That little schooner out there is still worth twice what we owes, so I don't want to see no tears! And I'll have Father's watch." Pius' hand trembled.

"All right," sighed Ashcroft. He took the gold watch out of his pocket and put it in Pius' hand. Ashcroft was beaten. "I'll strike the debt."

The merchant turned the Fogo account pages, stroking through them one by one. Pius watched closely. He knew every name in the ledger, had entered most of them himself over the years. He nodded as each page was painfully stroked. The men crowded into the door way grinned and winked. It wasn't often they had the pleasure of seeing Ashcroft bested in a bargain. Still, they also knew the truth; the schooner was worth more. Or was she? She was a small schooner compared to the cost in lives. Pius felt no satisfaction, only a sense of justice when Ashcroft turned to his own page and made the final stroke, writing *In Full* across the bottom of the page.

"Are you satisfied, Pius Humby? You've cost me a year's profits."

"My sonny boy! You're little sum's no more than the King's tax compared to what we've already paid for her."

Pius, took his Grandfather's carved cane off the counter and walked to the door, his head held higher than his body felt like carrying it. The crowd melted back to let him pass. He walked slowly to the wharf and shoved off for the schooner to gather his few belongings.

It would be a long pull across the open waters of Hamilton Sound to Fogo Island but Pius gave that small hardship little thought. He laid the Humby flag across the thwart of the dory and slipped away from the schooner, dropping down the harbour on the outgoing tide. The schooner, like a spurned lover, turned her back as she swung to the anchor. He tried not to look at the graceful lines, seen from her best angle as he rowed out the arm for Burnt Island Tickle, regretting that he had to leave the beautiful old ship's wheel behind. *The wheel's only an object*, he said to himself, or was he talking to the crowd of fishermen and boat builders along for the ride? *A small loss, compared to the rest, b'yes.*

End of Book One

Fiction by Patric Ryan

The Fogo's War Trilogy
Book One
Summer Wars & Winter Schooners
Book Two
Schooners Are Black & U-Boats Are Grey
Book Three
The Final Acts of Fogo's War

The Paris Shooter's Union

The Burning Islands

Surviving Well Is the Best Revenge: Cuba

Surviving Well Is The Best Revenge: Montreal

Surviving Well Is The Best Revenge: Newfoundland

Non-fiction

Closing The Newfoundland Circles

Screenplays

Winter Schooner, Fogo's War & Ellie's Boat

Short Stories
Rum Runners & River Rats, The Last Fisherman & The Man From Chicago

Made in the USA
Charleston, SC
01 November 2014